CAMOUFLAGE
VICTORIA JAYNE SAUNDERS

This book is dedicated to anyone who's ever felt underappreciated, ignored, or cast aside.

We see you. We need you.

Keep going.

CONTENTS

THE CHEHWINOO

Sit down, gather 'round, have a drink or two. If you wait and fill your plate, I'll
tell you 'bout the Chehwinoo.

The night is young, the wind is calm, the sky is still light blue.
If you think you're tough, then you're in luck. I'll tell you 'bout the Chehwinoo.

Long before we settled here before this town stood high,
A family man traversed this land, his pack heavy with wares.
He traveled with his wedded wife, with locks the colour of rye,
On her hip, her son did sit, sporting his father's raven hair.

The father, the mother, the son, the troop,
To Devil's Lake, their path would lead.
But misfortune fell on their little group,
On their sorrow, it would feed.

Quiet now, little ones, don't tell the flies to shoo.
If you're loud and make a sound, you might call the Chehwinoo.

Ten feet tall and made of ice, his claws turn your skin blue.
The air grows cold and you hear a scream- it must be the Chehwinoo.

Winter came before the frost, harder than ever before,
The father grew scared with every gust, as their store of food grew bare.
I must go and hunt, he said, one hand on the door,

The other reached for his young son, who screamed it isn't fair.

I'll be back before the sun,
The father unknowingly lied.
He tied his boots and took his gun,
While his wife and young son cried.

Hunger is a powerful foe, can leave you with nothing left to do.
Just be smart and play your part. Don't anger the Chehwinoo.

Where darkness lurks, where spirits hide in shadows of every hue,
Have no doubt it's lurking about. You'll find the Chehwinoo.

The father searched high and wide for signs of doe or buck,
He wandered far into the woods, where the rays of sun wouldn't touch.
He wandered as far as he dared, and when he thought he'd run out of luck,
The father came across a man, dying in a little hutch.

I have no food, he wept
I need your help, please.
From his cheeks, the tears he swept
Dripped on the father's knees.

I'll whisper now as the night goes on and the moon rises new.
It shuns the sun and fears the light, that sneaky Chehwinoo.

Quickly now, we must make haste, we have no time to lose.
Finish this tale and get inside where it's safe from the Chehwinoo.

The dying man knew not his fate as he begged for help,
The father had a terrible thought as his hunger screamed for blood.
The dying man could feed his wife, his strapping little welp.
With his gun, he shot the man and watched as he fell into the mud.

But the father had failed,
He wouldn't see his wife this night.
For if she knew, her skin would pale,
She'd stare at her husband in fright.

Hunger is a powerful foe, but you cannot let it win.
You'll lose yourself along this path, your humanity will grow thin.
What would you do to survive?
Would you sin so too?
The beast inside will come alive.

You are the Chehwinoo.

Chapter One

INTERLUDE

Somerton Town Hall

Working for a man like Adrian Stamkos was never boring; if nothing else, Jerry Leichester could never complain about his job being 'mundane.'

As a personal assistant to the most influential pharmaceutical empire in the United States' CEO, Jerry never knew what to tell people when they asked him what he did on a day to day basis. Answer phone calls, emails, letters? Yes, of course. Organize meetings, lunch dates, travel plans? Absolutely. The grunt work was expected, visible, even. When people asked Jerry about his job, they weren't asking about the time he juggled three different conference appearances in the same weekend, interspersed with media interviews and a particularly nasty court summons. No, they were asking about the aspects of his job that made working for Adrian Stamkos unique. Exciting. Scandalous.

Jerry could've told them any number of things, but the ancient, bloodthirsty ice demon was a bit of a crapshoot. Sure, it was easily the most noteworthy task Mr. Stamkos had ever assigned him, but getting anyone to *believe* that story was another matter entirely.

A notification buzzed on Jerry's phone, and he glanced at the screen. It was a follow-up from Mr. Stamkos' tailor, nothing urgent. Jerry refocused his attention on the tablet in front of him, alternating between updating his personal social media accounts and waiting to hear back from Tessa Greene. She came highly recommended for their purposes, but Mr. Stamkos would only accept her for the task if Jerry vetted her first. That brought him no small amount of pride; to have the trust of someone so powerful was a heady, almost addictive sensation. He refused to lose it.

Footsteps sounded outside their temporary office, and Jerry heaved a sigh. It was likely the interim sheriff, coming by once again to remind them that they didn't have permission to set up shop in the mayor's old quarters at town hall. He had done so several times already, but the fact that they remained meant he had no real authority to remove them. Jerry tried his best to keep the sheriff's nagging out of Mr. Stamkos' earshot, but the residents of Somerton weren't well-versed in the art of subtlety. To his relief, the footsteps walked past without pausing at their door.

God, he couldn't wait to leave this place.

Somerton was charming in its own way, with vast wilderness and a tight-knit community that genuinely cared for their town. It was also small, stupid, and smelled of rotting grass. Jerry didn't think it was possible, but he actually missed the factory fumes that accosted his high rise in L.A. If it weren't for the immense real estate potential of the Basin, he would've spent the last six months gently nudging Mr. Stamkos in a different direction, far away from this overly compli-cated negotiation. As it stood, there was simply too much money to be made in Somerton for the company to walk away.

Another alert sounded from his phone, this time from Tessa Greene. Jerry checked the time stamp of his initial inquiry, noting that she answered in approx-imately 12 hours. A little slow for his liking, but he could work with it. Not that he had much of a choice. Mr. Stamkos had given him a strict timeline, and Jerry would rather saw off his left arm than be late.

Tessa agreed to his suggested meeting time and date. Perfect. Jerry was slightly concerned that she'd insist on a virtual meeting, as per the guidelines on her website. That wouldn't do. In-person conversations were far easier to hide. Dis-creet. Secret. Ideal for what Jerry needed Tessa to do. He responded to her con-firmation with a compressed folder of documents, nothing damning, of course. Information that was all easily accessible online, compiled for convenience. He would explain what Tessa was to do with that information once they met and he confirmed she was well-suited.

With that done, Jerry leaned back in his chair and sighed.

Annoyance rippled through his stomach as he considered the monumental task ahead of him. Tessa's help would be instrumental, yes, but it was far from the only cog in the wheel. For this to work, Jerry needed everything to go smoothly. He needed to be at the right place, at the right time, talking to the right people, saying the right things. All of this could've been avoided if Mr. Stamkos had just let him handle the communications with James Carver from the beginning. Adrian Stamkos was a brilliant man, but covering up messes was *Jerry's* job. The most effective way to clean up any mess was to prevent it in the first place, starting with the cardinal rule of secrecy: never leave a paper trail.

Now, a literal piece of paper was threatening their entire operation, and Jerry was responsible for making sure that didn't happen. It didn't matter that he had a plan. Plans could fail. Then what would he do? He couldn't very well admit to Mr. Stamkos that he'd fumbled their last hurdle, not when the biggest, most obnoxious hurdles had been cleared. It would be like running a marathon and tripping on a shoe lace at the finish line. Dealing with the ice demon should have been the hardest obstacle to overcome. Jerry would never be able to show his face at Stamkos & Stein again if he let one flimsy note ruin their success at this stage.

While Jerry could understand the initial pushback to their presence in Somerton, he couldn't help but think that Mr. Stamkos was an unrecognized hero for the small town. He wasn't an unreasonable man, after all. His presence was felt significantly now that he was here, in person, directly involved, but it would fade when the factory was up and running. Then, Somerton would be bursting with job opportunities and new sources of income. The town would grow from a speck on the map to a bustling hub of industrial manufacturing, and the people would be rolling in more money than they knew what to do with. Eventually, they would see that. Jerry just hoped they could smooth out the wrinkles in their plans sooner rather than later and encourage that day to come quickly, before more eyes fell to their work here.

The Chehwinoo was a significant, if unexpected, hiccup. In truth, he hadn't believed the stories when Mr. Stamkos shared Mayor Carver's concerns. Why would he? It took a close encounter and a stubborn case of frost bite on his arm to convince him that they were dealing with something tangible and dangerous, not superstitious nonsense. When they first arrived in Somerton, Jerry was afraid he would need to start calling in favors from some of his more unsavory contacts, some of whom he had been warned never to speak to again if he valued his life. He did value his life, of course, but he valued his job more. Thankfully, the creature's attention had been drawn away from the factory construction by the other glaring obstacle in their way.

The enemy of my enemy...

Nyla Jameson. Jerry couldn't suppress a smile. He'd never admit it to Mr. Stamkos, but Jerry liked Nyla. A lot. He admired her ambition, her intelligence, and her heart. More than once, he wished that their plans didn't intersect. He pitied the woman, watching all of her hard work be wrenched from her white-knuckled grip no matter how hard she tried to fight them. Pity had to take a back seat, though. Jerry, like Nyla, had a job to do. He wasn't about to let compassion stop him. For now, at least, they were on the same side. Nyla and her friends were doing an impressively effective job at keeping the Chehwinoo's damage to a minimum, and that was exactly what Jerry needed her to do. He wasn't looking forward to the day that changed, and he had a feeling that time was approaching much faster than any of them realized.

In the meantime, Jerry had a meeting to prepare for. Ice demons, paper trails, and beautiful women would have to wait.

Chapter Two

EMMETT

Emmett heaved a sigh of bittersweet relief, dropping his head back against the lip of his father's truck bed. The dying screeches of another monster were suddenly drowned out by the steady thump of the opening riff to *Another One Bites the Dust,* immediately followed by a series of exasperated expletives.

"Sam!" Amelia yelled at the same time that Tyler snapped *"Fisher!"* The man in question crashed through the bushes, headbanging erratically and strumming an air guitar like he'd never seen an instrument in his life. Emmett suppressed a grin. Sam's antics were bothersome at times, but he couldn't deny the levity that accompanied each childish outburst. God knows they needed some levity these days.

"Do you seriously have to play that shit *every time?*" Tyler demanded, pinching the bridge of his nose between his thumb and forefinger. Emmett was used to seeing him in his typical FBI getup, but now he wore a dark green winter coat and splash pants to protect him from the wet ground. His cropped blond hair was dishevelled from where he'd shoved it under a beanie, although the hat was nowhere to be seen now. If Emmett squinted, he might be able to pick out a thin dusting of dark shadow along the edges of his jaw, a pale impersonation of the thick stubble covering the lower half of Emmett's face.

The others were joining them slowly, inching their way around the disintegrating Chehwinoo with care not to step in the growing puddle of slush. Amelia hopped out of Aaron's X5, controller in hand, looking as irritated as she did fond. She was dressed in a thin, plum-coloured hoodie and jeans, since most of her work kept her inside. Her hair was pulled into a loose ponytail, the dark purple ends making it look like she'd dipped them in paint. They were fading now, but that only served to make the colour stand out more against her dark brown roots. Sam was tailed by Nyla, who looked significantly less annoyed than everyone else. Emmett offered a shrugging chuckle to Aaron, who was seated next to him in the pan of Emmett's borrowed truck.

"It's a *theme song*, Ty. The point is to play it every time." Sam gave him an incredulous look, finally ending the song and slipping his phone into his jeans pocket. In contrast to Tyler, Sam had a bright red puffer coat on, designed to attract attention.

"We don't need a theme song."

"Au contraire, I believe we do." Sam made his way to where Amelia was leaning against the side of the SUV, hooking his arm around her and jostling the controller in her hands.

"Careful!" She righted herself as quickly as possible, glaring at Sam as she did. Holding up the controller, she pointedly scolded him. "Delicate, expensive, and *not ours*."

"Can whatever forest god is orchestrating all this take him next? Please?" Tyler pleaded, his head tilted back to face the sky. Sam made an offended sound, dramatically clutching his chest and flipping his sandy brown hair out of his eyes. It was longer now, brushing his eyebrows when it was weighed down with water or sweat.

"At least wait until I touch base with Roxy," Amelia interjected before Sam could. "I'm pretty sure you forfeit your bet winnings if Sam kicks the bucket before I get a chance to tell Rox that I've sucked her brother's di—"

"STOP." Tyler covered his ears in exaggerated disgust. "I know it's happening; doesn't mean I want to hear about it."

"I should've stayed on infidelity cases," Aaron said with a sigh, for only Emmett to hear. He chuckled, spotting the drone dipping into the clearing as Amelia expertly navigated it to the ground.

Acquiring the drone had been a game-changer that they didn't know they needed. After dealing with the immediate fallout following the second Chehwinoo's death, another one popped up in record time, setting off a chain of trial and error that ended when Amelia borrowed Tyler's vehicle and made off for

Chicago. She returned two days later with well wishes from Tyler's wife, Chia, and a drone that was far too advanced to be a commercial product. Initially, she was content to keep the specifics of her trip to herself, but after some needling from Tyler and Nyla, Amelia confessed that the high-tech piece of equipment was on loan from the Chicago PD. How exactly she managed to pull that favor remained a closely guarded secret, but Emmett suspected it was an under-the-table deal with someone on the inside, given the uncomfortable expression she donned when asked about it directly. Then again, maybe she'd stolen it. With Amelia, Emmett quickly learned not to rule anything out.

The drone itself was something Emmett would never dream of getting his hands on, nor did he want to. Technology in general wasn't his forte, and drones were as mysterious as the Bermuda Triangle as far as he was concerned. The only thing he understood about this model was that it came with a highly sensitive heat-mapping camera, and that's how they'd managed to fell five Chehwinoo in just under two weeks. Amelia would send the drone out into the Basin, coasting above the treetops to search for areas of intense cold. When they found one, it was just a matter of suiting up, heading out, and sticking to the plan. They'd reduced monster-hunting to a nearly infallible science: Amelia monitoring the creature's movements from inside the vehicle with the drone, Sam and Nyla luring it with fire into a clearing where Emmett and Aaron were waiting, perched in the back of Ephraim's truck with rifles at the ready. They were the best shots out of everyone present and were usually able to make a clean kill in less than three bullets. If that failed, Tyler was often on standby with a much larger gun, hunkering down in the brush so that the creature wouldn't notice him right away. Luckily, the fail-safe was almost never needed, since Tyler spent most of his days travelling between Somerton and Chicago to tend to a very-pregnant Chia.

It was efficient and effective, but they all knew it wouldn't last for much longer. The knowledge weighed heavily, hovering like a dark shadow over their group, looming closer with each passing day.

November weather in Wisconsin was cold. The closer they got to December, the less likely it would be for the drone to distinguish between supernatural cold and a winter wind. Despite their progress in taking care of the creatures with minimal bloodshed, they were no closer to figuring out why this was happening and how to stop it. It was wearing on all of them, Emmett could see it plainly. Sam's jokes were strained and got fewer laughs, Aaron's patience was running thin, Tyler hardly smiled anymore, Amelia spoke less, and Nyla had formed a constant wrinkle of worry between her brows.

That last one unsettled Emmett more than anything else. In all the years he'd known Nyla, she'd never been fazed by stress. Not visibly, anyway. They needed a breakthrough, and they needed it now.

Aaron alighted from the truck bed, landing on the hardened dirt ground with a decisive thud just as Nyla reached him, her golden hair shining rosy pink as the sun reflected off her locks. He wrapped an arm around her waist and pulled her into him, pressing a relieved kiss against her forehead. Emmett considered teasing him, but he let it drop. He'd needle Aaron later when they weren't a few seconds away from freezing.

"Have you gotten anywhere with Stamkos yet, Am?" Nyla asked, sinking into Aaron's side. Amelia shook her head, grimacing.

"He's not an easy man to get an audience with," she said, her words dripping in annoyance. "I think George has had more luck than I have, but not by much."

Emmett resisted the urge to roll his eyes. Adrian Stamkos showing his face in Somerton wasn't something they'd anticipated, but after the initial shock, they'd seen it as an opportunity. While the Chehwinoo was still active, it wasn't safe for people to be in the Basin. S&S's factory was putting a lot of people in harm's way, and the higher ups had no idea they were sending their employees into the lion's den. Aaron had suggested a stop-work order to be issued by the town, but George didn't have the authority. He was only the interim sheriff until a new mayor was elected and could sign the necessary forms to make his position permanent. Without a mayor, their hands were tied. Tyler spoke to Kelley about the issue, but that came with its own problems. With the Wildlife department breathing down their necks, pushing for a proper investigation of the Basin's fauna, Kelley had to meticulously plan her every move. Issuing a stop-work order due to present dangers in the Basin would give Wildlife the excuse they needed to go over Kelley's head and seal off the area while they took samples.

That left one feasible option: convincing Adrian Stamkos to pause his building plans.

'Feasible' was a bit of a stretch, but it was the only option that didn't result in a surge of preventable deaths. If they could sit down with Stamkos, persuade him to put his plans on hold for just a short while, it would give them the breathing room they needed to finally put an end to the Chehwinoo's reign of destruction. Asking a billionaire to voluntarily throw away tens of thousands of dollars in construction delays based on their word alone was its own obstacle, one they would need to face if and when they secured a meeting with the man in charge.

Emmett pressed his lips together, forcing himself to remain quiet. He wasn't great with the intricacies of corporate negotiations, but he'd done some research. Every night that he wasn't exhausted from a hunt, he was online, watching taped interviews and press releases with Adrian Stamkos. The man was impressive, and he certainly knew how to charm a crowd, but Emmett's digging rewarded him with the more accurate image of Stamkos' character shown in lesser known appearances and candid recordings. He was ruthless. Cold. Uncaring. He was a businessman, and the only thing that mattered to him was maintaining his image and profit margins. Getting him on their side was a hail Mary, and not one that he expected to work. Still, they had to try, didn't they?

A moment of silence passed, heavy and thick.

"Come on," Aaron announced suddenly, interrupting the cloud of doubt that was quickly gathering. "Let's go back to the Willow. It's almost time for supper. We'll relax, get a hot meal, and come at this again with fresh eyes."

Wordlessly, everyone followed Aaron's instructions. Emmett wasn't prone to envy, but Aaron was a hard man not to idolize, just a little. Leadership oozed from his pores, and he had the skills to back up his attitude. Worse, he had an impeccable sense of style. He almost rolled his eyes at himself for even thinking it, but it was true. Emmett didn't care how he looked as long as he was comfortable and could get his work done, but he couldn't deny that spark of irritation every time Aaron walked into a room looking like he'd stopped by on his way to a movie set. Even now, with his hair wind-tousled and pink colouring his nose and cheeks, covered in winter gear, he managed to look sleek and not just a little bit sexy. It was an infuriating test of patience.

Climbing into the driver's seat of Ephraim's truck, Emmett took a deep, heavy breath. The weight of responsibility pressed down on him until his head hurt;

from the beginning, Nyla did her best to keep Emmett on the periphery of the chaos. He had his ailing father to worry about, and Nyla could handle things with the group of friends she'd collected along the way. Now, though, Emmett chose to insert himself in the thick of it.

After the night that Sam drove his truck into the lake, Emmett committed to seeing this thing through. He trusted Nyla to reach out to him when she needed to, but why bother? If Emmett was *here*, actively helping them investigate the Chehwinoo mythos, she wouldn't need to reach out. He'd be ready and available whenever he was needed.

The toll on his nerves was more than he expected, and it was bearable most of the time. Emmett just needed a minute alone to collect himself and he'd be ready to tackle the next step. Whatever that might be.

Sending a text to Nyla letting her know about his planned detour, Emmett brought the rusted truck to life and pulled away from the shoulder of the road, heading directly for the Coffee Corner and some much-needed caffeine.

Chapter Three

CALLIE

Well, this was turning into a clerical nightmare.

Callie gulped the final dregs of her latte with a grimace. It had long since cooled, leaving a thin, gritty film of vanilla bean foam coating her tongue after she swallowed. Shaking herself free of the unpleasant aftertaste, Callie put her tablet down on the passenger seat and heaved a sigh.

Two hours. She'd been parked in the lot outside Somerton's lone cafe, the Coffee Corner, for two hours, poring over every document she could find related to the Lichen House acquisition. Between the stacks of paper files she'd swiped from the office and her notes and electronic folders, her borrowed vehicle looked like a tornado ripped through an office supply building. It was chaos, but organized chaos. By the time she'd finished her BLT, Callie had a deep understanding of the case ahead of her. To her relief, the paper trail for this contract was strong, with nearly every detail meticulously recorded by Orville (a miracle, really). To her frustration, it was largely useless.

Orville had burdened her with a monumental task, one that would require a combination of herculean effort and divine intervention to overcome. Their clients, the couple who'd purchased Lichen House, had a vision. They wanted to turn the property into a combination bed and breakfast and museum while preserving the history of the site, which wasn't an easy ask in and of itself. Their first hurdle, and the one that brought them to Orville in the first place, was obtaining the right to renovate the old buildings. That took a year. Then, they had to come up with a renovation plan that was approved by the town council while also satisfying their original image of the business. Callie counted no less than six contractors that were consulted, hired, and subsequently dismissed before settling on the company currently in charge, a process that took another year. Once all was said and done, the Lichen House contract had a longer shelf life than some of the paralegals Orville hired.

Now, they should be celebrating. Everything was in place to begin renovations, and on Callie's side of things, she need only handle the myriads of permits required in the hospitality industry. Liquor license, health inspector, electrical evaluation, all of these were agreements that Callie had done before. It should've been easy. In her mind, it was. Callie let herself daydream about a life where Orville was already retired and she was reshaping the business into what she wanted it to be; less a hodgepodge of legal grunt work and more targeted, specialized caseloads. She'd bring back some of the employees that Orville's cantankerous attitude drove away, building a team that she both trusted and respected.

Better yet, a team that respected *her*. She damn well knew Orville didn't.

All of that, everything Callie was working toward, now lay in the hands of a corporate titan, one that couldn't care less about Callie's hopes and dreams: Adrian Stamkos, the figurehead of Stamkos & Stein Pharmaceuticals.

It wasn't personal, Callie knew. She'd worked with enough mid-size companies to understand that business politics were impersonal and cutthroat by nature. Adrian Stamkos didn't bear her any more ill will than a McDonald's cashier does a Shake Shack line cook. Likely, Adrian Stamkos was completely unaware of Callie's existence, let alone the strife his business was causing with her clients.

Callie wouldn't be in this position if Stamkos & Stein had just waited another month or two before releasing their concept images of the new plant. Through blood, sweat, and tears, Callie convinced their clients that the plant wouldn't affect the appeal of Lichen House. It was too far away, hidden by the thick and impenetrable wilderness crowding the Basin. They likely wouldn't know the plant was there, let alone be negatively influenced by its presence.

Then the photos came out.

It was an intentional marketing move, one that Callie had seen before. S&S was getting backlash from the locals, delaying their building process. To counteract the bad press, their marketing team released idealized images of the final product, looking like some futuristic space station in the middle of the woods, cradled harmoniously amongst trees and wildlife alike. It was new, innovative, and unlike anything anyone in Somerton or Hatfield had seen before.

It was also a load of corporate bullshit.

Eco-structures were becoming more and more popular in the tourism industry, but in pharmaceuticals? No chance. It was impractical at best, and malfunctioning at worst. S&S knew their audience and they played to it, offering empty promises and false comfort along with a blueprint that would never see the light of day. After all was said and done, the factory up and running, it would be too late. Anyone curious about the original plans, the designs that had pacified them in the early stages, would be met with a wall of vague excuses ranging from budget cuts to incompatible landscapes. Capitalism – one, honesty – zero.

Callie knew that all too well, as did her clients. When the campaign began, they'd done a deep dive into the public permits already acquired by S&S. The information they found, coupled with their research on noise pollution and corporate expansion, resulted in no less than twenty frantic emails to Callie and Orville. If they were going to keep this contract, their biggest and longest-standing to date, something had to be done. It was now up to Callie to figure out what.

Bang!

"Orville, what the fuck are you— oh, shit."

The angry words were preceded by a hard smack on the driver's side window, startling Callie into fumbling her phone onto the floor of the car. She shrieked in tandem with her jump, throwing herself as far away from the window as she could.

"Callie? What are you doing here?"

The voice registered at the same time a face appeared in the window, and suddenly Callie's tongue-tie had nothing to do with her fright.

Emmett Coady. Bricklayer, son of Lichen House's interim groundskeeper, and the hottest man Callie had ever laid eyes on.

"Emmett!" Callie exclaimed in surprise, realizing belatedly that he probably couldn't hear her. The window was still up. Emmett's voice carried, but hers definitely didn't. Cheeks flaming, she used the manual crank to lower the window and braced herself for the strangely intoxicating scent of pine and gasoline that accompanied Emmett wherever he went.

Callie wasn't used to feeling so unsettled by a man. Orville liked his female employees to be mild, meek, and subservient. Callie's family hailed from Louisiana, and she went to school in New York. Mild and meek were not words most people would use to describe her. Through sheer force of will, Callie had tempered her fiery attitude into a hard outer shell of calm confidence that, while Orville didn't approve, he didn't object to either. Yet, whenever Emmett looked at her, Callie couldn't help but feel like he was seeing past that shell. The sensation made her squirm.

God, was he hotter now? How the hell did he get *more* attractive since she'd last seen him?

"Hey, Emmett," she tried again, praying her voice was steadier than her heartbeat. Emmett was her age, tall and broad, with piercing brown eyes that peeked out from beneath dark brows. Callie spent more time than she cared to admit examining Emmett's eyes; they were some of the only parts of himself he left uncovered. His clothes were heavy, tattered, and stained from work. His black hair was cropped short, mostly hidden beneath a baseball hat bearing his company's logo. His chin was obscured with thick stubble that was always visible, even after a recent shave. 'Sexy' probably wasn't the first word that came to mind when most people saw Emmett Coady, but those people simply weren't *looking*. Not like Callie was.

"Hey," Emmett raised an eyebrow questioningly, and Callie realized she'd been silently staring for much longer than was proper. She blushed harder. "Sorry for the scare, I thought Orville was here to harass Dad again."

"Oh, no," Callie swallowed, trying to get herself under control. She was a *lawyer*, damn it all. If her more aggressive clients didn't intimidate her, Emmett Coady's unfair jawline shouldn't. "Orville's out of town on a business trip. I'm just... trying to tie up some loose ends."

"You're still going ahead with the renos?" Emmett frowned, his expression troubled in a way that made Callie's stomach flip. She was almost annoyed at herself. Not *everything* the man did had to make her heart skip. "I thought the new owners weren't happy with this S&S bull."

"They're not," Callie agreed, finding her confidence again and relaxing into the conversation. "That's why I'm here. I'm hoping to speak to Adrian Stamkos, unofficially, and see if we can't work something out. There must be some assurances he can offer local businesses. He can't alienate *everyone*."

"Don't underestimate him," Emmett said, rolling his eyes bitterly. Callie bit the inside of her cheek, wondering at the familiarity of his reaction. It was almost like he'd met Stamkos already, but why would that be the case? Emmett had no reason to interact with the head of S&S. At least, none that Callie knew of. He worked for the company heading the Lichen House renovations, but that was a distant connection to the head of a pharmaceutical empire. "You heading back to Hatfield soon? Or do you have time for a coffee?"

Elation and shock struck Callie in equal measure. Their employers were closely intertwined— Callie through the Lichen House contract, Emmett through his father and employer— so she wasn't naive enough to assume he was asking her on a date per se. Still, any excuse to spend time with Emmett was good enough for her.

"I'd love that," she said, hoping she didn't sound too eager. From the way Emmett's face lit up, she thought she succeeded, or, if she didn't, he wasn't put off by her enthusiasm.

"Great," Emmett opened her door for her, stepping aside so she could get out, "I've got another half an hour before I need to get back to work. I could use a distraction."

"Tell me about it," Callie said, sighing. She alighted from the car, removing her black velvet beret and shaking her hair loose. It was cropped to her chin in a severe bob, the shorter style leftover from the summer months. "I've got a headache just from reading through all this crap."

"I take it negotiations aren't going well?" Emmett fell into step beside her, walking just slightly ahead so he would reach the door first. Callie smiled in gratitude as he held it open for her.

"Not so much," Callie confirmed. "The concept images really pushed Tara and Ed into a tailspin. They know a ploy when they see one."

"Downsides to working with people who know what they're doing," Emmett said sympathetically. "How's Orville taking it?"

Callie grimaced, schooling her features just in time for the barista to call them to the front. She ordered a tea and waited while Emmett ordered a black coffee for himself and a slew of other drinks. She raised an eyebrow.

"You caught me on a group coffee run," he explained. Callie opened her mouth to apologize, tell him not to be held up on her account, but Emmett silenced her with a withering look. "They can wait, Cal. I'm allowed to take a few minutes for myself."

Well, shit. Did he have to say it like that? Her stomach did a backflip at the stubbornness in his tone, and Callie once again had to stop herself from physically rolling her eyes at her reaction. Emmett was hot, yes, but she was a grown woman, not a crush-addled schoolgirl.

Emmett accepted the tray of drinks from the barista, balancing it in one hand while he passed Callie her tea. He caught her staring warily at the precariously placed tray, and answered her unspoken concern with a wink.

Okay, a grown woman she may be, but she still had a crush.

Emmett walked them to a booth near the window, facing away from the main dining room. Callie slid into her seat gracefully; she was used to being hyper-aware of her movements in client meetings, but she was typically more relaxed on casual outings. With Emmett, though, she was very aware of her body and the space she took up. Maybe she should just ask him on a date, get the rejection over with so she could focus on her real reason for being in Somerton. The idea fizzled almost as soon as it sparked; the theoretical sting of disappointment was already too much for Callie to swallow.

"Orville is... Orville," Callie said, suddenly remembering that she hadn't answered his question before they ordered. "I think he was expecting it. He said he was going to retire when the Lichen House contract is finalized, and it's turning into our longest negotiation in company history. Doesn't seem like a coincidence."

Emmett scowled, crossing his arms over his chest with a displeased grunt.

"I don't know why you still work for that prick," he groused. "Everyone knows what he's like. You've got more than enough experience to get a job with a different firm."

Callie took a deep breath, already feeling the exhaustion of having to defend her choices. Everyone always said the same things to her: just quit, find a new job, report Orville for his behavior. They meant well, but...

"Orville owns the only firm from here to Madison," Callie argued. "If I left, I'd have to move."

"Why not start your own firm?"

Something on her face must've given away her irritation, because Emmett uncrossed his arms and softened his tone.

"Sorry, I'm not trying to give you career advice," he said, lips quirking in a small smile. "I just hate that Orville gets away with treating you the way he does."

Callie released her breath, trying to dispel her instinctive annoyance.

"I've thought about it," she admitted, taking a sip of her tea. "The problem is that everyone in the area who needs a lawyer has already hired Orville. There aren't any clients left for me, and I'm not sure I'm cutthroat enough to start poaching."

"You wouldn't need to poach," Emmett said. "I meant what I said: everyone knows what Orville is like. I bet if you offered an alternative, clients would flock to you."

It wasn't a bad notion, but it wasn't quite that straightforward. Many of Orville's clients were elderly, set in their ways. The newer companies hired internal representation or remote freelancers. Callie might be able to attract some of their existing clientele to follow her, but not nearly enough to justify upending her career. No, waiting for Orville to retire, while exhausting, was better for her in the long run.

"Thanks, but it's really not that simple," Callie said, hoping he wouldn't push. Emmett was the kind of man who either didn't pay attention to the more nuanced aspects of career politics, or he didn't care. If he wanted something, he went for it. If he thought something, he said it. He'd crash and burn in the legal field, but as a person, his attitude was refreshing if irritating at times. "How's your dad? I dropped by to pick up some documents on my way in but I didn't get much of a chance to catch up. He looks well."

"For the most part," Emmett agreed, easing back into his chair and accepting her change in topic without protest. "His leg is getting worse. I keep trying to convince him to get a walker, but he's a stubborn geezer."

Callie laughed.

"You need to let him think it was his idea," she suggested. "He'll be a lot more open to it."

"How the hell am I supposed to do that?" Emmett asked, bewildered. Callie pressed her lips together to suppress another laugh.

"It's not as hard as it sounds," she said. "You just need to frame it in a way that makes it seem like you're hyping up his ideas. 'Hey Dad, I was thinking about what you said the other day and you're right, I worry too much. You can still be fully independent, and I need to respect that. Didn't you say something about getting a walker to help you move around easier when I'm not here? I think that's a great idea. I can pick one up for you on my way home from work.' That's a little ham-fisted in terms of actual application, but it works as an example."

Emmett was quiet for a moment, considering her words.

"Alright, I think I get it," he mused. "Let me try. 'Hey Cal, I was thinking about what you said earlier and you're right. Orville absolutely knew this Lichen House contract was going to be extended. Didn't you say something about starting your own firm? Great idea.' How's that?"

Callie's encouraging smile snapped into a frown, her brow raising in his direction.

"Seriously?" She rolled her eyes. "Ha ha, very funny."

Emmett just shrugged, looking entirely too pleased with himself. Callie deliberately ignored him, trying to swallow too much of her tea at once and nearly choking on it instead. The scalding liquid burned down her throat, making her eyes water.

Hot and irritating. Ironic, given her present company.

A buzz sounded from Emmett's jacket pocket, and he broke his smug eye contact to read the message. His face grew solemn, and he deflated a bit as he stood. "Sorry Cal, I've gotta get going. Seems I'm needed."

Callie checked the time on her phone, slipping it into her pants pocket as she stood too. "No worries! I need to get to the Willow before reception closes. I'm sure Nyla would stick around if I needed her to, but I'd rather not impose."

Emmett's step faltered, recovering quickly. He cocked his head to look at Callie in trepidation. "The Willow? Why?"

Callie moved to get the door for Emmett, but he beat her to it.

"I'm in town for a few days," she answered easily. "Adrian Stamkos isn't an easy man to get a meeting with. I wanted to be flexible with my schedule so I have the best chance at fitting into his. Nyla said she always has extra space, so I figured I'd stay there."

"You were talking to Nyla? Recently?"

The urgency in Emmett's voice took Callie aback as she tried to place it. Nyla and Emmett were friends, that was no secret. She'd even been a bit jealous, embarrassingly so, when she'd first found out how close they were. But Callie quickly abandoned that jealousy after spending a small amount of time with them. Now, Nyla was happily in a relationship with Aaron Klein, and Callie could see how committed they were to one another even after only a brief chance encounter at the gas station between Somerton and Hatfield. So, why would Emmett be nervous about her talking to Nyla?

Not that he would *care* what Callie thought about his relationship with Nyla. At least, she had no reason to think he would. As long as they'd known each other, Emmett never expressed any interest in Callie.

"Not since she borrowed Orville's flamethrower," Callie said. "I guess she did make the offer last spring, but I thought... well if she doesn't have room, I'll just go to the motel—"

"No."

The vehemence in Emmett's tone startled Callie into stopping in the middle of the sidewalk. Callie turned, blinking at Emmett in surprise.

"I'm sorry... did you say 'no'?"

"I said no," Emmett affirmed. "Callie, now is not a good time to be stirring things up around here. Nyla's been dealing with a lot since the factory was announced. You shouldn't bother her with *your* work on top of everything else she's got on her plate."

A spark of something— anger, spite, defiance— seared the back of Callie's throat. She stepped closer to the window, where they wouldn't be in the path of customers heading to the front entrance.

"I'm not," she insisted. "I only want a place to stay. My work is separate."

"Is it?" Emmett pressed. "You know as well as I do that Nyla isn't exactly celebrated around here. How is it going to look if you show up, badgering Stamkos about his project, and you just so happen to be staying at the Willow?"

Callie understood Nyla's position in Somerton well. Everyone did. The town hated her, due in no small part to ex-sheriff Bill Hannaford's influence, and made no attempt to hide it. Callie hated how unfairly Nyla was treated, even before they'd met. She also understood there was nothing she, or anyone else for that matter, could do about it. Once a small town made up their minds about someone, no earthly force would be able to change them. Staying at Nyla's property wasn't going to make anything worse, at least.

"It's a *lodge*, Emmett! No one is going to connect my meeting with Stamkos to Nyla. That's absurd."

"A lodge that's currently *closed* and owned by a woman who's known to go to unreasonable lengths for her friends."

Callie snapped her jaw shut, biting her tongue before she said something she'd regret. Emmett waited for her to relent, his expression unyielding. She counted to three, carefully composing her response to be free of venom.

"Well, I appreciate your concern, but I would rather talk to Nyla about this." Callie deliberately checked the time on her phone screen. "I need to get going."

"You need to go *home*." Emmett's voice hardened, crossing his arms over his chest. Callie blinked in shock, the urge to argue with him warring with the bewilderment at Emmett's seemingly unwarranted reaction.

"I can't," she said slowly. "I need to secure this contract, or Orville will work himself into the grave."

"You can sort it from Hatfield," Emmett insisted, shuffling around her with assertive movements. He put his hand between her shoulders, carefully but firmly pushing her toward her vehicle. Callie was so shocked that she let him, her brain running like mud. "Adrian Stamkos probably won't listen to you anyway. Save yourself the trouble and send him an email he can ignore."

"Excuse me?" Irritation and offense loosened Callie's tongue. She dug her heels into the gravel, forcing them both to a stop. "Are you saying that because he's an asshole, or because you don't think I can handle my job?"

"He's an asshole," Emmett said quickly. "And you have better things to do with your time. *Outside* Somerton."

"I don't recall giving you permission to dictate how I spend my time." Callie planted her hands on her hips, all of her nervous babbling gone in favor of her annoyance. Emmett may be attractive, but that wasn't an excuse to get away with whatever he wanted. Even if his attitude *did* make him clench his jaw in a way that made his cheekbones stand out.

Damnit, Callie. Focus.

"I'm not arguing with you about this, Callie. This is a fool's errand." Emmett turned away from her and headed toward a rusted old pickup that Callie recognized as belonging to Ephraim. "Adrian Stamkos isn't a problem you can solve over dinner, and Nyla has too much to worry about with S&S. She doesn't need you adding to it. Leave it alone."

"All the more reason for me to *stay*," she snapped. "If Nyla's being affected by this build, then having another business on her side will only help her cause!"

"And push her further into the role of town scapegoat!" Emmett barked back. "She's been through enough, Cal. Good intentions or not, you'd be more of a help if you'd just leave."

With that, Emmett hauled open the driver's side door of the truck. He didn't hop in yet, waiting to see what Callie would do, expecting her to listen and drive Orville's car back the way she'd come. Maybe he was right, and she should do that; clearly there was more going on here than she originally thought. But Callie was never good at following orders.

Her blood burned hot with indignation, churning uncomfortable feelings in her stomach. Before she knew what she was doing, Callie had her phone in her hand. She dialed, pressing the speakerphone icon and waiting as the rings sounded. One, two, three, four.

"Willow Lodge, we're not accepting reservations at the moment but if you'd like to leave your name—"

"Nyla? Is that you?"

Callie spoke pointedly, keeping her tone light for Nyla's sake but boring a glare in Emmett's direction. He met her gaze steadily, silently warning her to stop.

"Callie? Hey! Oh my God, how are you?" Nyla's voice lost its elevated professionalism, dissolving into her normal cadence. *"If this is about the flamethrower, I need it for just a little bit longer if that's alright?"*

"Totally fine," Callie said with a deliberate smile. "I was actually wondering if you were busy this afternoon. I'm in town and I was hoping to stop by to discuss some things."

Emmett's glare soured, realizing she wasn't going to be intimidated out of this. Callie held his accusatory look, daring him to try to stop her again.

"Sure! I'm here for the rest of the evening. We won't be alone if that's okay. I've got some friends here, and Emmett just went out for a coffee run but he'll be back soon. It's a full house, honestly. But if it's business, we can always go into the office."

"Emmett?" Callie repeated in surprise. "I thought he was working today?"

"Work? No, he's on PTO until next week." Callie quirked her brow at him from where she stood, filing the lie away for future examination. *"Why? Have you been talking to him?"*

"Just assumed," Callie said, shrugging. To any of the other customers in the lot, Emmett and Callie probably looked insane. They were locked in a silent standoff, Callie on the phone disproving at least two things Emmett told her and Emmett warning her with his body language to drop whatever thread she was pulling. She had no intention to, of course. "I'll head over now then, if that works."

"Of course! I'll see you soon!"

Callie dropped her phone into her pocket, still holding Emmett's glare. She used her key fob to unlock her vehicle, the unassuming beep sounding off like a war horn. Without allowing Emmett to speak, Callie returned to her car and, still seething, pulled out of the cafe parking lot and headed in the direction of the Willow.

Chapter Four

EMMETT

Shit.

Blood roared in Emmett's ears as he angrily shoved his truck into drive, reminding himself to keep to the speed limit as he followed Callie to the Willow.

She shouldn't be here. He didn't want her anywhere near here, not with the threat of imminent death lurking in every shadow. Visiting Somerton was one thing, especially in the daylight, but to *stay* here? For several days? It was a suicide mission, and Callie had no idea of the danger she was putting herself in. The moment Emmett realized she meant to remain in town, all reason left his body. He was running on pure instinct, and that instinct was to get Callie the hell out of harm's way.

That didn't mean he'd gone about it elegantly, though. The longer he drove in tense silence, the more the irritation in his stomach dimmed, making room for shame to take its place. What was it about Callie that had his emotions on a wire, ready to veer to either side at the slightest whim? He wasn't this volatile with anyone else, not even Nyla, who tended to intentionally pick away at his last nerve. There was something about Callie specifically that dragged out the caveman in him. Maybe it was her hair, so orange it practically glowed, cut in a severe bob that sharpened the otherwise soft planes of her face. Maybe it was her body, all lush curves and freckled skin. Maybe it was that little spark of fire in her eyes that she kept firmly hidden, buried beneath layers of propriety and business sense. Emmett wanted nothing more than to stoke that flame, to watch as it exploded into an inferno of Callie's true feelings. To make her let go. It struck him as a challenge, and that was a problem. Emmett craved a challenge, and this one came with the company of a stunning woman. How could he possibly turn the other cheek?

He remembered the day they met. Ephraim received the call from Ed and Tara that he was hired as groundskeeper, and Emmett was invited to accompany them on the tour of the property since his firm was in talks for the renovations. When Orville's ancient Cavalier pulled into the parking lot, Emmett was prepared for a standoff. He hadn't dealt with Orville Guttenberg personally, but he'd heard the stories. He crossed his arms over his chest, squaring his shoulders to make himself look bigger.

Then Callie stepped out of the passenger side door, and Emmett's breath left him in a whoosh.

She was stunning, quite literally. Every single word in Emmett's vocabulary fell out of his head as the sun caught her fiery hair, reflecting off the sheen of her lip gloss. God, her mouth was practically begging to be kissed. Or maybe *he* was practically begging to kiss it. Either way, Emmett's hands twitched in the crooks of his elbows, fighting the physical urge to grab onto the rounded curves of Callie's hips. If not for his father's timely snort of laughter at his expense, Emmett would've happily stood there, rooted in place, staring at Callie until she either slapped him or stalked away, leaving him changed and empty.

Emmett had crushes before, and none of them electrified his patience the way Callie did, leaving him struggling for air and a semblance of calm. As attractive as she was, Emmett couldn't entirely blame his hormones for his rash behaviour. He *wasn't* a caveman, after all. At least, not last time he checked.

Callie beat him to the Willow, which he was anticipating. He'd thought about calling Nyla ahead of his arrival and instructing her not to let Callie stay on the property, but that was a terrible idea. The quickest way to get Nyla to do anything was to explicitly prohibit her from doing so. Emmett smothered a huff of exasperation.

How did he end up surrounded by such infuriatingly strong-willed women? It was exhausting.

As he pulled into the parking lot, deliberately choosing a spot close to the front entrance, Emmett saw Callie emerge from Orville's rickety Cavalier, the very same one she'd stepped out of that first day. To his endless annoyance, she locked eyes with him and, in no rush, walked purposefully toward the Willow. Emmett held back a grumble. Strong-willed, stubborn, *and* defiant. What did it say about him, that he was both irritated and mildly aroused by it? Nothing he was prepared to examine at the moment.

Jerking the truck into park, Emmett vaulted from the driver's seat.

"Callie!" he barked, almost believing for a moment that he could manage a gentler tone. The roughness in his voice quickly dashed that hope. Callie ignored him, reaching the front door and pulling it open with more force than necessary. Emmett ground his teeth together, convincing himself that barging in and yelling was not the most efficient way to handle things.

It was tempting, though.

By the time he was greeted by the rush of warmth from the Willow's oil heating, Callie was across the room in an excited embrace with Nyla. In their current position, Nyla's back was to him and Callie was facing him, making eye contact over Nyla's shoulder. Emmett scowled, twitching his chin to the side in a subtle command even as he approached the pair. Callie raised a brow at him. Her words carried through the empty space between them, spoken to Nyla but with a defiance that Emmett knew could only be directed at him.

"Actually, I was hoping I could talk business with you. Do you have somewhere private we can chat?"

Don't you fucking dare, Callie!

"Hang on—" Emmett tried, his call swallowed by Nyla's enthusiastic reply.

"Sure! Let's head into the office. Suits?"

Aaron regarded Emmett with mild confusion as they made their way toward the front office. Emmett picked up his pace, trying to catch Aaron's shoulder before they all disappeared behind a locked door. He thought he was going to make it as Aaron seemed to hear his approach, pausing his stride, but Callie was one step ahead. She called out to Aaron just as Emmett was gaining ground. As quickly as hope sprung to life in his chest, it died in a puff of smoke and a door clicking shut. Emmett skidded to an abrupt halt in the middle of the lobby, breathing hard.

Shit.

He could knock. He thought about it, seriously, for far longer than he should've. He could knock, but what was the point? If he interrupted them, there was nothing he could say to convince Nyla that she shouldn't hear Callie's proposal. If nothing else, she'd want to hear it *more* simply because he protested. Whatever was going to happen now, he needed to let it play out without him.

A task much easier said than done.

After running through a series of scenarios, none of which resulted in Callie heading home to Hatfield without the use of physical force, Emmett finally took note of his audience. Amelia and Sam were standing by the large window on the eastern side of the Willow's main building, facing a wall of trees. They regarded him with a mixture of confusion and worry. Tyler was nowhere to be seen, likely touching base with Agent Kelley.

Amelia nodded to Emmett, signalling him to join her and Sam by the window. He did, a knot already forming in the pit of his stomach. Amelia's expression was grave, a far cry from her usual combination of amused and exasperated.

"Wanna talk about it?" she asked, not bothering to specify what 'it' was. Emmett shook his head. She nodded, accepting that answer without hesitation. That was something he appreciated about Amelia; she understood when not to push.

"What's wrong?" Emmett asked instead, noting the tension in the air.

"I sent the drone out while you were gone," she said under her breath, turning her phone screen toward him. Emmett muttered a curse at the clear circle of freezing temperatures nestled among the trees. "Last I checked, it was on a path that would take it by the cabin. We're staying here tonight."

"No point in risking it," Sam agreed, wrapping his arm around Amelia's hips and hooking his thumb in her belt loop to anchor her to him. "It's not dark yet, but the cabin's in a valley. No telling what kind of shadow cover the thing will have."

"I'm more concerned about how quickly this one popped up," Amelia said, biting her bottom lip. It was already red, like she'd been chewing it for some time. "Less than a day since the last one. It must've jumped bodies right away."

"If that's how this works," Sam added. "We don't know if this is the same baddie playing *The Exorcist*'s version of Hot Potato or if it's a bunch of different spirits. Maybe it's not possession at all. Maybe it's a disease, like *Cabin Fever*. Has anyone checked the water supply?"

"Ignore him," Amelia gave Emmett a half-smile, "we've been watching a lot of movies to pass the time. Sex is great and all but at some point, you start worrying about getting dehydrated."

"I've got something to keep you hydrated." Sam raised his eyebrows suggestively, earning himself an elbow to the ribs. Emmett was barely paying attention, his gaze flickering to the hall where Nyla's voice could be heard over the dull hum of the fluorescent lights.

"Better to stay put," Emmett agreed solemnly, guessing that he'd missed some crucial change in topic by the confused looks Amelia and Sam gave at his response. In truth, he hadn't heard a word since he'd seen the drone image. As soon as he'd registered the presence of yet another creature, his thoughts turned right back to Callie.

What was the likelihood of Nyla agreeing to let Callie stay on the premises? Emmett tried to put himself in Nyla's headspace, working through the risks and rewards of both options. If Nyla turned Callie down, then she would go to the motel. She'd said as much to Emmett, and he had no doubt she would say the same to Nyla. Nyla wouldn't want that. If Callie was going to stay in Somerton, Nyla would make sure she stayed at the Willow. Advising her to go home wouldn't even cross her mind.

But it *would* cross Aaron's.

It was no secret that Aaron and Nyla disagreed on one fundamental aspect of the impossible situation they found themselves in. Nyla wanted to be more open about what they were dealing with, bring as many people into the loop as possible to give them the best chance at finding a permanent solution and keeping everyone safe. She thought that if the townspeople understood what they were up against, they could take the proper precautions.

Aaron, on the other hand, was firmly in the camp of keeping things quiet. He doubted the townspeople would listen to anything they had to say, even if it came through George Mason. Worse, he suspected they would have a repeat incident of George's bounty hunt from last month. To Nyla, the problem with George's plan was a lack of transparency. To Aaron, it was a lack of discretion.

Emmett didn't know which side of the fence he fell on in general, but he knew for sure what side he'd pick concerning Callie. He had to trust that Aaron would emerge as the voice of reason, convincing Callie that now was not the time to be pursuing an audience with Adrian Stamkos. He just needed to do it *quickly*.

Sam's cabin may be in a valley, but the Willow wasn't. Callie could still leave, safely. Emmett just hoped he could convince her of that before it was too late.

Chapter Five

CALLIE

"Sorry for the sudden invasion," Callie said, folding her hands neatly in her lap. Emmett's rapid approach had rattled her, convinced that he was about to burst through the door and demand that Nyla reject her request. The longer they spoke, uninterrupted by angered knocking, the more Callie relaxed.

Whatever the hell Emmett's problem was, he wasn't desperate enough to drag Nyla into it directly. Good.

"Don't be," Nyla said, offering her a mini chocolate bar from an orange plastic bowl on her desk. It looked like leftover Halloween candy. Callie accepted gratefully. "Things are a bit... chaotic here right now, but I'll do what I can. What did you want to talk about?"

Callie hesitated, framing her approach carefully. While her primary motivation *was* to speak to Adrian Stamkos on behalf of her clients, she hadn't lied to Emmett. Working together would likely benefit whatever Nyla was trying to accomplish as well. But... on the off chance that she was wrong, the last thing she wanted was to make things harder for Nyla.

Emmett's bluster contained nuggets of truth. Callie wasn't sure she'd be able to handle the level of ostracization Nyla endured, and she certainly didn't want to add to her stress.

From the outside, at least, it seemed like Nyla was handling things well. She looked happy, as she always did, with a sparkle in her pale green eyes that hinted at some mischief brewing beneath the surface. Her pinkish-blonde hair dusted the tops of her shoulders, a bit longer than it had been the last time Callie saw her. Even her clothes were more or less the same, comprised of army-green cargo pants and a tight-fitting cropped t-shirt with bright blue lettering that spelled 'LOVE' across her chest. Nyla was unapologetically herself, and Callie was relieved to see that she wasn't openly suffering under public scrutiny.

Still, Callie didn't want to make more trouble for her. She'd have to be delicate about this.

"Do you remember the charity cook-off in Hatfield last March?" Callie began, fighting the familiar urge to fidget. "You mentioned that you often had free rooms. Is that still the case?"

"Now more than ever," Nyla said, laughing. "Every room is free, aside from mine. The Willow has been closed for months. It's... complicated."

"I understand," Callie interjected quickly. "You don't need to share if you don't want to, but if there's anything I can do, particularly from the legal side of things, please let me know. I know you've been struggling with Stamkos & Stein's new project. That's actually why I'm here."

"You have dealings with Adrian Stamkos?" Aaron cut in, his eyebrow twitching in the barest betrayal of surprise and interest. "Has he contracted you for negotiations with the town?"

"No, nothing like that," Callie assured him, and some of the tension released from Aaron's shoulders.

He was much harder to read than Nyla. In some ways, it was a mystery how they ended up together. Aaron seemed like Nyla's opposite in every conceivable way, even visually; he was tall where she was short, he had dark hair where she had light, his body was lean and hard where hers was compact and plush. Aaron gave off an air of seriousness that echoed in his image, including everything from his sharp features down to the clean lines of his charcoal grey suit. On the other hand, watching Nyla and Aaron together clicked everything into place. Instead of distancing them, their opposing traits balanced each other perfectly, bringing out Aaron's levity and grounding Nyla's optimism.

"My clients, the couple renovating Lichen House, are concerned that the factory's proximity to their property will kill any business they might attract before the project's even off the ground," Callie said, watching Nyla and Aaron carefully for their reactions. "They're panicking, and I have a feeling they're considering offering the land to S&S in an effort to recoup their losses."

"They'd sell Lichen House? To Stamkos?" Nyla repeated, blinking slowly as she processed the information. Callie waited a breath, letting the implications sink in. Her clients hadn't mentioned the possibility of selling yet, but Callie had to assume it crossed their minds. She needed to intervene before that passing notion became a full-fledged option.

If S&S purchased Lichen House, then the only property standing between their two lots would be the Willow. It was only a matter of time before the court of public opinion began pressuring Nyla to sell her business to Adrian Stamkos. With a corporate genius like Stamkos at the helm, how long would Nyla be able to hold him off? Not indefinitely. Nyla was stubborn, spirited, and resourceful, but she couldn't stand up against the tools in Adrian Stamkos' arsenal. If she refused to sell, he would simply put her out of business. Callie had seen those tactics more than once; it was how multi-million-dollar corporations kept themselves on top and forced small businesses in line.

"My goal is to prevent that from happening," Callie continued. "I've managed to track down contact info for Stamkos' office, but I haven't called yet. He's a busy man, I may only get one chance to speak with him and I can't afford to miss it. I wanted to make sure I'd be able to meet at the drop of a hat before I reached out."

"Where does Nyla come into this?" Aaron asked, crossing his arms over his chest. He was leaning one hip against the desk in a relaxed pose, but his body language was alert, ready, and paying very close attention to the words coming from Callie's mouth.

"I don't know much about your problems with Stamkos," Callie said. "All the same, I think we can help each other. If nothing else, I can give you some business for a short time. That's why I originally came by. I wanted to see if I could stay in one of your cabins for a few days. I'd pay you in full of course."

"Originally?" Nyla repeated, her attention flickering to the door so briefly that Callie wasn't sure it happened at all. "Why do you say it like that?"

"Oh," Callie shifted in her chair, "I... I ran into Emmett on the way over here. He mentioned that you were being affected by the S&S build. I didn't mean to pry."

Nyla and Aaron looked at each other, unreadable expressions on their faces.

"What exactly did Emmett say?" Nyla prompted. Callie couldn't stop the flash of annoyance that pursed her lips.

"What *didn't* he say?" she grumbled. "Sorry, our conversation wasn't exactly pleasant. Is he... is Ephraim okay? Is there something going on with Emmett's employer? He was very... abrasive."

"I think we're all a little on edge right now," Aaron assured her. "It's certainly been an interesting few months."

"Understandably," Callie agreed. "It just seemed like it was more than that. I've never seen Emmett so upset."

"I wouldn't worry about it," Nyla said, smirking. "Emmett isn't always great with the whole communication thing. He was probably trying to be serious and it just came off as dickish."

"If you say so." Callie had her doubts, but then again, Nyla wasn't there. "So, about the cabin. Would it be okay if I rented one for the week? I realize you're closed, so I'll take care of my own housekeeping and everything. I only need a bed."

"Normally that would be a snap yes," Nyla promised. "But..."

"But now is not a great time," Aaron finished for her. "Is it possible for you to drive in from Hatfield once you've scheduled your meeting with Stamkos?"

"I might have as little as a twenty-minute window from when I finally speak to him to attending the meeting. I need to be available to make any timeframe work. If I can't stay here, that's completely fine. I'll reach out to the motel on the interstate. They always have rooms, I just wanted to speak to you first. I'd much rather stay here if I have the option."

"You're not staying *there*," Nyla insisted, frowning. "That place is gross. If it's going to be here or the motel, you're staying here."

"Nyla."

At the warning tone in Aaron's voice, Nyla looked up at him. They held each others' stares for a breath, silently communicating. Callie tried to interpret their body language, but they were both too tense to give anything away.

Why *was* everyone so tense? Emmett, Nyla, Aaron... all three of them were disproportionately on edge for the situation. Financial and business troubles were undeniably stressful, but Callie couldn't shake the feeling that more was lingering beneath the surface. She just couldn't see it yet.

Eventually, Nyla lifted her chin, ignoring Aaron's minute head shake, and turned back to Callie.

"Of course you can stay here," she said, her tone final. "I'll get you a key."

By the time Callie's cabin was settled, she felt much better. Aaron was clearly unhappy with the way things had turned out, but Nyla was determined to ignore his frustration. She gave Callie a cabin close to hers, along with a list of important new safety rules in light of the bear attacks over the summer. Some of the rules seemed odd to Callie, particularly the curfew, but she was too relieved to question it now. She succeeded in securing lodgings for the week, and that was a win worth celebrating.

Her confrontation with Emmett was long forgotten, until they emerged from the office and were met with his agitated glare. Emmett was standing next to two others, a woman and man that Callie recognized as being the same ones Nyla was speaking to when she arrived. They hadn't been introduced yet, as Callie was in a rush to meet with Nyla before Emmett caught up to them.

"Well?"

Emmett's question was said to the three of them, but Callie knew it was directed at her. She met his scowl defiantly.

"I'll be staying here for the remainder of the week," she said proudly. "Is that a problem?"

Instead of responding, Emmett clenched his jaw tightly. Ignoring Callie's question, he locked eyes with Nyla.

"Can I talk to you for a minute?"

"Is everything okay?" Nyla pressed, looking confused. "Jesus Em, you look like you sat on a railway spike."

"I just need to talk to you," he insisted, rolling his eyes. "Alone. Now."

The blunt response clearly surprised Nyla, her eyebrows raising noticeably.

"Okay, Little Miss Sunshine," she deadpanned. "Talk. Office. Now."

Nyla mirrored Emmett's scowl, comedically harrumphing and stomping back toward the office, making aggravated grunting noises in a poor imitation of Emmett's low timbre. Callie covered her mouth to stop her chuckle. Emmett followed silently.

"I'll introduce you," Aaron said suddenly, gesturing to the two other people in the room. "Callie, this is Sam Fisher and Amelia Bradley. They're staying at Sam's family cabin for a while."

"Pleasure to meet you," Callie said with a polite smile. Amelia returned the greeting, while Sam saluted her.

Amelia looked like one of the girls Callie would've been afraid of in high school. Not the preppy, popular cheerleader type, but the ones that looked like they could either kick your ass or save your life, depending on their mood. She was average in height, a little shorter than Callie but much taller than Nyla, with long, dark-brown hair that hung in loose waves. The ends were dyed a deep plum purple that almost matched the half-zipped hoodie she was wearing on top of a plain black tank-top and light-wash jeans. But it wasn't so much her appearance that gave Callie her initial impression, it was the way she held herself. Confident in a way that was almost standoffish, while hanging back like she didn't want to be perceived.

Sam, on the other hand, was the embodiment of energy. Even sitting still, he practically vibrated with life. His hair, which was short, sandy-brown, and slightly curly, was combed through and styled chaotically to one side like he'd been sprinting in a windstorm before parking himself on the lobby couch. Callie got the impression that her imagined scenario wasn't too far off. Sam was athletically built, bulky, and muscled in a way that only came from consistent training. He would be intimidating too, if not for the beaming, lopsided grin he wore.

"I need to know how you did it," Sam asked eagerly. Callie frowned.

"How I did what?"

"How you pissed Emmett off!" Sam threw his arms up in exasperation. "I've been trying to rattle him for weeks and I haven't gotten more than a mildly irritated sigh. You spend five minutes with him and he's spitting brimstone. I'm so jealous. You need to tell me your secret."

"I don't think 'spitting brimstone' is a real phrase," Amelia pointed out. Sam waved off her comment.

"So, what'd you do?" he prodded. "Was it violent? Did you knee him in the balls? Or was it verbal? Did you insult his dad? Or— oh God, did you insult his *hat?*"

"Ignore him," Amelia said pointedly. "That's what we do."

"*You* can't ignore this dick," Sam teased, humping the air and earning a gentle punch to the arm from Amelia. Callie pressed her lips together to hide her laughter. Alright, so Sam and Amelia were a couple. That also made a strange sort of sense.

They made small talk for a while, waiting for Emmett and Nyla to re-emerge. Callie was enjoying herself at first, letting herself be distracted by Sam's outlandish anecdotes and Amelia's clear exasperation, both a sharp contrast to Aaron's calm tolerance. They all worked well together, even though it didn't seem like they should. Callie could easily picture the room becoming even more animated with Nyla's cheery optimism and Emmett's usual dry teasing. A pang of something echoed in Callie's chest, but she didn't have time to examine it. The clock on the wall chimed seven, and it occurred to her that Emmett and Nyla were taking a long time to join them.

When another ten minutes had passed and there was still no sign of them, Callie began to worry. Surely Emmett wouldn't change Nyla's mind after they'd already agreed, would he? Maybe she should try to politely excuse herself to settle in; if Emmett did manage to change Nyla's mind, perhaps Callie could guilt her into changing it back by having everything out of her suitcase before they left the office. Callie reached into her pocket to touch her cabin key in reassurance, but it wasn't there.

It was still on Nyla's desk.

"Crap," she muttered. "I left my cabin key in the office. Do you think they'll be much longer? I'd like to unpack my bag."

"Hard to say," Aaron said, humming in thought. "Nyla tends to go off track when Emmett is around. They're good at getting on each other's nerves. If I were you, I'd just go knock and ask her for the key."

"You don't think they'd mind?"

"Not at all," Aaron promised, giving her a polite smile. "They probably don't realize how long they've been gone."

"Or they're engaged in a hot, sweaty affair on the filing cabinet," Sam teased. "Listen carefully, maybe we can hear the metal shaking."

"The filing cabinet is too short," Aaron drawled, giving Sam a pointed look. "He'd have better luck with the bookshelf."

"And you know from experience?"

"At least three, give or take."

"Bullshit," Sam scoffed. "You would never defile the sanctity of proper organization practices."

"If you're trying to bait me into giving you office sex tips, all you have to do is ask."

Amelia snorted at the outraged expression that overtook Sam's face. Callie chose that moment to slip away, smothering her laugh as Sam demanded where Aaron learned such poor manners, and Aaron replied something about working with a man named Pratt for several years.

The office was just out of sight of the lobby, around the corner in a narrow hallway. Callie's stomach twisted to see that the door was still shut.

Sam was joking, but the image of Emmett and Nyla fooling around just out of earshot had left Callie feeling nauseated. She picked up her pace, lifting her hand to knock, when Nyla's voice sounded from the office, muffled and annoyed and definitely *not* wanton.

"It'll be *fine*, Em. The six of us can handle it—"

"Five." Emmett's voice cut in sharply, greeted with a beat of stunned silence. Callie pictured Nyla staring balefully at him, annoyed at his outburst.

"Six." As expected, Nyla's voice was jagged with warning. "Unless you want to handcuff Pratt to a light pole somewhere."

Another beat of silence, followed by Emmett's harsh exhale.

"Right. Tyler. I—"

"You thought I was talking about Callie," Nyla finished for him, her tone accusing and unapologetic. "What the hell is up with that, anyway? You've been a colossal jackass since she showed up. Did something happen between you two?"

Any guilt Callie felt about eavesdropping evaporated. She'd been wondering the same all evening, and she wasn't about to give up this chance to finally get answers.

"I don't have an issue with Callie." Emmett sounded closer now, like he was walking toward the door, trying to escape the conversation. Callie panicked, taking a huge step back, but then Nyla's dry laugh cut through the quiet.

"Okay, that's the biggest lie I've heard in awhile, which is really saying something." Shuffling sounds filled the room, like Nyla was approaching Emmett. "Wanna try that one again?"

"I don't," Emmett insisted, and Callie wasn't sure if he was answering her question or repeating his lie. "Callie's great. I've never had a problem with her."

"Is it difficult to walk with your pants on fire? I've always wondered."

Callie covered her mouth to stifle her snort of laughter.

"Look, do you want me to say it?" Emmett's words took on a defensive edge. "Fine. I don't want her here. There's no reason for her to be here, so I'd like her to leave. Happy?"

No, absolutely not. Callie was anything but happy. Emmett's curt dismissal of her stung, lancing through her chest and choking her with dismay. It shouldn't hurt as much as it did, but Callie couldn't ignore the sudden whoosh of air from her lungs, like she'd been struck hard in the chest. Frowning, Callie stared at the ground as she tried to unravel the feeling.

Nyla agreeing to let her stay here meant more than just a chance to speak to Stamkos. Callie wasn't sure where she stood with Nyla; she liked to think they were friends, but she'd been too afraid to test her theory. Callie didn't have many friends. If she showed up to the Willow and was rejected, Callie would've taken it hard. It didn't make any sense. Refusing a reservation was not a declaration that she wasn't a friend, but Callie knew that's how she would've felt. But Nyla *did* accept her, and the relief that brought was more than a simple victory over Emmett's head. It was confirmation that Callie was right. She and Nyla were, if not friends, then something like it. The foundation was there.

She hadn't realized how badly she wanted that connection, that security. Callie wanted *friends*, and the epiphany was both terrifying and absurd.

Independence was a cornerstone of her identity. Callie grew up in Louisiana, where everyone was loud and welcoming and buried their problems behind bright smiles and homecooked meals. Then, Callie moved to New York, where people were openly cold and dismissive. Graduating law school and entering the work force only solidified her dependence on herself. Her entire life, Callie understood that she needed to navigate the world on her own, suffer quietly and put on a brave face. She was good at it, in fact. One of the few things she *was* good at.

Callie didn't have friends. She didn't go out. She didn't have hobbies. She barely *lived*. If she couldn't be happy with that, then what did she have left?

She had Nyla. Or, at least, she *wanted* to have Nyla. Coming to the Willow unannounced, asking for a favor, wasn't something Callie would normally do. She'd taken a chance without consciously considering what it meant: an act of potential friendship, thin and fragile, and more important to her than she ever thought it could be.

Before she could escape unnoticed, the door to Nyla's office flung open. Callie hadn't been paying attention, so she missed whatever was said between Emmett's confession and their exit. She schooled herself quickly, donning a neutral smile that conveyed she didn't mind the wait, burying her hurt under a thick layer of professionalism.

Nyla stared at her in surprise, her hand still on the doorknob.

"Callie? How long have you been waiting out here?"

She was about to answer 'not long,' when the stark confusion on Nyla's face finally registered. Sure, she'd been standing there for a while now, but it wasn't long enough for Nyla to completely forget when she—

The realization struck her with the force of a lightning bolt. Oh god. She'd forgotten to knock.

When Emmett and Nyla's voices drifted through the door, Callie had completely forgotten to announce herself. She was just standing there in the hallway, obviously listening to a private conversation. What the hell was wrong with her?

"I'm sorry!" she exclaimed, praying her face wasn't as red as she suspected it was. "I was just coming to ask for my key. I think I left it on your desk."

"You did," Nyla said, smiling. She reached into her back pocket and produced the key, holding it out to Callie. "I was about to bring it to you. Come on, I'll show you to your cabin."

Callie caught Emmett's eye over Nyla's head, and the warning in them sparked a surge of defiance that fizzled much faster than she was expecting. Her stomach was still in confused knots about her feelings, and the hostility in Emmett's glare struck her harder than it would've 30 minutes ago. She and Nyla may be working toward friendship, but she and Emmett certainly weren't, and Callie hated how much that rejection bothered her.

Suddenly, her conversation with Aaron, Sam, and Amelia took on new weight. Were they just tolerating her presence? A slurry of awkward pauses and fumbled words flashed through her memory, and Callie couldn't tell if she was retroactively fabricating the irritation in their expressions or if it had been there all along and she was oblivious to it until now.

She was unsettled. Off-balance. Hang the contract, Callie needed some time to *breathe,* to figure out what the hell was wrong with her.

"Actually, Nyla," Callie interrupted, her heart racing with discomfort. "I don't think I'll be needing it after all. I... I got a call from Orville, and he needs me back in Hatfield right away. I'm sorry to have inconvenienced you."

The lie tasted bitter on her tongue, like she was admitting defeat. Part of her desperately hoped that Nyla and Emmett would argue with her, give her some explanation as to what she'd overheard. *If* they even knew that she'd overheard.

"You're leaving now?" Nyla frowned, her gaze darting to Emmett so quickly Callie almost thought she'd imagined it. Emmett may not know that Callie had been eavesdropping, but she was fairly certain that Nyla did. "What about Stamkos? I was going to ask you to spend the night here in the main building with all of us so we could talk strategy—"

"I'll walk you to your car," Emmett said, brushing past Nyla with a look of hard determination. Nyla bristled, and the look on her face told Callie that this hadn't been the plan, and she was about to let Emmett know just what she thought about his interference. Callie jumped in first, not wanting to cause any more trouble than she already had.

"No thank you," she said firmly. Emmett paused in his stalking to glance back at her in mild surprise. "I'm perfectly capable of walking thirty feet by myself."

"Seriously, Callie," Nyla called out, rushing after them as they made their way to the lobby. "It's getting pretty late. Even if you don't stay the rest of the week, I'd feel better if you spent the night. We were thinking about watching a movie—"

"Callie doesn't like comedies." Emmett spoke as if his word was final, which pushed aside some of the betrayal Callie was feeling and replaced it with anger.

"Did I ask you to speak for me, Emmett? Because I don't think I did."

"What's going on?" Aaron stood from his seat at the front desk, furrowing his brow in concern. His attention drifted between Nyla, Emmett, and Callie, gathering much more from his quick perusal than Callie ever could. "Is everything alright?"

"Callie needs to head home, but I was offering for her to stay the night with us," Nyla said urgently. "It's getting late, and I—"

"It's not dark yet—" Emmett cut in, but Nyla whipped around to him so fast that even Callie flinched.

"Coady, if you cut me off one more time, I'll *cut off* your dick and gag you with it." Nyla's threat was heeded, and for the first time since Callie arrived, Emmett looked chastised over his brutish behaviour. With his silent promise to let her speak, Nyla turned to Callie. "It's late. The roads aren't safe this time of year anyway, but it's worse at night. I'd feel a lot better if you waited until morning to head out."

Callie wanted to accept. Even now, she wanted to believe she had a reason to be here. She wanted to stay the night, watch a movie, eat snacks, and laugh. She wanted acceptance, comfort. One look at Emmett's irate expression told her she wouldn't find it here. Not now.

"Really, it's okay." Callie shrugged, hoping she looked nonchalant. "I promised Orville I'd leave right away."

Damn it, Quinn. Get it together. You barely know these people. You shouldn't care what they think!

"That might be better anyway." Amelia's voice startled her, interjecting from across the room. She wasn't looking at Callie though, her gaze was fixated on

Nyla, having an unspoken conversation. "If she leaves now, Callie can make it to Hatfield before nightfall. That's the safest option."

Nyla looked like she wanted to argue, but that was when Callie noticed that Amelia wasn't the only one staring meaningfully at them. Everyone in the room was watching Nyla warily, something heavy in the air between them, some secret they all shared. Callie knew then that whatever potential comradery she'd felt earlier was gone now, lost to an intangible connection that she wasn't a part of. Even Nyla was looking uncertain, caught between the silence and her desire to defy the group consensus.

Callie waited, and when Nyla still said nothing, she decided she'd had enough. Whatever this was, whatever insecurities she'd unearthed, Callie could process them at home, by herself. Then maybe she could call Nyla, go out for coffee, try again. Right now, she felt too raw. Too uncertain.

"It's fine. I've already overstayed my welcome. You guys have fun."

"Callie—" Nyla stepped forward as if to stop her, but Emmett got in her way. Callie gave him a chance to speak, to say something that would explain his hostility, to apologize or own up. He did nothing, just watched as her patience finally snapped and Callie stomped determinedly to the front door of the Willow, praying she could keep her tears at bay long enough to get inside her car and drive away. Before she could flatten her hand against the door and push, Nyla's shout shattered the air.

"There's a monster out there!"

The words stopped Callie in her tracks, turning to stare at Nyla in stunned silence. Her words echoed in the lodge lobby, panicked and loud. A... monster?

Callie was pleased to see she wasn't the only one shocked by Nyla's outburst. Amelia and Sam were staring at Nyla with open confusion, Amelia's mouth open in a slight 'o' of surprise. Aaron's expression was as close to outwardly shocked as Callie had ever seen, the earlier frustration seeping into his body language once again. Emmett had his back to her now, fully facing Nyla, but the tense set of his shoulders gave away his anger.

Nyla ignored them all, her gaze locked on Callie.

"Okay, I know that sounds insane." Nyla stepped forward, brushing past Emmett who didn't move out of her way, forcing her to push his arm aside to get to Callie. "And I would've liked to ease you into the idea more gently. I mean, ideally you wouldn't have had to find out at all. But given the circumstances, I don't think we have much of a choice. You *can't* go out there, Callie. Not now. Not when the sun is already starting to set."

"Because... there's a monster." Callie blinked, begging her brain to work faster.

"Yes." Nyla sighed, looking older and more exhausted in that small movement. "There's a creature out there in the forest and it's been hunting anyone who enters its territory for the last few months. It can't go out in direct sunlight which is why Emmett was trying to get you to leave before dark. The problem with that—" Nyla shot a venomous glare at the back of Emmett's head "—is that the sun is low enough in the sky that half the property is covered in shadow. I'm not sending you out there like a lamb to slaughter."

Nyla's attention turned to the others, lingering on Aaron. He was still visibly irritated, but something in her face softened his anger. Callie flinched as Nyla took her hand, pleading with her.

"You have every right to think that I'm completely crazy, that I need to be committed, that I'm on drugs, whatever your first instincts are. I don't need you to believe me right now, I just need you to listen and *stay*."

Silence descended following Nyla's wish. Callie didn't know whether to laugh or cry.

"She's telling the truth," Amelia said from her chair. She got up as Callie turned to face her, slowly making her way across the room like she was approaching a spooked animal. "We didn't believe it at first either, and we actually *saw* the thing before hearing the story."

"It's definitely safer for you here," Sam agreed. "Think of it like vampire rules. No sunlight, can't come in unless invited."

"We'll answer any questions you have." Aaron was speaking now, which surprised Callie most of all. He struck Callie as the reasonable one, the no-nonsense detective that grounded everyone around him. The fact that he was playing into this... this... whatever it was, confused Callie more than she could properly express. "I know this is a lot to take in, and Nyla's right, we would've preferred to explain everything more delicately. Will you give us that chance?"

Everyone fell quiet again, all staring at Callie and waiting for an answer. All except Emmett, who remained stubbornly facing away from her.

The urge to laugh suddenly overtook her, and Callie had to swallow it with bitter resentment. In the wake of their patchwork explanations, Callie could clearly see the root of what was happening. Not since high school had she worried over being the victim of cruel, childish games like this, nor had she ever been *so wrong* about a group of people in her lifetime. Anger, hot and devastating, tore through her heart.

"That's great," she said flatly. "Thank you, all of you, for your concern. If you wanted to keep me out of whatever private drama club meeting y'all have goin' on here, you could've just said so."

Callie cursed inwardly, her irritation drawing out her latent Louisiana drawl.

"Callie—"

"No, that's quite enough for tonight, thanks." She wasn't sure who'd called to her, her desperation to get away from the situation overtaking every one of her senses. Without giving anyone a chance to stop her, Callie shoved all of her weight against the Willow's front door and stomped into the fast-enveloping dark.

Chapter Six

CALLIE

She slammed the door behind her, refusing to look back. Callie had spent more than enough of her life dealing with bullies, people who got a kick out of stringing her along, giving her just enough information to make her think she was in on the joke when really she *was* the joke. Well, not anymore. Callie worked too hard to earn her place in life, and she wasn't about to devalue herself by associating with people who looked down on her.

Callie thought of Nyla, of how much she'd treasured the realization that they could be friends. She thought of Emmett and her stupid, *stupid* crush. Shame and anger whirled in her chest. At the barest hint of acceptance, she'd let herself get caught up in a fantasy. Was she really so lonely that losing even a slight chance of expanding her social circle struck her like a barb in the heart? Perhaps she was. Callie always thought of herself as independent and driven, but maybe she was a victim of circumstance. She'd spent so long making things work on her own that she'd convinced herself she didn't want or need a support network. Seeing Nyla surrounded by a group of people so clearly connected slashed open a deep-seated longing in Callie's chest.

Cursing, Callie stomped on a puddle of water that was crusted with a thin, newly-formed layer of ice as she walked. She was being dramatic. Overreacting. In pain over losing something she never had to begin with. Her grip on her carefully curated control was slipping, and Callie *hated* it.

The cold air was like a slap in the face, nearly whipping her hat clean off her head. Callie gripped the brim just before it took flight, striding toward her borrowed car in anger that was quickly giving way to hurt. When the Willow's door banged open again, she cursed herself for feeling hopeful.

"Callie!"

Emmett's voice carried easily on the frigid wind. The hope in her stomach turned to acid, and Callie latched onto the irritation that took its place.

"Leave me alone, Emmett." Her voice was harsh, annoyed. Good. "I'm too tired to play whatever game you guys are trying to sell me."

When he didn't respond immediately, Callie wondered if the wind was blowing too hard in her direction for him to hear her. She contemplated turning around, but that felt like a concession. Let him think she ignored him, then. That would be the petty thing to do. Callie wasn't usually petty. It was liberating and terrifying all at once.

She had about three seconds of reveling in her victory before Emmett collided with her with the force of a rogue bull.

"What—!" The air gushed from her lungs as Emmett snatched her off her feet, his arms like two iron bars locked in a vice around her stomach. Callie kicked out instinctively, thrashing her legs and driving her elbows into Emmett's chest. For all the good it did, she might as well have played possum.

"Put me DOWN!" Callie screamed, shock fading to fury in the time it took for Emmett to swing her around. "EMMETT! What the hell is wrong with you?! *Let me go!*"

"Emmett!" Another voice cut through the unrelenting wind, and Callie recognized Nyla with a pang of gratitude. Surely she was going to put an end to— "The truck!"

Callie felt herself be hauled in a new direction, away from the Willow and her car. Betrayal, sharp and bitter, coated her tongue.

"You're all insane!" She spat, hoping it would land on Emmett's shoe. Better yet, his face. "This is— this is kidnapping! You could be arrested for this! Unlawful detainment! Just— just— LET ME GO, NOW!"

"Shut up!" Emmett shifted her weight to one arm, her feet finally brushing the ground again. Callie took the chance, trying desperately to free herself from his grip. Emmett held fast, throwing the door of his truck open with one hand, holding her hostage with the other. Callie built a scream in her lungs, her throat burning with the urge to release it, but it was cut off by Emmett slinging her unceremoniously into the backseat of the vehicle. Callie scrambled to the other side of the cab, reaching for the handle. Emmett saw her target and cursed, clamoring into the seat after her and grabbing her again. The door shut behind him.

"You fucking *asshole*—" Callie's insults were interrupted by Emmett's hand clamping firmly over her mouth. She tasted a combination of pine, rubber, and gasoline on her lips before she could close them, struggling harder against Emmett's hold. He loosed an exasperated sigh, like he was trying to calm a flailing toddler, and pulled her flush against him, her back to his front. Callie fought, uselessly, until the adrenaline faded and her muscles ached from exhaustion.

"Be quiet," Emmett whispered in her ear, his short beard scratching her cheek. Callie turned her head to glare at him in outrage; it was the most she could manage. Emmett had her pinned in his embrace, utterly helpless in the face of his freakish strength. Her jaw twitched as she thought about opening her mouth to bite him, settling instead for an aggravated string of muffled curses. "Callie, *shut up—!*"

A crack, as loud and piercing as a felled tree, shook the ancient truck.

Callie froze, her entire body going rigid against Emmett's. He tensed behind her, squeezing her tighter to him, pressing his palm harder over her mouth. Was that a gunshot? Was... was someone *shooting* at them?

She tried to look back at Emmett, but he held her in place with the hand over her mouth. The world had gone quiet again, but it wasn't the peaceful forest night Callie was used to. The silence was suffocating, charged, like they were waiting for something to show itself.

Heart pounding, Callie tried to pinpoint the source of her unease. She was rattled from her altercation with the others, even more so from her battle with Emmett in the parking lot, but something more was creeping along her spine, caressing her basal instincts with icy fingers, drawing fear to the forefront of her mind.

A whoosh of air left her nose, clouding her vision. It was almost opaque, freezing instantly in the cold. When had the temperature dropped so significantly? She struggled in Emmett's grip again, trying to free herself, but he remained steadfast in his determination to keep her trapped. She summoned a burst of strength, preparing to throw everything she had into escaping his hold, when the ground shuddered so forcefully that the truck bounced.

Callie swallowed any remaining protests as the impossible sprung to life before her very eyes.

She wasn't sure what she was seeing at first. The night seemed to move through the truck's windows, rippling in disjointed shadows that refused to come together in her mind. Callie watched, wide-eyed and frozen in fear, as the blackness of the forest took shape, emerging from the wilderness like a wraith in search of souls. It *looked* like a wraith, too. The Willow's exterior lights illuminated the creature in fragments, refusing to give Callie a full picture of the walking nightmare before her. It was skeletal, with gangly limbs and jittering movements, its skin mottled with rot and decay. Its elongated skull seemed hollow except for the narrow, needle-sharp teeth that crowded its mouth. The only sign of life resided in its hard, gem-like eyes, shimmering like polished topaz in the dark.

"It can't get in here," Emmett murmured, his mouth pressed firmly against her ear, his voice low and stern. Suddenly, his hold on her wasn't so restricting. Callie felt herself latch onto his forearm, squeezing urgently, afraid he was going to let go now that she'd stopped fighting him. He didn't, pulling her more comfortably into the cradle of his body, settling into the space between the rear bench seat and the front passenger seat. Emmett dragged her into the tiny alcove of foot room on the floor of the backseat, as far away from the windows as they could possibly get in the confined space. When she was silent for long enough, he removed his palm from her mouth and wound his arm around her waist instead.

"You weren't lying." Callie's voice was flat, lifeless. Emmett's silence was more than enough confirmation. "I thought... you weren't lying."

Emmett released a tired sigh, weighed down with defeat.

"We weren't lying."

Chapter Seven

EMMETT

"Aspirin?"

The small bottle hovered tauntingly in the center of his vision, and Emmett accepted it with a grumble. Aaron handed him a paper cup filled with water, looking far too pleased with the situation.

Dick.

The aspirin went down hard, catching in the back of his throat before he was able to guzzle enough water to dislodge it. Emmett coughed, igniting a symphony of pain in his torso. He was going to have bruises from Callie's elbows and even more from her heels. *Why* did she have to be wearing heels?

"Your technique could use some work," Aaron said, settling into the chair behind the front desk. Emmett regarded him with an exasperated stare. "Next time you need to restrain someone, hold their arms behind their back. You'll suffer less injury that way."

"You're really getting a kick out of this, aren't you?" Emmett said drily. Aaron grinned in assent.

"You wouldn't be hurt if you hadn't been a jackass." Nyla sniffed. She stomped her way over to where Aaron sat, folding herself defiantly into his lap. Aaron instinctively pressed a kiss to the side of her neck, gathering her in his arms. Emmett waited until Aaron's attention returned to him and then rolled his eyes in an exaggerated display of disgust. Aaron answered by giving him the finger.

Despite appearances, Emmett liked Aaron. His initial wariness of Emmett's closeness with Nyla was understandable but had been dispelled quickly upon seeing them together. Emmett loved Nyla dearly, as a friend and nothing more.

The small nugget of jealousy between him and Aaron had swiftly morphed into a source of harmless entertainment for them both, a silent agreement of unconventional friendship. Truth be told, Emmett suspected they both kept it up merely because Nyla found it amusing. Their needling was surface-level, although Emmett couldn't deny the thrill he experienced when he managed to land a verbal blow that took Aaron by surprise.

Was that healthy? Probably not, but it was fun.

"I was trying to keep her out of it," Emmett said to Nyla, closing his eyes and dropping his head back onto the chair behind him. Nyla snorted. She was legitimately irritated with him, which obviously pleased Aaron to no end.

"Lot of good that did."

"I'm perfectly aware that my plan backfired," he groused. He'd messed up, and the evidence was in the closed and locked door of Nyla's office where Callie had hidden herself for the last few hours.

He should apologize. His boorish attitude had been a misguided attempt to keep Callie safe, and it failed spectacularly. Emmett's harsh rejection of Callie's presence resulted in her stomping off into the dark, and if Amelia hadn't rushed to check the drone, realizing the Chehwinoo was heading straight for them with just enough time for Emmett to barge out the door, Callie may have lost her life. He *should* apologize.

Except that he didn't want to.

It wasn't Callie's fault, he knew that, and yet he couldn't suppress the flickering spark of anger in his chest. Yes, his attitude had put Callie in danger. Yes, he'd made things unnecessarily difficult for everyone. That didn't change the fact that Callie shouldn't be here in the first place.

Why *was* she here? Nothing about the Lichen House contract needed to be settled quickly; Callie should be in Hatfield, far away from this godforsaken forest and its infestation of ice demons. Emmett felt aggravation coat the back of his tongue as he came to a decision. First thing in the morning, he was dragging Callie back to Hatfield whether she liked it or not. He'd already proven that he could maneuver her with ease. After their battle in the parking lot, she wouldn't fight him *that* hard.

His chest ached in response, telling him that was wishful thinking at best.

"Speaking of plans backfiring," Aaron cleared his throat in Nyla's direction, and she gave him a sheepish grin in response.

"Okay yeah, I know. I went rogue there with Callie. I should've talked to you guys first and I didn't, I'm sorry." Nyla made eye contact with Sam, Amelia, and Emmett on the apology, though the twist of her lips when she got to him told him he wasn't out of the woods in her books. She was still angry, but she knew she'd messed up and Nyla Jameson wasn't one to shirk responsibility. Emmett appreciated the effort, even with the tangible distaste in her expression.

"Callie's been helping us for a while now, anyway," Amelia said from behind her laptop screen. Emmett had no idea what she was working on over there, but it was taking up the majority of her attention. "Maybe it'll be easier with her knowing *what* she's helping with. I don't have an issue with her being in the loop."

"Neither do I," Sam agreed. "In the interest of sharing our feelings, I don't know why we're being secretive about this at all. Maybe we *should* be telling more people. The execution could use some work, though. Standing in the middle of town hall screaming about monsters is a bit on the crazy side, even for us."

"Sam's got a point," Amelia said, locking eyes with Nyla. Emmett knew she wanted to throw in her agreement as well, but her transgression with Callie was still fresh. Besides, they all knew where Nyla stood on the issue. "If we start telling people about this creature, wouldn't they be more likely to avoid the woods? Even if they didn't believe us, the paranoia might be enough of a deterrent. Fear mongering to our advantage?"

"We're not bringing anyone else into this if we can avoid it," Aaron interjected quickly, his tone leaving no room for argument. "I understand the sentiment, but you're putting too much faith in the general public. Spreading rumors about a monster living in the woods will only bring more people to the Basin— crypto-zoologists, ghost hunters, reckless teenagers, cocky hunters, the list goes on. None of which are equipped to handle the reality of the situation."

"Is *anyone* equipped to handle this shitshow?" Emmett muttered under his breath. After tonight, he was leaning toward Aaron's point of view. Whenever they brought another person into their circle of bootleg demon hunters, things got exponentially more complicated. It was exactly why he didn't want Callie getting roped into their escapades.

Not that it mattered anymore.

It was some time later, nearly daybreak, when Emmett's annoyance faded to concern. His reluctance to apologize had fizzled with his slowing heartrate, and now he was worried that Callie had somehow managed to escape the building through the pipes. Standing, he tried to be casual as he walked toward the office door.

"What the hell do you think you're doing?" Nyla snapped. Emmett flinched like he'd been caught in the middle of a crime, glancing over his shoulder guiltily.

"I'm going to check on her," he said, rushing to continue after Nyla fixed him with a challenging glare. "I won't be a dick, I promise. I'm just making sure she hasn't gone catatonic in there."

Nyla looked like she wanted to argue further, but Aaron gently squeezed her shoulder. Whether it was because he wanted Emmett to have a chance to make up for his behaviour or because he wanted to see if Callie would rip him a new asshole was anyone's guess, but Emmett was grateful regardless. He approached the door, gently rapping his knuckles against the wood.

"Cal? It's Emmett. I just wanted to—"

The door whipped open, and Callie's hand darted out. Emmett flinched, thinking she was about to smack him, but her fingers twisted in his jacket sleeve and tugged him sharply into the office before slamming the door shut behind him again.

"Start. Talking."

Callie crossed her arms over her chest, staring at Emmett like he was a misbehaving child. He blinked, taking in the blatant shadows under her eyes and the wrinkles around her mouth. Her lower lip was bright red, like she'd been chewing on it for some time. Emmett took a deep breath, searching for words— any words— but the English language had dropped clean out of his head the moment he'd stepped into the office. The room was filled with the scent of Callie's perfume, and he was having trouble concentrating on anything other than how delicious she smelled. What was it, lilies? Roses? Something floral. Emmett was never good with flowers.

"I'm probably not the best person to explain all this," he admitted, though it pained him. He really didn't want to leave this room, to invite someone else to take his place. He wanted to be the one to reassure Callie that she was safe, that everything was under control. Emmett felt his chest twinge in irritation at his own boyishness, shoving it down. "I'll get Nyla."

"No," Callie said, interrupting him. "I don't— I want someone to tell me I haven't lost my mind. And you're the best person for that. You won't sugar-coat it, or try to talk me down. If I'm acting crazy, you'll tell me."

Emmett's mouth snapped shut with an audible click, making Callie jump. It was then that he zeroed in on the subtle shaking of her arms, the way her knees were locked to keep herself upright. She was... scared?

Of course she's fucking scared. She was almost eaten by a demon less than six hours ago.

Wordlessly, Emmett pulled out one of the visitor's chairs, offering it to Callie before he took the other one. He didn't think she'd sit if he was still standing, so he promptly sank into the creaking seat. Thankfully, Callie followed suit. Once he was sure she wasn't going to pass out, Emmett tried his best to explain.

"You're not crazy, Callie. That thing you saw, it's a forest spirit of some kind. A demon, I guess. It lives in the Basin, and it takes over a human host to become... that. It's called the Chehwinoo."

"Sounds Native American."

"It is," Emmett confirmed, frowning at the way her voice cracked. Callie ignored it, her expression frozen in serious contemplation. "We've been trying to kill it for months now."

"Trying?"

"It's complicated," Emmett said, sighing. "Listen, Cal. You don't need to worry about this. The Chehwinoo can't leave the Basin, and it can't come out during the day. As soon as the sun comes up, you can leave and you'll never have to see it again. I'll call you when it's safe to come back to Somerton. In the meantime, do what you can for your clients, but do it from Hatfield."

She didn't respond right away, staring hard at the ground. Emmett waited, wondering if he *should* go get Nyla. When Callie still hadn't moved after five minutes, he stood. Before he could reach the door though, Callie's voice sounded from behind him.

"Thank you," she whispered, like she was hoping he wouldn't hear her but needing to say it anyway. "You saved my life last night. So... thank you."

Emmett grunted something noncommittal and then, feeling a confusing mixture of pride and unease, he left.

It was another two hours before Callie finally emerged from the office, looking far more put-together than Emmett expected. At the sound of the door creaking, he bolted upright in his chair, knocking his half-empty cup of water onto the floor. Nyla glared at him, but said nothing. All of the attention in the room was focused on Callie, waiting for her next words with held breath.

When she reached the end of the hall, just before she stepped completely into the lobby, she stopped.

"I have come to the conclusion that I am not crazy," she announced, lacing her fingers together behind her back. Emmett could clearly picture her in a courtroom in that moment, facing down a hung jury with poise and confidence even if the latter was hanging by a thread. "No matter how I try to examine the events of last night, I can't explain them away. You told me there's a monster. I saw it. I believe you."

"I'm sorry we couldn't have been more gentle about it," Nyla said quietly. "It's... we're all just doing our best with what we have."

"I know," Callie agreed, sending a quick smile Nyla's way before continuing. "I also know that *some* of you, no matter how ineffectively, were just trying to keep me out of harm's way with their uncouth behaviour yesterday."

Each word struck Emmett like a pointed barb, which was no doubt what Callie intended. He frowned, resisting the urge to roll his eyes. Apparently, all gratitude for 'saving her life' had faded in the early morning hours.

"Yeah, Emmett," Sam said, subverting Callie's attempt at performative subtlety. He elbowed Emmett's shoulder, jostling him into unfolding his arms to catch himself before falling from the chair. "Way to be uncouth, you heathen."

"Regardless," Callie said, ignoring their scuffle, "the attempt didn't work. I'm here, and I won't be leaving anytime soon."

"What about Orville?" Nyla prodded. Callie blushed.

"Uh… yeah, Orville didn't actually call me." She shuffled her feet, looking uncomfortable for the first time since she emerged from the office, reminding him that no matter how calm she looked, Callie was struggling with this. They all were. "I heard Emmett complaining about me and I got defensive. I have free rein until next week. You might as well use me."

"Use you how?" Emmett demanded, already feeling the instinct to fight her decision rising in his gut. Out of everyone here, barring perhaps Aaron, Callie was the most logical. Surely she would know that the smartest thing to do would be to go home. Aaron didn't have that option, Emmett knew. Nyla being at the center of everything, living in a constant state of danger, overruled any logical argument he could come up with. Aaron wasn't going anywhere, but Callie should.

"Emmett said you've been *trying* to kill the Chehwinoo for months now." Her attention drifted briefly to him. "I think I can help. I've been doing some light research on my phone for the past few hours using the creature's name and some of the email requests I got from Nyla over the summer. I don't know all the details so maybe I'm wrong, but it seems like you need information. I can get it."

The silence following Callie's speech was heavy with anticipation. Emmett caught Nyla smothering a grin, while everyone else was alternating between smiling approvingly at Callie and casting nervous glances his way. Emmett said nothing, fearing that if he opened his mouth, he'd say something he couldn't take back.

"And," Callie continued, sensing she hadn't quite won everyone over yet, "I believe I'm also right in saying that this whole thing ties back to Adrian Stamkos?"

The entire room tensed. Callie smiled humorlessly.

"Emmett tipped me off on that one too," she said, and Emmett got the distinct impression that she was tying her conclusions to him on purpose, letting him know not-so-subtly that *he* was the reason she was able to make these arguments. He was begrudgingly impressed. "He was all moody when we talked about Stamkos at the Coffee Corner. I figured he must be involved, and if that's the case, then you definitely need me. Bring me up to speed, and I think— I *know* I can be a valuable resource."

Emmett knew what was about to happen before he ever looked at Nyla, a firm stone of dread settling into the pit of his stomach.

"Then it's settled," Nyla cheered, jumping up from Aaron's lap. She rushed over to Callie, wrapping her in a tight hug. "Welcome to the team!"

CALLIE

As soon as the bathroom door clicked shut behind Callie, she fell to her knees and shuddered out several deep breaths. A monster. *Holy shit, an* actual *monster. What was that?! How is that real? How did I end up here?*

Before they delved into the specifics of their situation, Callie needed the restroom. She needed to splash some cold water on her face and celebrate the small hurdle she'd overcome by maintaining her feigned confidence in front of the others. In her scattered moments of calm, she'd known she couldn't walk away from this. It was too fantastic, too unreal, too absurd to ignore. Then, she'd remember the unnatural cold she'd felt, even tucked safely in Ephraim's truck.

Fear made bile gurgle in her throat, but she swallowed it down. Callie couldn't linger on those thoughts now. She'd spent the better part of the night oscillating between denial and hysterics, until Emmett knocked on the door. She was grateful for his intervention; if he hadn't showed up when he did, Callie might've done something monumentally stupid like climb out a window or call the cops. Emmett's attitude toward her was still cool, almost indifferent at times, but flashes of the Emmett she thought she knew were popping up sporadically, reminding her that there *was* a reason she liked him.

Despite her bravado in the lobby, Callie was still fighting back pangs of uncertainty, torn between the instinct to flee and the desire to understand, to help. Nyla and the others clearly had things under control, to some degree. They didn't need her here. Callie could go home, and no one would blame her, surely. She *wanted* to go home, she realized with a pang of shame. Deep in the pit of her stomach, fear broiled and lashed at her judgment. Her legs ached with the suppressed urge to run. But she couldn't. She wouldn't let herself.

You want friends, Quinn? Time to start acting like one.

Telling herself that she felt refreshed and remotivated, Callie straightened her shoulders and returned to the lobby, where a cluster of conversation had broken out in her absence. Emmett noticed her first, his gaze catching on her hands as they rested, clenched, at her sides. His brow furrowed in the slightest betrayal of concern, and Callie quickly relaxed her fingers.

"Welcome back," Sam shouted from across the room. He leapt onto one of the lobby chairs and gestured to the other free seats scattered around. "Put on your listening ears, because it's time for Sammy's Speedy Recap Special!"

Amelia groaned, grabbing Sam's wrist and trying to pull him into the chair properly.

"Samuel! We agreed that Nyla and Aaron would—"

"Let him do it," Nyla interrupted, suppressing a smile. "I kind of want to see where this goes."

Callie seated herself on one of the leather-wrapped benches in a daze, preparing to take mental notes. She had no idea what she was about to hear, but she knew that she needed to focus. As Amelia warned Nyla about what she was agreeing to, Emmett's body appeared next to Callie on the bench. His bicep brushed hers, and Callie noted the lack of give in his flesh. Emmett was hiding some considerable muscle under his lackluster wardrobe, reminding her of the way he'd manhandled her into the truck the night before.

Seriously? The man is already hot, does he have to be strong, too? There's no way he's that perfect. He has a physical flaw somewhere, and I'm going to find it. If only for my own sanity.

Callie let her attention drift to him for just a second, searching for anything that would make Emmett more human to her. Annoyingly, she found nothing. No weirdly-shaped ears, awkward bends in his thumb, or chipped teeth.

He has a small dick, she decided, ignoring the obviously substantial size of his shoes. *His genes are compensating for his cocktail sausage. His puny peen. Tiny undercarriage. Itsy bitsy teeny weenie.*

Feeling better, Callie finally looked up to catch Emmett staring at her... staring at him. She flushed scarlet, cursing her fair skin. She could try to blame her lack of decorum on the events of the last 24 hours, but it would be a lie. Callie knew that Emmett had the ability to rattle her just by being himself. The nightmare demon certainly didn't help matters, all the same.

"It all started at the height of summer," Sam began suddenly, lowering his voice to a theatrical timbre. "Hunting season was open in the Basin, tourists were making questionable life decisions, and Adrian Stamkos decided to open a factory."

Callie listened as Sam explained, surprisingly clearly, the events that set the ball rolling. Hunters began disappearing in the Basin, and Nyla was the first to realize something more was going on than a few unrelated accidents. She tried to get help from Sheriff Hannaford, but he rebuked her. Then, she contacted Aaron, and together they uncovered the truth of the danger. A creature made of ice and hunger, stalking the shadows of the Basin to slake its bloodlust. Nyla, Aaron, Emmett, Ephraim, and one of Aaron's FBI friends had been the first to encounter the Chehwinoo and live, and from that moment, they were locked in a never-ending war with forces they didn't fully understand.

"We don't know *exactly* what summoned the Chehwinoo," Nyla told her. Sam's solo performance had quickly devolved into a joint venture, the others jumping in with details and events that he either wasn't present for or had forgotten. "But given the location of the Hovel that Pratt found, and the first Chehwinoo being James Carver, I don't think it's a coincidence that this ramped up when construction began on Stamkos' factory."

"He confronted us after we killed the second creature," Aaron added. Sam rushed to clamp his hands over his mouth, preventing Aaron from speaking further.

"Wait! We were there for this part!"

Aaron looked like he wanted to argue, but he didn't get a chance. Sam barreled forward in his retelling, keeping his hands over Aaron's mouth until he was physically thrown off the chair. Aaron adjusted his suit jacket calmly, rolling his eyes as Sam never broke stride.

"It was just after my heroic sacrifice that nearly ended my life," Sam said seriously, scrambling across the floor to his girlfriend, dramatically clutching Amelia to his side. Callie wondered how he was able to have as much energy as he did after spending a sleepless night in a lodge lobby. "My stunning, beautiful, evil-mastermind of a girlfriend and I took pity on the poor FBI man and concocted a plan to use the Chehwinoo's weakness against it—"

"It was Nyla's plan," Amelia corrected.

"—but the plan went awry, and I was called upon to save the day—"

"Everything went exactly as intended until Sam's part," Amelia corrected again.

"—I used my innovation and quick-thinking to devise a foolproof plan to hit the Chehwinoo with my truck and send it into the lake—"

"It was a rental, and we still have to pay for it."

"—but there was a flaw in my perfectly thought-out maneuver. The airbag trapped me in the vehicle and I would've drowned had I not had the foresight to bring a knife—"

"Nyla had a hunch and snuck her pocketknife into Sam's jeans before we moved. Then Emmett and Aaron saved his ass from drowning."

Sam looked down at Amelia in exaggerated offense.

"Anyway," he sniffed, "by the time we got it all sorted out at the station, we were visited by the grim reaper himself. Adrian Stamkos."

Callie leaned forward, her fear long-forgotten.

"He introduced himself and told us, cackling evilly, that we were good-for-nothing, nuisance kids and we were ruining his business. Ordered us to take a hike, and took over the town hall."

Callie looked at Amelia, who shrugged.

"He's actually not exaggerating that much. No cackling, but the rest…"

Nyla and Aaron confirmed the validity of Sam's account, adding as much context as they could. Stamkos knew of Nyla and Aaron before he ever stepped foot in Somerton, because Nyla had been petitioning to cancel the factory build. She'd since amended her petition to simply *delay* the build until the business with the so-called rabid bear was resolved, but Stamkos was pushing on that front, too. They'd been trying to get through to him for weeks now, with no luck. He was staying in the area until the factory's foundation was complete so that he could address any hiccups personally, a tactic that was no doubt designed to intimidate. Callie suspected that his main motivation was bringing life to the face behind the company, dissuading local pushback by making his presence felt. It was harder for the public to villainize him if he were *here*, addressing their concerns himself, rather than some shapeless figurehead orchestrating a hostile takeover of their town from somewhere in LA.

It was smart. A business move. It was also a pain in the ass to counter.

They continued to talk logistics for a while, focusing on the fruits of their research. Nyla told her all about their efforts to take down the Chehwinoo, and the limited mythology they'd unearthed. None of them knew exactly why the creature kept coming back like some sort of cursed boomerang, and that's where Callie's expertise came in. They needed a lead, something to break up the monotony of dead ends and monster hunts. She could do that. Probably. Maybe.

Or I'll get eaten by a nightmare demon.

Callie needed sleep. Sleep, or wine, either one would work to keep her calm. Before even that, though, she needed her tablet. With a few stabilizing breaths, Callie felt the nerves begin to settle in her stomach. She had a task, something to focus her whirling thoughts on, and that was more of a comfort than anything she could tell herself. When she was confident that she wouldn't pass out, throw up, or worse, she stood from the bench.

"Okay. I think I get the gist of it. Now, I need to get organized."

"Aaron will grab the files from our room. We can go over everything we have whenever you're ready."

"The sooner the better," Callie agreed. "I'd like to get started right away. I just need to grab my tablet from the car."

Her hand was on the door, pushing just enough for a slight breeze to infiltrate the lobby, when she paused.

"Um... it is *safe* for me to go to my car... right?"

"Sun's out, guns out," Sam announced from his seat. "Or, I guess, guns... *not* out? That doesn't work as well as I thought it would."

"He's trying to say that it's perfectly safe," Amelia translated, rolling her eyes. "You'll get the hang of Sam Speak."

"I'll walk with you." Emmett's firm voice surprised Callie, but she didn't argue. As frustrating as he'd been the day before, she *did* feel better having someone accompany her. Even if it was supposedly safe in the sunlight.

The crisp mountain air was much colder today. December was on them, and with it, winter weather. Callie shivered, thanking her foresight to bring a warm coat. It was in the backseat of Orville's car, but at least it was here.

Emmett walked a step behind her, silence looming between them like a heavy fog. Callie watched her breath puff in front of her face until they reached the car, and then she couldn't take it anymore.

"How's your... uh, everything?" Callie winced, remembering the numerous points her feet and elbows made contact with Emmett's body during their fight the night before. His mouth twisted in the ghost of a smirk.

"I've had worse," he assured her. Callie chewed the inside of her cheek, tucking her tablet under her arm and reaching for the tan-coloured wool peacoat in the backseat.

"I'm not sorry, you know," she informed him, even as she fought the urge to apologize. "You tried to kidnap me. I think my reaction was perfectly reasonable."

"I never said otherwise."

Callie scrunched her nose in displeasure.

"You could've handled it better," she insisted. She wasn't sure what she was trying to solicit from him— an apology, maybe? Acknowledgement that his standoffish behaviour wasn't a result of his burning hatred for her? Whatever it was, Emmett wouldn't give it to her. He waited, silently, as she gathered her things in her arms and locked the car door behind her.

"Well," she continued, brushing her hair from her face. The wind was picking up, and she could feel ice in the breeze. "At the very least, I can understand why you wanted to keep people away from all... this."

"About that," Emmett interjected, stepping quickly in front of her before they got too close to the Willow's door. Callie stopped abruptly so as not to walk into him. "Look, you're right. I didn't handle any of this shit well. But that doesn't mean I've changed my mind."

"I'm sorry?"

"Callie, you shouldn't be here," Emmett said, his tone urgent but kinder than yesterday. "This isn't your problem to solve. Go home to Hatfield, where it's safe. You can always meet with Stamkos when this is over."

"Seriously?" Callie sighed, rolling her eyes. "I thought we were past this. Emmett, I can help. I *want* to help."

"Why?"

"Why not?" she shot back. "You don't live here. Your dad's only staying at Lichen House until the contract is settled, and you're on desk duty until the work permits come through. You could just 'go home to Hatfield, where it's safe.' Why are you helping?"

"Because people I care about are in danger," Emmett defended. "And I won't abandon them."

"Those same people *you* care about, *I* care about." Callie shifted her weight to one hip, adjusting her grip on her tablet and coat so she could cross her arms. "I may not know all of them well, but Nyla is my friend. Why is that reason good enough for you but not me?"

"Because I was dragged into this from the beginning," Emmett said hotly. "I've been here since day one, and I'm not backing out until it's over. You have a choice."

"So do you."

"No, I don't." Emmett huffed a frustrated breath. "Look, it's not the same, alright?"

"How?"

"It just isn't!" He shoved his hand beneath the brim of his hat, stepping closer until he was looming over her. Callie fixed him with her best expectant glare, straightening her spine and locking it in place.

"Emmett, you need to back up out of my space right now before I knee you in the balls. *Again.*"

He froze, blinking at her threatening tone. Emmett's attention flickered between his feet and her face, processing their position and pressing his lips together into a tight line. He took a sizeable step back, putting a respectful amount of distance between them.

"Sorry," he muttered, the word awkward on his tongue. "I wasn't— I'm not trying to use my size to make a point, but it did come across like that. I'll try to be more aware of it."

Surprise flooded her. Callie was expecting, at most, for Emmett to retreat with a possible eye-roll or derogatory snort, like she'd get from the male clients she'd said similar, albeit more polite, things to. An acknowledgement *and* an apology? It was almost enough to soften her anger at him. Almost.

"I just... I need you to understand." In lieu of pacing, Emmett propped his elbow on the car roof, tapping his index finger repeatedly on the cool metal. "Callie, you have no idea how much danger you'd be putting yourself in. This thing is... it's a killing machine. You shouldn't underestimate it."

"You've all managed to beat it, multiple times," Callie argued.

"We've spent weeks figuring out how to do it as safely as possible," he said. "and that's in no way a guarantee. We do everything we can to control the encounter, and things still go wrong. Every single one of us has come within an arm's length of death, and that's only going to get worse the deeper we dig. On the last hunt, Sam almost lost his arm. Half of Aaron's torso is scarred from the first attack, and Nyla discovers a new bruise or cut every day. Exhausted and stressed feels like a sugar-coated picnic in the park compared to what we are."

Callie opened her mouth to interject, but Emmett pressed on.

"Amelia is in danger of losing her job for all the unplanned time-off. She has students and family members flooding her email day in and day out, wondering where the hell she is and if she'll be back in time for the spring semester registration. The Willow is hemorrhaging money *and* reputation, to the point that even if we solved the Chehwinoo problem *right now*, I don't know if Nyla will ever be able to financially recover. This isn't a fun side project you can just join for fun and abandon when things get hard."

Indignation zapped through Callie, unfolding her arms and jerking her forward until she was in Emmett's space now. She was vaguely aware of the hypocrisy of her movements, but if Emmett cared, he didn't say so.

"I'm not interested in doing this for *fun*, Emmett!" Callie hissed, jabbing her finger into the middle of his chest. Emmett didn't move, glowering down at her. "I haven't forgotten last night, what it felt like when that *thing* walked by the window. I know this isn't a cute little outing with friends, and I'm not going to treat it that way. I'm not a fucking idiot. I understand that this is life or death!"

"Then you should go home!"

"So should you!"

"I already told you, I can't—"

"Then neither can I!"

Callie's breath was coming in fast huffs, clouding in front of her mouth in the chilly air. Emmett's chest pulsed beneath her finger in the same rhythm, his nose red from the cold, his cheeks red with adrenaline. Had she stepped closer to him? It suddenly felt like Callie was surrounded by Emmett's presence, his height, his scent, his warmth, even the light rasp of his breathing. She felt the proximity tickle the base of her spine, and her heart stuttered in her chest as she realized they'd both stopped talking.

One second dragged into three, then five. Callie was the first to come to her senses, inhaling slowly, letting the cold air cool her heated skin.

"There's nothing you can say to make me change my mind, Emmett," she said softly, averting her gaze. "You can either accept my help and work with me to end this as quickly as possible, or you can sulk. No matter what you decide, I'm not going anywhere."

Emmett didn't answer right away, the muscle in his jaw ticking in irritation. Callie waited expectantly, growing more and more satisfied the longer Emmett searched for a valid response. Eventually, she felt she'd made her point. Callie stepped deliberately around Emmett, and back into the Willow.

He followed soon after, closing the door with more force than necessary. Callie ignored his bluster, walking over to where Nyla was looking over a collection of documents.

"This is everything we were able to track down on the mythology behind the Chehwinoo." Nyla said as Callie reached her, pointing to the depressingly small pile on the left. Next, she pointed at the stack of file folders in the center. "These are all the criminal cases, accidents, missing persons, and natural disasters in the area that may or may not be related to previous monster sightings. And these," she pointed to the last pile, which was less of a pile and more a single folder stuffed to the brim with tattered pages, "are the resources we've been using. Maps, blueprints, copies of contracts, permits, town lines, and anything else we needed while we were investigating."

"It's organized alphabetically and then by date," Aaron supplied helpfully. "I have our notes here, too, but I thought you'd prefer to look at everything blind first. Form your own opinions before hearing ours."

"That's why we included the cases that we originally ruled out." Nyla tapped the middle stack again. "If we missed anything, you'd be the person to catch it, Callie."

Callie took everything in with careful mental notes. She already had a good idea of how she would approach the documents, and Aaron and Nyla had made things significantly easier than Orville ever did. Was this what it was like to work with competent people? A mixture of annoyance at her boss and longing for the future panged in her chest.

"Alright, leave this with me for a few hours," she said with a determined smile. "Can I set up shop here?"

"Park it, Quinn." Amelia smacked the arm of the chair next to her. She'd moved from the floor, her laptop sitting on the coffee table in front of her while Sam played basketball with a crumpled piece of foil wrap and an empty trash can in the hall. "I'll be following some leads of my own and, despite popular opinion, hacking involves a lot of waiting around. We can brainstorm while I work my magic."

"Sounds perfect," Callie said. "Let's get to it."

EMMETT

A hand clamped down on Emmett's knee, stopping it mid-bounce. He jolted in surprise, whipping his head around to look at Aaron, who was glaring at him with a degree of exasperation he'd only seen from his father.

He released Emmett's knee with stiff movements. "You're shaking the desk."

Emmett grunted a response, hooking his foot over the opposite knee to keep them still. He didn't bother defending himself; he knew he was being insuffer-able. The fact that Aaron lasted as long as he did before saying something was impressive.

With Callie now officially involved in their mess, Emmett felt a surge of moti-vation bubbling in the pit of his stomach. He wanted to get out there, knock out another monster before it had a chance to pose a real threat, but he fought the instinct back into a more manageable urge. Killing another Chehwinoo would only serve to make locating the next one a more difficult task. Right now, they knew where the creature was. Thus far, it'd steered clear of the more populated areas of the Basin, aside from the slight dalliance into the Willow's parking lot the night before. If they could avoid killing it right away, it might give them some time to determine how to permanently stop the transformation process here and now.

That didn't make it any easier for Emmett to simply sit back and wait.

Callie and Amelia were hard at work in the Willow's lobby. Nyla was on the phone with George, something that had become much more frequent as of late. George was doing his best to help, and he wanted to be up to date on any progress they made. He was also able to warn Aaron and Nyla of any hostility brewing.

The rush to supress the monster rumors had the dual effect of fostering distrust with the feds and pinning unfair blame on Nyla's involvement. Emmett wasn't surprised— the people of Somerton hated Nyla. When they needed a scapegoat, it almost always fell on her shoulders, whether it made sense or not. It soured his stomach to think of the bullshit she had to deal with, but what could he do? He stood up for her at every opportunity, defending her in his circles. It made no difference. The best Emmett could do was be there for her when Aaron couldn't.

His attention drifted to the front door, where he'd torn down and hastily hidden more than one derogatory note addressed to Nyla over the years. Emmett was sure she found plenty, but he still kept his personal discoveries to himself. No need to pile onto an already massive pile of stress.

As for the rest of their group, they'd branched off into individual tasks. He didn't know exactly what Tyler was doing, but it involved Agent Kelley. He'd texted Aaron and Sam nearly an hour prior to let them know he'd be working with the team for the rest of the day. With Kelley at least partially in the know, Emmett could only assume it was either relevant or important enough to drag Tyler away from the thick of things. Even Sam had found a way to make himself useful, emailing his family's attorney to determine if his parents' influence in the area could deter Stamkos' plans. Small business owners might not be able to change his mind, but the ire of a well-respected family legacy was a more promising threat.

That left Emmett.

Research wasn't his strong suit, Emmett knew that. He wasn't tech-savvy, nor was he particularly fond of academics. Trying to sift through the mountains of information that Amelia and Callie were organizing would only give him a headache and slow them down. Normally, he wouldn't be bothered by that. Emmett knew his strengths; he was practical, an action man. He wasn't ashamed of that. Now, though...

He glanced at Callie, furiously typing notes on her tablet. The urgency to act returned tenfold, and Emmett had to concentrate to keep himself still. It wasn't that he felt inadequate, he just needed to keep everyone safe. Sitting around and waiting wasn't going to accomplish that.

"I seem to recall," Sam announced suddenly, dropping his phone onto his lap, "long ago, in a kingdom far, far away, a certain knight-in-oil-stained-snapback promised to provide caffeine."

"That was *yesterday*, and I did in fact brought you coffee," Emmett snorted.

"And yet, we remain caffeine-less *today*."

"If this is your way of asking someone to do a coffee run, you need to work on your delivery." Emmett stretched, secretly grateful for the excuse to move. "But fine, text me what you want."

"My hero," Sam crooned, picking up his phone again and doing as Emmett asked. "Could I bribe you into upgrading to a lunch run?"

"What are you offering?"

"My body?"

"Already taken," Amelia interrupted, raising an eyebrow at Sam. "You may offer him one kiss, with tongue. That's all."

"Yes ma'am," Sam said with a purr. "Have I ever told you I love it when you boss me around?"

"It was implied."

Emmett rolled his eyes, standing up from his chair. A lunch run sounded perfect, giving him much-needed time away from the lodge to collect himself.

"Same instructions," he called over his shoulder, walking to the front door, "text me what you—"

Bang, bang, bang.

Emmett stopped dead in his tracks, everyone's attention whipping to the front door. It was glass, so there was no mystery as to what caused the noise. A man stood on the other side, fist raised from knocking. Emmett didn't recognize him and, from the silence in the room, neither did anyone else.

Nyla reacted first, pushing herself up from her seated position behind her desk and rushing to the front door, presumably to answer it. Emmett's attention was still locked on the man, something about him tickled the edges of his awareness, something that made him want to call out to Nyla, stop her from engaging. He couldn't put his finger on what, so he remained rooted in place, watching, evaluating. Searching.

One lock flipped open, then two. Nyla's fingers wrapped around the handle, ready to pull, when Aaron's voice cut clean across the room.

"Nyla! Don't—!"

She heeded his warning a second too late, opening the door a fraction. The man moved immediately, jamming his arm through the crack before she could slam it closed, tossing something into the middle of the lobby. It hit the floor with a bang and a hiss, and then the entire room exploded into a cloud of red mist. He'd deployed some kind of... paint bomb?

Nyla screamed in surprise, falling back against the door and shutting it in the process. She turned the lock, staring wide-eyed at the splatters of red paint that weren't there mere seconds ago. Amelia was frozen in her chair, staring at the smears of paint on her jeans and the back of her laptop screen. Sam, much like Emmett, was in shock, standing at the edge of the chaos and blinking as though the attack was a trick of the light. Callie was getting to her feet, watching Nyla with a worried expression pinching her features.

Aaron ignored the scene entirely, moving purposefully across the room with an air of carefully controlled anger. He gently moved Nyla aside, guiding her to a section of the lobby wall that wasn't visible from the large glass door, and surveyed her for injury. Finding none, he turned his head to Emmett.

"Get her a towel," he instructed, placing a gentle, reassuring kiss to the top of Nyla's head and then stalking outside. Before the door shut behind him, Emmett could hear a cascade of voices screaming increasingly vile insults.

Bitch. Slut.

Murderer.

"What the fuck is going on?" Amelia asked suddenly, shaking herself from her stupor. She stood long enough to glance out the window, where Emmett could see a small crowd gathering in the Willow's parking lot. "Nyla? You okay?"

She didn't answer right away, still staring blankly at the red paint staining the floor and walls. Emmett jolted into action, grabbing a fluffy, white spa towel from the lobby bathroom. He returned quickly, offering it to Nyla. She took it wordlessly, bunching the fabric in her hands and wiping the red from her face. Her movements were mechanical, stilted, like she wasn't really paying attention to what she was doing.

"Nyla?" Amelia tried again, her tone wary. Nyla wiped at her cheek again, more smearing the paint than cleaning it. After a long minute of silence, she nodded.

"I'm fine," Nyla murmured, almost shamefully. Emmett moved to her side, placing a comforting hand on her shoulder. Amelia cursed under her breath, returning to her computer and typing furiously. Callie approached the window, holding her phone aloft and snapping pictures through the glass. It was only when she moved that Emmett realized she'd been taking photos the entire time, not just of the people outside, but of the damage inside.

"I'll help you file a report," Callie explained, catching the confusion on Emmett's face but speaking directly to Nyla. "Pro bono. This is disgusting behaviour."

"Has this happened before?" Sam asked, his voice tight. Emmett looked at him, surprised at the tension in his face. Sam was always relaxed, always smiling. He'd only ever seen this serious demeanor a handful of times, and it still unsettled him.

"Not like this," Nyla said. She forced the blank stare from her face, trying for a reassuring smile. "It's usually just stupid notes or dirty looks. This is the first time they've ever..."

She trailed off, the false smile wobbling before breaking entirely. Aaron's raised voice sounded through the door, muffled but firm. Sam moved to follow him out, rolling his shoulders threateningly.

"I'll go help him," he said, ducking out the door without a glance back. Nyla closed her eyes, steadying her breathing. Emmett wasn't used to seeing Nyla unsettled; the hostility she experienced in Somerton was relentless and grating, but it was mostly harmless. She took it all on the chin, clinging to her refreshing optimism and cheerful approach to life. Emmett felt like he was getting a rare, unguarded glimpse into how all of the negativity really affected Nyla, and it hurt more than he was ready to accept.

"What's bringing them here *now?*" she whispered after an extended silence, her attention drifting between Emmett and Callie, deliberately avoiding the windows.

"I might have the answer to that," Amelia grimaced, carrying her laptop over to show Nyla the screen, "and it's not pretty."

Emmett released Nyla's shoulder to tilt his head toward Amelia's laptop. From his vantage point, the article was nearly illegible, but the headline jumped out at him.

Halloween Massacre-ade! Did Somerton's Inaction Lead to this Horrific Tragedy?

He didn't need to read the article to know what it was about. Malcolm Diamond's Halloween party.

"I thought George was keeping this out of the press?" Emmett demanded. Nyla's mouth formed a hard line.

"It was only a matter of time," Amelia answered instead. "The fact that he kept it quiet as long as he did is a miracle on its own."

"What do you mean?" Callie joined them, still jotting notes on her tablet. Emmett remained silent while Amelia explained everything; George speaking to the survivors and their families personally, pressuring them to keep details off of social media while the investigation was ongoing, reaching out to the victims' relatives and telling them a similar story, directing them to a support group the other family members formed so they had somewhere to air their grief without impeding the FBI, the impatience that led to a riot outside Somerton's sheriff station resulting in George's ill-conceived plan to placate the masses via an organized hunt. It was complicated, and information had been slowly leaking since the night of the incident, but the FBI and Somerton's government had collaborated to keep things under some semblance of control for over a month. Blog posts, a few videos online, and a handful of social media comments were all that made it to the internet for the better part of a month.

The dam had to break eventually, though. It seemed that time was now.

"What does any of that have to do with Nyla?" Callie asked when Amelia was done explaining. Emmett was wondering the same, though he knew from experience that Somerton didn't need much of an excuse to blame Nyla for just about anything.

Amelia skimmed the article, her dismayed expression morphing into rage.

"*...according to inside sources, the horrific turn of events was kept from the public at the behest of a local small business owner, who shall remain anonymous. Reports allege that this unnamed individual has been seen colluding with Sheriff George*

Mason, although this is unconfirmed. Contacts in Somerton's municipal assembly explain that the full details of the incident were suppressed due to negative aftershocks from the controversial bear attacks in July still impacting Somerton's tourism industry. Whether this was an act of compassion, as claimed by the Sheriff's station, or obnoxious self-preservation by certain individuals, as suspected by many, remains to be seen.

"There's no author," Amelia huffed, typing angrily again, "and the article link just leads back to a spam site. I'll need some time to figure out who posted it."

"Son of a bitch," Emmett muttered, squeezing his eyes shut. The fact that the article didn't name Nyla was irrelevant; rumors had been circulating for weeks that she was having an affair with George. In the town's eyes, that was the only possible reason he could have for entertaining her presence at the station. Never mind the fact that she was almost always there with Aaron in tow.

The article was basically a call to arms.

"How bad is it?" Nyla asked Callie, nodding to her phone. Callie pressed her lips together in a tight line, as though weighing the options of lying or telling her the truth. Eventually, she settled on the truth.

"There are about 10 people in the lot," she said, showing Nyla a picture of the crowd. The man who'd thrown the paint bomb was front and center, screaming in Aaron's face. Aaron, for his part, looked intimidating enough to keep the crowd from getting physical, but not quite enough to get them to leave. Emmett was glad Sam went out to help and was considering doing the same. "Has anyone called the sheriff?"

"Don't bother him," Nyla insisted, waving her hand in a dismissive gesture that was too jerky to be genuine. "This'll pass. Em? Can you go get Aaron and Sam? Tell them we're better off just waiting it out. I'll start on clean-up."

She was gone in a flash, walking quickly to the canteen where she kept some cleaning supplies in a hidden closet before anyone could question her. Emmett watched her leave with concern, but he knew from experience that there was no getting in Nyla's way once she made up her mind. Instead, he slipped wordlessly outside.

Sam's presence had certainly helped, a respectable distance now firmly in place between them and the gathered crowd. Aaron and Sam both glanced at Emmett when the door opened, nodding silently at him as he completed their three-man blockade. He quickly brought them up to speed, relaying everything Amelia had found online. They listened silently, an angry twitch in Aaron's jaw the only betrayal that he was registering what Emmett told them.

"Nyla wants everyone back inside," he said out of the corner of his mouth. The shouting had died down considerably too, only the occasional disgruntled bark breaking through the ambient sounds of people milling about in one place. "She says it's best to wait it out. Clean up the paint before it dries down."

Aaron didn't look happy with that answer, standing a little straighter.

"There's more than one paint bomb in this crowd," he muttered to Emmett, discreetly eyeing a man on the left side of the group with his hands stuffed in the pockets of his windbreaker. "Is she okay?"

Emmett didn't know how to answer that, so he said nothing. Aaron took a deep breath through his nose.

"She doesn't want us to call George."

"Too late." Aaron's voice was low and strained. While he was sure that Nyla would be angry about this development, he was relieved. Mob mentality was scary and dangerous, and he didn't want to be caught in the middle of a half-assed riot. "He'll be here soon. I've asked Pratt to call in a favor with crime scene clean-up. I'd like to get Nyla out of here for a while, let them work. She doesn't need to stew in it."

"We'll move to the cabin," Sam agreed. They were speaking quietly, keeping an eye on the crowd for any movement.

"We'll go in two vehicles." Aaron's attention snagged on something near the road, and Emmett heard the faint echo of sirens. "Someone should hang back and make sure we're not followed."

"Still up for a lunch run, Coady?" Sam asked, teasing. Emmett couldn't stop his smirk.

"Thanks for volunteering, Fisher."

"I always aim to please."

INTERLUDE

Somerton

Chapter Eleven

EMMETT

Once George arrived on the scene, the crowd settled immediately. They didn't leave right away, but the simmering threat of violence was gone, and George assured Aaron that he would hang around to prevent anyone following them to Sam's cabin. With their primary duty handed off to the sheriff, Sam and Emmett took their chance to pile into Nyla's jeep and set out on their lunch run, taking a roundabout route to Tinny's to make sure they weren't being followed, either.

On the drive, Emmett remained mostly silent, listening to Sam sing off-key renditions of various Disney songs and texting the others to remind them to send their food orders. By the time they'd reached the outer streets of Somerton proper, no one had responded to the message. The knot in Emmett's stomach grew tighter and tighter every second that passed, to the point that he was ready to wrench the wheel out of Sam's grasp and turn the vehicle around by the time Callie sent a short reply.

> We'll be late. Things are getting tense.

Emmett's heart sank and he felt like all the air in his lungs evaporated at once.

> What do you mean? Are they getting aggressive again?

> Not THEM. Aaron. If these idiots don't leave soon he's going to commit a felony and I'm not about to stop him.

Emmett barked a laugh at that, which Sam joined in on after Emmett brought him up to speed. Another text informed them that the assembly was finally breaking up and they were heading to Sam's cabin shortly, leaving in two vehicles now that they had George to cover their exit. Sam asked Emmett to remind Amelia to set the alarms on the property when they arrived, just in case. With all that done, they ordered food, taking guesses at what Nyla and Aaron might want as neither had responded to the text chain, and Emmett fell into his thoughts.

He'd never seen Nyla like that before. She was always quick on her feet, taking everything in stride no matter how unexpected or devastating. The frozen expression of shock on her face, made all the more grotesque by the streaks of blood-red paint staining her skin, was burned into his memory. She looked stunned, yes, but it was more than that. She looked... broken.

Emmett violently pushed the thought away. Somerton *would not* break Nyla. She'd never let it. It was the suddenness of the situation, that's all. Once the crowd dispersed and Aaron organized a clean-up of the lobby, Nyla would be okay. He had to believe that.

"I don't like it." Sam's voice startled Emmett so badly he nearly dropped his phone. He was clutching it in a white-knuckled grip, hoping to hear from Callie again soon that everything was well. Sam folded himself back into the driver's seat, swallowing a bite of food from the tinfoil-wrapped package he'd rescued from the brown paper bags in his arms.

"The surf and turf tacos? I told you they were trash. They don't even use real shrimp. Pretty sure it's imitation crab."

"Leave my fishy cow tortillas out of this," Sam said hotly, taking a deliberate bite of the offending dish. Emmett had had decent surf and turf tacos elsewhere, but the ones at Tinny's needed a biohazard label. How Sam could stomach, let alone enjoy, them was beyond him. Sam handed him the bags, which Emmett tucked safely onto the floor of the jeep. "I mean the news. That would be weird enough on its own, but to actually *attack* Nyla over it? Something reeks."

"You sure it's not the tacos?"

"I'm just saying," Sam shrugged, "Am and I are no strangers to this kind of thing. Our high school had this really obnoxious statue of our mascot, Lenny the Leprechaun. Don't ask me why it was a leprechaun. Something about the Irish mob donating a lot of money to the school board in the 70s."

"There is no way that's the real reason."

"Anyway," Sam continued pointedly, "During finals week one year, we decided to dress him up as the Kool-Aid man."

"How the hell do you dress up a statue like the Kool-Aid man?" Emmett asked, far too invested to further question the legitimacy of Sam's story. "Isn't he just... a juice jug?"

"Leave it to Am," he said, smiling proudly. "She got her hands on one of those giant inflatable hamster balls for people. Blew it up, painted the inside red, and drew a face on the outside with black marker."

"Hilarious, but what exactly does this have to do with our current situation?"

"The problem was that the statue is right in front of the principal's office window. We needed him out so we could get in, deface the statue, and leave without getting caught. So, Am enlisted Tyler for a distraction. He clogged the sinks in the boys' locker room next to the gym and let the faucet run. Thirty minutes later, the teachers were walking through puddles and Tyler was in the middle of his physics exam, totally in the clear. We put Lenny in his costume, and made it back to our respective classrooms before the janitors were finished mopping."

Emmett waited, but Sam didn't elaborate. When it was clear his point didn't get through, Sam sighed.

"The clogged sinks were a perfect distraction," he explained. "Time consuming to deal with, but ultimately no damage done. The kind of distraction that someone would come up with if they were familiar with weaseling their way out of trouble. Kind of like releasing a sensational story with just enough implied information to point fingers at Nyla. Annoying, time-consuming, but likely harmless and mostly untraceable."

"You think someone deliberately released information on Diamond's Halloween party to incite the locals as a distraction," Emmett concluded, furrowing his brow in confusion. "That's a bit of a jump, isn't it?"

"Is it?" Sam countered. "When was the last time anything happened in this town that was pure coincidence?"

He had a point, Emmett couldn't deny that.

"Alright, let's say someone orchestrated this," Emmett conceded. "That leaves us with two big question marks: who did it, and what are they trying to distract us from?"

"There's one way we could find out."

Emmett caught the mischief in Sam's voice far too late, and he realized he'd walked face-first into a trap. Sam's eyes darted over Emmett's shoulder, just for a second, but it was enough to make him curious. Turning, Emmett's gaze landed on the last thing he expected to see lingering outside of a borderline condemned taco truck.

"You've got to be kidding me."

Emmett was certain that the universe was conspiring against them now. Living in a small town like Somerton or Hatfield, Emmett couldn't leave the house without crossing paths with someone he knew. Still, this felt more like divine intervention than happenstance.

Across the parking lot, pulling away from Coffee Corner in his obnoxiously expensive Tesla, was Adrian Stamkos.

Sam interrupted the silence with a thoughtful hum, drumming his fingers on the dash. Emmett could see his brain working, and before he could fend off whatever insane idea was taking shape in Sam's head, the jeep was in gear and they were moving. "Wonder what he's up to on a fine day such as this?"

He phrased it as a question, but Emmett knew that they were already in for a penny, in for a pound. Besides, who was he to object? He wanted action, didn't he? Well, here was action, staring him in the face and dressed in designer slacks. There were only a handful of people Emmett could name with enough power and influence to pull off a stunt like that mob and news article, if it was a stunt at all, and Stamkos was certainly on that list. His motive might be unclear, but that's nothing a little digging couldn't solve.

And if they were wrong? Well, they'd take that loss with dignity. They couldn't possibly piss the man off more than they already had with their constant badgering over the factory permits.

"Shouldn't we check in with the others first?" Emmett pressed. Sam scoffed.

"Nah, we're on a solo mission already. Any decisions we make in the field are executive."

"Alright, but if this backfires, I'm throwing you under the bus. Nyla's already pissed at me, and that woman is terrifying."

"The scary ones are always the best though, aren't they?"

Following someone in Somerton was both easier and more difficult than in a bigger city, not that Emmett had been involved in many covert surveillance operations before. On one hand, there were less twists and turns to potentially lose the target. On the other, fewer vehicles on the road meant less cover and more opportunities for the target to notice they're being followed. Sam seemed to have everything under control, though, using his knowledge of the area to strategically navigate detours. He turned onto side streets that looped around to the main road, losing sight of Stamkos for no more than a few minutes at a time, always making mental notes of where he might have stopped if he wasn't where they expected him to be. After about twenty minutes of driving, they trailed behind Stamkos' Tesla at a leisurely pace along a narrow stretch of road leading just outside of town.

"Where is he going?" Emmett wondered aloud. The highway was in the opposite direction, and the road to Hatfield branched off nearly a mile back. Sam shrugged, easing his speed even more. If Stamkos was tracking their movements, hopefully he would assume that they were lost and second-guessing their location.

"There's nothing out here," Sam said. "Aside from a few rich assholes and their summer homes. Maybe he's visiting a friend?"

"Aren't your parents some of those rich assholes with a summer home?" Emmett pointed out, smirking. Sam laughed.

"Well, yeah, but at least our summer home is among the common folk."

"Unbelievable."

"Hey, it's not my money."

Emmett gave him a skeptical look.

"I have *access* to it," Sam clarified, "but it's not *mine*."

"Yeah, yeah," Emmett said, chuckling, "eyes on the road, nepo-baby."

At last, the Tesla's brake lights ignited. Sam slowed the jeep, keeping his distance until Stamkos completed his turn. Making note of the driveway, Sam drove past the turn-off until he was out of sight, then doubled back. He drifted to a stop several yards away from the mouth of the driveway, giving them the smallest chance of being noticed from the house.

It *was* a house, Emmett realized quickly. And he knew whose.

"That's interesting," he murmured. Sam looked at him in confusion. Emmett pointed to the mailbox, where the upper class had a habit of attaching a sign bearing their last names. Emmett never understood the appeal, but he was thankful for the trend now.

"What do we have here," Sam said, whistling low. The mailbox was just a few feet back from the shoulder of the road, half-obscured by a rhododendron that was badly in need of pruning before the snow fell. Hanging limply from the metal pole was a white wooden sign, decorated in black cursive.

Carver

"Well, what do you think, Coady? Is this escapade worth causing a distraction?"

Emmett didn't offer an answer; the conclusion was obvious. If Adrian Stamkos was behind the release of that article, then breaking into James Carver's old house absolutely counted as an activity he'd want to cover up. For a beat, Emmett wondered if Stamkos would really be that brazen before the understanding that yes, he *would* be that brazen, settled deep in his gut.

Men like Stamkos are used to getting their way through the sheer force of reputation. Like most titans in the industry, Adrian Stamkos came from money. His family had a disgusting amount of generational wealth; poverty hadn't brushed their bloodline in well over a hundred years. Old money, and lots of it. Stamkos himself had grown up surrounded by powerful people, all of whom were well accustomed to throwing money at problems until they went away. If someone caught Stamkos skulking around the dead mayor's house? Well, no, they didn't. Not after their conditional cheque cleared. If they turned down the money and went to the authorities? A convenient clerical error would surface, losing any official record of the report. Anything beyond that was hearsay, and unreliable hearsay at that. Company records would show Adrian Stamkos was in a meeting at that time on that day, so he couldn't *possibly* be the man they saw loitering around James Carver's abandoned bungalow.

While Emmett joked about Sam's family connections, he wasn't a true product of nepotism. From what he knew of Sam, he'd shirked almost all of his parents' attempts to help him financially and had built his career through his own merit, which is why he and Amelia lived modestly in a basic apartment in the middle of a student neighborhood; it was all they could afford on their shared incomes. Stamkos, though, had no issue calling in generational favors. The problem they faced with Stamkos was simple: they were playing with two different sets of rules. He was coasting with the boons of living among the one percent, and everyone else was facing the severe handicap of being lower to middle class. Emmett almost preferred battling the Chehwinoo; at least they were on even ground with the ice demon.

"What the hell could he be looking for?" Emmett asked aloud, easing the truck door open before Sam could speculate. Rather than chastising him, Sam followed suit. They pushed the doors gently shut, creeping through the foliage to circle the back of Carver's property.

Carver's house was still unoccupied. To Emmett's knowledge, it hadn't been touched since the mayor went missing. Stamkos would have no reason to come out to the property unless he was meeting someone or searching for something. Since his was the only vehicle in the driveway, it must be the latter. If they were lucky, maybe they could figure out what was so important to the S&S CEO.

"Take off your jacket," Sam murmured, shrugging out of his own bright blue hoodie. He bundled it into a tight ball and tossed it back in the direction of the truck. "He's less likely to spot your shirt from the window."

He was right. Emmett's t-shirt was a dark, army green whereas his jacket was a mix of khaki and red. He shucked the garment and threw it on top of Sam's. With that done, they continued through the trees until they could see into Carver's backyard. Stamkos was clearly inside, though it wasn't possible to tell exactly where. His vehicle was empty, and the police tape had been carefully dislodged. Emmett squinted through the kitchen window, searching for signs of movement.

"Let's try another window," Emmett suggested, nodding in the direction of the backyard. Sam agreed, and they slowly crept along the tree line. James Carver had an impressive fence erected around his property and while that would normally cause them problems, the land surrounding Carver's house was sloped. Emmett and Sam kept a steady distance from the fence, far enough to peek over it and survey the house. When they'd walked far enough to see into the south-facing windows, movement caught Emmett's eye.

"There," he whispered harshly, hunching his shoulders instinctively. Sam leaned forward, fishing his phone out of his pocket.

"He's definitely looking for something," he said. Stamkos was bent over what looked to be a dresser, or perhaps a desk, riffling through a cardboard box. "Any idea what?"

"Beats me," Emmett said, shrugging. "That's a question for Aaron."

"Come on, you rich bastard," Sam muttered, zooming in on the window as closely as possible with his phone camera. He'd managed a couple of photos with Stamkos' face clearly visible, but that gave them no indication of what he was actually doing here.

"It's gotta be legal documents, right?" Emmett guessed, stretching his arms behind his back and reveling in the soft crack of his shoulders. "What else could it be?"

"You'd be surprised," Sam said. "Dudes in power will go to crazy lengths to keep the most mundane shit hidden. Am and I broke into our principal's shed in high school and found a stash of porno mags under an old pool cover. Turns out the centerfold was the cafeteria lady back in the day. Embarrassing for him to have, maybe, but not illegal. Still, he bent over backward to keep it from being plastered all over the school."

"You guys blackmailed him? Did you have a personal vendetta against this principal or what?" Emmett raised his eyebrows in shock. Sam made a noncommittal noise. "Why didn't he just... expel you? Or call the police?"

"He didn't know it was us," Sam said with a shrug. "Don't ask me how; Am handled all the technical shit. I'm sure he knew it was a student, but he never figured out which one."

"You two are terrifying." Emmett paused, struck by the familiarity of the phrase. Realizing why, he clarified his statement prior to their arrival. "In a completely different way than Nyla."

"Do you have a preference?"

"I'll let you know when I decide."

They waited for another thirty minutes, watching the doors and windows for signs of movement. Aside from the occasional glimpse, they saw nothing. Stamkos was sticking to the less visible areas of the house, which was either coincidence or he was actively trying not to be seen. Emmett put his money on the latter.

"I don't think we're going to get anything," Sam said eventually. "Not unless he comes out with a sign that says 'I found the ledger' or something."

A weighted silence settled between them, and Emmett knew without asking that he and Sam were wondering the same thing: should they try to sneak in after Stamkos left? It was tempting. Even if Stamkos found and removed whatever drew him to Carver's abandoned residence in the first place, they might be able to find something among Carver's possessions to help in their own investigation. Carver was still the mayor when he died, it was entirely possible that he had town documents in his house.

They couldn't do anything with Stamkos still in the building, though.

They waited for a while longer, monitoring their phones for updates from the others. Amelia assured them that everyone was inside the cabin safely, with the perimeter alarms activated, but no one had followed them from the Willow. Emmett glanced back up at the house and spotted movement from one of the living room windows. Stamkos was unhurriedly making his way through each room, combing for something. Whatever it was, he clearly hadn't found it yet.

It was past noon now, and the sun was hanging low in the sky. Emmett and Sam shared a resigned look.

"We should get back," Emmett said. "He's still snooping around, and it'll be dark soon. If we can make it to the main roads before he leaves, he won't have any reason to think he was followed."

"Solid plan." Sam stood, his knees popping in a sound that echoed Emmett's spine. "This isn't nearly as easy as it used to be."

"We're getting old, Fisher," Emmett grinned, "it happens."

They crept through the trees, bent low despite their protesting muscles. When they reached the jeep, Sam gestured for Emmett to get in first. Before following, Sam pulled out his cell phone and made a call. He was only speaking for a few seconds before hanging up, seating himself behind the wheel and guiding the vehicle out of the dirt driveway.

"Who'd you call?"

"Am," Sam answered easily. "If Stamkos really did use the media to distract from this... whatever it was, then I'm not letting him off so easy. The sheriff is about to receive an anonymous tip that someone broke into Mayor Carver's house. I vote we hightail it before this place is swarmed with cops."

"You won't hear any complaints from me."

Chapter Twelve

CALLIE

By the time the Willow's lot was empty and they'd all migrated to Sam's, Callie was deep in problem-solving mode. She'd pre-emptively filed a complaint with Sheriff Mason, and was actively scrolling through the photos she'd taken to try to identify the individuals who'd run off without speaking to George. She was so engrossed in her work that Callie barely registered Aaron and Nyla leaving again, following up with George at the station and leaving her and Amelia to research in peace. The 'cabin' wasn't what Callie expected. It was a house, a *nice* house, and it made her wonder how well-off Sam's family really was.

She tried not to linger on it, worrying she'd come off as rude if she asked. Instead, Callie settled in the breakfast nook with her files and tablet, directly across from where Amelia was leaning over the kitchen island, watching a program run on her laptop as she slowly chewed a granola bar. The incident with the paint bomb had rattled them all, but it was much easier to push the troubled feelings aside now that they weren't standing in the middle of the mess. Amelia had changed her ruined jeans as soon as the arrived at the cabin, and Callie's outfit was mostly unscathed, shielded by a lobby chair. She couldn't remember Nyla changing clothes before she left with Aaron, but she must've. She was completely doused in red paint, having been the closest to the bomb when it went off. Surely, she took the time to clean up before rushing into the thick of things again.

Now, Callie needed to do the same; rush into the thick of things and find them a lead.

She started by reviewing everything Nyla and Aaron had provided for her. Some of it was largely useless, and even more only held loose promise at best, but by the time she was done, Callie felt like she had a solid understanding of what they were working with. Unfortunately, it wasn't much. Some old construction projects that had been abandoned for seemingly no reason, some missing persons cases that went cold suspiciously quickly, and a couple of newspaper clippings about odd weather patterns. It was a hodgepodge of potentially unrelated circumstances, but it was all they had. Changing that would be a monumental task, one that she was more than happy to take on.

Despite the danger and all the anxiety that came with it— and there was plenty of that to go around— Callie was having *fun*.

A brief flash of guilt rocketed through her as she was reminded that she told Emmett the exact opposite, that she *wasn't* doing this for fun, but she shoved the feeling down. It was still true. Fun was never the goal, just an unexpected side effect. It'd been a long time since she was able to tackle a project bigger than Orville's grunt work. Starting from the very base and working her way up, fitting bits of data together like a puzzle, forming a cohesive sequence of connected events... it felt like she was doing what she loved again. More than that, it felt like she was doing something that *mattered*. Something that could literally save lives. Callie hadn't felt that kind of passion since her internship with one of the larger firms in New York.

"Just sent you the contact info for a witness in one of the missing persons cases." Amelia reached over to a glass on the island beside her, taking a long gulp of her soda before continuing. "I'm still looking for others, but most of these cases are old. I keep getting tripped up by obituaries."

"That's more than I hoped to find." Callie sighed. "Thanks. I'll reach out tomorrow. Hopefully I'll get fewer questions if I'm snooping on a weekday."

"Tell them you're launching a true crime blog," Amelia said, shrugging one shoulder in Callie's direction without taking her eyes off her screen. "You'd be *shocked* at how much access that line will get you. Especially if you promise they can remain anonymous if they want."

"Does no one ask for proof?" Callie made a face. She'd like to think that if someone contacted her asking random, pointed questions, she'd be smart enough to ask some herself.

"Most people are just excited for an excuse to brag about their involvement," Amelia said. "But some do push back a bit. Just send them this." She flipped the laptop around to show Callie the homepage of a true crime blog.

"Is that... real?"

"Depends on what you mean by 'real.'" Amelia turned the laptop around again and resumed her work. She said she was busy infiltrating Stamkos & Stein's website, looking for any information that might be useful while she waited for another scan to finish. She was still investigating the source of the Halloween party article, but she hadn't made much progress yet. "It's a real website, but all the articles are pulled from Wikipedia. I've got a bio page on here about the history of the blog and some bullshit credentials. That's more than enough to satisfy the few people who ask for hard proof that I'm not a scammer."

Callie pondered that for a minute.

"So... what were you using this site for *before* the whole... monster... thing."

Amelia raised an eyebrow in her direction.

"You're right," Callie waved in dismissal, "I don't want to know."

With that, they resumed their work. Callie focused her energy on the few cases that she hadn't dismissed, ordering them from least to most compelling: the first was almost thrown out, but she kept it in the pile due to simple lack of information. The entire file consisted of a newspaper article from 1929, announcing the death of a family. While it wasn't a missing persons case, it mentioned something about a 'cold sickness' that piqued Callie's interest. The other three cases fell into the same category, all disappearances, all unsolved. In 1963, a couple went missing while camping with their friends. In 1970, a family of seven vanished overnight, the front door of their mountain home left open, everything untouched. Finally, in 1981, two teenage boys snuck out of their homes in the middle of the night and were never seen again. The contact information Amelia had given her corresponded to the 1981 case, and Callie was eager to explore that one more.

The other reference she made use of was the list of weather-related reports that Nyla pieced together. Out-of-season storms, unusual cold fronts, and yet another mention of the unhelpfully named 'cold sickness.' The details on that one were sparse, having occurred in the early 1910s, which was infuriating. Callie thought that, if anything, a cold sickness fit their situation the best and it was, of course, the singular event they had the least information on. The weather reports did offer some clarity, though. With a spark of determination, Callie pushed herself out of the chair and approached an old, dusty easel that had been tucked away in the corner of the room. One side was a whiteboard, the other a chalkboard and a small corner of both sides was covered in corkboard.

"Is this being used for something?" Callie asked.

"Sam found it in the shed," Amelia answered. "He brought it in because he thought it might be helpful. If you want it, it's all yours."

"Markers?"

Amelia stretched over the island, reaching blindly for the top drawer on the other side. When she found it, she jerked it open and rummaged inside for a few seconds. Eventually, she pulled her hand out and revealed two dry-erase markers.

"Help yourself."

Callie ran her sleeve-covered palm over the whiteboard, uncaring of the black stains collecting on the mint-green fabric. Her brain had grabbed onto a thread of connection, and she wanted to follow it before it vanished.

Popping the cap off of the black dry-erase marker, Callie began to plot out her timeline.

More specifically, she made three parallel timelines. On the first, she marked the years of unnatural weather phenomena. On the second, she recorded the dates of relevant case files. The third, she left open. Nyla had requested access to Somerton's previous construction logs and expansion projects, but she hadn't been approved. Callie was confident she could circumvent that roadblock, she just hadn't gotten around to it yet. For now, the construction timeline remained blank.

Next, she moved to the corkboard and started pinning papers, overlapping as little as she could manage. Across the top of the board, she placed all of the known Chehwinoo— the first page of their files, anyway. Each one had a small ID photo and basic information like their age, height, weight, address, and employment history. Below that, she pinned a list of known victims and did her best to match each list to the appropriate perpetrator. There was some blurring between the most recent three creatures, but Callie didn't think that would turn out to be overly important. Lastly, she reserved a small section of the corkboard for everything they knew about the Chehwinoo mythos.

They really didn't know much about this creature at all. The only information Callie was able to pin to the board consisted of a poem, a blurry photo taken from Sam's parents' security cameras, and a handful of short stories that Nyla found in a virtual museum archive. All together, it didn't amount to much of anything.

But it was a start.

"Aw, I missed the making of the conspiracy theory board?" Nyla's whine preceded her appearance, easing her way into the kitchen with an armload of folded blankets and towels. Callie hadn't even heard the approach of a vehicle, nor the opening of the front door. How long had she been fixated on her timeline? She turned, smile freezing on her face when she finally got a good look at Nyla.

She *hadn't* changed clothes before going to the station. It didn't even look like she'd washed her hands. Nyla was covered in patchy, dried, flaking paint, shedding from her body like an old skin.

"Have you added the yarn yet?" she asked casually, like she wasn't walking around resembling an extra from *Carrie*. "That's my favourite part."

"No yarn," Callie said, laughing awkwardly. She glanced at Amelia, who seemed just as shocked as she was. "I don't think I could connect it to anything even if I had it."

"Maybe not yet," Nyla agreed, "but the time for yarn will come. When it does, you'd better call me."

"Deal."

They fell into a tense silence as Nyla began to hum, kicking her shoes off absently. At first, it seemed like she was her normal, bubbly self, albeit covered in dried paint. Looking closer, Callie was unnerved by the forced, almost frozen expression of cheery optimism on Nyla's face. Her movements were jerky, almost *too* deliberate. Amelia and Callie glanced at each other and silently debated which of them should address the elephant in the room. Finally, Callie accepted the task.

"Nyla?" she began, keeping her voice gentle. "Are you... um. Did you get a chance to pack any spare clothes from the Willow? I have extra, if you want to borrow some."

"Same here," Amelia offered, nodding down the hall. "My suitcase is in the master bedroom, next to the fireplace. Grab whatever you need. You doing okay?"

"Of course, why wouldn't I be?" Nyla's voice was deceptively bright, even as she blinked paint flecks from her eyelashes. "I've been covered in worse things than red paint, believe me. I was just going to wash these in the shower, but a change of clothes might be nice."

"That's not really what I meant—"

"I told you you'd get itchy," Aaron's voice sounded from the front porch, exasperated and strained. "I'll go back to the Willow later this evening and pack a few things. You just focus on getting rid of that paint."

Nyla frowned, glancing down at herself as though she forgot the paint was there in the five seconds it took Aaron to interrupt.

"What's with the linens?" Amelia asked, nodding at the pile in Nyla's arms and drawing attention away from the odd atmosphere. Aaron appeared shortly after, carrying a stack of pillows. "We hosting a slumber party?"

"A gift from George," Nyla said, snorting in amusement. A flicker of genuine life returned to her demeanor, and the relief it brought was palpable. "Aaron mentioned we wouldn't be going back to the Willow for a few days while it's being cleaned, so he gave us some supplies just in case."

"I tried to tell him it wasn't necessary," Aaron dropped the pillows into a nearby chair, shaking his head at them, "but he wouldn't hear it. I think he's feeling a bit..."

"Useless?"

"You said it, not me."

Nyla gave him a sympathetic smile.

"Can you blame him?" Nyla shrugged. "We've killed, like, a dozen of these things and I still feel like I'm bailing water with a spoon."

"Speaking of water..." Aaron prompted softly. Nyla rolled her eyes, forcing a laugh.

"I know, I know. I'm going."

She disappeared down the hallway and it wasn't long before they heard the shower come to life. Safe in the knowledge that Nyla wouldn't overhear them, Amelia looked at Aaron.

"Is she... alright?"

"She's as alright as she's going to be," Aaron answered, sighing. He pushed his hand through his hair, staring blankly at the spot where Nyla was moments ago. "Nyla hates it when people worry about her. She can't stand it. As long as there are other things to be done, you won't hear a single complaint from her."

"That can't be healthy," Callie pointed out. Aaron shook his head.

"It's taking its toll." He looked older, suddenly. Lines cut across his forehead and wrinkled the corners of his eyes. "The sooner we finish this, the better. I'm keeping an eye on her, but there's only so much I can do when half the town is hellbent on tearing her down. I'll feel better when we can all put this behind us."

Callie couldn't agree more with the sentiment. Her mind was still abuzz with possibilities, none of which she could pin down. With the preliminary board finished, and when Nyla returned from her shower, looking much calmer in a borrowed pair of Amelia's sweatpants and tank top, Callie asked the others for their input. Amelia was able to supply a few more historical weather reports from her snooping, and Nyla suggested pinning up the maps that she and Aaron had made of the known attacks and sightings. Callie accepted both ideas eagerly. As impossible as it seemed, things were starting to take shape. That didn't mean she wasn't left with glaring holes in her knowledge, though.

What released the creature in the first place? Why won't it leave the Basin? How does it choose its host? And, perhaps most importantly, *how do they stop it?*

Callie's mind swirled with ideas and potential avenues of research, but she forced them down. Her eyes already hurt from all the reading she'd done. Before she started speculating, Callie knew she needed a break. If she threw herself into this investigation with no regard for her own exhaustion, she'd be no help to anyone by sundown. Rest, food, and distraction were of paramount importance.

Not to mention, the original reason she came to Somerton.

Callie swallowed a grimace. Dealing with Adrian Stamkos was the last thing on her mind, but it was something she couldn't ignore. Not if she wanted to get out from under Orville's thumb. Besides, it could be helpful. There was every reason to believe that the construction of the Stamkos & Stein factory was intrinsically linked to the Chehwinoo's resurgence. Maybe, if she could convince Stamkos to adjust his building plans, she could kill two birds with one stone. Move the factory out of monster territory and away from Lichen House, saving lives and her contract in one fell swoop.

She resisted the urge to snort. Speaking to Stamkos was a Hail Mary even before; Callie wasn't delusional. She knew there was virtually zero possibility of S&S adjusting their plans for the sake of a currently unprofitable small business. But Callie had a few tricks up her sleeve, tricks that would give Stamkos the illusion of being in the driver's seat. Would they *also* work to convince him of the dangers of continuing his plan as-is? She doubted it. Business collaborations were full of mind games and ulterior motives. Callie was entering the field with a losing hand, and bluffing would only get her so far. Time would tell if it was far enough to mean anything.

Lost in thought, Callie didn't notice the front door open again until Sam and Emmett were dropping huge paper bags onto the dining room table next to her.

"Hey, what took you two so long?" Amelia closed her laptop, pushing it to the far side of the island in favor of the food that just arrived. Sam handed her one of the paper bags, passing the other to Nyla. Emmett wordlessly dropped one of the two paper bags he was carrying next to Callie, his attention fixated on her whiteboard scribbling. She felt suddenly self-conscious and defensive at the same time, ignoring both feelings in favor of the hot meal waiting for her.

"We got a little sidetracked," Sam explained. "Did you call the sheriff?"

"He's been notified," Amelia said with a shrug. Callie blinked. She hadn't noticed Amelia making any calls. Then again, she was completely engrossed in her research for quite a while. It was entirely possible she'd missed Amelia excusing herself. "Wanna tell me what that was about?"

"Gladly." Sam made a show of clearing his throat, commanding the room. Amelia rolled her eyes, taking a massive bite of her burrito while her boyfriend warmed up his performance. "While dear Emmett and I were laboriously collecting nutrients for your consumption, we just so happened to notice a familiar face in the middle of an adventure of a decidedly suspicious nature—"

"We saw Adrian Stamkos heading into Somerton," Emmett interjected, ignoring the look of abject outrage on Sam's face. "We followed him to James Carver's old house. He broke in and was clearly looking for something, but we don't know what."

"*Never* enter showbusiness, Emmett Coady." Sam crossed his arm in exaggerated offense. "Your flair for the dramatic is decidedly lacking."

"What the hell was Stamkos doing at Carver's house?" Nyla demanded, frowning. "Did they even know each other outside of the factory build? Anything related to that would be at Town Hall, not Carver's *house*."

"That is the million-dollar question, isn't it?" Sam recovered immediately from his disappointment, stealing a curly fry from Amelia's takeout container. She smacked his hand away, but not before he managed to swipe one. "Is this the unveiling of a clandestine affair? A corporate conspiracy? Aliens? Personally, I'm hoping for aliens."

"Clandestine affair would be more interesting," Amelia disagreed.

"More interesting than *aliens?*"

"Aliens investigating the production of heartburn medication? Uh, yeah. Sex would be way more interesting than that."

"Alright," Sam conceded. "A clandestine affair *with* aliens."

"Now you're thinking," Amelia said, smirking.

"There might be more here than we thought," Aaron said, furrowing his brow in thought. He crossed his arms over his chest, staring hard at the floor. Callie could almost see the gears turning in his mind, making connections that she couldn't begin to guess at. "Do we know if anything was missing from Carver's property? Anything noted in his file?"

"I've been through this thing with a fine-tooth comb," Amelia promised. "There's nothing out of the ordinary. I'll have another look though, see if anything jumps out that might warrant Stamkos' attention."

"Do that," Aaron said with a curt nod. "Right now, we have too many questions and not nearly enough answers. It's starting to slow us down."

"Let's get to fixing that, then." Callie put her food aside, grabbed her tablet, and opened her notes app. She'd already started making a list of questions, and now that they were all here, she could finish it. "From the top, what do we need to know?"

Chapter Thirteen

EMMETT

"So, we've got Stamkos sneaking around Carver's house, a shit load of partial facts, and a vague mythos. In other words—"

"A whole lot of nothing," Nyla finished, blowing a raspberry in exasperation. "Well, that's not true. We have a lot of pieces, it's just that none of them fit cleanly together."

They'd been talking in circles for hours now, and it was starting to give Emmett a headache. After he and Sam gave a more detailed account of what they'd seen when they followed Stamkos, Aaron and Callie took over the conversation. They worked well together, using a lot of the same lingo and following the same processes. Once again, that spark of resentment toward Aaron reared its head, this time having nothing to do with Nyla.

For all his grumbling, Emmett was awestruck by Callie's abilities. In a short amount of time, she'd organized their patchwork of clues into a comprehensive plan. On her tablet, she had a list of the major questions they needed to answer, and each major question had a series of associated minor questions, some of which they had loose answers for. With so many blank spaces, though, it was impossible not to feel discouraged.

"And you haven't found a pattern with the victims?" Callie prompted, brushing Emmett's arm as she laid her drink down on the table and bringing him back to the topic at hand. He forced his attention away from the contact. "Or... the monsters, I guess?"

"Nothing that fits everyone," Aaron confirmed. He paused in his perusal of Callie's whiteboard, pointing to the list of Chehwinoo they'd been able to identify. "First, we thought they were victims of opportunity, but the substantial break between Carver and Diamond squashes that theory. Then we considered the fact that they were all S&S employees, but Carver and Diamond messed that one up again. Carver was the mayor, and Diamond worked for a contractor. You could make the argument that S&S employed the contractor, but that still leaves Carver."

"So, whatever pattern exists, it has to fit Carver and Diamond in a way we're not seeing yet," Callie said. She joined Aaron at the whiteboard, furrowing her brow in thought. "Could it have something to do with their personal life? Any connections there?"

"None," Amelia piped up from the corner of the room. "I'm still running some passive background checks, but nothing has turned up. The only links I've found have been recent, professional, and public. I *did* find out that Carver and Stamkos visited the same golf retreat in 2011, but they ran different courses. They might've interacted, although I don't know how that would be relevant now. I doubt the Chehwinoo is choosing people based on their average par."

"Could that explain why Stamkos was breaking into Carver's house?" Callie asked, chewing her bottom lip. "Maybe they were friends outside of their respective jobs?"

"I don't know about you, but I can't say I have a habit of breaking into my dead friends' houses," Aaron argued.

"Speak for yourself," Sam scoffed.

"I haven't found anything to indicate they knew each other outside of the factory contract negotiations," Amelia said, steering them back on track. "Whatever Stamkos was doing over there, I don't think it's going to help us figure out how the Chehwinoo spirit is picking its hosts."

"Maybe not," Aaron conceded, making a low, thoughtful noise in the back of his throat, "but I'd still like to know what exactly he was up to. If nothing else, we could use the information to persuade Stamkos to delay construction until we deal with the monster."

Emmett shared a look with Sam. They hadn't voiced their distraction theory yet, and Emmett wasn't planning to be the one to break the ice. He wasn't entirely convinced, for one, and for two, it had been Sam's idea in the first place. The credit, good or bad, belonged to him.

"Aaron Elizabeth Klein!" Sam gasped, clutching his chest in mock-surprise. "Are you suggesting we *blackmail* the CEO of the largest pharmaceutical manufacturer in the continental United States?"

"Yes," Aaron answered easily. "And don't ever call me that again."

"We need every advantage." Amelia glanced up from her computer screen, smirking approvingly at Aaron. "After what happened today, we can't count on the town making things easy for us. If we need to get a little creative to get things done, well, I'm not opposed to getting my hands dirty."

"We need to be extremely careful." Aaron's face was a mask of trepidation, his mouth pressed into a firm line. "Dealing with the public isn't the same as dealing with the Chehwinoo. If we make a wrong move with Stamkos, we can't exactly banish him with a flamethrower."

"Well, we *could*," Amelia argued. Aaron gave her a pointed look. "But we won't!"

"At least not while *Dad's* watching," Sam grumbled, eyeing Aaron while jostling Amelia with his elbow. She snorted a laugh, quickly covering it with a hum as she returned her focus to her laptop.

"Speaking of watching," Nyla said, "do you still have eyes on the Chehwinoo, Am?"

Amelia nodded, flipping her laptop to face everyone. The drone's camera feed was displayed in the bottom left corner, refreshing every 30 seconds. Amelia enlarged the thermal map, pointing to a cold spot in the Northeast.

"I've got the drone parked on a boulder to conserve its battery," she explained. "As long as the Chehwinoo is relatively stationary, we can monitor it for about three hours before I need to fly this baby back home for a charge break."

"Has it moved much?"

"Today? No. It's pretty much stuck to this small radius." She drew a rough circle over the map with the blunt end of her used fork. Her food was long gone, but she'd been fidgeting with the plastic utensil on and off. "No people nearby, as far as I can tell. A few deer."

"Good." Nyla sighed in relief. "The longer we can avoid killing this one, the more time we have to figure out if we can predict the next target. Or, even better, stop this entire thing before it ever gets to that point."

"I'll keep looking into the past Chehwinoo in the meantime," Amelia assured her. "If there's something hidden in any of their backgrounds that will help us identify this pattern and put a stop to it, I'll find it."

"She means that, too," Sam said proudly. "No dirty little secret can hide from Amelia Geraldine Bradley."

Nyla gave a soft snort. "Geraldine?"

Amelia eyed her disparagingly. "Got a problem, *Leanne?*"

"At least yours are unique," Callie joined in. "Do you have any idea how many other women I've met with the middle name 'Maria'? Too many."

"Mine's Peter, which happens to be my favourite slang for 'dick,'" Sam informed them happily. "And I guess it's also my great grandfather's name, but that's less fun."

"Ephraim," Emmett grunted before he could be accosted. "Family name. Dad's first name is technically Josiah, but he goes by Ephraim."

"Aaron has *three*," Nyla whined in despair. "Do you have any idea how long it took me to memorize them? I still get the order mixed up sometimes."

"It's common in Spanish-speaking countries." Aaron laughed, twining his fingers in Nyla's hair as he lounged next to her on the living room couch. She looked much more relaxed now that she wasn't covered in the evidence of what they'd endured at the Willow. "I'm named after both my parents and my maternal grandfather. Aaron Tomas Carlo Javier Klein. My *madré's* name is Carla, and my father's name is Thomas."

"I love your name," Nyla insisted, "I just can't remember it half the time."

"You'll just have to take his last name to help it stick," Amelia teased. "Get on it, FBI Man."

"You guys," Sam said in a high-pitched baby voice, "look at us! We're bonding!"

"And that's enough of that," Amelia said abruptly, elbowing Sam in the ribs when he tried to keep her in place. "Let's get back to work before I lose the lunch I'm still digesting."

"It would digest faster if you didn't inhale your food," Sam grumbled. "You need to eat more regularly."

"I'll eat *you* if you don't shut up and let me work."

"I've got something you can eat—"

"Okay!" Nyla stood, poorly concealing her laughter. "Serious investigation. Let's get it together, y'all."

The others dissolved into more relaxed chatter, taking a moment to destress before launching back into investigation mode. Aaron picked up the unspoken position of team lead. No one argued, given his experience as unit chief during his time with the FBI. After carefully reviewing Callie's list of unanswered questions while she visibly panicked behind him, Aaron divided each task among them. He and Nyla would focus on the Chehwinoo itself, and Tyler Pratt, Rebecca Kelley, and George Mason would take care of the legal routes. Investigating past incidents and dealing with Stamkos would be a joint effort between Sam, Amelia, Emmett, and Callie. Amelia was an expert on getting her hands on confidential information, but her powers could only stretch so far. Callie's connections and credentials opened a lot of doors for them, but it was more difficult for her to slip under the radar. Sam, despite his best attempts to convince them otherwise, was resourceful and street smart. Having his quick thinking adaptability at the ready would make in-person tasks much easier. As for Emmett, they needed someone local on their side. Someone generally well-liked and respected. Callie was still hoping to land interviews with some of the witnesses from the list Amelia gave her. Having both Sam and Emmett around for familiarity increased her chances of getting truthful answers, and it gave Emmett an excuse to be close to her, keep an eye on things.

Emmett remained silent as they continued to plan, taking in the sound of their voices, thankful that there was still enough happiness in his friends' lives that they could enjoy the quiet moments between strategizing. It occurred to him suddenly that one voice had grown notably absent, and he turned to see Callie still poised by the whiteboard, lost in thought. Emmett scowled, crossing the room to stand next to her.

"Cal? Everything okay?"

"Hmm? Yeah." The response was about as convincing as the smile she aimed at him. Emmett raised his brow, staring silently in answer. Callie lasted about 10 seconds before she relented, gesturing vaguely to the whiteboard. "It's probably nothing. I just feel like we're missing something."

"We're missing a lot of things," Emmett corrected. "What specifically is bothering you?"

Seating himself on a nearby dining chair, he stared her down for a truthful answer. Callie hesitated, watching him as though he were going to rescind his offer to listen. He bristled, knowing that reluctance was likely his fault. He'd been nothing but hostile to her since she arrived; why would she trust him to be genuine with her now? He waited, maintaining a calm, encouraging expression on his face. At least, he hoped he did. Eventually, Callie sighed.

"I can't explain it," she admitted, sounding frustrated with herself. "It's like... I don't know, it's like we're looking at two separate pictures that are supposed to connect, somehow, but I can't figure out how. I don't know how else to phrase it. It's not even a tangible problem, it's just a feeling. I know that's incredibly unhelpful."

She deflated as she spoke, her expression scrunching as she realized how futile her attempts to explain herself turned out to be. Emmett frowned, an uncomfortable feeling unravelling in his stomach. He wanted Callie to have the confidence to speak her mind with him, even if he'd done nothing to deserve that honor. He'd have to work on that with her, prove that he was worthy of her trust and she was deserving of support.

What the hell was he saying? That wasn't his job.

But damned if he didn't want it to be.

While he struggled with his emotions, Callie was blinking, unfocused, in the direction of the whiteboard. She opened her mouth, closed it again. And then she reached for her phone.

"Pictures..." she muttered, finding her thread of an idea and clutching tight. Emmett watched, afraid to breathe too loudly and distract her. She stared at her screen for a long, heavy moment, and then her eyes widened.

"Amelia!" she yelled suddenly, making Emmett jump. She smiled at him, timid and apologetic. It was so unbearably sweet that Emmett felt his heart clench in his chest. God damnit, the hold this woman had on him was both thrilling and terrifying all at once. Amelia lifted her head to look at the two of them. "I'm sending you a picture. Tell me if you recognize anyone in it."

Intrigued, Amelia reached for her phone. She stared at it in much the same way Callie had, scanning the screen until her eyes lit on something. A slow smile spread across her face.

"Top left corner, black jacket?"

"I thought so," Callie said, satisfaction and confusion warring on her face in equal measures. "Not to further complicate things, but does anyone know why Adrian Stamkos' personal assistant was at the paint bombing this morning?"

Chapter Fourteen

EMMETT

"Dad? You here?"

Emmett's head was pounding even before the steel door shut behind him, the resounding clang echoing through the barren halls of Lichen House. He flinched, listening for his father's reply to pinpoint his location. When a disgruntled shout sounded from the kitchen, Emmett sighed and made his way there.

He'd spent the past four hours feeling about as useless as tits on a bull. After the startling revelation that Stamkos' assistant was present at the Willow this morning, Sam revealed that he and Emmett had discussed the possibility of a set-up while they were staking out Carver's house. When asked why they hadn't brought it up before, Sam simply stated that it was a hunch and he had no evidence. He didn't want to cloud anyone else's judgment with unsupported theories. Now, though, they had reason to believe Stamkos was involved or, at the very least, had prior knowledge of the incident. Aaron excused himself to make a phone call, and soon after he and Nyla left to meet with someone named Andrews. Amelia and Sam were locked in some kind of silent communication that made Emmett nervous, not helped by their abrupt departure and vague reasoning. Then, it was just Emmett and Callie.

For the next four hours, Emmett did what he could to assist Callie in her research, but there wasn't much for him to contribute. He brought her a bottle of water at one point, and that was the most helpful thing he'd done all day. By the time Sam and Amelia returned from whatever it was they were doing, Emmett was ready to ignore his own wariness and throw himself at their feet for rescuing him. It wasn't that he didn't enjoy the time with Callie. He did, more than he thought he would. Emmett was never one for extended inaction, so he was concerned that sitting quietly while Callie worked would grate on his nerves. On the contrary, the atmosphere in Sam's cabin would have been downright peaceful if not for his clawing insecurities about being entirely out of his element.

They'd waited another hour for Nyla and Aaron to return, and then they decided that was a good stopping point for the day. Everyone else remained at Sam's cabin, dividing among the four available bedrooms, but Emmett was reluctant to stay. He hadn't checked in with his father since the previous morning. He could catch a few hours of rest here at Lichen House after making sure Ephraim was taken care of.

"I told you to leave the sink alone," Emmett insisted, squatting in front of the cabinet to see what Ephraim was working on. His father was sprawled on the floor, head resting on the wooden base of the kitchen cabinet, wrestling with an O-ring. "Tara said they were going to hire a plumber."

"They don't need a plumber for this," Ephraim grunted, dropping the little rubber ring directly onto his face. He cursed, slipping it over his thumb and shoving it back into place. Emmett didn't try to help, he would only get snapped at. "Damn thing won't stay put. Grab a light, would you?"

Emmett was already turning on his phone flashlight, aiming it at the pipe Ephraim was holding in his left hand.

"Water's not even hooked up yet," Emmett pointed out, knowing it was a useless attempt. "How will you know if you have it working?"

"I'll know."

Emmett pressed his lips together, holding his tongue until Ephraim hummed in victory, squirming out of the cabinet and pushing himself to his feet.

"There," he announced with a pride appropriate of a man who'd solved world hunger over the course of Tuesday brunch. "One less thing for Ed and Tara to worry about."

"You're not getting overtime for this," Emmett reminded him. Ephraim waved off his concerns, collecting his tools with deliberate force.

"It's not your money," Ephraim said. "Mind your business. It gets boring around here, gotta find something to keep this noggin sharp."

Emmett fought back the urge to question if his father's mind was *ever* sharp, taking an unopened water bottle from the stack on the counter.

Lichen House was a shell of its former self. The building had been around for longer than Emmett cared to remember, surviving decades of neglect and harsh weather. He wasn't sure what its original purpose was, although he was probably told at some point. History was never one of Emmett's interests. The house was old, and it wasn't built with electricity or indoor plumbing in mind. That was more than enough information for him.

Ephraim stretched, cracking his joints in quick succession. His father had been hired by Tara and Ed Gallagher to tend to the building while they worked out the logistics of their business model. Lichen House had gone through many proposals over the last few years, everything from a museum to a bed and breakfast. Emmett thought they'd settled on some kind of manor house, but in truth, he didn't care. The contractors he worked for had been hired to do the exterior restoration work. The function of the building didn't concern him.

"What the hell are you wearing, Em?" Ephraim groused, looking Emmett up and down with a critical eye. "Put on something presentable, for Christ's sake. This ain't *your* job site."

"You're critiquing my clothes?" Emmett raised an eyebrow in suspicion, taking a long drink from the water bottle. "Since when do you care what I'm wearing?"

"I don't, but other people might," Ephraim rebutted. "You never know who you could run into while you're out. You should try to make a good impression."

Emmett paused, carefully observing his father's body language. When he saw the slight twinkle of anticipation in his eyes, a sigh escaped him.

"Callie stopped by, huh?"

"Yesterday," Ephraim said, confirming Emmett's guess. "Said she'd be back later this week to go over some legal jargon. You're going to be here when she does, and you're going to look like you weren't raised in a barn."

"Dad, stop." Emmett turned away, stalking into the hall. Lichen House was empty enough that his words would carry no matter where he was. "Callie's not interested in me."

"But you're interested in her," Ephraim argued. "Maybe if you cleaned up a bit for once, she'd take notice."

"Can you drop it, please?"

His voice betrayed his irritation, making Ephraim pause in his assault. He regarded his son for a moment longer than Emmett was comfortable with, furrowing his brow in thought.

"What'd you do?"

"Nothing," Emmett said too quickly. Ephraim gave him a skeptical look, one that Emmett had been on the receiving end of too many times to count. "It doesn't matter," he amended.

"Why don't I believe that?" Ephraim muttered. "Did she get things sorted with Nyla? She mentioned something about staying at the Willow for a few days. Maybe you have time to fix whatever you fucked up."

"She talked to Nyla," Emmett grunted, reluctant to say more. If he knew his father, Ephraim would pick up on the tension surrounding Callie's presence right away. Better to avoid as many details as possible. "Not sure what they worked out."

"You're *not sure?*" Ephraim laughed, the rusty sound soothing to Emmett's ears even when it was directed at him. He always loved his father's laugh. He didn't hear it much as a child, with Ephraim working away for much of Emmett's life. Now, he treasured the moments they had together. He could do without the nagging, though. "Tell ya what. If you can find one piece of gossip that Nyla *hasn't* immediately blurted out to the nearest person, I'll believe that she didn't tell you what Callie's plans are for the next few days."

He had a point.

"As far as I know, Callie's staying at the Willow." Emmett's stomach twisted at the thought. That was up in the air now, after the incident with the reporters. Tonight, he knew they were all staying at Sam's. As for tomorrow, he wasn't sure, and he didn't want to speculate with Ephraim. "She... the Chehwinoo attacked her in the car lot. She's fine, but she wants to help us."

"And you want her as far away from everything as possible," Ephraim continued, "so you made an ass of yourself to push her away for her own good. Am I close?"

Emmett glared at him. Ephraim just smirked.

"Cheer up, son." Ephraim clapped a hand on Emmett's shoulder, shoving him toward the main stairwell. Lichen House was made up of two floors; a main floor with a communal kitchen, lobby, office, and storeroom, and a top floor with bathrooms, showers, and dorms. There was a cellar beneath the kitchen, but it was unfinished and no longer used. Most of the building had been gutted over the years, either by looters or contracted workers on behalf of various owners. The main floor kitchen consisted of cabinets and open spaces for large, commercial-grade appliances. The office was completely bare, and the storeroom held some boxes of junk collected over the course of Lichen House's operation, whatever it was. Upstairs had been neglected the longest, with Tara and Ed commissioning as little work as possible up there, just enough to make the building habitable for Ephraim. Two dorm rooms were insulated and furnished, along with one of the bathrooms containing a toilet, sink, and shower. The main water wasn't hooked up yet, but they'd rigged a temporary well pump for the sake of keeping Ephraim on the property. They didn't have an excess of water to work with, but it was enough to live.

"Easy for you to say," Emmett grumbled. "You're finally getting this project off the ground. Maybe when it's done you'll actually retire?"

"Fat chance," Ephraim scoffed. "Look, whatever happened with you and Callie, don't worry about it. I'm sure you'll have plenty of opportunities to make it right."

Emmett didn't like the mischief undercutting the sincerity of Ephraim's words, but he doubted he'd get anywhere by questioning him further. Instead, Emmett stomped up to one of the dorm rooms and collapsed backward onto the bed, staring hard at the ceiling.

After the shameful way he'd behaved, he wondered if it was even possible to make things right with Callie. Especially when he didn't altogether regret it. He still wanted her as far away from Somerton as possible, but it was increasingly apparent that the only way to do that would be to deal with the Chehwinoo for good. Before he could sink too deeply into his thoughts and, hopefully, drift off, his phone began to ping. And ping. And ping.

What the hell?

Emmett unlocked his screen to find a newly formed group chat with several notifications and growing. Frantically, he opened it.

Sam Fisher created the group

Sam Fisher named the group 'Bustin in the Basin'

Sam Fisher changed his nickname to 'Sexy Sam'

Sexy Sam changed Amelia Bradley's nickname to 'Amy Baby'

Sexy Sam changed Nyla Jameson's nickname to 'Mini Mayhem'

Sexy Sam changed Aaron Klein's nickname to 'FBI Man'

Sexy Sam changed Emmett Coady's nickname to 'Ball Cap Brian'

Sexy Sam changed Callie Quinn's nickname to 'Legally Ginger'

Sexy Sam changed Tyler Pratt's nickname to 'Prude'

Amy Baby named the group 'Group Chat'

Sexy Sam: Well that's boring

Amy Baby named the group 'Bite Me'

Sexy Sam: Happily <3

Prude: Wait, shouldn't I be FBI Man?

Sexy Sam: Not if you have to ask

Emmett suppressed a burst of annoyance, relief, and amusement all rolled into one complex emotional lump in his stomach. Honestly, he was surprised it had taken this long for one of them to make a proper group chat. The couple of group texts they'd sent were few and far between.

Amy Baby: Sam and I are ready to tell you what we were doing this afternoon

Sexy Sam: Aside from making hot, passionate love

Nyla, Tyler, and Amelia reacted to Sam's message with a barfing emoji. Emmett snorted.

Get on with it before I block you

> Amy Baby: Here's the thing. Some of you won't like it.

> Legally Ginger: Oh God, I'm 'some of you,' aren't I?

> Sexy Sam: You catch on quick!

> FBI Man: I already know it's illegal. Just rip the band-aid off.

> Amy Baby: We want to break into Adrian Stamkos' hotel room

The chat when abruptly silent. And then his phone rang.

"Are you out of your mind?" Tyler's voice snapped through the line. Emmett thought he'd dialled the wrong number, but then Sam's voice answered.

"No more than usual." Emmett could almost hear Sam's shrug through the phone. *"Amelia needs access to his laptop to install spyware. Where else are we going to get it?"*

"We've already cased the place," Amelia argued. *"It'll be a quick job, in and out in 20 minutes. And that's only if my program stalls."*

"We're not genuinely considering this," Aaron interjected suddenly. *"We're struggling enough just getting him to pay attention. If this goes poorly, he'll have us arrested. And there's not much I can do to prevent it."*

"I probably could," Tyler mused, *"but I won't. Because this is idiotic, even for you."*

The last comment was directed at Sam, who scoffed animatedly.

"Please. This is far from the dumbest thing I've done."

"He's right," Amelia said. *"I can list at least five that are way worse than a B&E."*

"Don't forget cyber crimes," Nyla's voice said cheerily. Aaron groaned.

"I don't think I should be on this call," Callie squeaked, *"I'm hanging up before I hear something I'll regret."*

"Wait!" Amelia's voice got louder, like she was clutching the phone closer to her face. *"You're an integral part of our plan!"*

"I'm what?!"

"*We need you to distract Stamkos,*" Sam explained. "*Schedule your meeting or whatever you were planning, and keep him occupied while we do our thing.*"

"Leave Callie out of your scheming," Emmett threatened, surprised by the low timbre of his words. He cleared his throat, trying to sound more like himself when he spoke again. "Her job is on the line, remember?"

"*I can do it,*" Callie assured them, her tone pointed. "*Unless you think I'm incapable, Emmett?*"

"That's not what I said!" Emmett pinched the bridge of his nose until the sting reached his cheekbones. "I just meant—"

"*Then it's settled!*" Sam said over him, sounding far too pleased with himself. "*We'll talk logistics tomorrow. Good night everyone!*"

There was a series of clicks, and then the line was quiet. Aaron sighed, complaining of a headache before hanging up. Nyla told them she'd better go make sure Aaron didn't pop a blood vessel, and then she was gone as well. Tyler had seemingly hung up around the same time Sam and Amelia had, probably to call them directly and express his concern. That left Emmett and Callie. At first, he didn't know what to do. Should he say goodbye? Should he just hang up? Should he apologize and try to explain that he only said what he said out of concern for her?

"*I'm sorry I snapped at you,*" Callie said, saving him from his panicked indecision. "*I know you didn't mean it the way I took it. It's just... it's been a long day.*"

Instantly, worry gnawed at Emmett's heart. He shifted on the bed, tempted to get up and drive himself back to Sam's cabin.

"It's okay," he dismissed. "I'm not good at controlling my tone. It probably sounded worse than I thought."

They fell quiet again, neither one willing to talk more or end the call. What did that mean? Emmett allowed himself the briefest moment of hope that, despite their rocky start, Callie hadn't completely written him off yet. Maybe he could still save whatever spark they'd shared.

If they'd shared it. Maybe Emmett was alone in his belief that they could be something.

"*Shit,*" Callie said suddenly. "*I totally forgot to tell Amelia that I heard back from Jodi.*"

"Jodi?"

"She's a witness in one of the missing persons cases we think is connected to the Chehwinoo." Callie shifted, the sound muffling her words momentarily. *"She agreed to meet."*

"That's great," Emmett said, and meant it.

"Yeah."

They fell into silence again. This time, it stretched far longer than could be considered comfortable. Emmett braced himself to say something, anything to break the tension, but Callie beat him to it.

"Well, I'd better get some sleep. Goodnight Emmett."

Before he could answer her, the line went dead.

Chapter Fifteen

CALLIE

Like most people her age, Callie hated speaking on the phone.

She'd grown up in a world of online chat programs, texting, and emails. Written communication was her norm, not to mention the benefits of having a paper trail in her line of work. Orville could never seem to wrap his head around that, and, once again, Callie found herself being woken up at an ungodly hour by her phone trilling the opening notes to *Jeepers Creepers*, Orville's custom ringtone.

"Quinn," Callie answered automatically, masking the sleepiness in her voice. She quietly stretched, rolling the stiffness from her shoulders. The Fishers' accommodations were comfortable, but they weren't as familiar as her memory foam mattress at home. Orville grunted into the phone, his only greeting before launching into an unnecessary summary of his weekend. The conference he was attending didn't affect her, it was for one of his investment ventures outside of the law firm. If he was simply trying to connect with her, she wouldn't mind so much. However, she knew that wasn't the case. Orville treated Callie like a glorified personal assistant, expecting her to remain up-to-date on all his comings and goings. They certainly weren't friends.

She listened to him ramble for the next half hour, getting herself ready for the day as she did so. When he paused to take his third dreg of coffee in a row, Callie knew he was winding down.

"When are you back in the office?" he demanded.

"Next Tuesday," Callie said decisively. "I have meetings lined up with the Brownes and Jill Morris for Wednesday, then we have a client coming in Thursday morning to discuss the—"

"We can worry about that when you're back," Orville interrupted. *"I need you to attend that seminar with Henderson today at 11."*

"Orville, I'm in Somerton," Callie reminded him pointedly. "I can't attend a seminar."

"It's virtual."

"I'm on vacation."

There was a pause. Callie knew Orville wouldn't say it verbatim, but she could almost hear the callous 'Should I care?' hovering on his lips.

"I'm not asking, Quinn," Orville said instead. *"I have an appointment with my chiropractor. I can't make it. You have to."*

"Orville—"

"I'll send you the link." Before she could argue further, the line went dead. Callie wanted to be shocked. She wanted to be outraged. Most people didn't put up with this kind of thing from their boss. If she confessed to the way Orville treated her, most people would tell her to quit.

She couldn't quit. Not when she was so close to her goal.

Taking a deep breath to calm herself, Callie checked her schedule. It was early, only 6am, so she had plenty of time to prepare for the seminar. The one silver lining to this whole thing was that Henderson had no time for pointless conversation. If the seminar was slated for 45 minutes, it would be 45 minutes. She could block off that time to make Orville happy, and then return to her current problem.

A memory struck her, hard and pointed. Callie *couldn't* make the seminar, because she was meeting with Jodi.

"Shit." Callie pulled out her phone to call Orville back, but the bastard didn't answer. She tried again, and the call went to voicemail. What the hell was she going to do? She couldn't skip the seminar; in all likelihood, it would be a very small group in attendance. Her absence would be noticed and it wouldn't reflect well on her professionally if she simply failed to appear. She couldn't reschedule with Jodi either; it was too last minute. If delaying the meeting by an hour meant that Jodi couldn't make it, they could lose their best chance at tying other open cases to the Chehwinoo.

Callie was left with only one option. Amelia already agreed to go with her to meet with Jodi, she'd just have to do it solo. Callie felt a bitter twinge of guilt in her stomach, but what choice did she have? It wasn't an ideal solution, but it would have to do.

If nothing else, the seminar would give Callie time to ruminate on the recent developments in their situation. The demonstration at the Willow sat heavily in the pit of her stomach, turning over and over until it was smooth as polished stone, and still she was no closer to understanding the why of it all. The implications in that news article, scam or otherwise, were a deliberate attack on Nyla's character and they were definitive grounds for a defamation suit if they could prove it.

Therein lay the true challenge, though. Proving it.

Defamation suits were notoriously difficult to win. Callie had yet to handle one herself, but Orville had taken on a dozen or so over his 50 year tenure. Out of all the cases that made it to court, only one ended in a settlement. The problem with securing a successful defamation suit was that the burden of proof focused on the defendant's intent. The prosecution needed to prove that, not only were the defendant's claims factually incorrect, but that the defendant spread the claims *knowing* they were incorrect. It was complex, to say the least, and most clients ended up dropping the case in the early stages. Callie was almost certain they'd never be able to prove that the article's author knew his publication would implicate Nyla. However, if they could find out who was behind the allegations, they might be able to get something rolling.

The picture of Stamkos' assistant flashed in her mind. It was pure chance that she'd recognized him at all; ahead of her attempts at securing a meeting with the industry titan, Callie had extensively explored the brand's social media presence. Jerry Leichester was tagged as the photographer in every one of Stamkos' personal accounts, and a quick dive into Leichester's profile explained why. He was a branding genius. When Callie was reviewing the pictures she'd taken at the Willow, his stance and positioning in relation to the other people gathered there had stood out to her, reminiscent of the poses she'd seen him take in the background of S&S marketing videos, capturing candid images for either his personal page or Stamkos'. She didn't fully place his likeness until a few hours later and, by that time, the mob had long since dispersed and they were safely tucked away in Sam's cabin. The strangeness of him being there, combined with Sam and Emmett's speculation, placed Jerry and, by extension, Stamkos at the top of the list of potential culprits. It was a loose theory, but it was the only thing they had to work with for now.

That still didn't explain *why* Stamkos was targeting Nyla. Was it simply for distraction purposes? Surely he could've found something less volatile to buy himself time to break into James Carver's house. Personal, then? Nyla had been vocal about stopping the factory build long before the Chehwinoo became a problem. Maybe Stamkos was acting on bitterness, killing two birds with one stone. Callie added that motive to her repertoire of bait topics to use if her meeting with him started to fizzle out; perhaps she could kill two birds of her own.

The reminder that she needed to pursue said meeting made her expression sour. To avoid Stamkos bringing his laptop to their meeting, she'd have to give off the impression that this was an informal conversation. Callie didn't like the idea. In fact, it made her sick with stress just thinking about it. But she also knew that their options were limited when it came to Adrian Stamkos.

She was putting herself at risk, she knew. Trying to organize a formal meeting with someone as successful as Stamkos was already a gamble; stressing the relaxed nature of their interaction would likely lead Stamkos to assume she was willing to explore under-the-table options to reach an agreement. That may work in her favor. It may also obliterate her already minuscule chance. Whatever the outcome, Callie had no choice but to try.

Getting Stamkos' contact information was difficult, but still significantly easier than it would've been for most other people. Orville's firm had enough pull to access that much, just not quite enough to secure a meeting without question. After emailing back and forth with a few of her contacts, she'd finally gotten her hands on Adrian Stamkos' office number. She just hadn't been brave enough to try calling it yet.

No time like the present.

Callie donned her best corporate voice, adjusting her posture and expression to better sell the illusion even over the phone. This was one of the few circumstances in which she elected to call rather than email. Time was of the essence, and with a massive corporation like Stamkos & Stein, an email was more likely to get lost in the flow of communication.

The line connected. Rang once. Twice.

"You've reached the office of Adrian Stamkos."

As soon as the male voice clipped through the line, Callie had the rather jarring realization that she was speaking with Jerry Leichester.

Of course, she mentally berated herself, *who else would be answering the phone? Get it together, Callie.*

"Good morning," Callie greeted cheerfully, tempering her enthusiasm with more difficulty than usual. The temptation to outright ask him what he'd been doing at the Willow yesterday was almost enough to waylay her plans, but she swallowed down the urge. She had a goal, one she couldn't ignore. "I understand Mr. Stamkos is out of the office at present. Is he still available to schedule a meeting? I'd be happy to go to him, so as not to interrupt his current business."

"Do you have an existing appointment?"

"No, I'm afraid we haven't had the pleasure of being introduced," Callie said, injecting just a touch of regret in her words. "However, I am a representative of Guttenberg Law, and we're very interested in negotiating terms for the upcoming factory build in Somerton, Wisconsin."

Callie heard typing, soft and efficient.

"Mr. Stamkos isn't entertaining offers in Somerton at this time."

"I understand," Callie said patiently; she expected some pushback. "We aren't looking to make an investment. My firm represents several small business owners in the area, and we're open to discussing possible purchase arrangements."

Not strictly true, but she wasn't committing to anything by floating the idea. Jerry paused, a series of mouse clicks filling the silence.

"Which businesses do you represent?"

"Lichen House," Callie answered, "and Willow Lodge."

There was a substantial silence following her words, and Callie suppressed a smile.

"Name?"

"Callie Quinn."

"Phone number?"

Callie rattled off her cell and Orville's office number. At least she could rely on Orville to pass along work when it came his way, including messages.

"I'll send this on to Mr. Stamkos," Jerry's voice told her. *"If he's free for a consultation, he'll reach out."*

"Thank you," Callie said. An idea struck her then, accompanied by a concerning flip in her stomach as an epiphany took over her mind. She waited for half a second to see if Jerry would hang up the phone right away. When he didn't, she took a leap of faith. "If you would be so kind as to include a short note in that message, I believe Mr. Stamkos will have a vested interest in what I wish to discuss."

"I can add a brief message, yes."

Now or never. It was time to see if the stone she'd tossed was on a collision course with multiple birds, or if her instincts were dreadfully wrong.

"Please inform him that I have a potential solution to his troubles with Ms. Nyla Jameson. I understand that recent events have made her more... amenable to discussion."

Jerry had been typing while she spoke. After Callie said Nyla's name, lowering her voice slightly to sell the illusion of secrecy, the typing paused. A slow, triumphant smile spread across Callie's face.

Direct hit.

"I... will be sure to mention it."

Was it just her, or did Jerry sound apprehensive? Her grin widened.

"Thank you. Have a wonderful day."

With the confidence that she was finally onto something tucked carefully in the back of her mind, Callie summoned the energy to leave her room. She heard shuffling coming from the direction of the kitchen, so at least one other person was awake. Donning an oversized sweater and leggings, she made her way toward the sound.

Aaron greeted her with a silent nod, holding his coffee mug aloft in question. Callie nodded enthusiastically, taking his cue to remain quiet. It seemed no one else was out of bed yet.

While Aaron poured her a cup of coffee, Callie wandered to the Fishers' massive living room window. The curtains were pulled tight, so she couldn't see the outside. Giving the fabric a soft tug, Callie had to stifle her gasp when the view came into focus.

The entire forest was covered in a thin layer of frost and snow.

On another day, the sight would've been beautiful. Ice crystals littered the tree branches, making them sparkle in the early morning light. It was almost magical to watch. Today, though, the pristine white represented danger. Worse, a danger that was getting more and more difficult to track with the coming winter.

"It'll melt before noon," Aaron informed her, keeping his voice low. He handed her the mug, already adorned with milk and sugar. He must've guessed from her coffee order.

"That won't be the case for long," Callie said, frowning. She took a sip of the coffee, letting it warm her. "Winter comes on fast around here."

"So I've been told."

They stood in silence, regarding the frost and emptying their mugs. After a few minutes, Sam's obnoxiously loud yawn preluded his appearance at the end of the hall.

"I smelled coffee," he announced, significantly less quietly than Aaron and Callie.

"In the pot," Aaron answered. "Get some before Nyla wakes up. I'm starting to think she bleeds the stuff."

"Pretty sure that's a girl thing," Sam said. "Amelia is the same way. Callie?"

"Guilty."

"See?" Sam yawned again, stretching and cracking his back in a wide, sweeping motion. "Something about women makes them instinctively addicted to caffeine."

"It's because we have to put up with men all day, we need the energy boost." Amelia's disgruntled voice appeared behind Sam, rubbing agitatedly at her eyes. Callie suppressed a laugh. Amelia clearly wasn't a morning person. "Can you pour me one too, please?"

"Anything for you, my terrifyingly gorgeous goddess of evil." Sam grabbed another mug. "Would you like cream or the souls of the damned?"

Amelia glared silently.

"I'm going to go see if Nyla's awake," Aaron announced, shaking his head with a bemused smile. "She doesn't usually sleep this late, but it's been a rough few days."

"Let her sleep," Sam argued. "Has she *had* a full night's rest since this whole thing started?"

"Hard to say," Aaron said. He furrowed his brow in thought. "I don't think so, but she's damn good at hiding it so I can't be sure."

"I have some sleep aids," Amelia said, already sounding cheerier now that she'd had a few gulps from her mug. "I used to have really bad insomnia before I went on my regular anxiety meds. They're not meant for long-term use, but a few nights in a row won't hurt."

"I'll mention it to her," Aaron promised, but the tone of his voice made it seem like he didn't expect Nyla to accept the offer. "Excuse me."

Ignoring Sam's suggestion, Aaron returned to the room he shared with Nyla the night before. Callie watched him go, a troubled feeling surging in her stomach. Nyla was taking this harder than any of them, especially after the paint incident. All day she'd been hollow and distant, noticeably quieter than her usual chatty demeanor. How much more could she take before the toll on her mental health became permanent damage?

The rest of them went about finding something to eat, making small talk, and discussing plans for the day while they waited for Nyla and Aaron to emerge again. Callie confirmed that Amelia was comfortable going to the meeting with Jodi without her, and Sam volunteered to take Callie's place for safety. That made everyone feel better, and when Aaron and Nyla joined them, the conversation shifted to logistics. During a lull, Callie reached into her pocket to check her phone for any follow-up from the nets she'd cast.

As she was wrapping her fingers around it, her phone buzzed, and Callie's stomach flipped at the sight of an unknown number. She then immediately felt foolish. What was she expecting? The Chehwinoo was hardly going to *text* her.

The reality wasn't much better. The text was cordial enough, but it represented a much larger battle she was preparing to fight.

> Good morning, Ms. Quinn. This is Adrian. I've been in-
> formed that you're interested in scheduling a meeting to
> discuss business in Somerton.

That was it. No invitation for further questions, no indication of whether he intended to agree to said meeting. Callie smiled humorlessly. As expected, Stamkos was keeping his cards close to his chest.

> Thank you for your prompt response, Mr. Stamkos. I
> would love to have a chat about your plans in Somerton
> if you're free. My clients are concerned about the effect
> your expansion will have on their business.

She sent that text, letting it sit for a moment before following up.

> However, I don't think we need a formal meeting to sort
> this out. Would you be available for coffee sometime this
> week?

There. She deliberately avoided any written mention of Nyla; creating a paper trail like that would reek of incompetence and she'd lose Stamkos before they even started.

With the bait set out, Callie had nothing to do but wait for Stamkos' response. She didn't wait long, nor did she suspect she'd have to. Men like Stamkos either gave their full attention or none at all, and the simple fact that he'd bothered to contact her personally told her which one he'd deemed her worthy of.

> I can meet you at Coffee Corner at 9a on Tuesday

Again, he didn't ask if that would work for her. Didn't offer an alternative, in case it didn't. Adrian Stamkos was used to having people work around him, which Callie predicted. And, she supposed, she did plan to do the same. Perhaps it was less his own doing and more the enabling of those around him. She toyed with the idea of trying to reschedule for a moment, just to see how he'd react. But this was too important to risk squandering. Instead, she sent him a quick acceptance.

> Perfect, I'll see you then.

After the text was sent, Callie checked her email again. She'd confirmed with Jodi the time and place of their meeting as soon as she'd finished her coffee and spoken to Amelia. Jodi's response came through while Callie was texting Stamkos, reaffirming her commitment. Callie forwarded the email to Amelia, cc'ing Jodi so that she was aware it wasn't Callie herself going to the meeting, apologizing profusely for the late change in plans.

Fuck Orville's stupid seminar.

Even on her own time, her boss was still interfering with her life. Callie couldn't wait until this contract was settled and Orville officially retired. Maybe then she could focus on fostering some of the friendships she craved.

"We have a hit," Callie announced, putting aside her annoyance at Orville. "I officially have a meeting with Adrian Stamkos."

"You're shitting me," Amelia deadpanned. "Callie, that's awesome! Send me the details and Sam and I will start working on a plan."

"Already done," Callie promised, typing on her phone. "I can't guarantee that I'll get anywhere with him in terms of his building plans, but I can at least distract him long enough for you guys to do what you need to."

The sound of tires on the snow-covered driveway interrupted them as Emmett's truck pulled into view. Callie felt a surge of discomfort war with her excitement. The confusing mix of feelings Emmett summoned in her was starting to give her whiplash.

"You've got this, Cal," Sam encouraged, holding his fist in the air in a triumphant gesture. "You know Stamkos won't be able to resist that Southern charm."

"Hopefully I won't have to turn on the charm," Callie said, laughing. "He probably already thinks I'm going to propose sleeping with him in exchange for what I want. Most execs do, when they find out I'm not a partner. They figure if this was a serious meeting, Orville would've handled it himself. The only reason he'd send me over him is because I'm willing to do things he won't.

"It's all bullshit," Callie rushed to add, although she didn't think anyone would assume it was the truth. "Orville sends me because he can't be bothered, not because I'm willing to flirt with the clients."

"Hey, don't underestimate the power of some timely flirting," Amelia countered. "You'd be shocked how many men will cave to a well-placed wink."

"I think there's a big difference between a little flirting and sleeping with your business partner," Callie said with an amused grin.

"I'm not saying you blow the guy under the table," Amelia amended. "But if he's being a little stubborn, you could always shoot him a look."

She demonstrated, donning a sultry smile that almost had butterflies stirring in Callie's stomach. She definitely couldn't pull off something like *that*.

"How about this," Callie started, stifling a giggle, "if it starts to go downhill, I'll make sure I'm wearing a low-cut top under my jacket."

"For what?"

The startled voice took her by surprise. Callie turned around to see Emmett, having finally joined them inside. He looked bewildered, only catching the last few pieces of their conversation.

"Seducing Stamkos," Sam informed him helpfully. "Callie is about to *blow* this whole thing wide open for us."

Chapter Sixteen

EMMETT

Sam was joking. Sam was *always* joking, and while it was sometimes difficult to know that for certain, it was obvious this time. That didn't stop the acidic burn of discomfort that coated the back of Emmett's throat when he locked eyes with Callie.

"I have a meeting with Stamkos scheduled for Tuesday," she explained, rolling her eyes to downplay the importance of her admission. "I'm just meeting him for coffee so Sam and Amelia can do their whole... thing."

"Break into his hotel room," Amelia pointed out happily. Callie visibly cringed, but she didn't try to press the issue.

"It's nothing formal," she continued. "The hope is that he'll leave his work computer, tablet, whatever it is he uses in the hotel room. If not, well..."

"We'll find a way to make it work," Amelia promised, and the conviction in her voice told Emmett that they had a back up plan in place, one they didn't want to share. Likely for Callie's sake. "While Callie is with Stamkos, we'll need someone on lookout. In case things go belly-up and she can't signal us in time to get the hell out of dodge."

"Let me get this straight," Emmett said, trying to keep his emotions in check. He ignored Amelia, staring directly at Callie. "You expect us to just sit back on our asses while you meet up with that psychopath for a *coffee date?*"

Callie stared at him, blinking as she processed his words.

"This was always the plan," Aaron pointed out, regarding Emmett with muted interest. "Meet with Stamkos to either buy ourselves time or convince him to amend his business model, the latter being more unlikely."

"Besides," Callie said, finding her voice again, "he's not a *psychopath*, Emmett."

"Could've fooled me."

"For Christ's sake, he's a businessman!" Callie huffed, the cadence of her words taking on the slightest hint of her Southern roots. He'd heard her accent lingering on the edges of certain words and phrases before, but the more time he spent with her, the more apparent it became that her accent intensified when she was worked up. He idly wondered if it was only when she was angry or if there were other kinds of stimulation that would make her slip into that delicious drawl. A flash of Callie using a low, sultry whisper with *Adrian Fucking Stamkos* brought him back to the present, reigniting the fire simmering in his gut.

"From his perspective, we're costing him money," Callie continued, bewilderment mixed with irritation on her face. *"Of course* he's not going to cooperate with us! If I can smooth things over with Stamkos while Sam and Am get access to his laptop, then we kill two birds with one stone. What's wrong with that?"

"She's meeting him in public, Em," Nyla interjected, catching his eye with a questioning look. Emmett ignored her unspoken question, his blood thundering in his ears too loudly to think straight. "He's an asshole, sure, but he's not *dangerous.* Committing the occasional corporate crime doesn't put him on par with serial killers. It's not like he's going to shove her in the back of his unmarked van and drive off."

"Thanks for that image."

"What's he going to do to me, Emmett?" Callie snapped, her vowels rounding in some words and sharpening in others, mirroring the way her expression hardened while her eyes pinned him in place. "I'm barely involved in all this, as far as he's concerned. If anything, he sees me as a potential ally. What can he do, besides be a colossal road block?"

"Are you forgetting about what happened ye—" Emmett cut off on a pained grunt as Aaron's shoulder drove sharply into his. With a pang of guilt, he realized that mentioning the paint bombing in front of Nyla likely wasn't the best idea right now, never mind that they hadn't *confirmed* Stamkos' involvement in that incident. It was certainly odd that his assistant was present, but odd didn't equate guilt. He glanced apologetically at Aaron, who dipped his chin in warning: *Get yourself together.*

"You're being ridiculous," Callie said, her own irritation feeding his, or maybe it was the other way around. She blustered past his near-slip, drawing attention away from the exchange. "I do this kind of thing all the time. This is my *job*, Coady. Do you have so little faith in my ability to be competent at it?"

"That's not—"

"Isn't it?" Callie snapped, losing the battle to keep her accent in check as her volume raised. Her rounded vowels expanded into clipped words and a soft drawl that would be hot as hell if he wasn't so angry. "Give me another reason for your bad attitude, please, I'm begging you. Right now, it sure as shit feels like you think I'm an idiot little girl in over my head."

"I never said that!" Emmett said hotly. "I'm *worried* about you, Callie! Is that such a bad thing?"

"You're makin' it a bad thing by actin' like a— a—"

"Caveman?" Amelia supplied helpfully. Callie jerked her chin toward her in acknowledgment, her glare burning holes in Emmett's face. He took a steadying breath, trying to calm his racing heart. He knew he was being an asshole. He *knew* it, he just couldn't *stop*.

"You're not going alone." Emmett crossed his arms over his chest decisively, as if that would stop Callie from arguing with him. He knew it wouldn't, but he tried.

"Oh, *fuck* that," Callie growled. "If you come with me, your overblown macho man routine will alienate Stamkos completely. People don't respond to meathead posturing in this industry, Emmett. It's all about money, connections, and manipulation. Do you bring any of those to the table?"

She didn't give him a chance to answer.

"No, you don't. You're stuck in this goddamn 'me man, me protect woman' mindset and it's driving me batshit. For the love of all that's holy, sit down, shut up, and *let me do my fucking job!*"

The room fell silent as electric tension crackled between Callie and Emmett, the only sound coming from her agitated breathing. Emmett wrestled with the urge to argue; that's what she wanted. He'd picked a fight, and she was giving it to him. But that wasn't going to get them anywhere.

He swallowed once. Twice. Emmett kept his lips pressed tightly together until the fire in his veins dulled, allowing him to speak with relative calm.

"I want to go with you," he began, rushing to continue before Callie went on another tirade. "I won't say shit to Stamkos, alright? You take point, I'll follow your lead. No questions asked. I just want to be there in case anything goes wrong. That's all."

He could see the gears turning in her mind as she considered him, weighing the options ahead of her. Emmett waited. He thought it was a reasonable request, but he didn't trust his own judgment right now. The fact that none of the others chimed in reassured him that he wasn't completely out of left field.

"Amelia said you'll need someone to keep watch," Aaron reminded her, surprising Emmett with his support. Maybe Aaron just wanted to get him away from Nyla so he didn't upset her. The words sat in the air between them, hanging, almost mocking in the silence. He could see Callie working through her options, considering each one carefully. Sam and Amelia were automatically ruled out as back-up; they were the ones breaking in. Nyla would draw too much attention, as would Aaron. Emmett was the only reasonable choice, he realized with a jolt of confidence. Callie was smart, surely she'd see that.

But would she be angry enough to fight back anyway? Emmett wouldn't blame her if she was.

Eventually, Callie sighed.

"You will listen to *everything* I say," she warned, her tone harsh. "I'm serious, Emmett. Adrian Stamkos is a difficult man to get to. We have one chance at this, and I can't afford to let you blow it for everyone. This is *my* meeting, and you will not interfere. Do you understand me?"

"You're in charge," Emmett agreed quickly, though the sentiment left his tongue with a bitter aftertaste. He didn't like relinquishing control. Just one more thing he was learning about himself with Callie around. "You're the expert here. What you say, goes."

"Well, bless your heart," Callie muttered, rolling her eyes. After a few deep breaths, she wrestled her composure back into place, her speech drifting back into the polite corporate cadence he was used to with only a scattered trace of Southern drawl in every other sentence. "We will arrive ten minutes early, no sooner, no later. Wear something smart casual. And for the love of God, *please* shave."

Chapter Seventeen

INTERLUDE

Amelia

"So, they're definitely going to fuck, right?"

Amelia suppressed a snort as she closed the front door behind them, stepping into the bracing cold. Even as it refreshed her, a sense of dread began to seep into her bones. The drone wouldn't be of use to them for much longer. She'd need to return it to Terrence soon, before he let his performative concern for her overwhelm him and did something stupid, like come to Somerton to check on her. Amelia didn't think she could bring herself to be civil to her abusive father's former best friend, patrol partner, and go-to alibi, no matter how guilt-ridden he claimed to be.

"The sooner the better," she agreed, rolling her eyes. "The bickering is starting to give me a headache."

"Our group only has space for *one* mean couple," Sam said, slinging his arm over Amelia's shoulder as they walked toward the vehicles parked in the driveway. "And we had that slot secured long before Red showed up."

"Really?" Amelia raised an eyebrow at him. "Red? That the best you can do?"

"Sometimes I need to go for the low-hanging fruit. I can't be hitting bangers every time; it would get boring."

When they left the cabin, the air was still tense. Callie and Emmett weren't outright fighting anymore, but they weren't exactly calm either. Aaron was doing his best to mediate while Nyla was doing her best to push every single one of Emmett's buttons, reminding him that he was being an idiot. Amelia hated to leave in the middle of everything, but they had a witness to interview.

Sam reached Nyla's jeep first, grabbing the windshield scraper from the trunk before setting to work. A thin layer of frost covered the glass, obscuring their vision. As much as Amelia felt like a sitting duck waiting around outside like this, she'd rather they not destroy a second vehicle on this trip.

"You know," Sam grunted, stealing a quick glance her way. "I usually charge admission."

Amelia blinked at him in confusion, trying to remember if he'd said something else before that. When she came up empty, Sam faced her, letting the scraper fall to his side.

"To the gun show," he grinned, raising his right arm and flexing. Amelia could see the muscles jump through the fabric of his sweater. She released an exasperated groan.

"Oh my God, shut up." She glared at him. "I wasn't even looking at you."

She was. Amelia found her attention drawn to Sam whenever she wasn't forcing it elsewhere. It shouldn't be embarrassing, he was her boyfriend, after all. She was supposed to be attracted to him. She just didn't want to give him the satisfaction of admitting it out loud. His ego was already almost too big to fit in their tiny apartment. Any bigger and they'd be forced to live on the street.

"Hey, no shame in ogling your investment," Sam said smugly. "All this real estate belongs to you now, Amy Baby. Stare as long as you want."

"I wasn't staring."

"Admiring?"

"Sam."

"Close," Suddenly, he was in her space, putting his hand on the jeep's passenger door, blocking her from opening it and caging her in. "Inject a little more wanton desire into that tone and we can make quick work of the backseat. Being surrounded by our friends for most of the day is making a certain body part very unhappy."

"Your 'body part' will have to wait. I'll make it up to him later," she promised. "We have shit to do,"

"In twenty minutes. That's enough for a quickie."

"We need to *leave—*"

"I need to get those damn jeans off you before my head explodes."

Amelia summoned her indignation, leveling Sam with a piercing glare.

"I'm starting to regret ever sleeping with you in the first place. I didn't think it was possible, but you've somehow gotten *more* insufferable."

"Then I guess I'll just have to remind you why it was a very, *very* good idea..." Sam teasingly pressed his knee between her thighs like he was going to guide her legs open. Amelia suppressed the little flip her stomach gave at the contact, but something on her face must've given away her reaction. Sam's grin turned wolfish, humming thoughtfully in the back of his throat.

"You talk a big game, Bradley," he purred, "but I affect you more than you let on, don't I?"

"All that shit you talk has trained your tongue well, I'll give you that." Heat flared in Sam's eyes, but she pressed on. "However, you and I both know which one of us has better control of their urges," Amelia challenged, her voice dropping to a dangerous whisper. "Do you *really* want to play this game with me right now, Fisher?"

Sam pretended to contemplate for a moment before dramatically grabbing her shoulders, throwing himself from side to side like he was in the middle of a tumultuous battle with his own body.

"I must... say... no," he crooned obnoxiously, shaking her as he wailed, "you're just... too hot! Can't resist... Need... relief!"

"SAMUEL!"

"Ooh, now that sounded like my mother." Sam shuddered, letting her go at last. Amelia stumbled against the jeep, laughing. "Alright, moment over. Let's go."

Jodi Prescott still lived in Somerton. That was perhaps the most surprising thing Amelia learned about her. Callie had arranged the meeting, but Amelia found most of the details they had on Jodi. When a work obligation forced Callie to hand the interview to Amelia, the short notice wasn't a problem. She had all the information she needed already. Jodi was married, with children, and a retired teacher. Initial research didn't turn up any solid connections between Jodi and the missing teenagers aside from the fact that they were classmates, and Jodi was one of the people Thomas's father contacted in the early stages of the investigation to ask after his son's whereabouts. On paper, Jodi had no reason to agree to talk to Amelia about this case.

All the more intriguing, then, that she was the only one who'd responded to their request. The logical assumption was that she was just curious; why would someone contact her about this case *now?* It'd been decades of radio silence. Maybe Jodi agreed to meet simply to see what Amelia and Callie were trying to get out of this interview. But what if it was more than that? Could Jodi just be after her five minutes of fame? Reliving one of the most exciting, albeit morbid, events in her young life?

The thought crossed Amelia's mind more than once before and it resurfaced as they pulled into the driveway of an unassuming bungalow. It was white, with hunter-green shutters and a garden that would no doubt be overflowing in the summer months. Now, it was littered with skeletal bushes and bound burlap.

Even more concerning was the possibility that Jodi knew exactly what they were dealing with. What were the implications of that? If Jodi Prescott knew about the Chehwinoo, she'd kept the information to herself. Why? Self-preservation? Lack of faith in local law enforcement? Fear? Impartiality?

Was she involved?

Amelia entertained the idea for a moment but ultimately discarded it. Everything they'd found thus far pointed to the S&S factory construction releasing the Chehwinoo. If a human was pulling the strings, they would've crossed paths by now. But maybe Amelia was thinking about this the wrong way. The Chehwinoo's *recent* release was an accident, but what of Jack and Tommy, the two missing boys from Jodi's past? If she'd known about the creature and, worse, was responsible for unleashing it, then she could be held responsible for the fate of the missing teens. That didn't tie everything together neatly either, though. She'd gotten away with manslaughter for decades, revealing herself now would be idiotic at best.

Or, the far more likely scenario, some dumb teenagers got themselves lost in the woods back in the 80s, and it had absolutely nothing to do with an ancient, bloodthirsty ice demon on a rampage.

A hard poke in the center of her forehead snapped her out of her spiraling thoughts.

"You're doing it again." Sam frowned at her in concern. "I can see the steam coming out of your ears."

"I'm just trying to be ready," she insisted, but he was right. Her concerns had shifted from risk calculations to anxiety scenarios. "Let's do this."

They exited the jeep with a shiver. The temperature was definitely dropping, quicker than Amelia would've liked. With a shake, she fell into step just ahead of Sam, reaching the front door before he did, and rapping twice.

Sam began to whistle, both because he was physically incapable of being silent for more than sixty seconds at a time and to distract Amelia from returning to her mental doom spiral. She suppressed a smile. As much as she hated it when people noticed her anxiety peeking out, it filled her with warmth whenever she caught Sam taking care of her in his subtle way. It was maybe the only subtle thing about him and it wasn't lost on her that he kept it that way for her sake. Why the hell had it taken her so long to realize she was crazy about him?

They waited for a full two minutes before knocking again.

"What?"

The voice met them before the door opened, revealing a woman in her late fifties, maybe early sixties. Her dark blonde hair was threaded through with silver wisps of grey, cut in a severe bob that softened the wrinkles around her eyes. Her make-up was equally flattering, highlighting her cheekbones and diminishing the smile lines carving around her mouth. Amelia recognized her from the ID photo she'd unearthed, but she was taken off guard by the formidable presence of Jodi Prescott.

"Mrs. Prescott?" Amelia began, donning her best Girl Scout smile. "I'm Amy Bradshaw, you responded to my colleague's email about an interview?"

"Don't bullshit me, girl," Jodi admonished, eyeing Amelia up and down with a critical stare. She felt Sam start to bristle at her side, but she quickly interrupted his intervention with a sharp elbow. "I know why you *say* you're here. No podcast or television show or video streaming jackass has ever been interested in Tommy before, and they're not about to start. Now, I'm going to ask this one time and I'd better get an honest answer or I'm shutting this door and calling the cops. Who are you, and what do you want?"

Amelia blinked, regarding Jodi with a mixture of annoyance and admiration. Out of habit, a list of backup plans and alternate stories flashed through her mind, and yet she believed that Jodi would accept none of them. Perhaps she recognized a kindred spirit. She shared a look with Sam and, after a silent agreement, Amelia met Jodi's hard stare with unflinching resolve.

"My name is Amelia. We want to talk to you about Tommy and Jack because we think that whatever happened to them might be happening again. And we want to stop it."

It was a little vague, but intentionally so. If Jodi knew anything relevant, she wouldn't be confused by the tidbits of information Amelia dropped into her plea. If this was a dead end, they would find out now. For a long moment, they simply stared at one another. Then, Jodi sighed.

"I was afraid of that."

The door slammed shut.

Amelia and Sam stood, facing the closed door with dumbfounded expressions. A beat passed, then two. Amelia didn't know what to do next; she didn't want to just give up, but Jodi didn't seem like the type of person she could convince with false innocence and carefully laid compliments. She was about to voice her concerns to Sam when the door opened again, revealing Jodi in a zip-up windbreaker.

"Do either of you smoke?" Sam and Amelia shook their heads. "Good. We'll take my car. Come on, I'll tell you the story on the way."

"The day that Jack and Tommy went missing," Jodi began, skipping the small talk and preamble that Amelia feared sifting through during this meeting. She was thankful for Jodi's no-nonsense approach; it was refreshing. "No one knew where they were supposed to be. Jack always had a habit of pulling Tommy into trouble, but it was never anything serious. When Tommy's father called around to our friends, none of us were very concerned. We should've been. Maybe if we'd taken the whole thing seriously from the get-go, we would've found real answers."

"You were teenagers," Amelia said. "They're not exactly known for making smart decisions."

"You've got that right," Jodi huffed, driving past the turnoff for the Willow and heading deeper into the forest road. Amelia and Sam both knew this route well as it was the quickest way to the Fishers' cabin, but Jodi took them farther still. "Monday morning rolled around and they held an assembly, handing out flyers with Jack and Tommy's faces on them. Told all of us that we wouldn't get in trouble, and if we had any information at all, we should come to the front office and speak to the vice principal or the guidance counsellor. We started to get nervous, then. For all the trouble Jack and Tommy got into, they'd never disappeared for more than a few hours."

"Did anyone talk to the vice principal?" Amelia prodded, carefully tapping notes into her phone from the back seat. Sam insisted on taking the front and, while he played it off like he was childishly demanding shotgun, Amelia suspected it was so that he was in a better position to intervene if Jodi was taking them somewhere they didn't want to go.

"Hell if I know," Jodi scoffed. "We were sixteen. As soon as school ended, a group of us met up at the bowling alley to gossip. My friend Ashley said she'd heard Tommy trying to talk Jack out of going into the Basin at night, but she didn't hear why they were going. Hannah said Jack was asking her about her father's jewelry business, and someone else said they heard something about an old mineshaft. It took the better part of a week and some strategically-worded questions, but we put the pieces together."

"So, Tommy and Jack went into the Basin, at night, looking for an old mine?" Amelia repeated back, organizing the information in her mind. When Jodi nodded, she continued. "Why?"

"Beats me," Jodi said, shrugging. She took a slow turn, her eyes scanning the trees as they blurred past. "If Jack got a whiff of something he shouldn't be sniffing around, he was on it like a bloodhound. He probably heard it was dangerous and wanted to explore. Whatever it was, we figured they'd gotten in over their heads and needed help. So, we followed them."

"You what?" Sam whipped his head around to look at Jodi, tearing his gaze away from the road for the first time since they left. "None of this was in the police report?"

Jodi eyed him dubiously.

"Can you think of a reason that might be the case, jumbo?"

"You didn't tell them," Amelia answered quickly, stifling the urge to jump to Sam's defense. Insults may be their love language, but that didn't mean just *anyone* could disparage her boyfriend. However, they still needed Jodi's help, and they were currently at the mercy of her whim as they were in her vehicle. Picking a fight over middle school name-calling seemed like a bad idea. "I think what Sam was getting at is *why* you didn't tell them."

Alright, she had to defend him at least a little.

Jodi met her barely-concealed glare in the rear-view mirror and Amelia swore the corners of her mouth twitched in a smile.

"Didn't I mention that we were sixteen? We wanted to go look for Jack and Tommy but if our parents found out, they'd ground our asses until college graduation. We set a meeting place and time well after our parents were in bed, and we went searching."

"And? Did you find anything?"

"You think I would've dragged you all the way out here if we didn't?" Jodi jerked her chin to the shoulder of the road where she was easing her car to a full stop. The trees here looked the same as any other stretch of forest, aside from a small break that looked like it could've been a trail. Amelia glanced at Sam. "Don't look so nervous. If I wanted to kill you, I wouldn't have left your car in my driveway."

"Comforting," Sam said sarcastically. "Where does this lead?"

"You're not very bright, are you?" Jodi muttered. "Context clues, jumbo. Your girlfriend has already got it figured out, I bet."

"The mine," Amelia answered, squeezing Sam's shoulder reassuringly. "You found it."

Jodi gave her an approving smirk.

"We found it."

Chapter Eighteen

CALLIE

"I think we should look at switching platforms. Our clients are getting younger, so we need to be catering to their expectations."

Callie nodded quietly, trying not to be too obvious about her lack of interest. The virtual seminar Orville forced her to attend was in full swing; she'd only just managed to get into her work email and follow the conference link before Henderson began his lecture on next-generation messaging platforms. With Sam and Amelia off meeting with Jodi, Callie set up her tablet in the dining room of the Fishers' cabin, her notepad open on her right, the page decorated with doodles.

Orville should be the one attending this seminar, not her. Callie was far more up-to-date on modern technology than he was. It was too late to argue, though. Another fifteen minutes of Henderson's droning voice and then she would be free to go back to her research.

The dining room door opened, and Emmett appeared, holding a mug of steaming tea in one hand and an orange in the other. He lifted them in her direction, a silent question on his face. Callie nodded quickly, sliding her notebook to the side to make space on the table. Emmett slipped into the room, closing the door softly behind him and placing the mug within her reach. He started to do the same with the orange, then paused when he saw her jot down a phone number that Henderson highlighted on one of his slides. Emmett considered her for a moment, then he started to peel the orange, placing the individual wedges next to Callie's mug.

She suppressed the little flip that her heart gave when she realized what he was doing. They hadn't spoken properly since their disagreement about her meeting with Stamkos, and Callie wasn't sure where they stood. The fact that Emmett approached her with a peace offering was a good sign.

She didn't *want* to fight with him all the time. She just couldn't help it.

"Ah, shoot," Henderson's voice crackled through the speaker, cutting out in between words. *"Sorry everyone, I think we're going to have to finish up early. There seems to be something going on with the Wi-Fi. I'll send out an email with the PDF version of the notes. Thank—"*

The connection cut before Henderson could finish his sign-off, the screen going blank. Callie sighed in relief, hastily closing the conference link in case it spontaneously came back online and she was roped into finishing the seminar.

"Done already?" Emmett asked, placing another orange slice on the table. Callie picked it up gratefully, popping it into her mouth. She expected him to hand the rest of the fruit to her now that she was free to peel it herself, but he made no move to do so.

"Got lucky," she said, shrugging. There was a pause, the only sound coming from Emmett's peeling. "Listen, about earlier—"

"That's on me," he interrupted, shuffling uncomfortably. "I was out of line. I know that. I don't trust Stamkos, and I didn't stop to think about what I was saying. I'm sorry."

"Apology accepted," Callie said. She watched Emmett peel her another orange slice, a smirk growing on her face. "Uh, Em?"

"Hm?"

"My meeting is over so... I can peel that myself, now."

Emmett froze mid-peel, and Callie swore she saw a blush peeking out over the neck of his t-shirt.

"I've almost got it done anyway," he mumbled, quickly removing the rest of the peel and dropping the orange as if it was burning him. He turned to Callie, uncertainty written across his face.

"Look, I'm not... great... at this stuff," he told her, shifting awkwardly in his chair. "Research and shit, I mean. I want to help, I just don't know how. But... if you need me for anything, I'm at your disposal."

Callie shouldn't like the way that sounded coming from him. The words shouldn't cause a small thrill to ricochet through her chest. He was being generous, that's all. Considerate, even. Nothing more. She absolutely was not thinking about what Emmett's hand would feel like wrapped around the back of her neck like she'd seen Aaron do with Nyla, holding her gently but firmly in place as he kissed her. She wasn't picturing Emmett's hand on the front of her throat instead, and the way her heart skipped at the implication.

Nope. Definitely not.

"I'll take all the help I can get," she said, trying to sound as normal as possible, like the very idea of working in close proximity to Emmett didn't make her heart flutter wildly against her ribs.

She should be over this. After the way he'd treated her over the last few days, Callie should be free from any semblance of a crush. She was, for a while. But then she learned the truth of why Emmett was being an ass to her and, while she still didn't appreciate his behaviour, she couldn't altogether blame him either. He was, in his own way, trying to look out for her. Misguided, sure, but borne of good intentions.

In all her adult life, Callie never struggled to connect with someone the way she did with Emmett. She wasn't social, but her job required a level of professional interpersonal skills that meant she could get along with just about anyone on the surface. Deeper connections were never her strong suit, but they were also not necessary for her to succeed in her field. After her emotional breakdown at the Willow, it wasn't lost on Callie that this penchant for shallow relationships had spilled over into her personal life, and it bothered the hell out of her. She wanted to fix it, even thought she was doing a good job with it when she considered Nyla, Aaron, Amelia, and Sam.

With Emmett, though, things were... different.

Emmett clearly had no time or tolerance for social showmanship. Whatever his feelings, good or bad, he wasn't going out of his way to hide them. That kind of blunt approach should have made navigating a working relationship with him fairly straightforward. However, Callie was quickly realizing that her indoctrination ran deep. She was so used to the song and dance of legal politics that, when presented with someone like Emmett who said what he meant, she struggled to take him at face value. It was confusing, unsettling, and left her feeling unbalanced. Callie didn't know how to handle that.

"Hey, you doing okay with all of this?" Emmett asked suddenly, oblivious to the nature of her inner turmoil. Callie nodded quickly, though she wasn't entirely sure what he was referring to. "You seem stressed. I mean, we're all stressed, but you seem... extra stressed."

"I'm fine," Callie insisted, trying to get a grip on herself. She was fine. She was. She would be.

Maybe.

Emmett regarded her with an expression that was just as skeptical as she felt. Callie heaved a tired sigh.

"I'm sorry," she muttered. "I really am fine, I'm just... I don't know, I'm out of my element here. I'm not used to that. After working for Orville for so long, I expect a fight at every turn. To have a group of people that just trust me to do my job and support me without question is almost overwhelming. I feel like I'm always waiting for the other shoe to drop."

It felt like admitting defeat, confessing her concerns to Emmett. He was the one who'd warned her in the first place, telling her that she didn't know what she was getting herself into. Callie wondered if she was even entitled to feel stressed after the adamant way she'd argued for her own involvement. And yet... talking to Emmett made her feel better, voicing her emotions took away the weight. Until she her gaze returned to his face. Emmett's expression scrunched, looking almost angry. Callie rushed to backpedal.

"And you didn't ask me any of that," she dismissed hurriedly, "I'm just rambling like an idiot. Okay, wow, yeah, I think I need to switch to decaf. Ignore me, I'm fine. I'll write up some quick notes from that seminar, and we can—"

"Callie."

Her jaw snapped shut. Emmett's voice had an intangible quality to it that made her react without thinking. He spoke, and she wanted to listen even though he wasn't yelling or demanding her attention.

"None of us have any idea what we're doing," he told her seriously. "We're feeling our way through this just as much as you are. Don't put so much pressure on yourself."

"I'm not putting pressure on myself."

Emmett raised an eyebrow.

"I mean, no more than usual," she corrected.

"Right," Emmett shook his head, a vaguely fond smile tugging at his lips. "Listen, between Sam's lack of impulse control and Nyla's chronic need to take the blame for everything, it's a miracle we've gotten this far. I don't need to be worried about you giving yourself a heart attack from work anxiety on top of everything."

His tone was light, teasing, laced with a note of concern. Callie's instinct was to interpret his words the way Orville would've meant them: pull yourself together, Callie. I have too much to worry about without you adding to my mental load.

But Emmett wasn't Orville.

He wasn't trying to manipulate her into feeling guilty. He was just... being Emmett. Showing his consideration for her wellbeing. Callie knew that. The thing she *didn't* know was why. Civility, or chivalry? Tolerance, or acceptance?

Friend, or more?

"Aaron and Nyla want to go over the plan for the next couple of days, if you're ready." His attention drifted to her unfinished orange, giving her the chance to decline until she was done, if she wanted.

Callie pressed her lips together to hide her smile, resisting the urge to poke fun at him. The emotional whiplash she felt whenever she was around Emmett was more than a little exhausting, but it was almost worth it for these rare glimpses of his softer side. If she didn't know better, she'd think there was a gentle, considerate man hiding beneath that aggravating exterior.

They left the dining room, meeting Aaron and Nyla in the kitchen where Aaron was contentedly preparing some kind of pasta dish. It smelled delicious, and Callie's stomach immediately began to rumble in response.

"I've had Pratt keep an eye on the Willow for us," Aaron said as they entered, getting straight to the point. "It looks like there won't be a repeat of the paint bombing, at least not any time soon. Nyla and I will be returning for the night as a test; if anyone is keeping tabs on the Willow, they should show up within 24 hours. Pratt will be on standby to help us if we accidentally summon a circus."

"That being said," Nyla picked up, facing Callie. She was seated on the counter near where Aaron was chopping vegetables, alternating between watching him work and stealing bites of green pepper when he wasn't looking. Callie was sure Aaron noticed, but he didn't stop her. "I think it would be better if you stayed here, at least until we have a better idea of how closely the Willow is being watched. Sneaking two people off the property is a lot easier than sneaking three."

"We haven't brought this up to Sam and Amelia," Aaron interjected. "I don't want to volunteer their hospitality, so this depends on their answer. If you staying here is a problem, we'll figure something out at the lodge."

"Don't stress about it," Nyla summarized, meeting Callie's gaze with a knowing glare. It was warranted. Callie was in the middle of doing just that. "We're not kicking you out."

"You can stay at Lichen House," Emmett said, drawing attention back to himself. "I'm sending Dad back to Hatfield for a while; it's getting too dangerous for him to wander the grounds alone. I'll use his room so you can have mine."

The room fell silent.

Callie eyed Emmett with a mixture of caution and surprise. The longer she spent with him, the less she felt like she understood his opinion of her. Emmett took every chance he could to argue with her, and yet he was the first to defend her. He went out of his way to avoid talking to her but would make note of her needs and quietly cater to them. It left Callie with a confusing jumble of feelings writhing in her gut— did Emmett like her, or not?

"Are... you sure?" Aaron asked skeptically, raising an eyebrow at Emmett in silent communication. Callie reminded herself that she wasn't the only one Emmett challenged on a regular basis. Aaron and Emmett fought like frenemies, while Nyla and Emmett fought like siblings. Neither of those options fit the chaotic nature of Callie's relationship with Emmett, but it was comforting to know that he wasn't singling her out *entirely*.

"It makes more sense than her staying here," Emmett said. He crossed his arms over his chest, shrugging to soften the gesture. "None of us should be alone at night, if we can help it. If we split up into pairs, we avoid that problem. You and Nyla, Sam and Amelia, Callie and me."

"Feeling a little lonely, Em?" Nyla teased, catching Callie's eye as she ribbed him. "You should've said something sooner. I'm still working on talking Suits into a threesome, but if we both start pestering him, I think we'll get somewhere."

Alright, Callie amended, maybe not *exactly* like siblings. Aaron gave Nyla a withering look.

"Not a snowball's chance in hell," Emmett snorted.

"My thoughts exactly," Aaron agreed.

Callie let them banter, considering the options available to her. She hadn't known Sam and Amelia long, but she was almost certain they would let her stay with them. If not, she was perfectly happy at Willow Lodge. The chances of a repeat paint bombing incident or something similar were slim to none without some kind of external influence, and Callie sincerely doubted whoever organized the attack would strike again right away. Even an untouchable billionaire has some semblance of tact.

And yet...

She glanced at Emmett, bickering happily with Nyla. He appeared relaxed, comfortable, until Callie looked closer. His shoulders were tense, his spine a little straighter than normal. More than once, he caught her looking at him and she could've sworn she saw a blush touch his cheeks before he looked away. He was nervous, she concluded. Nervous about his offer, her reaction to it.

Afraid that she would accept? Or afraid that she wouldn't?

"Emmett's right," Callie said, staring hard at the ground while she worked through her thoughts. "If there's an emergency, none of us should be alone. Emmett's been with Ephraim thus far, but if he's going back to Hatfield, then it makes sense for me to fill in."

Emmett's head swiveled to stare at her in shock, his mouth opening slightly before he clamped it shut again. He quickly shuttered his expression, a hint of a smile slipping out before he schooled his features. Something akin to happiness fluttered in her stomach. Whatever was going on, Emmett *wanted* her to accept his offer. Maybe it was a further attempt at keeping the peace, or maybe he was trying to make up for his behaviour. Either way, Callie wasn't going to dissuade him.

"Are *you* sure?" Nyla echoed Aaron's question, staring hard at Callie. "No offense to Ephraim, I'm sure he's done wonders with the place, but do you even have running water?"

"The plumbing in the upstairs bathroom is finished," Emmett answered quickly, eagerly. Callie's stomach fluttered again. "The shower, sink, and toilet all work. There are pipes through the rest of the house, but they're not hooked up to the well yet."

"I'm not picky," Callie assured Nyla, offering a smile. "Honestly, a working toilet is enough for me."

"Then it's settled," Emmett announced, moving to pick his coat up off the back of the couch. "Callie, grab your things. We'll get you settled in, get some lunch, and come back when Sam and Amelia are finished."

The scents wafting from the frying pan in front of Aaron made her want to argue. Whatever lunch they managed to scrounge up would surely pale in comparison to whatever he was cooking, but Callie didn't want to stress-test this tentative truce brewing between her and Emmett. She complied with his instructions, gathering her things and rushing to meet him at the front door. Maybe she was being too optimistic; with the amount of animosity between her and Emmett in a group setting, would they even *survive* spending the night in the same house?

Callie wasn't sure, but she was also dedicated to finding out. The small spark of hope taking root in her chest bloomed happily, despite her best attempts to temper it. This could all go horribly wrong, but it could also be incredibly *right*. Perhaps spending some alone time with Emmett would heal whatever was broken between them. And if that process came with the perfect opportunity for her to ogle him in his natural habitat then, well, that was just a bonus.

Maybe irritation and desire were intermingling in her mind a bit more than she'd like, but Callie couldn't deny that even through their worst confrontations, she was still attracted to Emmett. He was stubborn, impulsive, and pushy, all things she thought she hated in a man. With Emmett, the behaviour was more complex than simple male ego. His reasoning, however misguided, always centered around her safety. He tried to keep her from Somerton because of the Chehwinoo. He didn't want her meeting with Stamkos alone because he didn't trust him. And, more importantly, he seemed to genuinely regret his outbursts. That wasn't an excuse for him to continue, of course. If they were going to forge a path forward, Calle would have to set some ground rules.

And if they *could* reach an understanding... well, who knows? Even at his most irritating, Callie consistently fought back the shivers that tended to accost her spine when he loomed over her, jaw clenching and muscles taut. Was that wrong? Probably. Did she care?

Callie wasn't quite ready to answer that question.

The ride to Lichen House was quiet. Uncomfortably so.

Despite the fire of annoyance that Emmett sparked in her whenever they spoke, Callie could summon none of that now. She squirmed in her seat, searching for something to say, anything to break the awkward silence settling over them. Emmett made no move to help her, focusing hard on the road.

This may have been a mistake.

Callie pulled out her phone, tapping away absently. She wasn't doing anything specific, just keeping her hands busy while she waited for something to shift. Before that happened, Emmett was pulling into Lichen House's long driveway.

It really was a gorgeous property. Callie could easily picture it as a bed and breakfast or a historical experience, both ideas that Tara and Ed had considered. The stone exterior was dotted with patches of green moss, the edges worn from years of rapidly changing weather. Emmett pulled up as close to the front door as he could, shifting the truck into park and reaching behind Callie's seat to grab her bag.

"I can take—"

But he was already getting out of the vehicle. Callie felt a twinge of irritation.

Oh yeah, this was definitely a mistake.

Callie took a deep breath, following Emmett determinedly into Lichen House. He held the door for her, calling out into the empty hall.

"Dad! Callie's here."

Shuffling from the kitchen, and then Ephraim was standing before her.

"Well, come on in!" Ephraim grinned, holding his arms open for a hug. Callie returned his smile and his gesture, giving him a friendly squeeze. He was a stocky man, his torso thick and hard from years of living and working the Basin. His face was like an older version of Emmett's, with more laugh lines and prominent crow's feet. "What brings you out this way?"

"Callie's going to stay here for a bit," Emmett cut in before she could. "Nyla's having some trouble at the lodge. Think you'll be okay heading back to the house for a few days?"

"Kicking me out, are ya?" Ephraim raised an eyebrow.

"Yep," Emmett agreed, popping the 'p.' Callie looked frantically between them, panic bubbling in her gut. "Let me show Callie upstairs, then I'll bring you home."

"I'm not old enough for you to be bossing me around like this," Ephraim said, sniffing. Emmett rolled his eyes.

"You're old enough to remember when this place was built," Emmett countered. "Come on, Dad. I don't like you being here with that thing running around."

"But it's fine for *you* to be here?"

"I'm not recovering from a stroke."

Ephraim didn't have anything to say to that. Callie was fighting the urge to do damage control, but she couldn't sense any genuine upset coming from either man. She'd spoken to both of them about the business before, but that was primarily Ephraim taking the lead. Perhaps this was just how they interacted on a more casual basis.

Maybe Emmett really *was* blunt and bossy with everyone, not just her. The thought was oddly comforting.

"Alright, alright," Ephraim conceded, throwing his hands in the air. "I can see when I'm not wanted."

"I'm sorry," Callie rushed to add before Ephraim could walk away. "I didn't realize Emmett hadn't talked to you about this yet."

"Bah, you have nothing to apologize for," Ephraim insisted. "I could use a couple of days off, anyhow."

"I've been saying that for two years," Emmett muttered, rubbing his hand over his face as though he could scrub away the frustration building there.

"Well, you've convinced me." Ephraim ambled over to the stairs, carefully testing his weight on his bad leg. Callie resisted the urge to help; she'd done that enough times in the past to know that her offer wouldn't be accepted. Emmett watched him with a severe frown, like he was also resisting the urge to help but he was significantly angrier about it.

"Come on," Emmett gently nudged her shoulder, "I'll show you where you're staying."

After Ephraim was safely upstairs, Emmett and Callie followed him. The upper floor was less finished than the main floor, but it was secure and insulated. Callie could almost feel the difference in temperature as Emmett led her down the hallway. Suddenly, he turned, disappearing into a room on the right.

"I can get some clean sheets from the house," he told her, hastily plucking a few loose items of clothing from the floor and bed. "I haven't stayed here much, but still."

"That would be great," Callie said gratefully. "I appreciate it, Emmett."

"No problem," he said. "The bathroom is across the hall from Dad's room. It was the first door on your right at the top of the stairs. Feel free to use the shower, just try to keep it under 15 minutes, if you can. The water starts to go murky after that."

"I'll be quick," she promised.

Emmett paused, shuffling awkwardly as he summoned whatever words he wanted to say.

"There's a diner in Hatfield that makes good burgers," he said eventually. "I can pick some up for us on my way back, if you're hungry?"

"Starving," she confirmed eagerly. "I was just starting to wonder if my purse is edible."

He laughed, stepping out of her new room and into the hall.

"Give me an hour," he requested, "if you think you can wait that long."

"I'll manage." She delighted in the smile he gave her, feeling optimistic once again. "But if you take too long, you owe me a new purse."

Chapter Nineteen

INTERLUDE

Sam

Jodi Prescott was nothing like Sam expected her to be. Yes, she was snippy, and her no-nonsense approach to conversation bordered on rude, but he sort of liked that about her. He couldn't say the same for Amelia, who was clearly losing her patience with the veiled insults to Sam's intelligence. More than once, he'd caught Amelia's gaze during their hike, and the cold fury burning in her eyes made his heart do somersaults of happiness.

God, he was so in love with her.

As satisfying as it was to see Amelia jump to his defense, Sam wasn't bothered by Jodi's comments. He'd been called far worse by people who mattered far more. Besides, Sam got the impression that Jodi wasn't trying to belittle him. She was just... unused to the company.

They were well into the Basin now, thin layers of frost and snow crunching under their boots. Every few minutes, Sam would see Amelia out of the corner of his eye, reaching into her coat pocket and discreetly checking her phone. He had no doubt that she was monitoring the video feed from the drone, making sure the creature was well out of their way.

"Now, before either of you start pointing fingers," Jodi uttered from ahead of them, her breath coming out in solid puffs of white air, "we found this spot 40 years ago. If it's not what you're expecting, don't go blaming me."

"Luckily, we have no expectations," Amelia said. Sam slowed his pace so that she could walk ahead of him, putting Jodi at the front and Amelia in the middle.

If anything was going to sneak up on them, he wanted to be the first one in harm's way.

"I'm not sure if that's a good thing," Jodi admitted, her sigh so loud that Sam could hear it from several feet back. "You said you think what happened to Jack and Tommy is related to the missing hikers?"

"And the Halloween massacre," Amelia confirmed. "We... have good reason to suspect it's all connected."

"And you're not going to tell me what that connection is."

"Not if we can help it."

Jodi didn't respond to that, picking up her pace instead.

"I never believed the bear story," Jodi admitted after a pause. "Anyone who's lived here as long as I have would know that story was bullshit. Or they should've, anyway. Seems plenty of people are happy to swallow whatever lies the government feeds them so long as they get to stew in their own denial."

"Sometimes that's easier than the truth," Amelia said. She glanced back at Sam, her eyebrows raised. Sam made a gesture that vaguely resembled a tin foil hat being placed on his head. She grinned back at him. "If you didn't believe the bear story, did you make the connection with Tommy and Jack right away?"

"No, that suspicion came later," Jodi corrected her. "Somerton has more than its fair share of weird happenings. Most remote towns do. People aren't supposed to be this deep in the woods. The forest... it has a mind of its own. A way of balancing things that doesn't fit modern society. It wasn't until the unnatural cold started creeping in that I began to wonder."

"The cold?" Amelia stopped dead in her tracks, so suddenly that Sam almost collided with her. She gathered herself quickly, jogging to catch up to Jodi. "There was nothing in the case report about weather. Why did the cold tip you off?"

Jodi ignored the question.

"Jack and Tommy are dead," she replied. "They died the night they went missing. When we found the mine, it had very clearly collapsed. The entrance was crushed, half-buried under piles of rubble. We only knew it was the right spot because we found some of their things scattered around where the entrance used to be."

"I'm going to assume that, since none of this was in the police report, you didn't tell the sheriff that you figured out where Tommy and Jack went?"

"Even if we did," Jodi answered flippantly, "they wouldn't have believed us. So, no, we didn't tell them. Tommy and Jack were classified as 'Missing, Presumed Dead,' the case went cold, and that was the last any of us heard about it. Until your email."

"But that wasn't true, was it?" Amelia asked, her tone indicating it wasn't really a question. Sam watched Jodi's body language carefully; it didn't escape him that they were in the middle of the woods with a stranger, no car, no cell service, and no idea how to get home. Jodi didn't tense, nor did she look overly surprised. "If that was really the end of the story, we wouldn't be here. Why were you worried about the cold, Jodi?"

It was at that moment that Jodi stopped walking. At first, Sam was worried that he'd misread her body language. He tensed, readying himself for anything. Then he realized she was looking at the ground.

The terrain had leveled out, leading them into a small clearing. The ground was jagged and scattered with large, misshapen boulders, rotting tree stumps, and fallen logs. It would've looked like any other area of the Basin, if not for the remains of some manmade structure stabbing through the earth directly in front of them.

They'd found the mine.

From the shape of the stone, Sam guessed there used to be a small arch here, leading to a diagonal shaft that stretched underground. The entrance was completely destroyed now, weather and time warping the cement into barely distinguishable blocks of rock. If Sam really focussed, he could see where an opening *used* to be.

"You didn't think they could be trapped down there, alive?" Amelia pressed, watching Jodi with a suspicious glint in her eye. "You said that it was obvious the mine collapsed. Alright, fine, but who's to say that Jack and Tommy were dead? They may have found a pocket of stable tunnel and your choice not to tell the cops meant that they died of dehydration, or starvation, even hypothermia."

Jodi smiled approvingly, crossing her arms over her chest as she regarded Sam and Amelia in turn.

"You know, you *could* be an investigative journalist if you wanted. You're right, that was a distinct possibility. One that we debated, heavily, when we first found this place."

"But you decided against it."

"We did."

"Why?"

Jodi slowly stepped over to a decaying tree, staring forlornly at the crumbling bark. Its roots were embedded in the remnants of the mineshaft, clinging to it like a lifeline.

"I had the biggest crush on Tommy. High school was a long time ago, but those feelings stuck with me. Maybe it's because we never got our chance to try. I often wonder what would've happened if Tommy didn't go with Jack that night. Where we'd be. If we would've made it."

Jodi tilted her head back to look up at the sky.

"I love my husband. I love my children. I'm happy with my life. I just... wonder."

Sam and Amelia remained silent, letting Jodi's melancholy fill the air around them. Eventually, she took a sobering breath.

"We didn't tell the police what we found because it had been too long. We wanted to believe they could still be alive down there, but it just wasn't possible. It took us more than a month to find this place. If Jack and Tommy survived the cave-in, they were long dead by the time we figured it out."

Amelia closed her eyes, letting the gravity of the situation settle in the air.

"We could've told the sheriff anyway," Jodi continued. "If nothing else, they may have been able to recover the bodies. But... I can't explain it, not in a way that makes sense. There was a sense of finality to this place. Like... like it shouldn't be disturbed anymore. Even us stomping around the underbrush was stirring up energy that should be dormant."

Amelia caught Sam's eye, her expression wary.

"Not that I listened to my own advice. I used to come here by myself, for a while. After the others lost interest. Once they knew what happened to Jack and Tommy, this place became a black mark on what was otherwise a safe haven for us. Most of them went out of their way to avoid it, hating the reminder of what was taken from us. I could never stay away, though. To me, this is a grave. It's the closest thing we have to a proper burial site for Tommy and Jack. Yes, there are headstones in the cemetery, but they mark empty dirt. Here is where they truly rest.

"I'd been coming here once a week for nearly a year by the time I felt brave enough to explore. I told myself I wasn't trying to find a way into the mine, but I don't know if that's true. The energy in this clearing grew less and less intimidating the more I visited, and I think a part of me wanted to push my luck. If I'd found a usable entrance, I can't say for sure what I would've done. It's a moot point, though. I *did* find an entrance, but... well."

Jodi gestured for them to follow her to the tree, stepping over it and sliding down a small embankment. Sam held Amelia's arm to steady her, more out of a desire to keep her safe than a necessity. Once they were on level ground again, Jodi directed their attention to a small crater in the otherwise smooth hillside. From this angle, the mine was hidden by underbrush. The crater seemed to be the focus of their journey, so Sam stooped to have a closer look.

"Careful," Amelia warned him, quickly grabbing his jacket sleeve. "The mine is still under us. The ground might be weak."

"I wouldn't worry about that," Jodi sniffed. "Take a look in the center of the crater, near that red triangular rock."

Sam did, and when his brain finally processed what his eyes were seeing, he couldn't make sense of it.

The crater wasn't what it seemed. Instead of a solid, concave collection of rocks and dirt, it was more of a hole in the ground. The edges of the hole were surrounded by pointed rocks and severed roots, obscuring the true shape of the area. Sam squinted, working to separate the important details from the detritus. The hole wasn't open, not anymore. It was covered with a thick, crystal-clear layer of ice that had to be at least ten inches deep. Far too large to have formed naturally this early in the season.

"You asked why the cold tipped me off," Jodi supplied, her voice dipping until she almost sounded uncertain. Sam felt his stomach tighten. "Well, this is why. The ice there never melts. I took a torch to it once, and not even a light sweat."

Sam pressed his lips together in a hard line. The Chehwinoo's supernatural cold was impossible to contain, resulting in more than one permafrost forming in the Basin. They'd found several during their hunts, usually near the creature's temporary home. The thing that bothered Sam was that, once the creature was dead, the ice melted. If Jodi was to be believed, then this ice remained intact for 40 years.

"How can that be?" Amelia muttered under her breath, and Sam could tell by the troubled tone of her voice that she was deep in thought, singularly focused on the riddle presented to her. Sam extended his right arm, guessing correctly that Am was about to wander closer to the ice. She stopped short of colliding with his elbow, bending at the hips to get as close as she could without crossing his established boundary. She must've been closely chasing a thread of an idea, otherwise Amelia would've rebuked him for being overly cautious with her. He waited, letting her work through whatever she'd latched onto.

"I've been trying to figure that one out since the eighties," Jodi coughed a humorless laugh. "I stopped coming here when I went away for college and, to be frank, forgot about it. Then we had that strange drop in temperature over the summer and those men went missing and... well, it was all a bit too familiar for my liking. I made the hike again once things settled down, and all was exactly the same as the last time I was here back in 1992."

"Not *exactly* the same," Amelia interrupted suddenly, ducking under Sam's arm before he could stop her. He cursed, hovering, ready to grab her if anything went wrong. He didn't know *what* could go wrong, per se, but he wasn't taking chances. Amelia crouched, laying her palm gently against the ice. "The ice isn't uniform. If you move from side to side, catching the light at different angles, you can see that it's warped in places."

"And that's important because...?" Sam trailed.

"That means it wasn't frozen at the same time," she explained. "If it was, it would be uniform. Or, at least, close to it. If you lean down, you can almost see the layers that were added later. It's almost like... actually, yes, it's *exactly* like the ice started to melt and then refroze. Just the top layers are warped, and you can see that some moss and twigs got stuck in there. Everything below the first inch or so is clean."

"Amy Baby, I think we've already established that I'm the trophy husband of this relationship. I'm going to need you to fill in some blanks here. What does all that mean?"

"It means," Amelia said, ignoring Jodi's snort of laughter. She turned to face Sam, a hesitant hope blooming in her eyes. "I think we have a lead."

Chapter Twenty

CALLIE

Waiting for Emmett to return was the longest hour of Callie's life. It wasn't that Lichen House made her nervous— or, at least, she told herself it didn't— but the oppressive quiet was unsettling after spending the last few days surrounded by life. Sam's teasing, Amelia's quips, Nyla's cheerful optimism, and Aaron's exhausted attempts at keeping everyone on task had quickly become a staple in Callie's day-to-day life. Left alone with her thoughts felt unnatural in a way that it never did before.

While she waited, Callie pored over the casefiles again. She'd done so enough times now that she barely needed to check the source material, but it was something to keep her mind occupied. Questions crowded her thoughts, and she was no closer to figuring out the answers.

Her working theory was that the Chehwinoo had surfaced multiple times in the past. From the sparse details in the few cases she'd highlighted, it seemed impossible that this was the first time the creature terrorized Somerton. That didn't mean that events lined up cleanly, though.

One of the biggest issues she faced was determining just how many Chehwinoo there were before James Carver. Four was the tentative total she'd settled on, but there were problems with that guess. Many of the missing persons cases overlapped with strange weather patterns, and even more of them coincided with major environmental upsets; namely, construction. Callie felt safe in her assumption that the process of unleashing the Chehwinoo was roughly the same each time: a development project disrupts balance in the Basin, Somerton experiences an unnatural cold, people die or disappear, and then... nothing.

The biggest missing piece of the puzzle was the most important. No matter how Callie looked at Somerton's history, she couldn't nail down a definitive *end* to the Chehwinoo's reign. Stories petered out, weather slowly returned to normal, projects were abandoned, but no one specified the why or how of it all. Was the creature simply satisfied? Was there a threshold of bloodshed it needed to meet before returning to wherever it hibernated during peaceful periods? Were the people of Somerton caught in some horrific cycle that they couldn't break, one that didn't appear to follow any set rules?

Frustration pinched behind her eyes, and Callie forced herself to think about something else. Without more to go on, she'd never be able to solve this puzzle. Her biggest hope now was that Sam and Am got something useful out of Jodi.

Her phone pinged, mercifully drawing her out of her spiralling thoughts with a text from Nyla.

> Am just texted. Good(ish) news. When are you guys coming back to the cabin?

Callie glanced out the window near her bed. Emmett still wasn't back.

> Not sure yet. Em went to Hatfield. Urgent?

> Not yet. Can you ask Em to bring my walkie back with you guys? He's had it since August -.- I think we're going to need it.

She texted Nyla back confirming that she would ask, and then Callie heard tires on gravel. Through the window, she spotted Ephraim's truck pulling up.

"Thank God," she breathed, unfolding herself from her seated position on the bed. Callie forced herself not to run out into the hallway immediately, waiting until she heard Emmett's footsteps reach the top of the stairs before finally opening her door.

"Hey!" she greeted warmly, holding up her phone. "Just heard from Nyla. We can head to the cabin whenever we're ready. Sam and Amelia are back."

"Sure." Emmett shrugged. The tone of his voice surprised her; dull, hollow, defeated, like the air had been sucked from his lungs. Callie paused, examining his face as he stood at the top of the stairs, his eyes closed and the bridge of his nose caught between his thumb and forefinger.

"Is everything okay?" Callie asked tentatively, feeling like she was edging the toe of her shoe onto an iced-over lake. She'd seen Emmett in two moods: brooding or relaxed. This fatalism was new and unsettling.

"Yeah, sorry," he muttered, sighing heavily. "Dad— never mind, it's not a big deal."

Callie raised an eyebrow at him, waiting expectantly for him to continue. Eventually, Emmett relented.

"He tripped on the front step of the house," he explained. "It wasn't a full fall, just a little stumble. Enough to start another argument about his mobility. I'll get over it."

"I'm sorry, Emmett." Callie had never had to deal with a stubborn aging parent, but she'd handled some will disputes. The pain she'd seen, the weight of trying to ensure a loved one was taken care of, especially when they resisted, was unlike any other. Ephraim wasn't anywhere near the point of needing at-home care, but even a casual observer could see that his movement was labored. Callie couldn't imagine how much it hurt Emmett to watch his father suffer like that, even if it was his choice. "I know there isn't much I can do, but if you think of anything..."

Emmett offered her a grateful half-smile, ducking into his room without another word. The door swung on its hinges, closing at a snail's pace. Callie reached out with her palm, catching it before it cut her off. "I'll just grab a sweater, and we can go."

"I'll text Nyla that we'll be there in 20?" she asked, staring down at her phone as she updated Nyla with the plan after a confirming grunt from Emmett. Her attention snagged on the previous messages. Emmett was somewhere on the other side of the room; Callie wasn't really looking at him, only catching movement out of the corner of her eye. She stepped fully through the door, lifting her head at last.

"Before I forget, Nyla wanted me to—"

Callie skidded to a halt just over the threshold of Emmett's room, her mental function mimicking the abrupt stutter in her step.

"Wanted you to what?"

Emmett turned to face her, seemingly oblivious to the shock she'd received. Callie felt the door slam behind her, striking her in the back and forcing her to take another fumbling step forward.

"Hm?"

Callie's mouth felt dry as she stared at Emmett, openly and with unveiled appreciation. When he said he was going to grab a sweater, Callie assumed he meant to put one on *over* his current shirt. Apparently, she'd been wrong. Emmett stood by the bed in only his blue workpants, slung low on his hips. Without his shirt, Callie could clearly see the defined bunches of muscle that made up his torso and corded his arms, making him look impossibly bigger even without his massive jacket. She knew Emmett was fit, but she hadn't expected quite this level of bulk. More of a shock, though, were the lines of ink adorning his shoulder and part of his chest.

An ornate, detailed wyvern curled around Emmett's right shoulder, its tail weaving a mesmerizing pattern on the upper right portion of his back, its head slinking along his pectoral. The creature was once bright with a myriad of colour, but it had since faded over time. Now, the wyvern's black lines mingled with dulled greens and blues, making it look almost like the ink had been diluted with water. Callie knew she was staring, probably open-mouthed, but she couldn't look away. Every time she tried, a new detail caught her attention.

"Callie?"

"What?" She snapped her gaze up to Emmett's only to find him battling back a smile. A flush crept up her chest and neck, and Calle had to consciously stop herself from squirming.

"You said that Nyla wanted you to do something?"

"Uh... right. Yes. She did." Callie shook herself, trying to give the stunned hamster wheel in her skull a jolt back into action. "She wanted me to ask you about..."

Your tattoo? Your broad shoulders? How your back looks like it was Michelangelo's personal passion project?

"Her walkie!" Callie blurted suddenly, loudly. She clamped her mouth shut immediately, too late to stop the sound. "She said you still had her walkie from when she leant it to you in August."

"Right." Emmett scratched the back of his neck in thought, giving Callie an uninterrupted view of the lines along his chest, ribs, and stomach. She tried to distract herself by focusing on obscure patterns in the unfinished ceiling, failing every time Emmett made a noise or moved in any way. When he walked toward the dresser on her left, Callie was once again startled by a glint of something metal on his front. It took her a moment to understand what it was, and when she did, she couldn't hold back her runaway thoughts anymore.

"Em, do you have a nipple piercing?" Callie gaped, open disbelief in her voice. Emmett retrieved Nyla's walkie from the dresser, giving a self-deprecating chuckle before turning back to her.

"Yeah," he said, shrugging bashfully. "I got it when I was 18. Got drunk and lost a bet."

"You could've taken it out," she pointed out, still staring at the deceptively simple metal barbell.

"Thought about it," he admitted. "But... I dunno. Kinda thought it suited me."

"It does," she said too quickly, clearing her throat to cover the enthusiasm of her agreement. Callie blinked a few times, trying to rein in her attraction before she started drooling. Did she have a thing for guys with piercings? That was news to her. "I mean, I never thought about it before, but you seem like the kind of guy that would have one random piercing with a dumb story behind it. Not that you're dumb! I mean—"

Callie bit her tongue, inwardly cringing. She was never like this. She needed to pull herself together before she said something completely moronic. If Emmett was bothered by her lack of tact, he didn't show it. He laughed, a little uncertainly.

"No, I'm definitely dumb." He smirked. "If I was smart, I wouldn't have let them talk me into getting more than one."

"You have two?" Callie's gaze automatically fixed on the other nipple, but it was decidedly unpierced. "Did you take that one out?"

"No," Emmett said, looking amused.

Callie knew he didn't have any ear or facial piercings. His stomach was smooth and unmarked, and she couldn't see any studs or rings in unconventional places. She furrowed her brow, trying to remember if his tongue was pierced.

When he saw the confusion and unspoken question on her face, Emmett pressed his lips together to suppress a smile. He raised his eyebrows knowingly, his gaze darting downward before meeting hers meaningfully. It took Callie's mind longer than she would like to admit to figure out what kind of piercing he was talking about and when she did, her cheeks darkened.

"Right. Well. That's... cool." She reached behind her, fumbling with the doorknob. "I should go get my purse so we can go. I really didn't want to forget the walkie, so—"

Emmett held up the walkie, which she hadn't taken yet. Callie pressed her lips together in a firm line, mentally berating herself. She presented her open palm for the walkie, but Emmett didn't approach her. He wiggled the radio in his grip, offering it to her if she got it herself. Callie took a hesitant step forward, grasping the walkie uncertainly. Emmett didn't pull it away from her, but he didn't release it either. Instead, he held on for a second longer than he needed to, forcing her to stay in close proximity until he decided to let her go. Callie tried to swallow past the dryness in her throat.

This was ridiculous. She didn't even need to take the walkie from him. They were both going to the cabin, Emmett could easily slip it into his pocket. Callie ignored the way her skin burned with a bright red blush.

"Thanks," she murmured, afraid to look him in the eyes, not knowing what she'd see. "I'll be in the truck."

Callie spun, her attention firmly on the exposed chip wood floor. She reached for the doorknob, but Emmett beat her to it, leaning forward so far that she could feel the heat of him on her back.

"I won't keep you waiting," he promised, his voice low and rich in her ear. Callie felt his words caress the length of her spine, igniting shivers throughout her body. With a panicked waver in her gait, she rushed down the stairs without another sound.

"He has his *fucking dick pierced!*"

Callie uttered a string of unintelligible curses as she shut the passenger door with gusto, collapsing against the seat. She sank into it, groaning aloud as she turned the ignition and the truck roared to life.

"He has his dick pierced. Of course he has his dick pierced."

Of all the secrets Emmett could be hiding, Callie would never have guessed in a million years that he was pierced, in multiple places, and tatted to boot. Why was that so attractive? It shouldn't be. A dick piercing would be hard to clean, wouldn't it? And it might get caught on some unsuspecting hair if Emmett wasn't careful, so not only unclean but also painful. No, it shouldn't be attractive. Callie was losing her mind. She needed some sense talked into her.

"Tell me I'm crazy," Callie said before Nyla had even uttered a 'hello' into her cellphone. Callie stared hard at the front door of Lichen House, preparing to change the topic if Emmett appeared. "No matter what comes out of my mouth in the next two minutes, I need you to tell me I'm insane."

"You're insane," Nyla responded dutifully. *"But I'm going to need some specifics to really hammer it home."*

Callie sucked in a shaky breath, trying and failing to dispel the image of Emmett's naked torso branded into her memory. She realized belatedly that she was about to confess, however indirectly, that she had a massive crush on Emmett to one of his close friends, and that thought should've terrified her into making up an elaborate lie on the spot to protect her dignity. It didn't, though. Instead of scared, Callie felt relief. Nyla may be Emmett's friend, but now she was Callie's friend, too. And talking her out of stupid decisions about men was exactly the kind of thing she needed a friend to do.

"He has a tattoo," she confessed, knowing Nyla would figure out who she was talking about quickly enough. "A dragon on his shoulder. And a nipple piercing."

"Damn, Emmett," Nyla said, laughing to herself.

"There's more."

"Go on."

Movement in the upper windows told her she was running out of time. It also meant that Emmett was no longer shirtless. Callie shouldn't be disappointed about that.

"His dick is pierced."

Nyla's scream cut out halfway through, disintegrating into a fit of giggles.

"You're kidding! No way, I don't believe it. Emmett? *When? Why?"*

"On a dare, years ago," Callie muttered, burying her face in her hand. "Tell me I shouldn't find that hot. It's not hot, right?"

For her part, Nyla didn't seem the least bit surprised that Callie found *anything* about Emmett hot. It made her wonder how obvious her feelings had been from the very beginning.

"Are you serious?" Nyla scoffed. *"That's hot as fuck. I've always wondered what it would be like to have sex with a guy with a pierced dick. Wait, what kind of dick piercing? Prince Albert? Frenulum? Scrotal?"*

"Why do you know so much about dick piercings?"

"Don't worry about it," she dismissed. *"Just answer the question."*

"I don't know!" Callie nearly screeched. "I didn't ask!"

"Well, now you have *to bone him so you can tell me about it."*

"Nyla!" Callie said in outrage. "You're supposed to tell me I'm crazy and I shouldn't be attracted to Emmett, remember?"

"Right." Nyla hummed in thought. *"You're crazy, and you shouldn't be attracted to Emmett. Unrelated, hold on a sec."*

The sound of muffled movement came through the line, followed by Nyla's voice just a bit quieter than before.

"Suits? What are the chances you'd get your dick pierced for me?"

"Lower than me getting anything else pierced for you," Aaron's voice answered, unfazed by Nyla's blunt line of questioning. *"And before you ask, those odds are already painfully low."*

"Emmett has his dick pierced."

"Good for Emmett."

"Maybe I wrote him off too early," Nyla mused, sounding louder again now. Despite her inner turmoil, Callie couldn't help by smile. *"Cal? How does Emmett feel about one-night stands with taken women?"*

"You'll have to ask him," Callie said, falling into a more relaxed posture. Nyla may not have confirmed her insanity with the certainty she'd hoped for, but calling her had been the right decision. Callie felt better already. "I, apparently, forget half of my vocabulary when I'm in his presence."

"Oh yeah, you're definitely smitten," Nyla agreed sagely. *"You know the cure for that?"*

"Don't say sex."

"It's sex."

"Why do you hate me?"

Nyla laughed again, and, despite her grumbling, Callie smiled.

"I *am* crazy though, aren't I?" she pressed, her stomach churning with nerves and vulnerability. "He's been such an ass lately. Crushing on him should be the last thing I feel."

"You answered your own question," Nyla pointed out, much to Callie's confusion. *"He's been an ass lately. You've spent enough time with him to know he isn't normally like this. Aside from the obvious, Em's been pretty overprotective ever since Ephraim's health scare, so I'm sure that doesn't help matters. He's a colossal idiot, but he's not a bad guy."*

Callie let the truth of that sink in, calming her emotional turmoil. Nyla was right, of course. Emmett wasn't normally like this, at least not in the relatively short time she'd spent with him before now. Perhaps that's why she was so upset by his hostility toward her. It wasn't just that it was undeserved, it was also out of character.

"Just keep putting him in his place until he sorts his shit out," Nyla continued, and Callie could hear the smirk in her voice. *"And if that doesn't work, I've heard threesomes are a great way to improve a man's mood."*

"Something you *will never experience firsthand,"* Aaron's sharp voice muttered in the background. Nyla cackled.

"Good*bye*, Nyla." Callie shook her head in amused exasperation. The front door of Lichen House swung open, revealing Emmett in his ballcap, winter jacket, and a thick grey sweater. Callie tried to ignore the little shock of adrenaline that coursed through her as they made eye contact through the windshield. He held up a brown paper bag, reminding her of the reason he'd been gone so long in the first place. Her stomach rumbled appreciatively. "We're leaving Lichen House now. We'll talk more when we get there."

Chapter Twenty-One

EMMETT

Maybe it was boyish of him, but Emmett couldn't get the smile off his face after his run-in with Callie at Lichen House.

She was stubbornly quiet on the drive to Sam's, her attention fixated on inhaling her burger as quickly as humanly possible. Emmett didn't mind; smugness had settled comfortably in his bones and he was sure Callie could sense it.

He'd never seen her cheeks that red before.

Her embarrassment was adorable. Emmet's crush on Callie was always a nagging presence in his mind when she was around, but now it was screaming at him to wake up, make a move, do *something*. She was clearly attracted to him, that much was obvious. Did her disdain for him overwhelm her curiosity? Emmett wanted to ask, but he doubted it would go well. Any time he tried to bridge the gap between them, the olive branch caught fire and burned to cinders in his hand. The only reason their earlier conversation didn't end in a verbal brawl was likely because Callie was too stunned to summon any anger.

Did Emmett even *want* to date Callie, if their relationship was always going to be this volatile?

Call him a masochist, but Emmett knew the answer was a resounding yes. Callie pushed every single one of his buttons without trying, buttons he didn't think he had. She was able to claw her way under his skin with a single word, set his blood blazing with a defiant look, and make his heart pound just from her proximity. Callie was everything Emmett didn't know he needed in a woman. She was someone who would match his energy, challenge his impulses, and put him in his place when he was out of line. Why was the thought of that so goddamn hot?

Emmett didn't have time to ponder it for long. Sam and Amelia were already at the cabin by the time they arrived, and whatever they learned was exciting enough to forgo pleasantries.

"Jodi knows more than we thought," Amelia explained, quickly relaying the version of events that didn't make it to Tommy and Jack's police report. Callie sank into a dining room chair, typing furiously on her tablet. "I don't think anyone, aside from us, suspects the extent of the danger, but a lot of the older residents know that *something* is happening and has been for a long time."

"Any idea how long?" Aaron pressed. Amelia shook her head.

"Nothing concrete, but I have a theory." She pulled out her phone, showing them a picture of what looked like a porthole carved into the mountainside. It was an almost perfectly circular chunk of glass formed into the dirt.

Not glass, Emmett realized belatedly, *ice*.

"We know the Chehwinoo leaves a trail of ice wherever it goes," Amelia continued, pulling up a new image. This time, it was the live feed of the surveillance drone. On the screen, they could see harsh, jagged ice growths spiking the terrain around a deep crevice where the current Chehwinoo had been hiding during the day. "We also know that the longer the Chehwinoo stays in a certain area, the thicker and more permanent the ice becomes."

She glanced at Nyla for confirmation.

"The Hovel was completely iced over. It didn't melt when the Chehwinoo left the cave, not like the usual frost trails do. It only started to melt when the Chehwinoo was dead, and then it was pretty instant."

"Exactly," Amelia said, excitement making her bounce on her heels. "You've segued into my next point perfectly. The ice covering the mine shaft entrance is supernatural, we know that. Jodi told us she'd tried to melt it before and had no luck. The ice was roughly ten inches thick. The first eight inches were clear, almost like glass, which means it likely formed all at once. The top two inches were more warped and dirtied with twigs and leaves. They formed later and in much smaller, more frequent layers.

"I think we can safely assume that all the frequent melting and refreezing in the top layers is a result of our intervention. Before that, though, for the ice to still be that thick and resistant to melting over the last four decades, it would've had to have been sustained by the creature. That could only be true if the Chehwinoo had been alive, trapped in the mineshaft, since the collapse."

"In 1981?" Callie frowned, her eyebrows pinching together. "You're trying to say that the Chehwinoo was trapped in an abandoned mine for *forty years?*"

"At least, yeah." Amelia grimaced. "Honestly? I think it was longer. From the files I sent you, no other strange events were noted in Somerton in the late seventies or early eighties. That makes me think Jack and Tommy stumbled across it when they went spelunking."

"But if that's true," Aaron said quietly, speaking for the first time in a while, "that means the first Chehwinoo wasn't James Carver. It would've been someone from the eighties, maybe even earlier depending on whether Jack or Tommy *became* a Chehwinoo or *found* a Chehwinoo, like Amelia suggested. The spirit then took over Carver after it was released, probably having its old host body crushed during the first wave of construction."

"I'm leaning toward 'found,' too," Callie added. "Nothing about either kid makes me think they'd be a target."

"So, then, they found a Chehwinoo that was trapped in the mine, released it, and trapped it again, dying in the process, all in the same night?" Nyla's expression twisted in thought, like she wasn't sure how to feel about her own question.

"It's not as far of a stretch as it sounds," Amelia reassured her. "I was talking to Jodi about the kind of things Jack and Tommy would get into together. Jack was particularly stubborn, so if they came across any barricades or walls, he would've knocked them down before turning back."

"Let me get this straight," Emmett took a deep breath, "Chehwinoo is trapped in the mine until Jack and Tommy accidentally find it, sacrifice themselves intentionally or otherwise to keep it trapped, the monster hangs out in an abandoned mine for forty years, then Stamkos & Stein come along, digging up shit they shouldn't be digging up, and the Chehwinoo is either killed as a result of the construction work or its spirit or whatever it is gets loose and takes over Carver? Am I getting that right?"

"I'm not saying it's clean, but it's a theory," Amelia said, looking grave. Emmett glanced at Callie, who was staring at her unfinished timeline on the whiteboard. "The important take-away is that it *can* be trapped, at least semi-permanently. The big question now is can it be trapped *anywhere*, or is the mine special, somehow?"

"I'm glad you brought that up again," Nyla said. She scrunched her brows together in thought. "I didn't know there was a mine in the Basin. It must've closed ages ago, right? Do you know what they were mining?"

"Topaz, I think," Amelia answered, pulling out a piece of paper and unfolding it carefully. "I don't think it was a very large operation."

"For it to not appear on any of our preliminary searches, it must be old." Nyla crossed her arms, staring at the ground in thought. "Like, *old*, old. Maybe even older than Somerton."

"Information on it is scarce," Amelia agreed, tapping the paper in her hands, "but I found this map. It isn't dated, but judging by the style and some of the landmarks noted, I think it's from the late 1800s. Definitely pre-Somerton. And it *did* reveal something interesting."

She smoothed the paper, revealing a blurry printed image of a rudimentary map with red circle drawn in permanent marker. Emmett stared at the location, struck by familiarity, until the realization hit him with the force of a freight train.

"The Hovel," he muttered at the same time Nyla gasped. "The Hovel is part of the old mining tunnels."

Not even Emmett could miss the significance of that revelation. The Hovel, where the Chehwinoo had resided during its initial reign of terror over the summer, had contained several relics with depictions of the creature. It had *also* been intentionally closed off after the Chehwinoo was killed, though they didn't know by whom. The logical assumption was that it was done as part of the ongoing construction, since the Hovel was technically on Stamkos & Stein's property, but they hadn't had the time or resources to confirm. In light of the increase in murders, the Hovel's secrets had fallen to the back burner. Now, though, they were front and center.

"That can't be a fucking coincidence," Sam said under his breath. "How is it that everything we find ends up leading back to that damn factory? Are they manufacturing Ouija boards in there? Spirit bottles? Hex bags? Who invited them here anyway?"

Amelia elbowed Sam sharply in the ribs and he cut off on a hissed yelp of pain. When he looked down at her in bewilderment, she widened her eyes and glanced briefly in Nyla's direction.

Despite Amelia's quick action, Nyla had heard Sam's frustrated words. She gave a tilted smile, half-raising her hand in the air.

"Guilty," she joked, forcing a chuckle. "Although if I realized that drug manufacturing was the kind of business James intended to bring in, I would've kept my mouth shut. Bit late for that now, though."

Her tone was dismissive and self-deprecating with an air of humor that didn't reach her eyes. Emmett wanted to argue with her, to tell her she was wrong. That this wasn't her doing. But Nyla had already blown past the brittle moment to examine the map more closely.

It *wasn't* her doing, that was the worst part. Nyla's vision for Somerton was built on wilderness retreats and eco-tourism, an economy that highlighted the natural beauty and isolation of the Basin. James Carver, no doubt aided by Bill Hannaford, had taken her vision and warped it, focusing on industrial expansion that destroyed the very forest she wanted to feature. And when she challenged them on it? The town called her ungrateful. Fickle. Impossible to please. They all turned on her, painting her as the villain trying to stop Somerton's municipality from creating much-needed work for the locals. It made Emmett's stomach turn, even more so when he realized that Nyla might *believe* that filth.

She was good at hiding it, but Emmett was starting to wonder just how much pain Nyla had been in during the last four years.

"Hey," Amelia said gently, laying an awkward hand on Nyla's shoulder. She was rescued from offering more affection when Aaron silently wrapped his arms around Nyla from behind, murmuring something in her ear that none of them heard. "You're the only reason there's a Somerton left to save, at this point. This isn't your fault."

"You don't owe the people here shit," Sam agreed wholeheartedly, trying to recover from his blunder. "Honestly, you *should* leave them to clean up this mess on their own. If they listened to you in the first place, none of this would be happening."

"We've put too much into this to stop now," Nyla insisted. "I'm not giving up. But... if anyone wants out, I won't hold it against you. Any of you. I mean that."

She did, and Emmett knew it. Nyla's biggest fear had always been someone getting hurt on her watch. The Chehwinoo was basically a twisted manifestation of that fear, and Nyla wouldn't fault a single one of them for pulling out now. That was also exactly why none of them ever would.

"No one's going anywhere," Amelia scoffed. A series of nods around the room echoed her sentiment. "We've come this far. What we need to do now is find some way to force the Chehwinoo into dormancy and keep it there, if we can't outright kill it."

"Getting into that mine might be a good place to start," Callie agreed, staring at the floor with her brow furrowed in thought. "It doesn't sound like the entrance Jack and Tommy used is viable anymore, but this map might help us locate other access points. The Chehwinoo was trapped there for decades without incident. There must be *something* that kept it there, stopped it from trying to dig its way out."

"The Hovel is still closed," Aaron added. "So, that's not an option."

"Leave it with me for a while," Nyla said. "I've been all over this mountain. If I can get a map of the Basin to fill in any gaps in my memory, I can pick out the spots most likely to be alternate entry points."

"How would we even know what to look for?" Sam asked, sounding calmer now. "Its trail has been pretty obvious so far, but who's to say the thing keeping it in the mine isn't something stupid, like a rust allergy, or a really strong aversion to the colour orange?"

Amelia rolled her eyes at him, but before she could say anything, Nyla perked up.

"I know someone who might be able to help us with that," she said slowly, sneaking glances at Aaron. He scowled, and Emmett knew what was coming before the words ever left Nyla's mouth. "The Chehwinoo is from the Onaqwe culture, right? We've been looking for old sources this whole time, trying to find historical records of the Chehwinoo and how to deal with it. But maybe we're coming at this from the wrong angle. For starters, I don't speak Oki-qwe. That's already made things difficult even before getting into the sheer lack of documentation. More than that, though, the Onaqwe people practise verbal records. Most of their stories won't be written down anywhere."

"It's the biggest roadblock we've been facing," Aaron conceded, his jaw tight. "One we can't overcome without bringing in outside help."

Nyla and Aaron shared a silent communication, ending only when Aaron gave the slightest nod.

"Lucky for us," Nyla grinned excitedly, "I know just the person."

Chapter Twenty-Two

CALLIE

To Emmett's credit, he proved to be very good at following directions.

The meeting with Stamkos had fallen to the back of Callie's mind in light of the revelations from Jodi, but the next morning came with a renewed sense of uncertainty. Part of her was still angry at Emmett for insisting he accompany her to this meeting. Another part of her was relieved that she wouldn't be going into the dragon's den alone.

When he emerged from his room that day, Callie almost did a doubletake. Emmett was clean-cut in a way she'd never seen before; he wore suit pants, a light blue button-up, and a navy sports jacket. He'd ditched his baseball cap, loosely styling his short hair to give it more volume. Lastly, he'd shaved. If she was being honest with herself, Callie preferred the unrefined version of Emmett, the one with grease-stained clothes, dark scruff, and an unwavering commitment to hats. Still, this version of him was... intriguing. And not just a little easy on the eyes.

They arrived at the Coffee Corner exactly ten minutes early, just as Callie planned. The place was busy with the late breakfast crowd, but they were able to secure a table near the window. Maybe it was smart, or maybe it was paranoid, but she wanted to be able to see the parking lot.

As Emmett waited in line, Callie caught movement across the café. She spotted a blonde woman around her age staring at Callie with calculating eyes. Unease blossomed in her stomach. Callie spent considerable time convincing herself that people *weren't* staring at her whenever she went out in public, and this woman was single-handedly unraveling her hard work. She looked to the counter to see if Emmett was finished ordering yet.

He wasn't, so Callie busied herself with her phone until the chair opposite her scraped against the tile, and Emmett sat down. Callie breathed a sigh of relief, accepting her drink from Emmett's outstretched hand.

"What's the plan?" Emmett asked, taking a long gulp of his coffee. Callie considered him for a moment. As angry as she'd been when Emmett first insisted he come along, she had to admit that he seemed to be in an agreeable mood today. Maybe having someone on her side wouldn't be such a bad thing.

"We want to keep things friendly," she said, glancing at the blonde woman again. She was still looking in their direction, but her attention wasn't on Callie anymore. It was on Emmett, and her expression was far angrier than it had been a moment ago.

"And...?"

Callie jumped, forgetting for a moment that she was in the middle of a sentence.

"Right, sorry," she said, blushing. "This isn't an official meeting. We want casual language, no promises, no commitments, and absolutely nothing that could be considered a verbal contract. If you're not sure of your phrasing, it's better to keep your mouth shut."

"My plan is to let you do the talking," Emmett said with a smirk. "I don't feel like having my ass handed to me with a high-heeled boot."

Callie laughed, reflexively clicking her heel against the floor in response.

"Good plan," she teased. "Although, I gotta admit, handing your ass to you is proving to be pretty fun."

Emmett's eyebrows shot up.

"Is that so?"

"Maybe," Callie said, her voice turning shy. She took another sip of her drink to stop herself from filling the silence with something stupid. Again, the blonde woman flickered in the corner of Callie's vision. She skirted her attention away the second that Callie turned her head, but it was clear she'd been staring. Callie frowned, looking between the blonde and Emmett with a confused expression.

"Uh, Emmett?" He met her gaze. "Any reason that blonde woman keeps looking over here like she wants to throttle you with her bare hands?"

Emmett whipped his head in the direction Callie indicated, groaning when he caught sight of the woman. She was with a group of two others, seated in a booth with a trio of ceramic mugs cluttering the table. Her friends would cast their attention on Callie and Emmett every few seconds, expressions ranging from curious to indifferent.

"Ah, that." Emmett cleared his throat, taking a long dreg of his coffee before answering. "That's my ex, Kelsey. We didn't exactly end on good terms."

"What happened?" Callie prompted, pulling her attention back to Emmett. Knowing who Kelsey was, she didn't want to give her the satisfaction of acknowledging her. "If you don't mind my asking."

Emmett shrugged one shoulder, but the movement was stiff. He may be acting nonchalant, but Callie had no doubt there was some resentment buried there.

"It was a while ago now," he said, forcing a smile. "I caught her sleeping with one of her coworkers. She tried to play it off like it was a one-time thing and it wouldn't happen again, but I went through her messages. Not proud of that, but it is what it is."

"I'm sorry," Callie said sincerely. She'd been cheated on before, and she knew the kind of lingering pain it inflicted. "How long were you together?"

"About a year," Emmett answered. He took another sip of coffee, more relaxed now having gotten the hardest part out of the way. "Kelsey was always fickle, but I didn't think she'd... well, you know. I guess that was on me."

"None of this is on you, Emmett." Callie glared at him, frowning into her doughnut. "Kelsey is responsible for her own actions. She's an adult."

"Didn't stop her from trying to blame me," he said with a sardonic grin. "Told me that I was neglecting her needs, that I worked too much, that I didn't care about her or what she wanted. It was all a sympathy ploy but... I'll be damned if it didn't work. Took a long time before I was able to accept that she was just trying to save face. I wasn't perfect, but I *know* I didn't neglect her."

Callie nodded along sympathetically, having no trouble believing him. Emmett may be one of the most infuriating people she'd ever met, but she never felt like she was vying for his attention when she spoke to him, even in a group. And it wasn't just her. Aside from the few heated exchanges they'd shared, and the more recent arguments with Nyla, Callie had never seen Emmett talk over anyone, cut anyone off, lose interest in the middle of a story, or anything. Even in their contract meetings, Emmett always made sure she had her turn to speak.

Stealing another quick look in Kelsey's direction to ensure she was still looking their way, Callie shifted forward in her chair. She deliberately dragged her hand across the table, tracing patterns across the back of Emmett's hand with the tip of her nail. Emmett jolted in surprise, furrowing his brow at her in confusion.

"Just act natural," Callie murmured, donning what she hoped was a flirty expression. "If she feels like staring, may as well give her a show."

Emmett's snort of laughter was genuine, even as he shifted his chair closer to hers and covered her wandering hand with his own large, calloused palm. Callie's stomach flipped at the contact, the strength in his grip contrasting with the gentle way he held her.

"It was Nyla that pulled me out of my funk, actually," Emmett said, easing into his role. Callie answered him with a smile, encouraging him to continue. It was the longest she'd spoken to Emmett without devolving into an argument, and she wasn't ready for it to stop. "We knew each other before the whole Kelsey thing, mostly through Dad, but we weren't exactly friends. Then I went 'full Eeyore,' as she put it, and she decided enough was enough. Asked me out for drinks the next weekend, and we've been friends ever since."

"You guys fit together well," Callie said experimentally, recognizing that she was fishing. Emmett picked up on it immediately, coughing a harsh laugh.

"Sure we do," he said, snorting. "If by 'well' you mean like warring siblings. Nyla is amazing, but she's basically family. Even if Aaron wasn't in the picture, me and Nyla? Ew."

Callie didn't like the flood of relief that moved through her at that admission. She took another determined bite of her doughnut.

"What about you?" Emmett asked, startling her. Callie swallowed, hard, trying not to choke on her dessert.

"What?"

"Any crazy ex stories to share?" he clarified, regarding her with a gentle smile that set her heart fluttering. Callie silently warned it to knock it off, washing down the doughnut with some more of her drink.

"Not a lot of time to date," she said easily. Emmett casually reached over to brush a stray lock of her hair away from her face, tucking it behind her ear as though it were the most natural thing in the world. Callie forced herself to focus on her words. "I've gone out for the odd dinner, but my last boyfriend was nearly five years ago. Not that I would mind dating again, it's just..."

"Just...?"

Just that the one person I want to date is sitting across from me, and I still don't know how to feel about that.

"The opportunity hasn't come up," she settled on eventually, trying to fight down her blush. Emmett regarded her curiously for a moment, his hand squeezing gently over hers, the motion so small Callie almost thought she imagined it.

Silence fell between them, heavy and tense. Callie squirmed in her seat, wondering if she should remove her hand from his. A glance across the cafe told her that Kelsey and her friends were gone, so there was no reason to keep up their little performance. Emmett was looking anywhere except her, tapping his foot under the table, keeping his hand firmly over hers. After too long a pause to be comfortable, Emmett made a small sound in his throat, like he was gearing up to say something. Callie sat straighter, forcing her gaze back to his face.

"Cal—"

"Well, this is a pleasant surprise!"

The commanding, deceptively polite greeting came from over Callie's shoulder, making her jump. She jerked her hand away from Emmett's, smoothing her palms over her thighs to distract from the absence of his comforting warmth on her skin. Adrian Stamkos circled their table, decisively taking the chair to Callie's left.

"So sorry I'm a bit late," he continued, snapping his fingers in the direction of the counter. The barista nodded, moving to the espresso machine without a word from Stamkos. "Meeting ran late, you know how it is. I can't say I was expecting this to be a group setting, Ms. Quinn. Who am I required to share your lovely company with today?"

"Emmett Coady," Emmett said, his voice hard. "My father works at Lichen House."

"Ah, Coady, yes," Stamkos hummed. "The name is familiar. Well, the more the merrier, as it were. What can I do for you?"

Chapter Twenty-Three

EMMETT

While Callie exchanged pleasantries with Stamkos, Emmett checked in with Sam and Amelia.

There was something thrilling about knowing he was aiding in the closest thing to a heist he would get in his lifetime. Emmett knew that, between the six of them, they'd broken the law several times over the last few months, but this felt different somehow. Sitting here, in public, distracting Stamkos while Amelia and Sam broke into his hotel room felt more substantial than anything they'd done previously. It eased his mind, finally feeling like he was contributing something meaningful to their goal.

Even if it meant sitting quietly while Callie and Stamkos engaged in verbal warfare.

With confirmation that Stamkos was at the coffee shop, Sam texted Emmett that they were moving. He was being vague on purpose, on the off chance Stamkos caught a glimpse of Emmett's phone screen. It wasn't exactly professional-level espionage, but it felt cool none-the-less.

"I appreciate you taking the time to meet with us, Mr. Stamkos," Callie began, smiling politely. Emmett watched her with a careful kind of awe; he used to think that Callie's default persona was her professional one, leaving him feeling like she never truly let her guard down even among friends. Seeing her now, though, flipped that assumption on its head. Callie's demeanor around Stamkos was starkly different than what Emmett had grown accustomed to. She was bright, bubbly, but reserved and almost coquettish in her interactions with him. It was both fascinating and unsettling, and it made him wonder if the professional, polished Callie he was used to was even more of a shield than he previously thought.

"Please, call me Adrian," Stamkos corrected, reaching behind him to accept the mug of black coffee being handed to him. Emmett wanted to roll his eyes; when had he established the expectation that the baristas would provide him table service? "Unless this meeting has gone from casual to formal, of course."

"Not at all," Callie said. "Feel free to call me Callie. I hope you've been enjoying your time in Somerton?"

"It's been an enlightening experience," Stamkos hummed, leaning back in his chair. Emmett chose to remain silent, following Callie's instructions perhaps a bit more faithfully than she had intended. "Somerton has quite the personality."

"It's a unique town," Callie agreed. She mimed Stamkos' posture, easing back in her seat. To anyone on the outside looking in, their conversation appeared relaxed, easy. Emmett knew better. Both Callie and Stamkos had a sharpness in their eyes telling him that they were seeing everything, hearing everything, and evaluating their next move carefully. Emmett had never watched a professional chess match, but he imagined the energy was much like this.

"It certainly has its charms."

"And its challenges," Callie said, nodding. "I understand you've had a few hiccups since your project began?"

It wasn't a question, but Callie phrased it as one. Emmett watched Stamkos closely, looking for anything that would give away his thoughts.

"Comes with the territory, I'm afraid." Stamkos' smile turned sugary, almost condescending. "Although I admit I've had more individual pushback than I'm used to."

He was talking about Nyla, his anticipatory expression almost baiting either one of them to address the elephant in the room. Callie neatly maneuvered around the tactic.

"Somerton is expanding," Callie said pacifyingly. "Growing pains are to be expected. I can certainly relate."

"Oh?" Stamkos regarded her with a knowing glint in his eye. "You mentioned you were representing the new owners of Lichen House. Running into a few roadblocks?"

"Comes with the territory," Callie agreed, repeating Stamkos' words back to him. "Without beating around the bush, I was hoping for your input. Unfortunately, it's the Stamkos & Stein factory plans that are causing the biggest upset for us at Guttenberg Law."

Stamkos nodded slowly, taking a sip of his coffee while he considered his response.

"Given the nature of this meeting, I take it that you're not here as Orville's representative?"

"I'm not."

"Nor your clients?"

"That's right."

"And do they know of your intentions to speak to me?"

Callie hesitated. It was just for a second, barely long enough to notice, but it was there.

"I didn't consult them beforehand, no. Since this isn't an official business negotiation, I didn't deem it necessary."

"Hm." Stamkos pressed his lips together, saying nothing more.

Emmett didn't even try to understand the significance of that exchange. Whatever was happening between Callie and Stamkos was far beyond him now. He checked his phone as discreetly as possible, noting with concern that he hadn't received a single update from Sam or Amelia.

"I'm sure you can understand the awkward position I'm in," Callie pressed onward, picking up her drink in a deliberately casual gesture. "My clients are concerned about the effect this building will have on their business model moving forward."

"The presence of modern architecture doesn't take away from the significance of historic building sites," Stamkos argued lightly. "There are a number of successful museums, hotels, restaurants, and many other categories of historic businesses located in the heart of metropolitan centers. New York, for example, has more than you can count."

"That *is* true," Callie conceded, "but the appeal of Lichen House is intrinsically tied to its remote location. We can hardly advertise it as an 'isolated piece of history' when there's a bustling production facility next door."

"I sympathize with your predicament, Callie, I do." Stamkos once again donned a pitying smile. "You're not the only one to express concerns about modernizing Somerton. Unfortunately, this is the direction the world is moving. Without new business bringing job opportunities, Somerton will never be able to attract young families to supplement their aging population. Besides, it's *one* factory. Somerton is completely surrounded by untouched wilderness. I doubt we'd be able to make a dent with *ten* factories, let alone one. This is a good move, for everyone."

"Not everyone," Callie pushed, frowning. "I see your point, Adrian, but I have to disagree. Bringing in business is important, yes, but the *kind* of business matters. Somerton is a prime space to build a thriving eco-tourism sector, and having a drug production operation so close to town borders hinders the locals' ability to take advantage of Somerton's natural assets."

"I've yet to see evidence that the town *wants* to take advantage of Somerton's natural assets," Stamkos pointed out. "The residents have had decades to do something with the resources they have at their disposal. They didn't. It was only a matter of time before someone like me noticed the abundance of wasted potential around here. I'm not in the business of waiting for others to snatch up the things I want."

Emmett tensed. A slight wrinkle had formed in Stamkos' forehead, wedged directly between his eyebrows. Callie must've noticed it too, because she immediately softened.

"No one with any sense would question your judgment, Adrian," she said gently, her expression almost... coy? Emmett shifted uncomfortably in his chair. "You're an incredibly successful man. And I would never presume to know your business better than you do."

"Then why are we here, Callie?"

The question wasn't rude on the surface. Stamkos kept his tone light and curious, but his features were guarded. Emmett wasn't brazen enough to assume they had him on the back foot. He was calculating something.

Callie considered his question carefully before turning to Emmett.

"Em?" she said shyly, "would you mind getting me another doughnut?"

Emmett blinked at her in shock. He'd fallen into the background of their conversation, just like Callie wanted. Now she was trying to get rid of him? Why? Had he done something?

He opened his mouth to argue, but a quick flash of warning in Callie's eyes told him that now wasn't the time. He forced his mouth to close, his movements stiff as he stood from the table.

"Sure," he muttered, glancing briefly at Stamkos. "Want anything?"

"No thank you, Mr. Coady," Stamkos dismissed with a tight smile. Emmett bristled, something about his tone rubbing him the wrong way. Silently, he walked toward the counter. What the hell was Callie thinking?

Even as he waited in line, Emmett strained to hear the conversation at the table. To his relief, the café was quiet enough that he could make out most words if he focused hard.

"...to ask you a favor," Callie said, her voice airy and inviting in a way that Emmett had never heard before. "I know it's not my place..."

The line shuffled forward, obscuring the end of her sentence.

"Callie, you know that S&S is an outspoken advocate for small businesses," Stamkos said placatingly, "but you're dangerously close to overstepping. This is a multimillion dollar project. I can't ax it for the sake of a beautiful woman."

Emmett's stomach knotted in disgust. Stamkos was exactly the kind of corporate slime Emmett thought him to be. He wished he was at that table right now, so he could see the look on Stamkos' face when Callie ripped him a new asshole.

"I would never ask that of you," Callie answered, matching Stamkos' syrupy tone. Emmett froze, his task completely forgotten. "...can I be candid with you, Adrian?"

Emmett didn't hear Stamkos' reply. He was too busy trying to work out what the hell was happening. The Callie he knew would've slapped Stamkos across the face for pulling that condescending bullshit. Instead, it was almost like she was... reciprocating? Encouraging?

"This is a big case for me," she continued, and Emmett risked a glance over his shoulder to see that, to his horror, Callie had reached across the table and was absently toying with Stamkos' coffee cup, her fingers tracing an eerily similar pattern to the one she'd danced over his hand before they were interrupted.

Stamkos was watching her with a newfound interest, an almost predatory spark in his eyes that hadn't been there before. "Orville needs to retire. He's well past his prime, and our firm is suffering under him. If I finalize the Lichen House contract, I have a real shot at taking over for him."

"Guttenberg Law would certainly thrive with a smart young woman like you manning the wheel," Stamkos agreed, his voice dropping so low that Emmett had to strain to hear. "It seems like you have a monumental task ahead of you, though."

"I do," Callie agreed, sighing. "I understand that your hands are tied, Adrian. So are mine. My clients won't want to move ahead with the renovations knowing that this time next year they'll look out their windows and see smokestacks. But..."

It was Emmett's turn to order, but he found his legs refused to move. He stood, rooted to the spot, frozen in shock at the words coming out of Callie's mouth.

"I was reviewing the sale records for the property you purchased," she said. "The land east of your construction site is untouched. It belongs to the town, but I'm sure you could negotiate something with Somerton's new mayor, whenever they're appointed. If you were to move your factory plans east, then my clients would never see the finished product. You get your factory, my clients get their business, I get my contract, and Orville gets to retire with peace of mind knowing that his firm is in good hands. Not to mention,"

Callie's voice dropped to a quiet purr.

"I would be inclined to show my gratitude," she intoned, inserting a deliberate pause after her statement. "In an unofficial capacity, of course."

"Of course," Stamkos answered, and Emmett could practically hear the cocky smirk on his face. "You know, Callie, I have an unrivalled appreciation for women in this business who aren't afraid to use every advantage to get what they want. I respect your drive. I *will* do you a favor."

Emmett's heart stopped. He was halfway through the process of spinning around to intervene when Stamkos started speaking again.

"I'm going to give you an opportunity to come out the other end of this in a better position than you would be if you took over for Orville." Stamkos told her, the subtle flirtation unmistakable in his words. "I'll give you this advice for free, and you let me know if you want to take advantage of it."

Callie remained quiet. The urge to turn around to see her face was burning like a hot coal in the pit of Emmett's stomach.

"There is an alternative to your predicament, perhaps it's one you've even considered," Stamkos continued. "We employ a sizeable legal team at S&S. We're not currently hiring, but that means nothing to me. If I want to add employees, I simply create a position."

"You're implying you would give me a job?" Callie clarified, surprised.

"I'm not implying anything, I'm stating it outright." Stamkos must've shifted, the sound of a chair scraping muffled his next words. "...as an associate attorney for Stamkos & Stein. Our salaries and benefits packages are more than generous."

"That's a round-about way of fixing my problem," Callie said slowly. Stamkos laughed.

"For now," he agreed cryptically. "In time, I think you'll understand the nature of my offer. In the meantime, do tell Tara and Ed I said hello."

Emmett wasn't sure what happened. In a matter of seconds, the atmosphere in the coffee shop shifted. The barista had long-since stopped trying to get his attention, the other patrons simply walking around him to reach the counter. Callie didn't answer Stamkos' request, the air turning icy even as Emmett finally relented and turned around.

She was frozen in her chair, stiff-backed and staring at Stamkos with a carefully blank expression. Emmett felt his phone buzz and, if not for the knowledge that it could be Sam or Amelia, he would've ignored it. As it was, Stamkos was standing from his chair, looking like he was getting ready to leave. If Sam and Amelia weren't done...

Abruptly, Callie recovered from whatever freeze she'd been trapped in. She plastered a cool smile on her face, matching Stamkos' predatory demeanor with a look that could curdle milk.

"I'll be sure to pass your message along," she said casually, picking up her coffee mug and taking a deliberate sip. "I've been meaning to call them about a potential purchase agreement with Willow Lodge. Thank you for reminding me."

Stamkos paused in his retreat, long enough to make Emmett wonder if he'd missed something. When he regained his composure, Stamkos regarded Callie with renewed interest.

"The Willow Lodge would certainly add substantial value to Tara and Ed's vision," Stamkos conceded, watching Callie with unveiled intensity. "I was under the impression that Ms. Jameson wasn't interested in selling."

It wasn't a question. Callie hummed with a slight shrug.

"She's had some complications come up recently," Callie continued, carefully avoiding looking at Stamkos, as though he were dismissed. It was a subtle move, but one that placed her firmly in the upper hand of their conversation. "It's the strangest thing. Some sensationalist article appeared on a gossip forum and incited a mob. Ms. Jameson is concerned for her safety."

"Oh?"

Callie put down her drink, meeting Stamkos' gaze again. Something passed between them that Emmett couldn't quite name, but it wasn't friendly.

"I can't blame her," Callie said slowly. "Maniacs were throwing paint bombs into the lobby, all over some baseless rumors that she's involved with the sheriff's department. Haven't the faintest idea where they came up with that nonsense, but it's causing her problems. Last I heard, she was thinking about moving out of Wisconsin entirely."

Another buzz from Emmett's phone, and he scrambled to check it before he was distracted again by the silent war playing out before him. The text flashed across his screen. A simple text from Sam with a thumbs up emoji. They'd done it.

The relief hit him like a tidal wave, unlocking Emmett's limbs. He stepped forward, his task forgotten, and that seemed to rouse Stamkos from his thoughts.

"Sorry for the abrupt departure," Stamkos said amicably, turning to smile at Emmett as well. "I have another meeting coming up soon and I need to stop by my hotel first to grab a few things. It was lovely meeting with you, Callie, Mr. Coady."

Leaving a tense and brittle silence in his wake, Adrian Stamkos walked out the front door.

Chapter Twenty-Four

CALLIE

That slimy, disgusting, conniving, underhanded, dirty son-of-a-bitch!

Curses that Callie hadn't used in *years* ran through her mind, some she'd picked up in New York, some she'd learned at far too young an age visiting her mother's mother in Louisiana. She was vaguely aware of Emmett staring at her long after Stamkos' departure, his expression wary. Before he could speak, Callie shook herself out of her stupor.

"Tell me we got what we needed," she snapped, her vowels rounding as her accent peeked through her anger. If she didn't calm down soon, she'd start spewing broken French that even her Cajun grandmother would be proud of.

"We did," Emmett said slowly, watching her for some sign as to why she was so flustered. Callie couldn't explain herself right now, not with the bombshell Stamkos just dropped on her fresh in her mind. Instead, she gave a tight nod, silently standing up and walking to the door.

Tell Tara and Ed I said hello.

That fucker. That *motherfucker!* Callie folded herself into the passenger seat of Ephraim's truck, seething. In one sentence, Adrian Stamkos undermined everything Callie was working toward, and the bastard *knew it*. He did it intentionally, Callie had no doubt. He kept that little tidbit in his back pocket and waited for the perfect moment to drop his mic. Too bad for him that Callie had her own mic drop ready and waiting, but the revelation still stung no matter how satisfying it'd been to see the shock he couldn't hide quickly enough.

Tara and Ed. Not 'Mr. and Mrs. Gallagher.' Not 'Theresa and Edwin.' Tara and Ed. The only way Stamkos would know to call them that was if he'd met them before. If he'd met them before, then that means *someone* was keeping Callie out of the loop. Adrian Stamkos was in talks with *her* clients and she didn't know about it.

Bullshit. Complete, utter bullshit.

Callie didn't have time to feel embarrassed that Stamkos had the upper hand on her the entire meeting and she had no idea. She knew going into this that she had no leg to stand on. The entire point was to get him out of his hotel long enough for Sam and Amelia to do their thing, not to actually convince Stamkos to bend to their will. It was a losing battle from the start; it didn't matter *how* she lost. She was expecting it. The fact that she'd been able to throw a last minute sucker punch with the Willow was never meant to swing the meeting in her favor, just to buy them more time. It worked, and she'd even managed to imply that they were suspicious of his involvement with the news article fiasco, but it was far from a resounding victory.

Now, she was just angry. Angry and betrayed. If Orville knew about the Gallaghers' meeting with Stamkos and he didn't think to inform her, Callie didn't know if she'd be able to stop herself from screaming. If it was Tara and Ed that kept it from her, she'd be more hurt than angry, but no less frustrated.

Emmett started the truck and began driving in silence. Callie closed her eyes, trying to calm her racing heart.

The contract was done. Callie had been in the business long enough to see the writing on the walls. If Tara and Ed were entertaining offers from Stamkos & Stein, they'd already decided to sell. Maybe they hadn't realized it yet, but deep down, they weren't committed to the project anymore. That meant Ephraim was out of a job. It meant Emmett's company lost a huge contract. It meant Orville wouldn't retire.

Callie wanted to cry from the unfairness of it all, but she couldn't. They had a job to do, and crying wasn't going to help any of them.

"Sam and Amelia are back at the lodge," Emmett said after a while, testing the waters. Callie nodded stiffly. "They said they ran into some trouble with the front desk staff, but otherwise it went off without a hitch. Amelia is sifting through Stamkos' dirty laundry now."

"Awesome." Callie cringed at her own bitterness, forcing herself to take a breath. "I mean, that's great. Really, it is."

No matter what she did, her words sounded forced. She groaned, dropping her head back against her seat.

"Sorry, I know I'm being a dick right now," she huffed. "I just wasn't expecting... it doesn't matter. I'm happy the plan worked."

"Only because you kept Stamkos' attention for so long," Emmett praised, perking up at her subtle shift in demeanor. "This was only possible because of you."

"Yeah, right,"

"Seriously," Emmett insisted. "You got the meeting in the first place. You kept him engaged long enough for Sam and Amelia to get in and out unseen. This win is largely on you, Cal."

She paused, considering Emmett for a moment. He was being kind. Awkward, yes, but kind. Despite her festering mood, Callie smiled.

"Thanks, Emmett," she said sincerely. "And thank you for keeping your word."

At that, Emmett's shoulders went rigid.

"Right," he said, his cheek twitching in irritation. Callie frowned, wondering what she'd said that bothered him. "It wasn't exactly easy."

"I'm sure it wasn't..." Callie trailed, watching Emmett closely. "Stamkos is the special kind of sleazy that makes you want to punch a hole in his teeth, I get it. I appreciate you listening to me, though."

"A huh."

Emmett didn't elaborate, staring pointedly out the front window as he drove them to the Willow. Callie was about to drop it— she didn't have the emotional energy to tease out whatever was bothering him— but Emmett abruptly started speaking again.

"Did you have to throw yourself at him?"

Callie blinked, slowly processing Emmett's question. When she'd determined she hadn't misheard, that spark of anger flared in her stomach again.

"Excuse me?"

"I was at the counter, Callie. I'm not deaf. I heard that little proposition of yours." His grip tightened on the steering wheel until his knuckles turned white. "That wasn't in the plan."

"The 'plan' was to keep his attention," Callie argued. "Look, I don't like it anymore than you do, but it's pretty common in most industries for the men in charge to *expect* women to be willing to sleep their way to the top."

"I didn't think you were one of the willing women."

"I'm not," Callie snapped. "I just needed Stamkos to think I was."

"What if he accepted? Would you have slept with him?"

Callie felt insult and outrage burning in her veins, making her breath come in quick bursts.

"I would've tried to get out of it, obviously." She rolled her eyes. "Seriously, Emmett. I told you before, guys like Stamkos, people in big business, they're all about mind games. You play the game, you win, and you'll never have to make good on any of the 'promises' you made to get where you are."

"And if he insisted?" Emmett demanded, "What then? He's a powerful man, Callie. Adrian Stamkos is not the kind of guy to let you get away with tempting him and ditching. Fuck, what if he *forced*—"

Callie groaned in exasperation, spinning in her seat to face Emmett properly. The seatbelt dug into her collarbone, but she ignored it.

"You think I didn't consider that? I lived in *New York*, Emmett. I couldn't check the mail in my own building without a taser. Chances are, Stamkos wouldn't resort to violence for the sake of sex. He's got power, and a lot of it. Coercion would be much more likely, and that's only if he bothered with me at all. I'm sure the man has an entire backlog of women at the ready. But fine, let's say he absolutely insists that I make good on my promise. He's not *un*attractive. Sex wouldn't be my first choice, but I've suffered through some pretty atrocious sex in my life."

"I thought you wouldn't use sex to get ahead in your career?" Emmett shot back, his voice rising. "Does that only apply to the ugly corporate executives?"

"This isn't about my *career*, you jackass!" Callie resisted the urge to scream. "People are *dying*. If I have to sleep with Adrian Stamkos to save literal lives, then yes, I'd suck it up. Hell, I'd do a lot worse than that."

"No, absolutely not." Emmett snapped, pulling the truck to a jerky stop in the Willow's parking lot. "You're not sleeping with him."

"Obviously not," Callie sneered, "but—"

"No. Buts." Emmett threw the driver's side door open, stomping toward the Willow's front door. Callie was aware they were about to have an audience, but she didn't care anymore. Maybe it was because she and Emmett hadn't fought for while, but her anger was nearly explosive. He picked a fight knowing she was in a bad mood, even if he didn't know why. Now, he was getting a fight, and she wasn't going to be the one to make peace this time.

Callie ran after him, reaching him just as he pulled the front door open.

"God, I knew this was a mistake." Emmett muttered. "You should never have gotten involved."

"I beg your pardon?" Callie gaped at him. "We just got our first big break in weeks because of me! You *just said* this was only possible because of *my* involvement! Don't you dare try to walk that back now!"

"We got our first big break *since you joined,*" Emmett growled, doubling down. "We've been doing this a lot longer than you, and we'll keep going after you're safely back in Hatfield."

"Keep going with what, Emmett?" Callie absently threw her hat onto one of the lobby chairs, crossing her arms over her chest and glaring hard at Emmett. "Before I got here, you guys were floundering around in the dark blasting ice demons with a borrowed flamethrower *that I got for you*. You can't keep punching blind forever!"

"Guys, what—?" Nyla appeared in the corner of Callie's vision, looking worried and confused, but Emmett continued his angered tirade before Nyla could finish her question.

"We're sure as shit not going with your ideas."

"My ideas got us the information on that laptop!"

"Guys! What is going on?" Nyla yelled, forcing Emmett and Callie to acknowledge the room. "I thought the meeting went well. Amelia said—"

"It went swimmingly, thank you, Nyla," Callie said, sniffing indignantly. "We got exactly what we needed."

"At what cost, Callie? Wanna explain that part?" Emmett challenged.

"At no cost! Emmett's just being a pig, as per usual."

"Does someone want to bring the rest of us up to speed?" Amelia said, appearing next to Nyla with Sam hot on her heels. "I've been neck-deep in files since we left the motel. What kind of dumpster fire did I miss?"

The room fell silent as everyone waited for Emmett or Callie to explain. Callie had no intention of saying a word. Emmett started this, he could finish it.

To her shock, Emmett thought for a moment, and then turned to face Nyla.

"Nyla?" he started, still breathing hard.

"Uh," Nyla hesitated, unsure where this was going, "yeah?"

"Would you have sex with Adrian Stamkos?"

There was a split second of complete silence, and then the room erupted.

"I'm sorry, *what?*" Nyla demanded, her mouth falling open in shock. Aaron, who'd been silently observing up until that point, strode purposefully across the room, putting himself directly between Emmett and Nyla.

"Absolutely fucking not," he snapped. "Have you lost your mind, Coady?"

"Alright, what about you, Amelia?" Undeterred, Emmett took a half-step back from Aaron and looked at Amelia instead. "Willing to hop in the sack for the sake of a lead?"

"You've got about three seconds to explain yourself before I 'hop' on the dark web and register you as a sex offender in 48 States," Amelia responded, a deadly calm descending over her face.

"She's not kidding," Sam added helpfully.

"My bad, I thought this was a commonplace solution we were using around here." Emmett spun back to Callie, apparently feeling like he'd made his point. "Callie certainly seems to think so, since she offered herself up to him on a silver platter."

Callie seethed.

"I did not! I *flirted* with him, for fuck's sake. We hadn't heard from Sam and Amelia yet and I felt like we weren't getting anywhere with the conversation, so I *implied* that I would sleep with him if he did me a favor. I had no intention of following through!"

"But you would've, right?" Emmett pressed. "That's what you said in the car."

"I said that I'd *consider* it, if it came down to brass tacks. That's very different from throwing myself at him, as you so aptly put it. Lives are at stake, Emmett! It's not like I'd do it for a BOGO coupon at Denny's."

"Hold on, can I just interject here for a second?" Amelia said, having recovered from the shock of Emmett's question. "Callie is a single woman, is she not? If she wants to sleep with Stamkos, what's stopping her? Not my type, but no judgment. A dick is a dick, you know? Get it when you can, girl."

"Is that all my dick is to you?" Sam gasped, affronted. "A sex toy that just so happens to be attached to the embodiment of charm and wit?"

"*I'm* stopping her," Emmett snapped, redirecting the conversation back to Callie and Stamkos. "You're not having sex with that man, Callie. I'm not allow-ing it."

"You're not *allowing* it?" Callie bristled, rage turning her cheeks red. She put aside the fact that there was no need for her to have sex with Stamkos now, focusing instead on the audacity of Emmett's phrasing. "And who the fuck do you think you are? You have no say over who I sleep with, Emmett! You're not my boyfriend!"

"Maybe I should be!"

Callie's mouth snapped shut.

"Oh shit," Sam whispered, laughing incredulously. Emmett immediately be-gan to flounder, his ears turning red as he stammered through an explanation.

"I mean— just— I didn't mean it like that," he muttered. "I meant I should be able to stop you from sleeping with corporate jagoffs like Adrian Stamkos. The boyfriend thing— that was— it was irrelevant. That's all."

The room remained silent, the ticking of an analog clock somewhere in the building the only sound.

"So, just to be clear," Nyla said, clearing her throat. "No one's having sex with Adrian Stamkos?"

"No," Aaron growled. Pulling Nyla into the protective circle of his arm, he leveled Emmett with a glare that could cut glass. "And when Coady is back to his senses, he owes every woman in this room one hell of an apology for treating you like a solution to his fucking insecurities."

Emmett visibly flinched, but Callie couldn't find it in her heart to care.

"Klein—"

"Right now, I think we all need to cool off." Aaron caught Callie's attention. "Callie? Cabin three is unlocked. Feel free to use it if you need a minute."

"Thank you, Aaron," Callie said pointedly, bumping Emmett with her shoulder as she stalked past him. She paused at the end of the hall, listening.

"I think a break is a good idea," Amelia said with a strained smile. "Meet back here after supper?"

Instead of answering, Aaron gave her a small nod, and then he led Nyla out the back entrance to their cabin, passing Callie on the way. She offered them a reassuring smile. Sam shouldered both his bag and Amelia's while she clutched her laptop tightly to her chest, as though she was afraid it would disappear.

"Hey, Emmett?" Sam clapped a hand to his upper back. "Remember how you said Aaron didn't *actually* hate you? After this whole... whatever it was, I'd maybe rethink that."

"And that's not to say anything about how pissed off Nyla is." Amelia's voice sounded bitterly amused. "And Callie, of course. You're on a roll today."

"Are you not included in that list?" Emmett said dully. Amelia snorted.

"Oh, I am," she scoffed, "but my anger is more of a slow burn. You'll wake up one day with your kidneys missing and someone using your identity to commit insurance fraud."

"She means she's more upset about what you said to Nyla and Callie than what you said to her," Sam offered. "I, on the other hand, don't get mad. Luckily for you."

"Do either of you have anything helpful to say, or can you leave me to my misery?"

"Good luck Coady," Sam said, a twinge of bitterness in his voice despite his assurance that he wasn't mad. "You'll need it."

Callie waited until Sam and Amelia were gone. The room was quiet for a few seconds, and then she heard Emmett give a bone-weary sigh. She told herself she didn't care, that he deserved to feel like shit after the way he'd acted, but there was no venom behind the feeling. Gathering herself, Callie opened the back door of the Willow and made her way to cabin three without a word.

Chapter Twenty-Five

INTERLUDE

Nyla

"He didn't mean it, you know." Nyla smoothed her fingers through Aaron's hair as he lay on the couch, his head in her lap. His eyes were pinched shut in irritation, massaging his temples with the heels of his hands. "He wasn't *actually* suggesting anyone have sex with Stamkos."

"That's not the point." Aaron's grunt was aggressive, expelling the all the air from his lungs. "Whether he meant it or not, it was disrespectful to you. You deserve better than that from someone you consider a friend."

Nyla pressed her lips together to hide her smile. If anyone else had said the same things Emmett did, she'd be seething. As it was, Nyla had every intention of tearing into Emmett when things calmed down, but her anger was mostly surface-level.

"He's... frantic." Nyla hummed in thought, searching for the right words. "I'm not excusing his behaviour. He *was* being a prick, and I'm still upset at him for it. Emmett just isn't used to feeling helpless. He's always been a practical person, and being forced to sit around while we do the heavy lifting has to be driving him insane. Not to mention, he is head-over-heels in love with Callie."

"I fail to see how that's your problem."

She laughed, nudging Aaron with her knee to signal him to sit up. When he did, Nyla crawled across the couch and curled herself into his embrace, sighing contentedly as she felt him relax beneath her. With her face buried in the crook of Aaron's neck, she could almost pretend that everything was alright.

"It's my problem because he's my friend and I care about him," Nyla said, nuzzling the warm skin at Aaron's throat. He made a contented noise that gave her goosebumps. "Emmett doesn't do well when things are out of his hands. Give him some time to adjust and he'll be back to normal before Amelia can ruin his digital footprint."

"I hate seeing you being taken advantage of, *mi cielo*." Aaron's hoarse words were muffled against her hair, but she had no trouble picking them out. "I didn't think I had to worry about that with Emmett. And I definitely didn't think I'd have to worry about him telling you to fuck anyone but me."

"You don't, I promise," Nyla said, squeezing him in reassurance. "This is a unique situation and emotions are high. Emmett has *never* said anything like that to me before, and I have every confidence that he won't again. Certainly not after I'm done with him."

A small laugh broke free from Aaron's chest, and triumph inflated in Nyla's heart. She always felt a surge of victory when she managed to pull Aaron from a slump, even if he rarely entered them.

"I never would've predicted how delightfully possessive you are, though," Nyla mused. "Do you have any idea how hot it is?"

"Don't," Aaron said firmly, tightening his grip on her until her arms were pinned to her sides, stopping her hands on their slow journey to the front of his pants. Nyla pouted. "We have too much to do today, I can't let you distract me."

"But I'm so good at it."

"Too good," Aaron agreed, his voice coming out with just a hint of roughness that let Nyla know how affected he was by her. She'd barely done more than suggest, and already Aaron was tense beneath her. It was a powerful feeling, one that she had trouble ignoring in favor of their busy schedule. "Let's go meet with Pratt and Clary, then we can catch up with the others. You can distract me all you want later tonight."

"You drive a hard bargain, Agent Klein," Nyla purred, knowing full well that the sound of his title on her lips went straight to his dick. Aaron sucked in a breath, and she smiled. "But you're right. I need to bring Clary up to speed on everything before you change your mind."

Nyla stood, fixing her shirt and avoiding Aaron's assessing gaze.

Consulting with Clary had been a contentious topic since the very beginning. Nyla hated keeping secrets of any kind, but especially from her best friend. With how complicated their lives had become lately, Nyla had less and less time to spend with Clary, and the added veil of secrecy just made the growing wedge between them wider. It hurt, but Nyla understood that it was necessary.

Now, though, things were changing.

They were on the brink of a breakthrough, Nyla could feel it. Amelia had successfully infiltrated Stamkos' laptop, Callie had built a usable timeline of events from their hodgepodge of research, and Jodi filled in some of the blanks. They'd gone as far as they could with the resources they had, and now it was time to bring in an expert. Nonna Isa may have given them their starting point, but it was Clary's help they needed this time around.

That didn't mean Aaron was happy about it.

They'd never fully agreed on a proper course of action regarding Clary's involvement. They'd argued about it, sure. More times than Nyla cared to admit. But in terms of a resolution, they hadn't found one. It was a series of circumstances that led to the decision to bring Clary into the loop and ask for her help, not a clearly defined discussion. A subtle tension formed between them whenever the topic was broached, and Nyla didn't know how to dispel it without accidentally making everything so much worse.

Aaron watched her fidget for longer than she would've liked, and then he stood. Stepping into her personal space, he cupped the side of her neck, tilting her head back to kiss her. Nyla melted into him as she always did, clinging to that little spark of responsibility that stopped her from saying to hell with it and tearing his shirt from his body. When he pulled away, there was a troubled look clouding his expression, and Nyla frowned up at him.

"Let's go," he murmured, straightening his tie. Nyla watched him walk toward the front door, a pang of unease echoing in the pit of her stomach. Now wasn't the time to question him, though.

Silently, Nyla followed Aaron to the parking lot.

"Still no baby?"

Tyler Pratt greeted them as Aaron pressed the power lock on his key fob. Despite the long hours and delicate operations Pratt had been dealing with for the last few weeks, he looked as cheerful as ever. Nyla skipped up to him and enveloped him in a hug, one that he happily returned.

"No baby," he confirmed, sighing in relief. "Thank God. I mean, I know Chia's miserable, so I want this to be over for her sake, but I hate the thought of leaving you two to clean this up on your own."

"On our own?" Nyla repeated, laughing. "We have an army at this point."

"Oh yeah," Pratt said, snapping his fingers. "That attorney joined you guys recently, right? Quinn?"

"Her name is Callie," Nyla confirmed. "Her presence has been invaluable in both the investigation and driving Emmett to an early grave."

As they approached the sheriff's station, Nyla and Aaron gave Pratt a brief overview of everything they'd accomplished since they last spoke. With Rebecca Kelley holding off the Wildlife representatives for as long as she could, most of the fieldwork fell to Pratt and his colleagues. They'd seen little of him since Adrian Stamkos came to town, but they all knew he was working just as hard as the rest of them.

"German is covering for me this afternoon," he explained, checking his phone. "Kelley has another video call with the higher-ups in Wildlife tomorrow morning. They're getting pushy, Klein. We need to make some progress, and we need to do it yesterday."

"I know," Aaron huffed, pressing his lips together in a tight line. "We're getting there, Pratt. We just need more time."

"You've had more time than anyone expected to get." Pratt shoved his hands in his pockets in frustration. Nyla knew he wasn't berating Aaron; he was worried. "Kelley says that Jim is getting a team together to run sample analysis on the bodies we managed to get our hands on. Pretty soon, they're going to find out that rabies was never on the table to begin with. Then, we're going to have scores of people traipsing through the Basin. If we haven't stopped the Chehwinoo by then, it'll be the biggest bloodbath this country has ever seen."

"*I know,*" Aaron said again, his own frustration bubbling to the surface. "We're close. Closer than we've ever been. I just need you and Kelley to hold the line a little longer."

"We're doing what we can." Pratt shook his head, regarding Aaron with a worried expression that echoed Nyla's feelings. "Whatever you're going to do, do it quickly. That's all I can say."

They'd reached the main entrance of the station. Two officers were visible through the glass, both with their attention trained on the three of them. Nyla waved politely, though neither of them acknowledged the gesture. She wasn't surprised, but it still stung.

"We're meeting with Clary after this," Nyla interjected, hoping to relieve some of the tension brewing in the air. "From everything that Jodi told us and what Callie was able to piece together, we think the Chehwinoo is much older than Somerton itself. If we can figure out how it's been existing for long periods without hurting anyone, we might be able to put an end to this."

"Is Clary some kind of immortal vampire?" Pratt asked, raising an eyebrow. "How the hell is she supposed to know what happened a hundred years ago?"

"She's indigenous, you dolt." Nyla rolled her eyes. "The Chehwinoo poem is Onaqwe in origin."

"I thought you said Clary was Maliseet?"

"She is," Nyla conceded. "Both the Maliseet and Onaqwe cultures have Algonquin roots. She can definitely read more of the Oki-qwe language than either Aaron or I can. Besides, she might know where we can find an Onaqwe elder willing to speak to us."

"Willing?" Pratt repeated dubiously.

"They're a private people," Nyla explained patiently. "They were almost completely wiped out by European colonizers when Wisconsin was settled, so they keep most of their culture to themselves now as an act of preservation. That's a big part of the reason we've been struggling to find any concrete information about the Chehwinoo."

"So, it seems we've nixed the 'Keep Clary Out of It' plan," Pratt said with a smirk. Aaron said nothing, instead glancing at his watch and nodding toward the station door.

"Five minutes," he said, pulling on the handle.

"Do you want us to come with you?" Nyla asked, looking from Aaron to the door. They'd stopped by on their way to Clary's to meet up with Pratt and check in with George; the latter she assumed they'd do together.

"Not necessary," Aaron insisted, offering her a tight smile. "Wait here. I won't be long."

Before either she or Pratt could argue, Aaron disappeared into the building. They were quiet for far too long, the sense of unease in Nyla's stomach growing with each passing second. She wanted to believe that Aaron only left her outside for her sake, to prevent her from being subjected to excess scrutiny and open hatred from the deputies. She wanted to believe that she wasn't a burden to him and the investigation.

"Alright, how'd you fuck up?" Pratt asked after a while, crossing his arms over his chest and raising an eyebrow at Nyla. "I didn't think it was physically possible for Klein to get mad at you, so what'd you do? Did you like... stab him, or something? Unless he's into that."

"I didn't," Nyla said, frowning. "I didn't stab him OR fuck up. He's just sore about the whole Clary thing. He'll get over it."

The words left her lips with a confidence that she didn't feel. Nyla was in unfamiliar territory here; her disagreements with Aaron rarely evolved into genuine fights or emotional standoffs. They weren't screaming at each other by any means, but this was the closest they'd ever come to a serious bump in the road. She didn't know how to handle that.

"Right," Pratt said, his voice laced with skepticism. "Walk with me, Nyla."

She didn't need to be asked twice. Nyla fell into step beside Pratt, making their way to Aaron's X5 at a leisurely pace.

"Klein doesn't get butthurt." Pratt shoved his hands into his pockets, looking at her out of the corner of his eye. "He's annoyingly mature that way. Baiting him into petty arguments is a challenge fit only for a masochist. If something is bothering him, there's a damn good reason. I'd bet money on that."

"We've been on opposite ends of this topic since the summer," Nyla confessed. "He doesn't want to bring *anyone* else into this, and Clary is the one I've been pushing for since the start. It's totally understandable that he'd be upset about losing this battle. I'll just... give him some space to process."

"Are you sure that's all it is?"

"What else would it be?"

Pratt paused, leaning against the hood of the X5 while he considered his answer.

"What's the one thing Klein absolutely cannot live without?" he asked suddenly.

"Dry-cleaning?"

Pratt snorted a surprised laugh, shaking his head.

"Seriously." When Nyla didn't answer right away, he rolled his eyes. "*You*, baby girl. I've known Klein a long time, and the man doesn't have a casual bone in his body. Whatever has him on edge to the point that *I'm* noticing, I can guarantee it has everything to do with you."

Nyla let the words sink in, glancing back over her shoulder to where the station stood silently, like it was watching them with its huge, reflective windows.

"I'm not used to doing things as a team," she murmured, biting her bottom lip. "I know it stresses him out sometimes, but I can't help it. I've always been independent. Until I met all of you, I didn't have a support group to lean on even if I wanted to. Do... you think that might have something to do with it? Could it be bothering him that much?"

"Who, Klein?" Pratt said dubiously. "Retired, top of his class at the academy Agent Aaron Tomas Carlo Javier Klein? The youngest guy to make Unit Chief of the Chicago Field Office since the seventies? The man who muscled his way to the top of the department because nobody knew how to say no to the guy? Why would he have an issue with someone undermining his authority?"

"I feel so much better, thank you," Nyla deadpanned. The feeling of unease twisted into a knot of dread. Pratt looked like he was about to make another sarcastic quip, then thought better of it.

"Look, as frustratingly well-adjusted as Klein is, he's still human. Hard to believe, I know. I spent the first three years of our friendship looking for concrete evidence that he's really an android."

Nyla laughed in spite of herself.

"Whatever's on his mind, he'll talk to you eventually." Pratt laid a comforting hand on her shoulder, pulling her attention away from the station just as she saw Aaron emerge and spot them next to his vehicle. "He is *disgustingly* in love with you. Pretty sure you could threaten to carve out his internal organs and he'd offer to do it himself so you wouldn't get blood on your hands."

"Your brain scares me sometimes, you know that?" Nyla teased. Pratt shrugged, ruffling her hair before pulling his hand away.

"I grew up with Amelia, remember?"

"Good point."

Aaron joined them then, looking between the two with a wrinkle between his brows. Nyla offered him a small smile, one that he returned after a slight hesitation.

"Are we ready to go?" he asked. Nyla and Pratt nodded, piling into the X5 and mentally preparing for a long afternoon of convincing Clary they weren't insane.

Chapter Twenty-Six

EMMETT

It took nearly two hours for Emmett to summon the courage to knock on Callie's cabin door.

The first hour was spent alternating between lingering irritation at the thought of Callie and Stamkos in bed together and berating himself for being an idiot. Again. The second hour was filled with panic and guilt, wondering if he'd finally broken things beyond repair.

He needed to apologize and he needed to do it in a way that at least partially conveyed how badly he meant it. The idea of begging Callie's forgiveness didn't frighten him in the usual sense; Emmett wasn't bothered by the concept of admitting he was wrong. Some of the men he worked with seemed to have a personal vendetta against taking accountability, but he wasn't like that. He was more than willing to own up to his mistakes and even more willing to prove that he wouldn't repeat them.

Emmett just hoped that would be enough to fix this mess.

His hand hovered above the door, bracing for impact, when the sound of Callie's frustrated voice caught his attention. Her words were muffled by the wood, but Emmett could make out the gist of the conversation.

"You didn't think that was relevant?" Callie snapped, sounding louder now. Emmett guessed she was pacing the room. "Do you have any idea how *stupid* you made me look?!"

A pause, then Callie cursed.

"Go ahead and fire me, then!" Emmett heard a thud, like something had dropped. "I fucking *dare* you, Orville. Fire me and see how long you last before your firm falls apart at the seams. It's already halfway there!"

More silence. Callie laughed bitterly.

"Yeah, I gathered." Emmett wished more than anything that he could see her face right now. "No, I don't want to hear another word from you until I'm back in Hatfield. I don't care— No. How about this: when I get back to the office, you can tell me if I still have a job, and *I'll* tell *you* if I still want it."

There was an aggravated huff and another thud, and Emmett determined that was probably her phone. Callie let out a muffled scream of anger, and, for some reason, that was the push Emmett needed to knock.

"What?" Callie snapped, yanking the door open with enough force to make Emmett step back. When she saw who was on the other side, she scowled. "I have nothing to say to you right now."

"Wait!" Emmett put his hand on the door, stopping her from slamming it in his face. Callie's expression flickered with outrage, and Emmett felt hope slipping through his fingers. In desperation, he dropped to his knees in the dirt, despite every facet of his brain rebelling at the submissive pose. The action was enough to make Callie pause.

"I'm sorry," he said, holding her gaze unflinchingly. "That's not nearly good enough, I know. 'Over the line' doesn't even begin to cut it. I was an asshole. A raging, idiotic, pathetic, controlling asshole. And you deserve so much better than that from your— from your friends. I *want* to be friends, Callie."

"You've got a weird ass way of showing it," Callie muttered. Emmett's lips quirked.

"I know," he said, rubbing the back of his neck absently. "I never said I was good at it."

Callie regarded him for a minute, the gears spinning in her head. Emmett waited, trying not to fidget.

"You really hurt me, Emmett," she admitted, almost glaring at him. "You insulted me, Nyla, *and* Amelia."

"I know, and I'm not just apologizing to you. Everyone is getting an apology."

"A sincere one?"

"Yes," Emmett exhaled, letting some of the distress he was feeling show on his face. "I've said and done a lot of stupid shit since you got here, Cal. I know I can't make everything better with words. I want to show you that I'm committed to doing better. But I can't force you to let me, and I won't try. If you tell me to fuck off right here and now, I will. I can't walk away from this until Somerton is safe again, but I will do everything in my power to steer clear of you."

"Why?"

Emmett furrowed his brows in confusion.

"Why have you been acting like this?" Callie clarified, wiping subtly at her cheek. Emmett's chest constricted. Was she crying because of him or because of what he overheard? Was it both? "I know we were never close, but I thought we were at least friendly."

"We were. We are."

"Are we?" Callie demanded, crossing her arms over her chest. "From what I've seen, you can barely stand to be around me."

"That's not true," Emmett insisted, anxiety making his limbs itch with the need to move. He stood, resisting the urge to grab Callie's hands. "I love being around you. Too much. That's the problem."

"That makes absolutely no sense."

"I know," Emmett groaned, pinching the bridge of his nose until the sting became too much. "I know. I can't explain it in a way that makes sense, Cal. Something about you makes me lose my fucking mind, apparently. I want you here, I do, but I also want you to be safe. I *need* you to be safe, and God knows it's not safe in Somerton right now. It's like... I don't know, it's like you somehow manage to override all the logical parts of my brain. That's not an excuse. I didn't mean to make it sound like this is your fault. Shit."

Emmett closed his eyes, took a deep breath, and tried again.

"This is all on me," he said with conviction, taking a breath before speaking again. He wouldn't let his emotions get the better of him. Not this time. "I've been... off kilter lately. Ever since Dad's stroke. I'm not trying to get sympathy," he rushed to add, seeing the slight suspicion creeping into Callie's face.

"What does Ephraim's stroke have to do with anything?"

What, indeed.

"I don't like not being in control," he admitted, even that over-simplification feeling like a massive concession. "It's not easy for me to sit back and let things play out. I hate that I haven't been able to help Nyla with the people here. I hate that people I know, people I've worked with, people I respect have died to the Chehwinoo and I can't stop it. I hate that Bill fucking Hannaford almost murdered one of my best friends with his bare hands and I had no idea. Dad *needs* help, help that I can actually provide, but he won't let me. It's been difficult. And it's spilling over into the rest of my life. If I can't keep my own father safe, then how do I expect to protect *anyone?*"

The frustration and helplessness festering in Emmett's chest boiled over, making him struggle for breath as sweat condensed on the back of his neck. He inhaled slowly, willing his heartrate to calm.

"I'll do better," he promised, pouring every ounce of sincerity into his words. "I'm asking you for the chance to prove I can do better."

Callie scrutinized his features, searching for any indication that he was merely trying to save face. Emmett let her examine him at her own pace, letting all of his emotions flicker openly, hiding nothing. When Callie pursed her lips uncertainly, Emmett felt his heart lurch.

"I... believe you." Callie sighed, her expression souring. "I shouldn't, but I do."

"Really? You do?"

"I do," she said, a reluctant smile spreading across her face. "I mean you literally got down on your knees and begged me to forgive you. How could I not?"

"Ah, yeah," Emmett winced at the reminder, "maybe don't mention that to anyone? I don't *beg.*"

"And yet, here we are."

"I had to prove I was serious somehow," he defended, his cheeks getting hot, "I panicked."

"Well, you proved it. For now, anyway."

"I'll earn that," Emmett promised, feeling like a weight had been lifted from his shoulders. He cleared his throat to smother the excited grin threatening to take over. "And I'll start by kicking Orville's ass."

Callie looked confused for a beat, and then she seemed to figure out what he was talking about.

"Ah," she mumbled, shuffling her feet, "you heard that, huh?"

"Parts of it. Do you want to talk about it?"

"Not with the door open like this," Callie said, smirking. "Come in before I lose my fingers to frostbite."

Emmett was only too happy to oblige, following her into the cozy cabin. It was one of Nyla's smaller dwellings, with only a bed, a chair, an end table, and a bathroom. Callie climbed onto the bed, sitting cross-legged, facing the chair. Emmett folded himself into the seat, leaning forward, giving Callie his full attention.

"Turns out Orville already knew that Tara and Ed have been talking to Stamkos," Callie said bitterly, staring hard at the bedspread. "They've met with him twice now. Tara and Ed didn't mention it to me because they figured Orville would've. He *should've*."

"Hang on." Emmett held up a hand, bewildered. "What do you mean? Are the Gallaghers in talks with Stamkos? Since when?"

"Oh, right," Callie said softly, her cheeks flushing an adorable shade of pink. "I didn't get to explain why I was so mad after our meeting. Stamkos implied he was friendly with Ed and Tara, meaning he'd been speaking to them outside of my knowledge. I called Tara to ask her about it, and she said Orville already knew. Then I called him to tell him to go to hell."

Callie sighed, biting her lip.

"I shouldn't have. It was impulsive and stupid, but I was just so *angry*. He gave me this contract knowing damn well the clients already had one foot out the door and he didn't even have the courtesy to tell me. He *wanted* to undermine me, make me look like an idiot."

She fell backward on the bed, knocking her head against the wall with a smack that sounded painful. Emmett flinched forward, but Callie wasn't fazed.

"He's never going to give me the firm," she whispered, staring at the ceiling. "I should've known that from the start. He's been dangling it in front of me for years and I've been following along like a horse after a carrot."

"Are you going to quit?" Emmett asked softly. Callie considered her answer.

"I don't know," she admitted. "I should. Orville has always been a terrible boss, but I put up with him to take over the business. Now, I doubt that will ever happen. If he hasn't already fired me."

"I'm sorry, Cal," Emmett told her, unsure what else to say. Callie lifted her head to give him a half-smile.

"Thanks, but we have more important things to worry about now." She sat up again, looking at Emmett with a serious expression on her face. "Your company is out of a contract, and your dad is out of a job. Not to mention, with Stamkos owning both Lichen House *and* his existing properties, he's in a much better position to push Nyla into selling the Willow."

"The Gallaghers haven't sold yet, have they?" Emmett asked. Callie shook her head.

"No, but from the sounds of things, they've pretty much made their decision."

"Then we have time," Emmett said with determination. "Don't worry about me. The boss has contracts lined up through 2027. Dad will be fine; he should be retired anyway. Right now, we need to focus on helping Nyla, and the best way to do that will be to deal with this whole ice demon fiasco. Property disputes can wait."

"I've been working on that," Callie said, swinging her legs off the bed and jumping up. She hurried past Emmett to the end table, grabbing her tablet and flipping the case open. "Amelia sent me a scan of the topaz mine map. I made a few calls and I think I have something."

She focused on her tablet for a while, her hair falling into her face as she searched for whatever she wanted to show him. Emmett resisted the urge to reach out and tuck the wayward strands behind her ear. He doubted his touch would be welcome right now.

"The mine *is* older than Somerton, just like we thought, but not by much" she told him, reading from an email app. "It started as a very small excavation in 1893, barely extensive enough to be called a true mine. It was originally intended to provide a source of trade between the indigenous population and European settlers, but when the Europeans arrived to assess the value, they decided to stay. That's how Somerton was founded. The settlers worked the mines for about a decade, and then reports of topaz exports completely vanish from town records.

The mine stayed closed until 1947, when the U.S. was looking for ways to boost the economy after the war. Again, it stayed open for about ten years, and then it closed again, this time permanently."

"And none of this is readily available information?" Emmett prodded, confused. "I find it hard to believe that Nyla and Aaron would've missed this. Even harder to believe that Amelia did too."

"They missed it for a good reason," Callie informed him, a small, proud smile tugging at her mouth. "I have a contact at the local history museum in Milwaukee. He mostly studies personal documents, like diaries, journals, letters, things that could give us some insight into life before proper record keeping. They've got a whole collection from Somerton's archives, they just haven't been properly sorted or evaluated yet. When I asked him about the mine, he went digging."

She paused to read more.

"Somerton's 1965 mayoral council ordered that all record of the mine be wiped from town resources. Seems like they didn't want to risk anyone reopening it in the future."

"Which means they had cause for concern," Emmett said, mirroring Callie's smile. "Concern that might very well be the reason we're in this mess."

"I'd bet money on it."

Chapter Twenty-Seven

INTERLUDE

Aaron

"Nyla!"

Clary swung the door open before Aaron could knock, reaching past him to pull Nyla into an enthusiastic hug, squeezing tightly. She gave Aaron the same, then Pratt, welcoming them into the spa. It was empty, save for the four of them. A lack of clientele in the middle of the day would normally indicate that business wasn't great, but Aaron knew that Clary's spa was maintaining a steady income. Clary must've freed up her afternoon for the purpose of meeting with them.

Clary led them to the staff room out back, where she had a number of creature comforts, including two couches and a low-slung coffee table. Nyla took a seat next to her on one couch, with Aaron and Pratt seating themselves across from them on the other. With the small talk out of the way, Nyla glanced at Aaron.

His chest tightened. Nyla looked at him warily, and he knew that was his fault. Nyla wasn't stupid. She realized Aaron was troubled by something, she just wasn't sure what. He hadn't helped in that matter, but what could he say?

"So... why do I feel like this isn't a friendly visit?" Clary asked hesitantly, glancing between Nyla and Aaron suspiciously. Her gaze settled on Nyla, silently communicating her concerns. Nyla shook her head quickly, dismissing Clary's unasked question about her safety.

"It's not," Nyla confirmed with a sheepish smile. "I know I've been AWOL lately. I promise I'll fix it as soon as we deal with... this."

"'This' being...?"

Clary raised her eyebrows at Nyla, again asking her a question without uttering a word. Nyla looked guiltily at Aaron, who sighed. He'd known. Deep down, he'd long since figured out that Clary wasn't as in the dark as he wanted her to be. He just hadn't been willing to admit it to himself.

"You don't need to be cryptic, Clary," he said, rolling his eyes. "I know you know."

"Well, damn," Clary huffed, crossing her arms over her chest. "Who told you?"

"She doesn't know everything," Nyla cut in quickly, locking eyes with Aaron. She couldn't hide her emotions if she tried, staring openly at him with a mixture of guilt and pleading on her face. "Honest. I didn't tell her. And I didn't tell him that you knew at all," Nyla said to Clary, biting her bottom lip. "He's just eerily perceptive."

"I'm a detective, *mi cielo*, it's my job."

"She's telling the truth!" Clary defended hotly, turning on the couch to fully face Aaron. "I wasn't about to sit back and do nothing after you two hit me up about cannibalistic demons and a strict before-dark curfew. How was I supposed to stop myself from digging? I figured out a lot of it without Nyla ever uttering a single word to me—"

"It's okay, Claire," Nyla said, suppressing a smile. Her best friend was nothing if not protective of her. "We came here because we need to tell you everything. Suits is just upset that I'm making his job more difficult."

"His job being what, looking all haughty in a tailored jacket?"

"Keeping her *safe*," Aaron corrected, his voice tinged with exasperation. Pratt shifted on the couch next to him, catching his eye with a concerned pinch between his brows. Aaron shook his head, silently dismissing his worry.

Nyla had, unintentionally, struck the heart of the problem. She *was* making his job difficult, and most of the time it was completely unintentional. Nyla's safety was always at the forefront of his mind, distracting him from just about everything else. However, that didn't mean she was entirely free from fault.

Aaron loved and admired Nyla's independence, resourcefulness, even her impulsivity (although it caused him considerable stress at times). It all came together to make Nyla who she was, and he adored her. Aaron just wished that she would stop and think more often than not. He wouldn't be so worried about her wellbeing if he could trust that she wouldn't throw herself into a dangerous situation on a whim. Somehow, it ruffled him even more that she was aware on some level of how her recklessness affected him. He wasn't angry, exactly. Just... unsettled.

While Aaron worked through his turbulent thoughts, Nyla brought Clary up to speed with everything that had been going on. It quickly became clear that Nyla hadn't lied to Aaron when she assured him that Clary had discerned most of the information about the situation with the Chehwinoo on her own. The details Nyla filled in were mostly from their experiences with the creature. Clary listened to the events of the summer and fall with rapt attention, even as Nyla skimmed over some parts. The entire time, Clary listened with a serious frown, absorbing everything silently.

"After Amelia and Sam spoke to Jodi," Nyla said with an embarrassed sigh, "we realized we've been unintentionally ignoring a huge piece of the puzzle. We've been too reliant on our understanding of the world. The Chehwinoo comes from a culture that doesn't belong to us, but we've been using *our* knowledge to try to fight it. It's no wonder we're failing miserably."

"We need all kinds of help," Pratt agreed. "And right now, you're our best lead."

Nyla pressed her lips together in a thin line. Aaron knew this was difficult for her in a number of ways. Keeping Clary in the loop about her life was one thing, but bringing her into their fight was another entirely. Not to mention, they were asking her to cross cultural lines that they had no right to ask her to cross. Nyla's relief at confessing the reality of their situation was tinged with the inherent worry of putting her in harm's way.

"This isn't my mythos..." Clary began, but Nyla quickly grabbed her hand, threading their fingers together reassuringly.

"We know," she promised. "And we're not asking you to do anything you don't want to do."

"You can tell us to get out of your hair and we will." Aaron leaned forward, clasping his hands together to keep from tapping his fingers in a nervous tic. "We want to be respectful, but we have no idea what we're doing. Any kind of guidance would be helpful, if you're willing."

"And if not, then we're all going to die." Pratt shrugged. Aaron shot him a pointed glare.

"I'm obviously going to help you, idiot." Clary snorted, giving the three of them a withering look. "This is my town, too. I'm not about to stand by while some ice monster picks off my clientele. I'll see if I can contact someone from the band in Madison. They'll have more resources than I do. *If* they'll talk to me. I'm not Onaqwe, and I don't know how much of this will fall under closed practice. But I'll try."

"That's more than enough," Nyla assured her, pulling Clary into a hug. "Thank you. And I'm sorry I acted like a dumb white person."

Clary laughed, hugging her back.

"Nyla, we've been friends for years. You *are* a dumb white person," Clary teased. "I knew what I was getting myself into. Now quit staring at me like you accidentally ran over my dog. It's making my skin crawl."

They dissolved into their regular kaleidoscope of conversation, freely catching each other up on the little things they normally communicated daily but had been pushed to the wayside in recent months. Pratt was content to jump in with occasional questions and playful comments, but Aaron remained determinedly silent.

He should have felt relief. If anyone could get access to the information they needed, it was Clary. He should feel happy. Delighted, even. Watching Nyla and Clary catch up, chattering like excited squirrels, Aaron didn't feel happy. A lump settled into the pit of his stomach, festering into something unpleasant. He knew Pratt was looking at him, but he kept his gaze averted.

"I have to make a call," Aaron said suddenly. The lump in his stomach was morphing into a suffocating dread, and he needed air. The spa was too closed in, too congested. Without waiting for acknowledgment, he walked swiftly to the door.

The crisp, early winter air sobered him instantly. Aaron wasn't used to this; keeping a level head was something he prided himself on. He could logic his way through most things, even most emotions, if he tried hard enough. Right now, he was standing on unsteady ground, and he didn't know how to get his bearings. That alone was enough to invoke a spiral.

"Suits?"

Nyla's soft voice tugged at the pit in his stomach, giving him a lifeline to clutch. He looked back over his shoulder as she closed the door gently, watching him with a worried waver in her gaze.

"Hey," she said, her words hesitant. "Listen, I'm really sorry about Clary. I didn't mean to hide anything from you. Truthfully, I didn't realize how much she managed to figure out on her own until today."

"I'm not upset at you," Aaron assured her. The sentiment left his lips easily, so he knew it was true.

"But you are upset," Nyla pressed.

Was he?

Yes, he supposed he was. 'Upset' didn't quite fit his emotions in the way he wanted, but it wasn't incorrect. He was upset, and the reason was lingering just outside his awareness. He didn't plan on pulling the thread until they were home, or maybe when the Chehwinoo was dealt with.

He also couldn't lie to her.

"Maybe a little," Aaron admitted softly. Nyla was quiet for a moment, and then he heard her footsteps beside him. Her soft hand curled around his, lacing their fingers together comfortably.

"Will you tell me?" she asked. "I like to know what I'm apologizing for."

"You have nothing to apologize for, *mi cielo*." Aaron did his best to offer her a smile. "I'm not upset at something you did."

Nyla watched his face, waiting for him to explain. Aaron looked up at the sky, taking a deep, measured breath. Whether he intended to pull at the thread or not, it was unravelling inside him and, suddenly, he felt like he needed to let everything out before he imploded.

"I'm upset at everything you do," he concluded, smirking so she knew he wasn't being entirely serious.

"...Thanks? I think that's better?" Nyla said, scrunching her nose in confusion.

"Every time I think I have you figured out, you find some new creative way to prove me wrong." Aaron wasn't thinking anymore, he was just talking. The mess of thoughts rattling around his brain spilled out, filling the air between them.

"That's not a bad thing. In fact, it's one of the things I admire most about you. You're spontaneous and creative in ways I just can't be."

"But...?" Nyla prompted.

"But that makes it very hard for me to keep you safe. I spent the better part of my career learning how to read people, and I'm good at it. You walked into my life, took everything I thought I knew, and set it on fire. You're unpredictable in the most absurd, incredible, awe-inspiring way. But if I can't predict what you'll do next, how the hell am I supposed to protect you?" Aaron cursed, the helplessness he felt at the thought of failing to protect Nyla welling in his chest and making his throat tight. "You're the single most important thing in my life, *mi tesoro*. I can't stand the thought of losing you."

"Aaron, you have to know that if I'm in danger, you're my first call. My only call." Nyla moved to stand in front of him, holding his hand between both of hers. "I know that I haven't always been the most upfront with you. I know it bothers you, and I'm working on it. But it's... difficult. I've had to rely on myself for most of my adult life. I'm not used to having anyone in my corner, let alone someone competent. I guess that affected my communication skills more than I thought."

"I know," he said, sighing. He'd seen firsthand the lack of support network Nyla had here in Somerton. He saw the way the townsfolk treated her, the way they ostracized her. The paint bombing was extreme and he wanted to believe it was an outlier incident, but he also knew that once the line had been crossed, it was much easier to cross it again. Somerton was becoming *less* accepting of Nyla, not more, and he suspected it would only get worse with time. It pained him in a way he couldn't properly articulate.

And then, it clicked.

Everything he'd been struggling with, all of his tumultuous thoughts, came together in a startlingly clear realization. Aaron brought his other hand to their joint ones, covering Nyla's with his palm.

"Move to Chicago with me."

Of all the things Nyla was likely expecting him to say, it was clear that wasn't one of them. She blinked at him, momentarily stunned into silence.

"I... I'm sorry, say that again?"

"Come to Chicago," Aaron repeated, determination flooding him as he found the source of his anxiety and held on tight. "It doesn't need to be permanent. I know there's not much in the city for you. But when this is over, I want you to move in with me."

"Where is this coming from?" Nyla asked, still visibly shell-shocked. "Aaron, I can't just move to Chicago. The Willow—"

"Sell it."

Silence descended between them, thick and heavy.

"What?" Nyla murmured, but he knew she'd heard. Aaron took a steadying breath, preparing to explain himself.

"The Willow is a beautiful property," Aaron said, dispelling any notions of him disliking the lodge. "And I know how hard you've worked to make it what it is today, but Somerton isn't good for you. Come stay with me until we can figure out something more sustainable long term."

"The Willow is everything," Nyla said adamantly. "Everything I've built, everything I've been working toward, is in that building. I have a *life* here, Aaron. I can't just leave."

"What life, Nyla?" he pressed, feeling like a jackass for putting it so bluntly even as he knew that nothing less would get his point across. "The people here hate you, *mi cielo*. They don't want you here, and they sure as hell don't deserve the effort you've put into saving this place."

"So, what, I'm supposed to just abandon everything?" Nyla pulled her hands away, planting them on her hips as anger and indignation sparked in her eyes. "Give up? Let them win?"

"*Yes,*" Aaron said. "Who cares if they think they've won? You're an amazing person, Nyla. You could accomplish so much if you didn't have to deal with superficial roadblocks at every turn. Sell the Willow and start over."

"Don't say that like it's simple, Aaron," Nyla snapped. "If I give up now, everything I've done for the last four years will have been for nothing. I'll be a failure!"

"You are *not* a failure!" Aaron practically growled, the sentiment alone infuriating him. "You're surviving in a town that has done *everything* to cast you out. Imagine what you could be if you were somewhere else? Somewhere you don't have to fight for your place at the table. You wouldn't just survive, *mi cielo*. You'd thrive, and it would be a beautiful sight to behold. Somerton would kick themselves for ever letting you go."

"After everything I've been through, if I let the Willow go now, it *will* be a failure," Nyla insisted, her expression hardening. "And if I sell the property, who do you think will buy it? I refuse to make anything easier for Adrian Stamkos. I'd rather set the lodge on fire than let it fall into his hands."

"Why does it matter?" Aaron countered. He thought he heard the sound of a door, but he ignored it. "Adrian Stamkos is going to find another way to get what he wants. You're only hurting yourself by refusing to even consider other options."

"That's *my* choice to make." Nyla's attention darted over his shoulder, and Aaron knew this conversation was over. "We have to meet up with the others. Thanks for your help, Claire."

Aaron heard Clary mutter a soft farewell, followed by an equally tentative greeting from Pratt. He closed his eyes, breathing through his nose.

He didn't handle that well. He knew that before locking eyes with Pratt, who gave him a small, disapproving frown. Aaron hadn't meant for their conversation to go that way, but he'd been thrown off guard by the realization that Nyla was limiting her own potential by staying here. More than anything, Aaron wanted Nyla to be happy. Whatever success looked like for her, he would support. But she couldn't be happy in Somerton. The town wouldn't let her.

If only she could accept that.

The sound of the X5's passenger door slamming shut rattled him from his thoughts, and Aaron opened his eyes to see Clary staring hard at him. He prepared for a verbal assault like he'd never experienced before, but to his surprise, Clary turned her attention to the parking lot where Nyla and Pratt were settling into the vehicle.

"She thinks that if she proves herself, they'll accept her." Clary sighed, frowning. "She's always said that she just needs to get through to them, make the Willow profitable, prove that she's not the enemy. She said she knows it's possible because I did it."

Clary turned back to Aaron, her expression unreadable.

"My family has lived in Somerton for generations," she told him. "If it weren't for my nonna, I would've left years ago. It weighs on you, you know? Always looking over your shoulder, going the extra mile just to be recognized for attending the race. The people here, they tolerate me because of my family. Nyla doesn't have that."

Aaron swallowed a hard knot that formed in his throat.

"You're right," she said, surprising him again. "Somerton doesn't deserve Nyla. You might be the only one capable of making her realize that."

Clary reached for the door, preparing to depart. Aaron stopped her.

"Somerton doesn't deserve either of you," he clarified, offering a smile. Clary returned it.

"You offering for me to come live with you too?"

"I'd charge you rent, no offense."

"None taken," Clary said, laughing. "Can't say I'm willing to do whatever it is Nyla does behind closed doors to get free room and board from you. No offense."

"None taken," Aaron repeated Clary's words back to her, feeling marginally better. "Have a good night, Clary."

"It's Claire," she corrected, surprising him for a third time. "Good luck, Suits. I'll call if I find anything."

Chapter Twenty-Eight

CALLIE

Calling Orville was a mistake. An impulsive one. Callie had never spoken to her boss like that before but, to be fair, she'd never felt so disrespected before, either. Orville was never a good boss, she had no illusions about that. He'd been rude and disrespectful to her more times than she cared to count, and yet he'd still managed to surprise her with his blatant disregard for her role as an employee. Every other legal representative that Orville employed over the years had walked out after a similar show of insult, but not Callie. Callie always did her best to swallow her pride and bear Orville's slights for the sake of her future and paycheck. Perhaps it was the stress she was under, or maybe she'd finally reached her limit, but Callie couldn't swallow her pride on this one.

As frustrated as she'd been to see Emmett on the other side of her door, she was glad he'd come by. Reconciling with him had been the boost she needed to get back into focus. Now, with Sam and Amelia back from their break and Aaron and Nyla on their way to the Willow with Agent Pratt, Callie felt optimistic for the first time in days. Maybe that optimism was to blame for her accepting Emmett's apology so readily.

She *wanted* to stay angry at him. He'd behaved atrociously, insulting not only her but also the people who were quickly becoming her closest friends. She wanted to make him suffer a little; he certainly deserved it. But then she'd looked into his eyes, saw the sincerity in them. Hearing him speak about Ephraim, seeing the pain on his face, Callie finally felt like she understood him a little better. Looking back on their various arguments, they always seemed to happen after near-misses, high risks, or when he returned from checking on his father. She believed he was telling the truth, that his behaviour was borne of a more complicated mess of emotions than she'd originally thought. In truth, Callie didn't have the energy for grudges. Besides, ever since their talk, Emmett was making a genuine effort to fulfil his promise to her, and that was hugely reassuring.

Amelia and Sam both got an apology as soon as they walked through the door, and it was just as honest and awkward as Emmett's apology to Callie. Sam accepted with a flippant wave, but Amelia made him squirm a bit. Callie wished she'd have had the foresight to do the same. Eventually, Amelia put Emmett out of his misery and accepted his apology. When Aaron and Nyla walked in with a man she didn't recognize, presumably Agent Pratt, Callie almost thought the tension in the air came from Nyla's lingering anger at Emmett. That confused her, because Nyla didn't seem all that upset in the first place. Irritated, yes, but not outright angry. It was only when she noticed that Nyla and Aaron were putting deliberate distance between them that she realized the tense atmosphere had nothing to do with Emmett at all.

"We haven't met, which is a shame," the man interrupted her musings, drawing her attention to him. He was a conventionally attractive man, with blond hair and dark roots that made Callie think he dyed it. His features were boyish, making it difficult to assess his real age, but the FBI badge on his jacket dispelled the illusion of youth. "If you went the rest of your life thinking Klein is an accurate representation of FBI agents, I'd never forgive myself."

"Callie, this is Tyler Pratt," Amelia yelled from across the room. "Ignore everything he says. He was best friends with Sam all through high school."

"Please don't hold that against me," Tyler groaned, rolling his eyes. "I was young and stupid."

"And now you're blond and stupid," Sam shot back, confirming Callie's theory about the hair dye. "Pretty stereotypical of you, Ty."

Callie watched the scene play out, thinking that she was the only one who noticed the distinct silence coming from Aaron and Nyla. As she met Emmett's gaze, though, she realized she was wrong. Amelia, Sam, and Tyler were likely pulling attention away from the couple on purpose. Callie felt warmth bloom in her chest.

"You guys came back at a great time," Callie said, joining the effort. Amelia smiled approvingly, and Callie felt her heart do a stupid flip at the experience of being included. She went on to explain the information she'd gathered on the mine, including why the information hadn't shown up in their initial searches. Amelia grumbled something about how she should've realized something like that had happened, but it wasn't said to disparage Callie's efforts. As Nyla stared at the map, which was now flattened on the front desk, she started to speak.

"They found artifacts in the Hovel," she murmured, squinting in thought. "Indigenous artifacts depicting the Chehwinoo found in one of the entrances to a forgotten mine where the creature was trapped for at least a few decades. That has to mean something. You said the mayoral council ordered the destruction of the records, right? Could it be possible that James Carver knew about the mine and that was the main source of the permit conflicts with Stamkos?"

"It wouldn't have been Carver's council that made the original call, but that doesn't mean he wasn't aware. It's possible."

"It would make sense if he did," Tyler added, humming as he worked through his thoughts. "Uncovering any of those tunnels would be a massive headache for everyone involved. He probably set the borders of the land he sold to Stamkos deliberately to avoid exactly what happened with the Hovel. He wasn't expecting Stamkos to go back on his word after the contracts were signed."

"So, Stamkos started construction outside the limits of his agreed upon permit, accidentally blasted a hole into old mining tunnels that he may or may not have known about, and then rushed to cover it up by sealing off the Hovel and banning public access, all while ignorant to the fact that his greed released an ancient, murderous ice demon on the town." Sam crossed his arms over his chest, tapping his foot in time with his words. "Can we prove any of that?"

His question was addressed to Amelia, who'd been quietly sifting through the information she'd stolen from Stamkos' laptop whenever she had a free moment. She glanced up briefly to acknowledge she'd heard Sam, and then she was peering at her screen again.

"Maybe," she said slowly. "I mean, we have the original permits. We can prove that he went outside of his approved land, but that will only result in a fine and maybe the tear-down of the work he's done already. I doubt that, though. As for him knowing about the mine tunnels beforehand, if I can find proof of *that*, we might have something."

"If he started construction without disclosing the potential danger of the terrain with his workers, he would have a major lawsuit on his hands," Aaron agreed, nodding at Callie for further confirmation. "We could use that."

"I haven't found anything yet," Amelia muttered, sounding frustrated with herself. Callie understood that feeling all too well; struggling to swallow the fact that she *should* be able to solve a given problem, and not blaming herself if she couldn't. "For a corporate guy, Stamkos has horrifically messy file organization. I'm still trying to sort the relevant information from the random garbage stored on here."

"Just be careful you don't stumble on any nudes," Sam warned gravely. Amelia grimaced at him.

"Too late."

A chorus of gagging sounds echoed throughout the room. Tyler shook his head to clear whatever image had taken over his brain, and then he turned to Aaron.

"I've been meaning to tell you," he began, "I got clearance from Kelley to go back into Carver's house after Stamkos broke in. It all looked pretty much the same as before, except the home office. It was completely ransacked, to the point that I have no idea if anything was missing."

"Searching Carver's office implies that we were right about one thing, at least," Emmett grunted. "He was probably looking for some kind of incriminating document. Maybe something that proved his knowledge of the mine?"

"That's the most likely scenario, *if* he knew. Without some kind of written record, we can't prove—"

Aaron was cut off by a high-pitched shriek that made them all jump. After the initial shock wore off and the realization that they weren't in danger restored their senses, every eye turned to Amelia, who was responsible for the scream. She sat bolt upright in her chair, swinging her legs off of the armrest and turning in the same motion. She clutched her laptop in a white-knuckled grip as though it would disappear if she gave it the chance.

"Holy *shit!*"

"What?" Nyla gasped, clutching her chest as her breathing slowed. "Please tell me you found something that'll justify the heart attack you just gave me?"

"I found something alright," Amelia confirmed, finally looking up from her screen to hit them with a beaming, triumphant grin. "But I don't think you're going to believe it."

She spun the laptop to face them, scrolling through a long list of files. Nyla and Callie shared a discreet look, wondering if they should know what they were seeing. Emmett looked just as confused, and Sam, while beaming with pride, didn't offer an explanation either. Aaron wasn't even looking at the screen. Amelia, noting the definitive silence, rolled her eyes in good-natured exasperation.

"These are chat logs," she explained, highlighting various files with her mouse. "The messages came from a private email address belonging to James Carver. This folder has years of communication between him and Stamkos."

"*Years?*" Nyla repeated incredulously. "I didn't know they were in contact for that long... What were they discussing?"

"I only just found this." Amelia turned the laptop back around to face her, quickly scanning a small section of the content she'd unlocked. "I haven't gone through the older messages, but the recent ones are all about the factory. It's weird, though. Stamkos was almost treating Carver like *he* was in charge. He sent him everything from budget proposals, contractor interviews, even employee portfolios."

"*Just* employee portfolios?" Callie straightened, but Amelia winked at her before the question could spring to her lips.

"Oh, you *know* the contractor portfolios are in here too," Amelia said, grinning. "And yes, that includes one of our obvious outliers, Mr. Diamond."

"God, you are so hot," Sam crooned from where he was leaning casually against the wall. "Keep talking tech to me, baby."

Amelia shook her head in amusement, otherwise ignoring Sam's teasing. She clicked and typed for a few breathless seconds while Callie waited, anxiety churning her stomach. This was it. If there was anything important about Mac Diamond and his involvement in the project, they were about to find out what it was. After what felt like an eternity, Amelia's eyes rounded.

"Oh, *hell* yes," she whispered, typing frantically. Callie resisted the urge to prod her for more, knowing she would give it the moment she had it. "Oh my God, this has to be it. Callie—"

"Yes?"

Amelia gave her a knowing smirk.

"I would like to formally introduce you to Mr. Malcolm Diamond, contract employee, heavy equipment certified, and..."

The laptop flipped again, showing a blurry, frowning image of Diamond against a white background, clearly an ID photo of some kind. Callie scanned the screen, taking in the personal information next to the picture, confirming that it was an ID card. Specifically, it was an employee identification card from Mac Diamond's previous employer. The name of the company was vaguely familiar to Callie, but she couldn't place it. As it turned out, she didn't have to. The longer she stared at the screen, the more of it she took in. The ID was included as part of Diamond's hiring paperwork for S&S and, tucked inconspicuously in the bottom corner of the digital file, under a text box labelled 'Employer Access Only (Employee Cannot See),' Callie found their smoking gun.

Assign to Lewis for back-hoe operations. Any adjustments in schedule go through AS.

Note: employee record from Granite Shore Blasting Co. can be found under file name '71129_MD_Experience_Verification'

Granite Shore Blasting Co. was a company Callie knew well, having spoken to them many times for construction clients. They were a small company, having no more than ten employees at a time, including the owner and admin, both of whom Callie knew by name. The rest of the employees were trade specialists and since Granite Shore Blasting Co. only offered a certain category of work, Callie knew without a doubt what Mac Diamond would've been hired for.

He was a demolition expert. Whatever Adrian Stamkos was planning involved the unauthorized use of blasting equipment.

"Demolition..." Nyla muttered under her breath, thinking hard. "I don't remember any blasting going on when the factory build started."

"That's because there wasn't any," Emmett said, frowning. "The guys at work were talking about it. S&S applied for a blasting permit but they were denied, so they brought in the heavy equipment to dig. Do we know what Diamond was hired to blast? Does it say?"

"You've asked the million-dollar question," Amelia cheered, looking more animated than Callie had ever seen her. She snuck a glance at Sam, who was watching with a fond smile. "We don't know *what* he was hired to demolish, but we do know *where*."

"No way," Nyla whispered, a grin spreading across her face. "It can't be that easy, can it?"

"It can," Amelia confirmed, pointing to a list of coordinates. "If I'm reading this map right, then the spot Mac Diamond was hired to blast is right on top of our mine."

"More than that," Nyla said, her expression both hopeful and confused. "That looks like it intersects perfectly with one of the potential entrances I pinpointed. But... this area of the Basin is *way* outside of the construction zone. I know Stamkos is brazen, but this is going beyond playing it fast and loose with property lines."

"It's almost certainly deliberate," Aaron murmured, lost in thought. Nyla glanced at him warily, but said nothing. "I'd suggest that he was trying to discreetly access the topaz deposits, but I can't see why. The Stamkos family has multiple businesses, none of which have anything to do with mining. Not to mention, there isn't exactly a shortage of topaz in the world."

"But why else would he be targeting this area?" Callie wondered aloud. "Unless he—"

She cut herself off abruptly, internalizing the ridiculousness of what she almost said. As insane as the situation was turning out to be, the possibility that Adrian Stamkos knew about and deliberately sought out the Chehwinoo was astronomically absurd. Callie told herself that, repeating it for good measure.

So then why was the idea sticking in the back of her mind?

"I don't know," Amelia said, answering her question and saving Callie from her own paranoia. "But there's one way we can find out."

Chapter Twenty-Nine

EMMETT

The next morning was sunny and crisp, warmer than it had been the previous few days. Emmett took that as a positive sign.

Once they'd determined with relative certainty that they knew where the mine entrance was, the planning began. While they were going underground where the sun wouldn't be able to protect them from the creature, they decided that starting their trek in the early morning was best. With any luck, the Chehwinoo would be asleep, or at least unaware of their movements during the better part of the day. They set out from the Willow, since that was the route Nyla knew best, and wound their way into the depths of the forest.

Emmett was on high alert. Amelia had her tablet with her, checking on the Chehwinoo's location regularly as they walked. It still hadn't moved from its temporary den, and Emmett was starting to get a bad feeling about that. Everyone was, though no one had admitted it out loud. The Chehwinoo remaining stationary for so long *should* be a good thing. No disappearances or deaths had been reported, and that was allowing Agent Kelley to give them more time by holding off the Wildlife investigation. The problem that Emmett had with the whole thing was *why*.

Why hadn't it moved? Was something stopping it? Should they check?

He couldn't begin to guess, but it didn't matter. The lead on the mine entrance was the biggest break they'd gotten so far, and Emmett needed to focus his full attention on making the best of it, which came with its own onslaught of questions. What was Stamkos looking for out here? What did it mean that he'd been communicating with James for far longer than anyone thought? Emmett wasn't much of an intellectual, but from his perspective, they had three separate problems that were, somehow, connected: Stamkos & Stein's factory build causing problems in town, the Chehwinoo posing a risk to anyone and everyone that entered the Basin, and now the topaz mine. It felt like all of the pieces should fit together, but not in a way that Emmett could pinpoint.

The factory freed the Chehwinoo, they were almost certain of that much. Construction meant more people in the Basin, putting them at risk. Stamkos wasn't a man who could take no for an answer, and his ambition was both stepping on peoples' toes and, worse, getting them killed. That had all fit cleanly up until Amelia found Malcolm Diamond's employee records. Now, Emmett didn't know what was coincidence, what was a red herring, and what was important to ending this madness.

"What are the chances Diamond managed to clear the way into the mine before he was possessed?" Sam asked. Six of them were currently making their way through the Basin; Tyler had gotten a call from Kelley late last night that demanded his immediate attention. None of them held it against him; he was still actively working for the FBI, and he'd taken as many liberties as he possibly could. The fact that he'd been able to help them even half as much as he had was more than they expected.

"His contract started well before Halloween," Amelia answered, reading something on her phone. Before they set out, she'd managed to find one more important piece of information tucked away in Diamond's file. According to the official records, he was hired *after* the initial construction began. With that revelation came even more questions, and Amelia had been reluctant to leave her laptop at the cabin, desperate to sift through the mysterious chat logs between Carver and Stamkos for some kind of explanation. In the end, her curiosity about the mine won out. "I don't know if he would've finished blasting, but I'm guessing he at least started."

"We'll find out soon," Nyla called back over her shoulder. "We're almost there."

Emmett peered through the trees ahead, vaguely recognizing the area. He couldn't remember ever coming across a cave.

They walked in silence for a time, and Emmett contemplated hurrying his way to the front of the line so he could apologize properly to Nyla. With the excitement of finding a potential mine entrance, he'd forgotten to do so when she, Aaron, and Tyler came back to the Willow. Looking at her now, maybe it was for the best.

Nyla was upset about something and, judging by the way she and Aaron avoided eye contact with each other, it had everything to do with him. Emmett couldn't remember Aaron and Nyla ever fighting before. They had their disagreements, but he didn't think it had ever turned into a point of contention like this. Maybe they were usually better at hiding it, but Emmett had his doubts. Nyla was an open book, and if she was having problems with Aaron, he'd like to think he would've known about it.

When he wasn't distracted by his own concerns about the Chehwinoo and Nyla, Emmett's attention was firmly dragged to Callie.

She hiked alongside him for most of the trip, not talking much. Emmett didn't mind, he was just happy to be near her, to feel the occasional accidental brush of her hand against his arm. Every opportunity to be with Callie was a gift, something he didn't properly appreciate before. He hadn't expected her to accept his apology. God knows he didn't deserve it. Maybe she'd seen something in his confession that softened her anger at him, or maybe Callie was a much kinder person than most, but Emmett wouldn't squander this chance. He had a feeling it was his last.

Soon, the downward sloping terrain evened out. Nyla slowed her steps, gingerly pushing through a cluster of young evergreens to reach a clearing on the other side. Instinctively, Aaron reached out to hold the branches back for her. Emmett saw her give him a tight smile, which he returned. Worry welled in Emmett's stomach.

He hated seeing them like this, and he clearly wasn't the only one. Callie had the same worried look on her face watching Aaron and Nyla interact. Emmett couldn't see Amelia and Sam's expressions from here, but he'd caught them stealing glances at each other every now and then. Even Tyler had seemed more subdued than usual before he left.

"Good news," Nyla yelled back to them, her tone sounding lighter. "Mr. Diamond managed to do us a favor before his untimely demise."

They hurried forward to see for themselves. The clearing was scattered with abandoned equipment, including shovels, pickaxes, and even a rusted backhoe. Emmett blinked in surprise. How had Stamkos managed to transport all of this?

Searching the clearing for answers, Emmett's attention snagged on a clear-cut path to the west. He suppressed a snarl. Clear-cutting was illegal in this part of Wisconsin, not that he was particularly surprised Stamkos would stoop to such tactics. If he had to guess, the path led to one of the old cabin roads, likely one that connected to the Hatfield highway.

Ignoring the butchery, Emmett returned to examining the equipment. From here, he could see evidence of blasting. It must've been contained and planned to correspond with other construction work, otherwise people would've been suspicious of loud bangs coming from the Basin. As it stood, they'd seemingly accomplished their goal. The cave mouth was pitch black, diving deep enough that daylight couldn't reach the end of the tunnel.

"Did everyone do their homework?" Sam asked, clapping his hands together. When he received blank stares in response, he rolled his eyes. "I *said* we all needed a refresher on *The Descent*. I'm not losing my life to some creepy ass cave crawler. Do none of you read my newsletter?"

"He doesn't have a newsletter," Amelia clarified, seeing Callie's confusion. "And I'd rather go down to a cave crawler than take a single piece of Sam's advice."

"You know," Sam said, sniffing, "words hurt, Amy Baby."

"So do fists."

"Not if you stretch properly."

Emmett snorted a laugh, watching Nyla shine her flashlight into the cave mouth. Darkness reflected back at her.

"I think he managed to break through to the mine," she determined, considering their options. "Normally, I wouldn't suggest descending into an unknown system. But..."

"We have a map," Amelia reminded her, "and we need answers."

"I don't think we have much choice," Aaron agreed, squinting into the cave. "All the same, we should take precautions. I doubt there will be cell service down there. Someone should stay topside with a walkie."

"I can," Callie volunteered, and Emmett jolted in surprise. "I know my strengths, and cave exploration is not one of them. I'll just slow you all down."

His first instinct had been to suggest Callie stay behind, but he'd squashed the urge deep down in the pit of his stomach. He'd made enough of a mess of things in trying to keep Callie safe; part of proving to her that he was sincere in his apology was to trust her. Emmett expected to swallow protests, bite his tongue, and suffer his worry in silence. Maybe he was just accustomed to dealing with Nyla, but it never once crossed his mind that Callie was perfectly aware of her own limitations and was content to work within them.

God, he really had been a fucking asshole, hadn't he?

"Here," Nyla handed her a walkie, passing the other to Emmett. "Do you still have a copy of the map on you? It might be easier if you're directing us on top of our own navigation. Hopefully we won't need to travel too deep..."

"But we've already exhausted our good luck for the day," Emmett finished for her, "and we don't want to push it."

"Exactly."

"I'll stay with you," Amelia offered, tapping her tablet screen. "I can monitor the Chehwinoo and get a head start on these chatlogs. Besides, if there's trouble, you'll need someone who can shoot."

"Fingers crossed it won't come to that," Callie said, smirking. "I appreciate it, all the same. We'll set up shop in the backhoe. Should give us some shelter from the wind, and a bit of protection from anything else."

"Good idea," Amelia agreed. She paused to give Sam a quick kiss before heading to the backhoe, the tight lines around her mouth revealing a hint of worry. Callie followed her, giving the group an encouraging smile.

"Don't miss me too much," Sam lamented, dramatically flipping his short hair. "I won't forget you, Amelia Geraldine!"

"Who are you again?"

"Ouch, my pride," Sam cried. "Your words are but laced daggers, poisoning my blood with undying devotion to you!"

"Get in the damn cave before I lose my breakfast, Fisher."

Emmett grabbed Sam by the back of his sweater, hauling him toward the cave behind Aaron and Nyla.

"I love you, dark angel of nightmares!" Sam wailed, clawing at his chest like his emotions were liable to burst from him at a moment's notice. "Queen of torture, Goddess of pain, Mistress of giving *incredible* head—"

"Alright, now *I'm* going to lose my breakfast," Emmett muttered, shoving Sam ahead of him. "Seriously, were you dropped on your head as a child?"

"Several times," Sam confirmed, "but that's irrelevant. I have a skull of steel."

He sauntered into the cave, coming to a stop just beside Aaron and slinging an arm over his shoulders. Emmett watched, perplexed, until he caught sight of Amelia out of the corner of his eye. Despite her exaggerated annoyance at her boyfriend's antics, she was clearly suppressing laughter.

It clicked, then, what Sam was doing. Suddenly, Emmett looked back on all the times Sam made a fool of himself in an entirely new light.

"He really loves her, doesn't he?" Callie said softly, having realized the same thing Emmett did. He nodded silently, wondering when she'd reappeared beside him. He glanced down at her, and Callie made sure to look anywhere but his face. "Be careful down there, okay?"

Emmett smiled, the sentiment warming him almost as much as the shy look on her face as she said it.

"Don't tell me you're actually *worried* about me, Cal?"

"As if," she said, pouting. "I'm not finished making you grovel your way back into my good graces yet. You need to be alive to do that."

"You have my word," he assured her, jostling her shoulder with his own. "Try not to go off on anyone until I get back?"

"Please," Callie said, snorting. "I save all my animosity for you."

Emmett knew she was joking. Still, a troublesome happiness spread through him at the idea that she might just be telling the truth. That he was special to her in some way.

"I'll hold you to that," he promised, and then he was following Sam, Aaron, and Nyla into the darkness.

CALLIE

The backhoe's cabin was cramped with only one seat, but Callie and Amelia made it work. They each sat on opposite sides of the floor, using the chair as a sort of table between them. It was a tight fit, their legs constantly bumped into one another, and the cold metal beneath Callie's thighs made her shiver. Still, she'd rather have the close quarters than be sitting out in the open.

Amelia's phone was perched on the seat, angled so they could both see the drone feed. The Chehwinoo hadn't moved, and Callie found herself feeling less and less comforted by that.

"Making a left," Emmett's voice crackled from the walkie. Callie held up the map, tracing their path with her index finger.

"You're coming up on a slight bend. Follow it until you hit a T, then take the path on the right."

"Got it."

Callie put the walkie down, scanning the map for any potential hiccups. She wouldn't find any, she knew. She'd been studying it ever since the others disappeared into the cave.

It hadn't been long; barely ten minutes. In that time, Callie was sure she'd sprouted a handful of grey hairs.

"Relax," Amelia insisted, giving her a knowing smile. "They'll be fine. I know he doesn't seem like it, but Sam is a good person to have around in a crisis. He used to play tight end, so he's great at taking direction. You basically have a giant, sentient sack of muscle to do your bidding."

Callie laughed, some of the tension easing from her shoulders.

"I'm not worried about that," she promised. "Everyone in our group is beyond capable of handling themselves. I'm just... worried. In general."

"Preaching to the choir," Amelia said in a self-mocking tone. "I'd offer you some of my anxiety meds, but I've been on these babies so long now that the dosage is enough to knock out a cow."

"You're exaggerating," Callie said, although her voice wavered a bit in apprehension. Amelia chuckled.

"Yeah, I am, but they *would* give you a splitting headache."

Amelia only laughed harder at the relieved look on Callie's face. She scrunched her nose in protest, staring down at the map again. Nyla had looked at it more closely on the way here, determining that it would take them approximately four hours to reach the center, if everything went smoothly. They planned to turn around well before that, giving them enough time to make it back to the Willow before full dark. Still, six hours of sitting in a backhoe, fretting over what could go wrong, was a daunting prospect.

To distract herself, Callie looked over at Amelia's tablet. She'd opted to leave the laptop at the cabin for ease of transport, transferring the chat logs to her email so she could review them while they waited.

"Anything interesting?" Callie prompted, resisting the urge to drum her fingers on her knees. Amelia frowned, staring at the screen.

"Maybe..." she paused, reading another message. "Hand me the walkie?"

Callie did.

"Nyla?"

"Yeah?"

Amelia sat up a bit straighter, almost glaring at the text in front of her.

"You said Carver was pushing for the factory contract, right?"

"He was," Nyla confirmed bitterly. *"Bill said it was his idea, but that was just him blowing hot air. He and Carver both tried to play it off like they were organizing the contract to appease me."*

"I was afraid of that," Amelia murmured. "According to these chat logs, Carver was actively fighting *against* Stamkos on this project."

"What? Why?"

Callie leaned forward, scanning the text upside down. She couldn't make out much from this angle, but the short messages she could see supported Amelia's claim.

"He doesn't say why specifically," Amelia answered. "It's all just vague references to phone conversations, which of course weren't recorded. From the look of things, though, Carver was fighting *hard*."

"I don't understand," Nyla huffed, frustrated. *"Why would he fight back against a project* he *organized?"*

"Based on this conversation log, I don't think he *did* organize it. In which case, why would he suddenly start pretending that he did?"

"Do you think it's because of the mine?" Callie suggested. Amelia pressed her lips together in a tight line. "Maybe we were wrong and Carver didn't want Stamkos building in the Basin at all."

"Maybe," Amelia said, shrugging. "I'll keep reading. Maybe they'll let something slip."

They sat in silence for a few minutes, until Callie couldn't stand the waiting. Checking to be sure the walkie was muted, Callie nodded to the tablet in Amelia's hands.

"Anything in there about the whole... paint bomb thing?" Her voice dropped, even knowing that Nyla couldn't hear her. Amelia glanced at the walkie too, shaking her head.

"Nothing on Stamkos' device, it was the first thing I checked," she whispered, matching Callie's tone despite the fact that they were currently alone. "I suspect a lot of this happened through text or phone call, especially if Stamkos' assistant was involved. The article is still up, but it hasn't gotten much traction in the last couple of days."

Despite the implied positive of her statement, Amelia looked more troubled than before.

"What? What is it?"

"I haven't found anything on *Stamkos'* computer," she said slowly. "But I did find this."

Amelia showed Callie a post on Somerton's official social media account. It was a progress picture of the S&S factory, but the comments were all about... Nyla.

Surprised they got this far with that shrew kicking up a stink!

Take that, Jameson. Keep crying about it.

Somerton Strong!

Maybe she'll FINALLY get the hint and LEAVE!!!! Give the Willow to a REAL Somertonian!!!!!

Someone call the cops! S&S are making more jobs for Somerton residents! ALERT THE MEDIA! WE'LL NEVER SURVIVE!

Who's gonna tell #NuttyNyla that her idiot petition did jack shit? Can you film it??

The comments had been turned off, but not before the townsfolk said their piece. Callie felt a hard rock of despair form in the pit of her stomach.

"Please tell me she hasn't seen this."

"She's blocked from the town's social media page," Amelia assured her. It was a double-edge comfort; on one hand, it was likely Nyla hadn't seen the cruelty lurking on this page. On the other, blocking her from Somerton's official social media was yet another slight against her.

Callie fell silent as Amelia returned to her tablet. There was nothing either of them could say or do that would make the situation better in that moment. Later, when the Chehwinoo was dealt with, Callie promised herself that she would do everything in her power to fix whatever was broken in Somerton that prevented the people from seeing what a treasure Nyla really was. How much she loved their town. What she would do for them if they'd just give her a chance.

And if they never did?

She was about to voice some of her concerns to see if Amelia had opinions to offer when she caught movement out of the corner of her eye. Callie looked over Amelia's shoulder, through the backhoe's mostly-glass door. She only had a split second to register what she was seeing before someone climbed onto the machine.

"Amelia!" Callie screamed, lunging forward. Amelia reacted instantly, dropping her tablet and spinning to face the door. By that time, the man had ripped the cab open, grabbing Amelia by the back of her sweater. She fought viciously, lashing out at the man with her legs. Callie reached for Amelia's elbow to stop the man from pulling her out of the backhoe, but she wasn't quick enough. Amelia's body slid across the metal flooring, her jeans catching on the seat base before tearing free. The man hauled her to her feet, shoving her off the landing of the machine and jumping down next to her. Amelia hit the frosted ground with an audible smack, a string of curses erupting from her mouth.

Callie scrambled to intervene, but the second door behind her opened before she could gain any ground. A fist twisted in her jacket, yanking her backward. Callie screamed, flailing for purchase. Her hand connected with the walkie and she grabbed on, searching for the comms button—

She slammed into the dirt, hard, knocking the air from her lungs. Callie rolled, gasping, the walkie flying from her grasp as she struggled to breathe.

"I expected better from you, Ms. Quinn."

Callie froze.

No. No way.

A series of colourful expletives cluttered the air before Callie could answer, Amelia appearing from the other side of the backhoe, guided by the man that pulled her from the cab. He had her hands pinned behind her back, but that wasn't slowing her down. She kept fighting, threatening her captor with a myriad of creative outcomes.

"You're trespassing," Adrian Stamkos continued, looking down at Callie like a disappointed father. "In a dangerous location, no less. I thought you were smarter than this."

"What the fuck are you doing here?" Amelia demanded, pausing her verbal assault. Stamkos was flanked by three other men, two of which were dressed like the men that had attacked Amelia and Callie. They were wearing dark blue windbreakers and black pants. Some kind of security, no doubt.

The last man was wearing coveralls and a safety helmet.

"You're both lucky I spotted you in that cab," Stamkos said, staring absently at the backhoe. "We're still working in this area."

"You don't own this land," Callie argued, pushing herself up onto her elbows. As soon as she did, the guard closest to her pulled her to her feet, gripping her upper arms and pinning them to her sides. Callie suppressed a yelp of pain. "This is public property!"

"Is it?" Stamkos shrugged. "Too bad. I'll have to adjust the legal budget."

"What do you want, anyway?" Amelia snapped. Callie was too stunned to think clearly. Stamkos shouldn't be here. He had no reason to be here. The blasting was done, they'd found the mine. Why would he come back? What was here that he needed so badly?

"I'm just doing a little clean up," Stamkos explained, reading the confusion on Callie's face, shoving his hands in his pockets. "Turns out, there are several tunnels running through this area. Opened one up while we were scouting. Horrible luck, really. Unfortunately, our demolition expert was among the casualties over Halloween weekend. Took me ages to find someone to come in and finish the job."

Callie didn't understand. Finish what job? They weren't close to the new factory, and the mine was open. What could he be...?

The man in coveralls moved toward the mouth of the cave, where he spent some time searching through the discarded equipment. Finding what he wanted, he waved to Stamkos.

"Looks intact, Mr. Stamkos," he announced. "I can set it off as soon as we're clear. If it doesn't fire properly, I have a few more charges back in the truck."

"Wait!" Amelia's panicked shout startled Callie into the realization that this was much more serious than she thought. Willing her brain to work faster, Callie forced the pieces together until they fit into some semblance of an explanation. When they did, her heart dropped.

"You can't destroy it!" Callie yelled, tugging against her captor. "You opened it in the first place! Why would you want to close it?"

"Opening it was an accident, Ms. Quinn." Stamkos gave her a small, condescending smile that told her every word from his mouth was a lie. "It would be irresponsible to leave it here for anyone to stumble into."

"There are people inside!" Amelia cut in frantically. She wasn't fighting the guard anymore, focusing her anger on Stamkos instead. "If you blow it up, they'll die!"

"No one is in there," Stamkos insisted. "This is a private construction site, and I don't believe anyone has signed in aside from us. Isn't that right, Mr. Verne?"

The man in coveralls nodded, still tinkering with the electricity line that had to be connected to some manner of explosives inside the mine.

"That doesn't matter," Callie argued, her eyes darting to the walkie. It was about five feet from where she stood, and, while it had been blessedly quiet thus far, Emmett and the others were bound to request directions soon. "I can confirm that there are people inside, authorized or not. You *can't* set off that charge!"

Mr. Verne rejoined them, holding the controller aloft.

"All set, Mr. Stamkos."

"Excellent." Stamkos waved to the men to position themselves behind the backhoe, regarding Amelia and Callie with pity.

"I don't know what you girls were trying to accomplish out here," he said, "but I advise you to stay clear of the Basin for the next few weeks. I have big plans for this town."

"Stamkos, *stop!*" Callie begged, frightened tears welling in her eyes. "Please! Our friends are in there, you can't just—"

Callie locked eyes with Stamkos, her frantic gaze colliding with his cool indifference and setting off an explosive realization in the pit of her stomach. In that brief moment, Callie knew. She knew that Stamkos believed her, knew that he understood the repercussions of flipping that switch.

And he didn't care. He was going to do it anyway. Adrian Stamkos was less than a breath away from committing second-degree murder, and Callie couldn't stop him.

White hot fear lanced through her body, giving her a burst of unrefined strength. Callie ripped herself free from the arms restraining her and dove to the ground, scrambling for the discarded walkie. Movement closed in around her— she didn't have time. Her fingers grazed the hard plastic, and she dug her nails in, clutching the device with every ounce of energy she had left.

Amelia screamed from somewhere behind her, and then another scuffle broke out. Callie had just enough time to glance behind her to see that Amelia had knocked one of the guards off her, buying Callie precious seconds. She scrambled forward in the grass, trying to wrestle the walkie into her grip.

A hand clamped onto her leg, and she kicked blindly, her heel colliding with something hard— a knee, or a chin, judging by the string of expletives following the impact. Fumbling the walkie into her palm, Callie drove the pad of her thumb into the comms button, relief flooding her at the familiar crackle of static connecting her to her friends. Someone else made a grab for her arms, but Callie ignored them, emptying the air from her lungs in a desperate plea.

"EMMETT! *RUN!*"

Chapter Thirty-One

EMMETT

"If I never see the inside of another cave for the rest of my life, I might be able to die happy."

Sam's complaint was laced with just enough sincerity to undermine the teasing lilt in his voice. They hadn't been walking for long, approximately half an hour by Emmett's count, but it was long enough for the cold and damp to seep into their bones.

It didn't help that they were moving *slowly*. If they were hiking at a normal pace, they'd be far deeper into the mine by now. As it was, none of them knew exactly what they were looking for, so progress was continuously halted by pauses to evaluate markings, abandoned tools, and anything else that looked out of place. Emmett idly wondered if they were even deep enough to escape the lingering sunlight.

As they moved, he contemplated calling Callie again, just to see how things were going on her end. He resisted, not wanting to bother her or, worse, make her think he didn't trust her to keep herself out of harm's way. What could possibly happen to her in an abandoned backhoe, with Amelia not two feet away? Besides, he really just wanted a distraction from the heavy task ahead.

"I think this is topaz," Nyla said idly, trailing her finger along a vein of rock that was discoloured compared to the surrounding walls. "Funny, I always thought it was naturally yellow."

"Depends on the origin," Aaron offered gruffly. Emmett gave him a reassuring pat on the back. It felt awkward and stilted, but it had the desired effect. Aaron gave him a strained smile in return. "Some are yellow, others are white. Most look like a muddied brown until they're refined."

"Weird," Nyla hummed, momentarily distracted from her silent feud with Aaron by the curiosity burning in her eyes. "I wonder if there's enough here for the mine to still be operational. Not that I think it *should* be, but there could be a wealth of resources down here."

Emmett slowed while Nyla examined the topaz vein, scanning the cave with his flashlight for anything else of interest. He hated that it was too dark to see properly without a light; flashlights didn't light the entire room. Whenever he was forced to use one, he always felt like he was missing key details.

Swinging the light to the far wall, he spotted something embedded in the rock. Emmett frowned, approaching. Whatever was shoved up there had a long string connecting it to... something. The string trailed to the ground and disappeared into the dark, toward the entrance. The entire set-up was eerily familiar, but Emmett didn't know why until he was close enough to see clearly.

Emmett recognized the bundles immediately, having come across them at numerous job sites. Dynamite charges, professionally laid and wired to the cave entrance. This cave was still rigged for blasting, and they were smack dab in the middle of the danger zone.

Shit.

They'd assumed that the blasting was done, with Stamkos moving his focus to Lichen House and Diamond having died in the Halloween massacre. That could still be true, and these charges were leftover from the initial work, abandoned and useless in the cave wall. Leaving rigged dynamite unattended was against code, though. Any demolitionist worth their salt would have a heart attack knowing that a prepped charge was unaccounted for.

Then again, Stamkos wasn't exactly a stickler for proper channels. Regardless, the situation had changed drastically with the discovery. It wouldn't be safe for them to continue without confirming that these charges were removed and there weren't more littered throughout the mine. Getting them removed posed its own risk, not the least of which being that drawing attention to this spot might mean they can never access it again. For longer than he expected, Emmett considered keeping his mouth shut. The detonator would be outside the cave, and neither

Amelia nor Callie was dumb enough to go around pressing random switches. Most of them needed a key, anyway. They should be relatively safe to continue.

The 'relatively' and 'should be' were his undoing, though. If Emmett was down here alone, he might stay. But he couldn't bring himself to knowingly put the others in danger.

"Klein?" Emmett cleared his throat, dispelling the nerves that had collected there. Aaron's brows furrowed slightly, picking up on the disguised urgency. He made his way to where Emmett stood, his attention quickly finding the explosives. He stiffened, the only betrayal of the seriousness of their situation. After a heavy moment of silence, Aaron turned back to the group.

"We should head top side," he said calmly, no hint of fear or stress in his voice or posture. Emmett was impressed, not to mention a little envious. "Emmett just got a text from Callie. She's got something for us."

"We've barely made a dent," Nyla argued, frowning. "If we turn back now, we won't have enough daylight to reach our halfway point goal. Can you call her on the walkie?"

"She says it's urgent," Aaron insisted, his words taking on a firm tone that still didn't hint at the danger they were in but discouraged further argument. Nyla narrowed her eyes in suspicion. "We'll have to come back another time."

"You heard the man," Sam said, hoisting his backpack into a more comfortable position on his shoulder before whistling a familiar tune. Emmett guessed he was too focused on leaving to question the weak explanation, or he picked up on the tension and trusted that Aaron had good reason to insist. With Sam, he never could tell. "*High-ho, high-ho, it's home from work we go...*"

Nyla, on the other hand, wasn't ready to let it go. She fell into step beside Aaron, just behind Sam and Emmett. They were moving faster now than they had been, but now that they'd committed to leaving, he felt urgency nipping at the backs of his heels, encouraging him to run. He fought the instinct down. Running blindly through a cave, even a fairly straightforward one, wasn't a good idea.

"What's wrong?" she demanded, her attention flickering between Emmett and Aaron. Emmett tried to keep his gaze forward, ignoring the burn of Nyla's stare in the back of his head.

"Something came up," Aaron told her, his hand moving to the small of her back and encouraging her forward. "I'll explain when we're outside."

They moved in silence for a while, Nyla watching Aaron and Emmett out of the corner of her eye. The closer they got to the mouth of the cave, the more Emmett relaxed, but he wouldn't be completely calm until they were all safely outside. Thankfully, they'd been moving slowly enough on their descent that their clipped pace was rapidly bringing them to the surface.

"Is Callie okay?" Nyla pressed, having remained quiet for as long as she possibly could. She maintained her pace, understanding that, whatever the reason, it was important for them to keep moving. "Why didn't she use the walkie?"

"Callie's fine," Aaron said, catching Emmett's gaze as he glanced back over his shoulder. "We should check in with her and let her know we're on our way back, though."

Emmett fished the walkie from where he'd stored it in his pants pocket, finding the comms button and preparing to press down. Before he could, static screeched from the speaker, disrupting the silence in crackled waves of unintelligible voices.

"What the fuck?" Emmett muttered, skidding to a stop.

"EMMETT! RUN!"

Callie's warning cut off in a garbled scream, interrupted by a chorus of male voices. Emmett stabbed the comms button, holding the speaker to his mouth as his steps grew faster.

"Callie? What's going on? Callie!"

"Move!" Aaron's palm appeared between Emmett's shoulder blades, shoving him hard toward the cave entrance. Emmett complied without thinking, panic surging in his blood. Something was wrong. Something was *very* wrong.

The sound of pounding footsteps drowned out the beating of his heart as Emmett let his body do what it wanted, falling into a sprint, danger be damned. Sam was ahead of him, having bolted as soon as he heard Amelia's voice among the screaming. Emmett overtook him, and then he lost track of who was where. All he could focus on was Callie's screaming, which they were now close enough to hear without the walkie. She was alternating between cursing and pleading, struggling against restraints of some kind. Amelia skipped pleading and went straight to threats, and he heard Sam swear under his breath somewhere behind him. Emmett felt rage boiling in his stomach— he had to get to them. *Now.*

The light of the afternoon sun brought no warmth, but at least it signalled their exit. Summoning the rest of his strength, Emmett burst from the cave, pausing only a second to take in the scene before him. Six men, Adrian Stamkos among them. Amelia, fighting against a man with a torn windbreaker, and Callie, being pinned to the grass by a beefy jerk with a fade. Emmett skidded to a stop just in time, nearly tripping over them as he grabbed the man by his jacket, ripping him free from Callie and throwing him into the nearest bystander, another guard with a bad attitude and douchebag sunglasses.

"What the *fuck*," Emmett spat, helping Callie to her feet. A sharp crack followed by a pained yelp and a heavy thud drew Emmett's attention to where Amelia had thrown her captor off with a well-placed elbow, darting toward the cave. He whirled to Stamkos— this was his doing, it must be— just as a deafening boom sounded through the air, and everything went still.

For one terrible second, Emmett thought it was the Chehwinoo. The sun was still out, but the trees were providing decent shadow. The creature *could* be lingering, waiting for one of them to venture too close to the dark. That fear was soon dispelled and replaced with a new, more bone-chilling realization as the boom gave way to a rumble, followed by a high-pitched whine as sound slowly became muffled, then clear again. The ground shook, and a shockwave passed through the earth and up Emmett's legs, destabilizing him. He stumbled, catching Callie as she too lost her balance.

The dynamite. They'd set off the dynamite. And they were going to do so when Emmett and the others were still inside. His rage would have to wait, though.

"Are you okay?" Emmett asked Callie, gently prying her hands away from her ears. She nodded mutely, wincing. Emmett let out a relieved sigh that was cut short by a scream that pierced his very soul.

He spun, searching for the others. They'd been right behind him! They couldn't still be—

No, thank God. He spotted Amelia first, on the ground but conscious, clutching her side. She was dirtied and bruised, much closer to the cave mouth than he and Callie were when the explosion happened, having ran for Sam the moment she freed herself. Sam was nearby, pushing himself up from the dirt, shaking his head to clear it. Emmett turned further, his gaze landing on Nyla as she struggled to stand, tripping and trying again, an anxiety to her movements that had him pausing. Was she hurt? Is that why she screamed? Where was—

Emmett's eyes widened in shock, horror dawning as he understood.

Where the fuck was Aaron?

The cave rumbled again, more debris falling loose as the earth settled. Nyla had managed to get to her feet and was running toward the cave, off-kilter from some unknown injury. Emmett took one step toward her before realizing he wouldn't make it in time.

"Sam!" he barked, running for Nyla anyway. Sam followed Emmett's shout, processing the situation with impressive speed for someone who'd just been thrown from an exploding mine shaft. He crouched and sprang, closing the distance between him and Nyla with smooth efficiency, tackling her to the ground with admirable precision indicative of his skill as a former football player. Nyla fought viciously, clawing at the dirt, kicking at Sam, begging him to let her go, but it was no use. Sam was bigger, stronger, and had a firm hold on her. Nyla wasn't dislodging him no matter how hard she tried. Once Emmett knew she was safe, he let himself listen.

Her screams, heart-wrenching, guttural, and raw, sent nausea roiling through him. Nyla's broken voice cried Aaron's name with such pain that Emmett felt it as his own. He'd never heard screams like that. He never wanted to again.

"No," Callie whispered, catching up to Emmett and grabbing his sleeve. "No, it's not... Aaron's not still... he can't be..."

But he was. Emmett knew, without a shadow of a doubt. Ever the protector, Aaron had pushed them all ahead of him, making sure they cleared the blast area in time. His first priority had been to get the rest of them to safety, placing his own on the back burner. He'd succeeded; they'd all made it out relatively unscathed.

Except for him.

"Call George," Callie demanded, pushing her shock aside and taking charge of the situation. "Get the fire department out here. We need to move the rubble, quickly. If there's any chance he's alive, he'll run out of air soon. We need to—"

"You *need* to explain what all of you are doing here," Stamkos interrupted, looking at them with potent disapproval on his face. "This area is dangerous. You shouldn't be poking around things you barely understand."

"You've gotta be fucking kidding me," Emmett snarled, taking an aggressive step toward Stamkos. "You almost killed us! You—"

Amelia's voice cut through the animosity, speaking urgently into her cell phone as she told whoever was on the other end that they needed fire and ambulance immediately, giving the coordinates to their location.

"I did nothing wrong," Stamkos insisted. "This mine was cleared for destruction weeks ago. Unforeseen delays put a hold on our work, but it's perfectly safe for us to blast out here."

"Bullshit! This isn't part of your contract!"

"By the time anyone gets around to checking, it will be." Stamkos permitted himself a small, pleasant smile that was drastically at odds with the situation. Emmett felt anger surging through his blood like fire, burning him, sizzling along the lengths of his limbs until he was vibrating with it.

"You."

The growl startled Emmett, and he turned in time to see Sam helping Nyla stand. Her face was tear-streaked and mud-stained, her skin pink and bruised. She was clearly the closest to the cave when it erupted, with blood and dust collecting on her clothes. Rage, pure and primal, darkened her normally bright eyes. Sam still had a hard grip on her, holding her back from running to the cave and putting herself in danger to get to Aaron. But when her attention shifted to Stamkos, Emmett could've sworn he saw Sam deliberately give her an opening, a chance to break free from him and launch herself at the man responsible for her pain.

And launch herself she did.

Nyla collided with Stamkos before his staff could intervene, her hurt and anger transforming her into a creature of unrestrained fury. She clawed at Stamkos' face, drawing long streaks of blood across his stubbled cheek, driving her elbow into his stomach, and forcing him to the ground. Stamkos yelled in pain and surprise, barely able to raise his arms in defense before Nyla was on him again, slamming his head into the ground and throwing wild, unending strikes at every inch of him that she could reach. The attack lasted less than a minute, with Stamkos' men snapping out of their shock long enough to pull Nyla away from him by her elbows, though not before her heel connected with his knee in a satisfying crack. Restraining her limbs did nothing to quiet her, though.

"YOU SON OF A BITCH!" Nyla screamed, spitting on the grass next to Stamkos' foot. "YOU *MOTHERFUCKER!* YOU KNEW WE WERE IN THERE! YOU KNEW!"

"I knew nothing." Stamkos struggled to his feet, wiping the blood from his face and neck. He was winded, his voice coming out strained. Emmett hadn't seen it, but it sounded like Nyla tried to choke him as well. "No one was permitted to enter that mine. It's not my responsibility if a trespasser was killed by his own reckless decisions."

Nyla threw herself at Stamkos again, an animalistic scream in her throat. His men were ready this time, tightening their grip on her. She thrashed in their hold, spitting a stream of curses and insults, some in English, and some in Spanish. Sam stepped in between her and Stamkos, clutching her shoulders gently, commanding the men to let her go. They did, but only once Nyla stopped resisting them. With her free, Sam guided Nyla further away from Stamkos, catching her gaze and whispering something to her. Emmett was too far to hear what it was, but it seemed to have the desired effect. Nyla's expression crumpled, the anger falling away to a broken kind of sorrow that made even Emmett want to cry.

"You *will* be held liable for this," Amelia snarled, taking over for Nyla in berating Stamkos. "You set off that charge *knowing* that people were inside. Permitted to be there or not, that's still murder."

"It's my word against yours," Stamkos said, shrugging. "You can certainly try your best, but I wouldn't expect anything to come of it."

"You're a pathetic bastard, Stamkos," Amelia hissed. Her rage was quieter than Nyla's, more restrained, more subtle. And yet Emmett had no doubt that she was just as capable of murdering Adrian Stamkos as Nyla was. "We're not letting you get away with this. You have no idea what you're dealing with."

"You *will* see the inside of a cell," Callie interjected, taking a stance next to Amelia, forming a human shield between him and Nyla and Sam. "I'll spend the rest of my career making myself the biggest pain in your ass I can."

"Good luck, Ms. Quinn," Stamkos droned, checking his watch. The sound of sirens interrupted the newfound silence, announcing the arrival of the fire department and Sheriff Mason. "Now, excuse me, I have a business to run. Tell George to call me when he needs a statement."

It gave Emmett a small sense of satisfaction to watch Stamkos limp away from them, the blow Nyla gave to his knee causing some damage. But when he was gone, all satisfaction fell away. Without Stamkos, nothing was distracting them from the reality they now faced. The mine was destroyed, their only lead gone in a cloud of dust and smoke. Worse than that ,and the truth that none of them were ready to accept, they'd lost one of their own. After everything they'd been through, their group took the one blow no one thought possible.

Aaron Klein was gone.

Chapter Thirty-Two

CALLIE

Callie watched numbly as the first responders arrived, led by George Mason. She watched as George strode directly up to Nyla, watched as Amelia explained the situation, and watched as the firefighters began to move with more urgency. She watched, because it was all she could do.

Emmett took control of the situation in Nyla's stead. She was broken, tears streaming endlessly down her cheeks as she stared, wide-eyed, at the rescue workers. Amelia remained by her side as Sam kept a firm hand on Nyla's shoulder, ready to catch her if she collapsed or tried to put herself in danger. Callie didn't know what else to do, so she stood silently, waiting to be directed.

She saw Emmett out of the corner of her eye, talking to George in a hushed tone. His expression was grave, but maybe that was just Emmett. He was always a bit gruff. Maybe the pale colour of his skin didn't mean anything.

As the rescue workers continued to assess the situation, another vehicle pealed down the clear-cut path. Emmett had briefly explained to her what it was and, initially, she'd been just as annoyed as he was at the blatant disregard for regulations, but she was happy for it now. If the path hadn't been cleared, how long would it take responders to reach them?

The vehicle screeched to a stop and, before the dust had settled, two people flew from the front seats. Callie recognized Tyler Pratt, looking gaunt and in disbelief. The other person looked vaguely familiar, but she couldn't quite place her until the woman found Nyla in the crowd and let out a choked sob. It was Clary Poulette.

Clary rushed to Nyla, gathering her in a smothering hug. Tyler headed to George and Emmett first, then to Nyla, crushing both her and Clary in his arms. Callie felt something shatter in her chest.

Hours. They waited in the clearing for hours while the firefighters called in help from Madison, slowly moving debris out of the way. No one would say what they were thinking, but Callie stubbornly refused to think of it as a bad thing. They *had* to find Aaron. He was alive, trapped in a pocket of rubble somewhere, waiting patiently for them to free him. He had to be.

By the time the sun started to sink behind the trees, they had a decision to make.

George told the seven of them to go home. There was nothing they could do to help at this point, and they'd already been standing around in the cold for the better part of the day. They were freezing, hungry, thirsty, and injured. The paramedics had seen to the worst of their injuries, but they needed rest. Emmett and Tyler argued with George that, with night approaching, they'd need help keeping the area safe. George dismissed him, insisting that he could handle any complications with the Chehwinoo, should it make an appearance. Callie didn't know if George had faced the creature before, but she was inclined to believe him. Expectedly, Nyla refused. She fought hard, arguing loudly enough to draw attention from the paramedics. In the end, it was Tyler who convinced her to return to the Willow.

After that, there was no reason for Callie to stay. Emmett told her to wait with Sam and Amelia while he left with Tyler to get his dad's truck, and then he brought them all to their respective homes. Tyler and Clary went with Nyla to the Willow, Sam and Amelia returned to Sam's cabin, and Callie followed Emmett to Lichen House. George told them to get some sleep, but Callie doubted she'd be able to.

Lichen House was far too quiet. Emmett didn't say anything as he unlocked the front door, letting them both inside. The stairs loomed before her, and everything in her body protested as she tried to take a step. Like going to bed would solidify the events of the day, like she could still go back and undo it all if she only stayed awake.

"Cal?"

Emmett's voice startled her into the realization that she was blocking the way forward. With a shuddering breath, she raised her foot and tried to lift herself up, but her muscles betrayed her. She was frozen, utterly incapable of forcing herself even one inch closer to her bedroom. A choked sob of frustration squeaked from her throat, and then she was surrounded by overwhelming warmth.

Callie stumbled backward into Emmett, his arms winding tightly around her torso, pinning her arms to her side and squeezing her, keeping her together as she fell apart. Callie's smothered cries turned into desperate, gasping breaths as she gripped Emmett's forearm, her nails digging into his skin. He didn't stop her, accepting more and more of her weight as her legs slowly gave out from under her. Callie's knees hit the floor with a dull thud, cushioned by Emmett bearing the brunt of their descent. She hunched forward over his arms, dropping her forehead and trying to focus, to breathe.

"It's going to be okay," Emmett murmured against her hair. He was still holding her, his torso blanketing hers like a shield against the reality they faced. Callie started to shake her head, her eyes shut, her ears pounding. "I've got you, Cal. We're going to get through this."

She was being ridiculous. Callie rebelled against the spectacle they made, curled up on the floor of a hollow building, crying into the concrete. She wanted to push Emmett away, to stand up, brush herself off, and apologize for overreacting. She wanted to be Callie Quinn, paralegal, lawyer, professional. But she couldn't.

Here, now, with Emmett's comforting embrace drowning out the buzz of responsibility and appearances, she wasn't Callie Quinn. She was just... Cal.

Emmett held her until she stopped shaking, stroking her hair with gentle murmurs of reassurance. When her spine began to ache and her knees felt numb, Callie finally pulled herself free of him. He didn't go far, helping her stand until she was steady on her feet and, even then, keeping his arm around her waist as they silently climbed the stairs to the second level of Lichen House. She knew Emmett was guiding her to her room, quietly making sure she was alright before he disappeared, the door to his own room shutting behind him with a click that made Callie jump.

Reality felt warped, like she wasn't truly present. Callie didn't remember sitting down on the bed, but suddenly her head was on the mattress and she was staring at the ceiling.

Aaron isn't dead. They're going to find him.

She grabbed hold of the thought and held on tight, pushing back the overwhelming grief that threatened to drown her. Callie couldn't let herself consider the possibility of Aaron being gone. If she did, she didn't think she'd have the strength to finish what they'd started.

Tears gathered in the corners of her eyes, dripping silently down her cheeks.

Chapter Thirty-Three

INTERLUDE

The Basin

As the sun fell behind the jagged mountain, the forest creaked to life.

There was a disturbance earlier, something loud and destructive and manmade that scattered the wildlife, hushing even the most rowdy residents. By nightfall, the tense silence gave way to sleepy relaxation as the Basin settled, content that the disturbance would not be repeated.

Winter wind whispered through the stiff branches of the evergreens, dying their needles a translucent shade of white, frost swallowing the lingering damp of autumn rains. A storm raged just on the other side of the mountain range, too far for the effects to reach the Basin. Still, a soft electricity sparked in the air, signalling a change.

The deep grey sky gave way to a navy-blue canvas of stars, blinking in endless sight, observing.

Underneath the protective canopy of a fallen oak, the Chehwinoo slept. Its skeletal body, lithe and deadly in its speed, had frozen to the snow-covered ground. Clear, deathly-cold ice crept over its joints, cementing it in place as it slumbered fitfully, its breathing erratic. Something poked and prodded at its awareness, something that wasn't there before. The Chehwinoo whined, a series of crackling protests erupting from its blackened skin as it forced its eyes open.

The Basin was the same, but the wind was different. The Chehwinoo scented the air, summoning its strength. The strange black bird still watched from its perch, its hard, unyielding skin reflecting the moonlight. Soon, it would fly off on its rotating wings, only to return with its shimmering red eye changed to green.

Vibrations crept through the dirt and snow, brushing the Chehwinoo's torso where it remained frozen to the ground. The vibrations told a story of pain and disruption, of unnatural intervention and unshackled chaos. The Chehwinoo's mouth widened, its tattered lips stretching into a morbid imitation of a grin. Soft, choking wheezes escaped its throat in an uneven tempo, like rusted metal gliding over sand. Its laughter rippled through the air, low and feral.

It was almost time.

CALLIE

Callie didn't remember falling asleep. She was tracing patterns in the unfinished ceiling, waiting for the tears to dry on her cheeks, and then she was startled away by a gentle knocking at her room door.

Summoning her strength, Callie stood. She knew who was on the other side—who else could it be? Sure enough, as Callie pulled the handle, Emmett's disheveled face swam into focus. He looked as tired as she felt, with his hair a mess, stubble coating his neck and chin, and a pair of dark red pajama pants slung low on his hips. It was the only piece of clothing he wore, Callie realized belatedly, and she had to stop herself from openly ogling his tattoo and piercing.

"It's late, Emmett," Callie whispered, too tired to worry about why he was here, if something else had gone wrong. Her arms and back still felt the ghost of his touch, and she almost wished he hadn't left her before. "What do you want?"

"You."

The short, simple answer shocked her so much that she was sure she had misheard.

"You... what?"

Emmett huffed an aggravated sigh, shoving his hand roughly through his damp hair. Had he showered? He must've. How long was she asleep?

"Look, I'm done tiptoeing around this shit," he growled. The sound sent shivers down Callie's spine. "I'm fucking attracted to you, Callie. And today has been literal hell. I'm pent up, I'm frustrated, I'm *pissed*, and I need a distraction. Desperately."

Emmett stepped into the doorway, into her space. Callie resisted the instinct to back away, instead letting him crowd her. His breathing was ragged, rattling through his chest at an uneven pace.

"I *need* you," he murmured, his attention falling to her lips. "I need you so bad it's making me insane. And I can't just stare at the ceiling all night, wondering if you're awake, if you're crying, if *you* need *me.* I can't make this all go away, but I can take your mind off it. If only for a while."

"Emmett—"

"Are you attracted to me?"

Callie reeled, blinking in time with her racing heart. Hell yes she was attracted to him! Did he really not know that?

"Wh— I—" she stammered, heat rising in her cheeks. It was one thing to *think* that Emmett was attractive, but to say it out loud? Emmett didn't let her flounder for long, his hand coming up to grip her chin and force her to look at him.

"Answer."

Fuck, that should not be as hot as it is. Callie's breath caught in her throat, staring up at Emmett with wide eyes. He watched her with an intensity that made her squirm, but she couldn't look away.

"...Yes, I'm attracted to you."

"Do you want to have sex with me?"

Did she?

The obvious answer was a loud and enthusiastic yes, but that was before their friend went missing. It felt wrong, in a sense, losing herself in Emmett when everything was so horribly messed up. What could she do about it, though? There was nothing to be done about the cave-in now. They needed to wait for the first responders to do their job. The Chehwinoo had to wait, too, until daylight when they could move about freely. Callie could either curl up in bed and utterly fail to get some rest, or...

"You can say no," he teased, a smirk pulling at the edge of his mouth. "I won't just up and vanish, not if you don't want me to. Cuddling *is* much less strenuous. Not as effective as a distraction, though."

Callie must be dreaming. There was no way this was happening. She had delved into full psychosis. Emmett wasn't actually here, he was in his room, and she was dreaming. Or delusional. Or—

"Answer me, Callie," Emmett whispered, his voice a low rasp that she felt in the pit of her stomach. "Do you want me?"

She wet her lips.

"I... yes."

Emmett's mouth twitched. He flinched forward like he was going to pull her into him for what would no doubt be a knee-weakening kiss. Callie placed her palm flat on his chest to stop him, which was a mistake. His skin was warm, pulled taut over impressive muscle. She swallowed. "Wait."

"Something wrong?" Emmett quirked an eyebrow at her in a look of confusion that was both irritating and endearing.

Yes. No. Callie wasn't sure anymore.

"You've been an asshole since I got here, and we're only just now starting to get along" she said, narrowing her eyes at him. "Don't think that if we do this, it means you have free rein to push me around again."

"Never," he swore, grasping her hand and bringing it to his mouth. He placed a soft kiss on the back of her knuckles, his stubble tickling her skin in the most fascinating way. "I trust you, Cal. I've been shit at showing it, but I do. I've got my issues, and I'm figuring them out. I won't put that burden on you."

"I didn't say that," she said. Callie frowned up at him, watching his mouth as it continued to explore her hand, providing an infuriatingly effective distraction. "You don't make my decisions for me, Emmett. If you're concerned about something, I need you to talk *to* me, not *at* me. We work it out together, got it?"

"Yes ma'am," he murmured, his lips ghosting over her palm. "Whatever you want. Whatever you need from me."

He meant it, as much as she didn't believe she'd ever hear such a commitment from him. Emmett watched her, waiting, as she worked through her feelings. Callie took control of her limbs again, pushing the hand he held into the thick of his hair, holding his head so that he couldn't look away from her. Her eyes sparkled in the low light.

"Prove it."

Emmett's eyebrows went up in surprise, questioning her with his silence. A smirk spread across Callie's face as she tugged gently on his hair, pulling him to within a few inches from her as she whispered to him.

"Beg."

Emmett froze, every muscle in his body tensing at once. He'd told her before that he was never one to beg, and in a moment of pure genius, Callie realized that was the test. The one thing he could do to prove to her that they weren't about to make a massive mistake. He seemed to realize it too, as his face transformed into an impressed smile, relenting to her demand with as much grace as he could muster. Emmett held her gaze firmly as he lowered himself to his knees, taking her hand from his hair and guiding it to—

Callie sucked in a sharp gasp as Emmett led her fingers to wrap around his own throat, her thumb pressed against the strong thrum of his pulse.

"Callie," he rasped, his already deep voice hoarse with undisguised want. Callie's stomach flipped wildly, *feeling* the words as they scratched their way out of his mouth. "I want you so fucking much. I've wanted you for *months.* Put me out of my damn misery, please. *Please.*"

Callie didn't know exactly what expression she wore, but it must've clearly shown Emmett the effect those words had on her. Before she'd fully recovered from the surge of heat roiling inside her, Emmett stood and shoved the door open fully, throwing her off balance. She stumbled into him, catching herself on his chest, and then she was in the air. Emmett hooked his hands around her thighs, hoisting her into his arms and pinning her against the wall.

His mouth was on hers before Callie's brain could catch up. She let out a surprised hum, linking her arms around his neck and crossing her ankles behind his back. Emmett grunted in approval, using his hips to keep her in place and freeing one of his hands to grip the side of her neck, his thumb resting beneath her jaw, tilting her head back and reclaiming the control he'd relinquished to her. Callie fought against the disbelief coursing through her.

She was kissing Emmett. She, Callie Maria Quinn, was *kissing. Emmett.*

None of her daydreams even came close to the real thing. She'd always thought he'd be a little shy in bed— in her experience, the more outgoing men tended to be gentler in sex, while the quiet ones took her by surprise. Emmett was single-handedly flipping that rule on its head. His quiet confidence and teasing arrogance gave way to a domineering control that Callie didn't dare push back against. She'd never been manhandled quite like this before, and it was thrilling.

"Do you have any idea how many times I've thought about this?" Emmett murmured into her ear, letting Callie catch her breath while he peppered the side of her neck with nips and licks. "How many times I had to stop myself from losing control?"

"Emmett..." Callie whined, twisting her fingers in his hair. It was too short to really get a good grip, but it was long enough for her to gently tug. Emmett groaned into her feverish skin, his hips jerking slightly in response to her touch. For one fleeting moment, Callie believed that she could forget the horrors of the day and lose herself in mindless pleasure.

Thump.

Callie shivered as Emmett's teeth grazed her pulse.

Thump. Thump.

"Do you hear that?" Callie asked absently, peeling her eyes open. Emmett grunted something that didn't sound like words. "Emmett?"

"Cal, I'll be honest, my attention is pretty firmly focused elsewhere."

"No, I'm serious." As intoxicating as this was, she *had* heard something. After the utter chaos they'd endured earlier in the day, she wasn't taking chances. Sensing her resolve, Emmett paused, turning his face away from her neck to listen. For a time, all Callie could make out was their labored breathing. As her gasps evened out, another sound made its presence known— a soft banging, inconsistent and echoing through the building.

"The front door?" Callie guessed. Emmett shook his head.

"The front door is steel," he whispered back. "It wouldn't make a sound like that. Whatever it is, it's coming from somewhere inside."

That simple knowledge sent a shot of ice through Callie's veins. She gestured for Emmett to let her down, which he did without protest. Fixing her shirt, Callie rounded the bed in search of her phone.

"Don't call Nyla," Emmett instructed, searching the room for his shirt before realizing he hadn't worn one. "She's been through enough today."

"I wasn't going to," Callie said. She flipped the phone around to show him her messaging app. "I'm texting Amelia."

Mollified, Emmett crept into the hall, listening while Callie waited for a response. It came quickly, in a series of short texts.

"The Chehwinoo isn't near here," Callie said, frowning. "Sam and Amelia are at the Willow with Nyla and Tyler. Tyler just got off the phone with George, and he's still with the search teams. They're making progress, but it's slow, especially now that the sun's down. By rights, no one should be here but us."

"I was afraid of that," Emmett muttered. He cursed under his breath, inching further into the hall. After a beat of silence, he gestured for her to follow him. "Come on, it might be something simple. A pipe or a loose tile."

Callie nodded, falling into step behind Emmett. Lichen House was never fully quiet; it was an old building with drafts and creaks as common as roaches. This sound was different than the regular settling noises of wood and concrete. The banging had a rhythm to it that wasn't quite perfect, faltering in uneven intervals. At some points, it seemed to drop off altogether before starting again, louder for a few bangs and then growing steadily weaker. Something moving with the wind?

They stalked silently through the building, checking each room in succession. Most were empty— even the drywall was absent more often than not. The sound got louder as they descended the main stairs and for one fleeting moment, Callie thought Emmett was wrong and that there *was* someone knocking on the door. Then they entered the kitchen, and it became clear that the banging was coming from somewhere lower still. Through the floor?

"Is there a basement?" Callie murmured, making Emmett jump at the abrupt disruption. He thought for a second before pointing his chin toward a lightly concealed door near the gas stove.

"There's a cellar at the back of the pantry," he said, having come to the same conclusion she did. "I didn't think there was anything down there except dirt."

"Well, there must be *something*," Callie insisted, striding to the pantry door. Emmett made a grunting sound that she took to mean displeasure before he overtook her, reaching for the handle before she could. "Does the plumbing run through it?"

"I doubt it." He reached into his pajama pants pocket, pulling out the master keys. "The plumbing was added later. The cellar would've been used as cold storage at the time."

Finding the right key, Emmett jiggled the lock and revealed the barren pantry. As soon as the door was opened, the banging became significantly louder. Callie followed him into the small space, her attention zeroing in on a wooden square nestled in the back corner of the room, covered in dust and debris. The banging sound, whatever was making it, was coming from the other side.

"An animal?" Callie asked quietly. At the sound of her voice, the banging picked up in speed and volume. Emmett cursed again, holding out his arm in front of her.

"Stand back," he instructed, palming the master key again. Callie searched for any telltale signs of danger— sudden cold, mysterious frost, crackling sounds— and found nothing. She didn't know if that made her feel better or worse.

Emmett crouched in front of the cellar door, gently wiping the dirt from the padlock. He held it up, angling the keyhole toward the light spilling in from the kitchen. After some trial and error, he found the correct key and carefully clicked open the lock. It was then that Callie realized the banging had stopped.

There was a breathless moment of silence during which neither of them moved, both listening intently for any signs of what had brought them down here in the first place. Just when Emmett began to reach for the handle on the hatch, another bang sounded, this one dislodging the door enough to produce a blast of cool air and dust from the newly-formed crack. Callie screamed in surprise, jumping backward into the kitchen. Emmett grabbed the lip of the door before it could slam closed, flipping it open and readying himself to grab whatever he found. In a rush of clarity, Callie saw the source of the sound, saw Emmett about to throttle it, and let the urgency to stop him take hold. She rushed at Emmett before he could reach into the cellar, grabbing his arm and yanking it back.

"Don't!" Callie snapped. "Look!"

Emmett looked like he was about to argue, to insist Callie back away from the cellar door, but he stopped as movement caught their attention. The dust settled, revealing the most welcome sight Callie had had in days.

"Holy shit," Emmett breathed.

There, huddled against a packed dirt wall, was Aaron. Caked in mud, blood, and dirt, scraped and bruised, exhausted to the point of barely conscious, and very much *alive*.

Chapter Thirty-Five

EMMETT

Jesus fucking Christ. What just happened?

"Careful," Callie chastised, helping Emmett lift Aaron out of the cellar as gently as they could. He groaned in protest, fighting to get his bearings. Emmett's mind was still stuck on the fact that he was alive in the first place. He didn't have the mental capacity yet to ask questions.

"Where are the others?" Aaron coughed, soil and soot staining his lips. "Nyla—"

"She's fine," Callie assured him quickly, rushing out to the kitchen to grab a paper towel. She wet the corner with a newly-opened water bottle, clearing some of the mud from Aaron's face. It was good that she was here; Emmett was proving to be utterly useless in his stunned state. "Everyone made it out of the cave alive."

"Thank fuck." Aaron's breath rattled in his chest. Emmett couldn't tell how injured he was, but the fact that he wasn't trying to stand up told him more than enough. Callie pulled out her phone.

"They're at the Willow," she said, more to herself than Aaron. "I'll call Nyla right now."

"Don't," Aaron wheezed. At her bewildered look, he clarified. "It's dark out, right?"

Emmett thought he was just confirming, but when Aaron didn't continue, he realized he genuinely didn't know. Wherever he'd been, he had no sense of how long he'd been gone.

"It's night," Emmett admitted in Callie's stead.

"It's too dangerous for her to rush over here," Aaron explained, closing his eyes on a pained expression. "As long as she's safe, this can wait until morning."

"Aaron, she thinks you're *dead*." Callie's voice sharpened in anger, but Aaron was already flickering out of consciousness again. Emmett caught her eye, shaking his head just enough for her to notice. Pressing her lips together, she pocketed her phone and helped Emmett carry Aaron into the foyer. At least there, they could lay him on a rug instead of the concrete floor.

"Call George," Emmett said, trying to keep his voice low. Aaron was wavering in and out of awareness, and Emmett didn't know what would be best. Let him sleep? Wake him up? Call an ambulance? "They're still searching the cave-in. They need to get somewhere safe now that we know Aaron's not buried under all that rock."

Callie nodded, slipping back into the kitchen to make the call. As she did, Aaron startled awake again.

"What happened?" Emmett prodded, taking the water bottle Callie abandoned and helping Aaron drink some of its contents. "How'd you end up in the cellar?"

"Long story." Aaron winced again, this time as a result of trying to sit himself up. Callie chose that moment to return, rushing to help him and pulling over the only piece of furniture in the room, a wooden lawn chair that had seen better days, for him to lean on. "Just... give me a chance to rest, and I'll explain everything. I don't think I'd be very coherent if I tried to tell you right now."

"We should take you to a hospital," Callie insisted. Emmett was thinking the same but hadn't gotten around to voicing it. Now that some of the initial shock of finding Aaron in Lichen House's cellar had worn off, his common sense was returning.

"Callie's right," Emmett said. "It's a damn miracle you're alive at all, who knows what kind of damage you've got going on under the surface?"

"I'm fine," Aaron rasped. When Callie and Emmett only stared at him, he amended, "I don't need to go to the hospital right now. I've survived this long; I can wait until morning."

"I'd feel better if we didn't," Callie pushed. Emmett didn't bother to argue. He knew Aaron well enough to understand that if the man didn't want to go to the hospital until morning, no force on Earth would succeed in making him. Sure, they could call an ambulance, but every first responder in the Somerton-Hatfield area was already searching for Aaron. After Callie's phone call to George, they'd be returning home. It would be a long time before someone came to transport Aaron to the emergency room and, at that point, they'd be better off doing it themselves.

Aaron took a steadying breath, letting his eyelids drift shut. He looked like hell, but Emmett wondered how much of that was simply the result of being covered in dirt. Aaron's movements were jerky and slow, like he was in pain, but he mostly seemed exhausted. He needed rest above all else.

"Do you remember what happened?" Callie asked, resigned to the fact that they wouldn't be calling an ambulance tonight. "After the explosion?"

"Most of it," Aaron mumbled softly. "My memory gets a little fuzzy after the blast."

The sound of screeching tires interrupted them, and Aaron's attention whipped to Callie.

"I told you not to call her."

"You would've wanted me to call if the situation was reversed."

Aaron looked like he wanted to argue, but before he could, the front door banged open revealing a disheveled and grief-stricken Nyla. She skidded to a halt, letting the door swing shut behind her as her gaze landed on Aaron, breathing hard and clutching his side as he struggled to hold himself up.

"...Suits?" Nyla whispered, her voice nearly inaudible in the relatively small room. Aaron caught his breath, staring disapprovingly up at her. Even confined to the ground, he managed to look stern and commanding.

"What the hell were you thinking, *mi cielo*?" Aaron scolded. "It's too dangerous; you should've stayed—"

Nyla was across the room in a blink, dropping to her knees beside Aaron and reaching out to touch his cheek, her fingers freezing before making contact as though she was afraid he'd vanish if she touched him.

"You're right," she said, tears collecting in her eyes and spilling over into thick trails down her cheeks. "I let my emotions get the better of me, and I didn't think, I just reacted."

With the weight of those words, Emmett didn't think Nyla was still talking about leaving the Willow.

"I was stupid and reckless, and you can yell at me all you want," she continued, choking on a laugh. "As a matter of fact, *never stop* yelling at me, Aaron. Never stop yelling at me ever again. Please—"

Nyla's plea died on a choked sob, and then Aaron was pulling her into his arms. He sucked in a harsh breath, the movement clearly hurting him, but he didn't stop nor did he let Nyla pull away. He buried his face in her hair, squeezing her as tightly as his exhausted body would allow.

"I'm so sorry, *mi vida*," Aaron whispered, his voice cracking as Nyla shook in his embrace. "I'm here. I'm okay. I've got you. I'll never leave you like that again, *mi amor*, I promise."

Callie and Emmett shared a look, distorted through the tears streaming down Callie's face. Emmett slipped his hand around hers and squeezed.

"You can have the room at the top of the stairs, on the left," Emmett told Aaron softly. "Do you need help getting there?"

"I can manage," Aaron assured him, smiling weakly. "I'm just going to gather my strength a bit down here first. We'll make our way up soon."

"Thank you," Nyla whispered, leaning back enough to give them a watery smile. "For this."

Emmett gave her a gentle smile, linking his hand with Callie's and pulling her toward the stairs. She fell into step beside him easily, and he was struck again by just how perfect it felt to have her near. Disorienting, emotional, and tumultuous, but perfect.

"Thanks for giving my room away, by the way." Callie elbowed Emmett as soon as they were out of earshot. "Where am I supposed to sleep?"

"With me." Emmett raised an eyebrow at her. She missed a step, catching herself on the rail as she stumbled. "Where else?"

"I— I thought that—"

"You thought that whole thing killed the mood?" Emmett chuckled. "Callie, I would crave you in the middle of an apocalypse. If you think I'm letting Klein stop me, you've seriously underestimated how horny I am for you."

Her skin flushed an adorable shade of pink, and Emmett suppressed a smirk. God, he loved making her squirm.

"Come on, Cal," Emmett whispered against her ear, "let me show you that my tongue can do more than just piss you off."

Chapter Thirty-Six

INTERLUDE

Aaron

Aaron had suffered more than one head injury in his life, but none that knocked him out as suddenly and as resolutely as the one he received in the aftermath of the dynamite blast.

He had no idea how long he'd been out. Aaron's memories stopped abruptly once the explosion went off. The last thing he could recall was the sound of tumbling dirt. Likewise, when his consciousness returned, the first thing he registered was a dull whining in his ears. Slowly, his mind fought to put the pieces together, sorting through the fog to find flashes of confusion, fear, and anger before finally settling on resolve. Aaron could breathe, albeit not well. He could move, though not much. He could hear the rocks shifting around him, smell the faint wisps of smoke and earth, and taste the dirt packed in his mouth. He was alive, and that would have to be enough.

Lessons from the FBI Academy flooded him, warning him off moving or trying to free himself. It was smarter to stay put, wait for rescue. He could have spinal damage, or a severe brain injury, and moving would just aggravate his already questionable condition. But Aaron was familiar with the basics of cave rescue, having spent a summer in college absolutely fixated on survival documentaries. It wasn't uncommon for the trapped individual to die before rescuers could reach them, either of asphyxiation, hypothermia, heart attack, or stroke. If he could get himself into a relatively safe position, he would be much more likely to survive until someone found him.

And so, Aaron made the, admittedly ill-advised, decision to move.

He started slow. His fingers twitched, igniting a series of pins and needles along his arms and shoulders. From that sensation, he was able to determine that he was lying face down with one arm above his head and the other folded behind his back. Broken? He flexed the muscles in his back and tried to wiggle his limbs. Pain rocketed through him, but it was dull and pulsing. Not broken, but one shoulder was dislocated.

Gritting his teeth, Aaron shifted his knee forward, trying to push himself onto all fours. Dirt and rocks shuffled around him, resisting his movements. Discouragement forced its way into the back of his throat, choking him with a sob, but Aaron fought back. If the dirt was moving, then that meant he was near a pocket. There was an open space *somewhere* nearby, and he was determined to find it. Collecting himself, he began to move again, testing the debris trapping him for even the smallest amount of give. His breathing was short, shallow, and rasping, sapping what little endurance he had left. Still, Aaron tried. He had to *try*—

With a desperate shove against the hard rock beneath him, Aaron emerged from the rubble.

His first unimpeded breath was a blessing, and he greedily filled his lungs without thinking. A sharp stab of pain erupted near his ribs, and the breath dissolved into a fit of coughs that had him clutching his stomach, tears streaming from his eyes. Aaron knew it was no small miracle that he was alive, yet his body was taking every opportunity to remind him. After the coughing settled, Aaron took more controlled breaths, letting his mind catch up to his reality while he pulled and shimmied himself out of his rock tomb. He was still in the cave, but he could move now, and that was a blessed relief. When he could think clearly again, a sliver of cold dread worked its way into his chest.

He was alive, but what of the others? What happened, after the blast went off? Did they make it? Aaron was confident he was the last of their group to make it to the exit, but does that mean that they did, in fact, make it to the exit? Aaron had no way of knowing how close he was to the outside world, he just knew that he was still underground. Nyla hadn't been all that far ahead of him, refusing to leave him behind. Was she...?

Aaron clamped down on that thought. He couldn't let it enter his mind. If it did, he wouldn't have the resolve to get himself out of this. Nyla was safe. She had to be.

Turning his head to the right, Aaron willed his eyes to pick up any shred of light. There shouldn't be any, he knew, not if he was completely sealed in. Yet, the longer he stared, the more he could see of his surroundings. It wasn't the equivalent of a flashlight or even the moon lighting the sky, but *something* was providing enough of a glow for him to form a loose picture of where he was trapped. The cave had indeed collapsed, with the old passage barely discernable from the debris. Still, if light was coming from somewhere, then there had to be a path. An exit. Something.

Time passed. Aaron didn't know how long. He drifted in and out of consciousness, gathering his strength and hoping that rescue would find him before he had to go in search of it. By the time he felt ready to move, he'd heard no signs of imminent rescue. Between periods of troubled sleep, he'd been staring at a pocket of nothingness that seemed to be the source of the glow. If freedom was anywhere, it would be there. Steeling himself against the pain he was sure to experience, Aaron shuffled onto his hands and knees, remembering too late that his left arm was still outside its socket. He faltered with a harsh gasp, cursing himself. Setting his jaw, Aaron used his right hand to shove his left arm back into place, biting back an injured yell as his joint settled. With that taken care of, and his breathing evening out, he began to crawl.

❧

Nyla listened to Aaron's story white-faced and tight-lipped, carefully cleaning the grime from his skin with a damp cloth. Aaron's voice grew steadily stronger the more he talked, alternating between taking sips of water and gingerly nibbling a saltine cracker. He didn't know if he could handle more than a few morsels of food, but he was starving.

"The hole in the dirt turned into the tunnel we were following," Aaron explained, wincing as Nyla dabbed at a streak of crusted blood on top of a bruise the size of his palm. "I couldn't remember the way exactly, but I remembered some of Callie's directions. I hugged the left side of the tunnel wall and just kept going until I reached a dead end."

"And that was the cellar?" Nyla prompted, brushing his hair out of his face and smoothing it back into place. He was sure he looked like death incarnate, but Nyla showed no signs of recoiling from him.

"That was the wall leading to the cellar," he corrected. Aaron shifted on the bed, trying to sit up. Nyla helped him, propping a pillow behind his back. He paused to catch his breath before continuing. "I could hear noise coming through the dirt. I took a chance and started chipping away at it with my hands. About 6 inches in, it started to give way. That was the cellar. When I saw the trap door, I just started banging hoping someone would hear. I had no idea I was in Lichen House."

"So, the tunnel connecting the mine and the Chehwinoo's lair is also connected to Lichen House..." Nyla frowned, her eyebrows pinching together. "What does that mean?"

"I have no idea," Aaron said honestly. He sighed, his body starting to relax under Nyla's careful attention. He was sore, he was tired, and he was in more pain than he cared to admit, but Aaron was finally calm. "But it's a start."

After he was finished explaining his side of things, Nyla told him what happened with the explosion and Callie's panicked warning. Anger, hot and vicious, swirled in his stomach like bile. Adrian Stamkos had put them all at risk without a second thought, all for the sake of his business. Aaron was no stranger to the drastic lengths people in power would go to secure their own fortune, but even he was unsettled by the blatant disregard for human life that Stamkos displayed.

Worse, Aaron wasn't the only one who didn't quite make it out unscathed. Nyla was closest to him when the blast went off, and it showed in the bruises colouring her arm and leg. She was scraped and dishevelled, although significantly less so than Aaron. It looked like she'd at least managed a shower, while he was reduced to a bedside sponge bath.

"Are you okay?" he whispered, cupping her cheek with his hand. Nyla scoffed something between a laugh and a sob, covering his hand with hers.

"I'm perfect," she assured him, squeezing his fingers. "I might get arrested for assault, but I think that's a worthy price to pay."

"Assault?" Aaron repeated, alarmed. Nyla laughed in earnest now.

"I may or may not have tried to kill Stamkos," she said with a shrug. "In my defense, Sam was supposed to hold me back."

"You *tried to kill him?*" Aaron blinked, struggling to process what he was hearing. An absurd image of Nyla with her hands wrapped around Stamkos' throat struck him. "How? With what?"

"My bare hands." Nyla was unapologetic, flickers of rage lighting her eyes as she remembered. Evidently, Aaron's imagination was closer to the truth than he'd expected. "I hope the bastard scars, too. Let him have a permanent reminder of the time he was almost throttled to death by a tiny, angry wilderness guide."

Aaron didn't want to laugh. He really, really didn't want to laugh. The pain in his ribs *screamed* at him not to laugh.

"At the very least, he's going to have a fucked-up face and knee for a while," Nyla said, a smug smile creeping onto her face. "And I think they make you get a bunch of shots if another person draws blood with their nails. Or is it just teeth? I should've bitten him."

Despite his best efforts, Aaron laughed.

"You're incredible," he said through chuckles, wincing with every inhale. Nyla laid her hand on his stomach, soothing him with gentle caresses. "And incredibly reckless."

"Callie said I was 'not in my right mind because of the trauma,' so I shouldn't get more than a slap on the wrist if he presses charges." Nyla placed the washcloth down on the nightstand, moving instead to help Aaron out of his ruined shirt. "I just won't mention that I've been waiting to do that for weeks."

"Probably not in your best interests," Aaron agreed, still smiling. With his tattered clothing removed and a borrowed pair of lounge pants covering his legs, Aaron stopped Nyla from picking up the cloth again. "Lie down with me."

She did, curling into his side and testing the weight of her head on his chest. Aaron braced himself for a burst of momentary pain and then tugged her abruptly into his arms, plastering her body as close to his as he could in his weakened state. Nyla gasped a protest, but Aaron ignored her, burying his nose in her hair and inhaling deeply.

They stayed like that for a few precious moments, Aaron letting the warmth of Nyla's body seep into his skin and imprint on his soul.

"Aaron?" Nyla's voice came out muffled against his skin. He hummed in response. "About what happened before... at Clary's..."

"Don't," Aaron insisted, squeezing his eyes shut as guilt pulsed in his throat. "I never should have sprung that on you."

"I overreacted," Nyla argued, her arms twitching like she wanted to hug him but was afraid of hurting him. "I should've let you explain your point of view."

"We don't have to talk about it right now," Aaron said, rubbing his palm gingerly over her spine. "We'll figure it out, together, alright?"

"I'd like that," Nyla said, her words wavering.

"I love you," he murmured against her forehead, closing his eyes and basking in the comfort of holding Nyla like this, her warmth soothing the ache in his chest where he'd hidden the possibility that she was dead. "I love you so fucking much, Nyla."

"I love you too," she wrapped her arms around him as tightly as she dared, and Aaron felt wetness staining his skin where her face was pressed against him. "If you *ever* scare me like that again—"

"I won't," Aaron interrupted her threat, hating the way her voice broke on the words. "Never again, *mi vida*. I swear."

"That's a new one," Nyla said, sniffling. She tilted her head back to look up at him, tears glistening on her flushed cheeks. Aaron wanted to wipe them away, but he couldn't bring himself to release her long enough. "You said it downstairs, too. What does it mean?"

"My life." Aaron kissed the pleased surprise from her face, his soothing gesture quickly turning feral, devouring her mouth with all the desperation and fear he'd put aside to survive. Nyla returned his kiss with passion of her own, always conscious of his injuries, stopping him when he tried to pull her on top of him. When they broke apart for breath, Aaron pressed his forehead to hers. "You are everything to me, Nyla Leanne Jameson."

"Then you'd better not leave me again, Aaron Too-Many-Middle-Names Klein."

He laughed again, full and unrestrained, ignoring the pain it caused. It didn't matter, not now, not to him. All that mattered was Nyla, here, safe, and his. Whatever happened with the Chehwinoo, with Stamkos, with the Basin, they would find a way to deal with it. Aaron would do whatever he had to, whatever it took to protect the pocket of happiness Nyla brought to his life. She was his world, and, now that they were together again, nothing was going to tear them apart.

Chapter Thirty-Seven

CALLIE

Heart pounding out an uncontrollable rhythm, Callie silently followed Emmett to his bedroom. With every step, she struggled to find words, her anxiety increasing the longer she struggled. Callie wasn't inexperienced, but she'd never been with a man like Emmett. He held himself with such quiet confidence that it was almost intimidating, nerves sneaking up on her until her breath caught in her throat. What should she do? Should she say something? Was she overthinking this? The answer to the last question at least was a confident yes, but Callie couldn't quite convince her brain to stop.

By the time the door closed behind her, Callie had worked herself into a fidgeting panic. She'd almost convinced herself to jump ship, but then Emmett's hands found her waist, spinning her to face him. He kissed her slowly, tenderly, but with a firm determination that had her wondering if he'd sensed her rising uncertainty. A little pang of affection echoed in her chest as she reached up to wrap her arms around his neck—

A sharp sting exploded across her behind, making Callie jump and yelp. Emmett broke the kiss to smirk down at her, his smile growing as realization dawned on her. He'd slapped her ass. Irritation sparked in her chest, and Emmett's entire expression settled into a lazy satisfaction, almost smug. He was *trying* to piss her off. He enjoyed it.

Callie felt a jolt in her stomach, surprise mixed with annoyance and... excitement?

Ah, hell, she thought, *I don't have time to examine* that *right now. At least the nerves are gone.*

Before Callie could chastise him, Emmett scooped her into his arms, hooking her legs around his hips. She sucked in a gasp, stabilizing herself with her hands on his shoulders as Emmett carried her to the bed, exploring her neck and chest with his mouth as he moved. Callie had forgotten about her state of dress until the rough heat of Emmett's palms grasped her bare thighs, his fingertips brushing the hem of her pajama shorts.

"Do you have a safe word?" Emmett asked, his voice scratching from his throat in a way that made shivers erupt along Callie's spine. A spike of alarm sent her stammering.

"Do I need one?" she squeaked. Emmett laughed, easing the tension that had begun to form.

"Not this time," he assured her, pressing a soft kiss to her lips as he laid her down on the bed, supporting his weight on his forearms and settling between her legs. "Later. We'll talk about it."

Callie didn't have time to wonder at the implications of that before he was kissing her again, slow and languid, peeling away her thoughts until all she could do was feel. The strangeness of the situation struck her absently, how the fire between them fluctuated so seamlessly between anger and desire. It was strange, yes, but also natural. As easy as breathing, as exciting as taking an unfamiliar leap.

Reality faded away slowly, falling back to the recesses of her awareness until all Callie could focus on was the feeling of Emmett's weight on her, the movement of his lips against hers, the subtle shifting of his leg between her thighs. Callie squirmed, demanding more from him, and he answered by pulling his knee away from her entirely. Callie made a noise of protest, and Emmett laughed.

"Can you not be a jerk for once in your life?" she muttered, hooking her leg over his hips and squeezing, encouraging him to give her the friction she craved. Emmett held firm, moving to place lingering kisses on the slope of her neck.

"I could, but it's more fun this way."

Callie scoffed, opening her mouth to argue, but her retort died on a gasp as Emmett's fingers slipped beneath the waistband of her shorts. She'd been too focused on what he was doing with his hips to take note of where his hands were.

"Better?" he teased.

"Screw you," Callie murmured, but there was no venom behind the words. Emmett laughed again, increasing the speed and pressure of his touch.

"Not yet, but we'll get there."

They fell into a rhythm of back-and-forth, give-and-take. Callie fought against the haze of pleasure clouding her better judgment to return Emmett's teasing, succeeding in drawing several sharp inhales and muttered curses from him before he inevitably took hold of the reins again. By the time she saw him reach for the drawstring on his pants, Callie was panting like she'd run a marathon. She shimmied out of her own clothes, preening at the look of pure appreciation that overtook Emmett's face as he took her in.

"Fuck me," he breathed, rubbing his palm over his chest absently. Callie smirked.

"I'm trying," she quipped. Emmett shook his head in amusement, reaching for the toiletry bag he'd dropped on the floor beside the bed. A condom was pinched between his fingers when he drew his arm back, and Callie waited anxiously as he slipped it on. She tried not to watch him; she sincerely doubted Emmett was self-conscious about his body, but who wants to be examined while they're wrestling a tight piece of rubber onto their sensitive bits? A flash of silver caught her attention before he was finished, and Callie suddenly forgot why she wasn't looking.

Pierced. Emmett had a dick piercing. How could she have forgotten that?

Covered only by the thin rubber of the condom, the piercing was on clear display. Two steel balls rested on opposite sides of the head, connected by a bar that ran through the middle. Callie blinked. In her mind, the piercing was somewhere less invasive, through a layer of skin somewhere perhaps, not directly through the most sensitive part of his dick. It must've been painful to heal. Was it still painful? Sudden hesitation burst in her stomach at the thought of hurting him.

"It doesn't hurt, Cal," Emmett assured her, sensing her rising concern. "I barely feel it most of the time. If anything, it's a little more sensitive than it was before, which isn't a bad thing. Trust me."

"I do," Callie answered easily, surprising even herself. "Trust you, I mean."

"Good. Took you long enough."

Outrage pushed aside her lust, and Callie inhaled to unleash a tirade reminding him *exactly why* it took her 'long enough' to trust him, but her words caught in her throat as Emmett pushed inside her in one steady thrust. She choked on her irritation, releasing a strangled sound of pleasure as unfamiliar sensations rocketed through her. *What the fuck?*

Emmett released a breathless laugh at her surprised moan, seating himself more comfortably inside her.

"Never had a pierced guy before, I take it?"

"Is that *just* your piercing?" Callie asked, shocked. In answer, Emmett rolled his hips, dragging his piercing against her in a way that made her legs quake and tore another moan from her throat. "Holy *shit*."

"That's just *one* of my piercings," he corrected. At her widened eyes, he chuckled again. "Don't worry, you'll feel the other one later. I don't want to tip you over the edge too soon. We're just getting started."

"You said you only had two!" Callie accused, shock colouring her expression.

"No, I said I had more than one. You assumed two."

Thinking back, Callie realized that he was right. Emmett had only ever emphasized that he had more than one piercing. Callie herself had made the jump to two. Her chin immediately fell to her chest as she looked for the other piercing, but Emmett's hand quickly grasped her chin, tilting her head back up to meet his heated gaze.

"Eyes on me, Cal."

She didn't even consider arguing. Emmett began to move, the deliberate drag of his metal piercing against her walls was almost too much, teetering on the line of overstimulating. Emmett must've known that, because his thrusts were deliberate, reading the expressions on Callie's face as he adjusted his speed. As much as he teased her, as happy as he was to push her buttons, Emmett clearly cared for her. Callie felt a swell of affection amidst the physical sensations coursing through her.

At one point, Callie was sure she heard the sound of footsteps on the stairs, signalling Aaron and Nyla making their way to her old bedroom, but the noise was quickly drowned out by her own muffled cries. Emmett groaned, his hips moving in erratic patterns, abandoning his careful, measured rhythm. Callie felt the beginnings of an orgasm creeping up on her, forcing all other thoughts from her mind. Emmett propped himself up on his elbows, shifting his body and hers until they were pressed tightly together, his pelvis grinding against hers. A shock of cold against her clit made her jolt, an inhuman sound tearing from her lips. Emmett swallowed her moans with his tongue, meeting her frantic movements with swift, shallow thrusts that repeatedly pushed his third piercing— what else could it be?— against her.

It wasn't long before Callie fell apart, her nails digging sharply into Emmett's shoulders, her face buried in the crook of his neck to muffle her screams. Emmett followed her soon after, suppressing his own satisfied grunts in the pillow beneath Callie's head.

They remained there, locked in place, until the sweat began to cool on Callie's skin. She squirmed, and Emmett took the hint, carefully extracting himself from their tangled embrace. Radiating wordless satisfaction, he disappeared into the bathroom and returned with a damp washcloth. He took his time cleaning the mess they'd made of her thighs, all but humming happily to himself.

"If I'd known this is all it took to shut you up, Coady, I would've suggested it ages ago."

Emmett snorted a laugh, continuing his task. Callie followed him to the bathroom this time, taking the opportunity to comb through the tangled nest of hair that had formed on the back of her head before getting ready for bed. When she was clean, redressed, and barely able to keep her eyes open, she flopped unceremoniously on the mattress next to where Emmett lounged, still naked. Curiosity took hold of her before sleep did, and Callie peeked at his third and final piercing: another set of two steel balls resting at the very center of his pelvis, just above his dick.

"You could've warned me," she pointed out, fighting back a smile. Emmett raised his eyebrow at her.

"And miss the look on your face when you found out? Not a chance."

They fell into a comfortable silence, their breathing measured, their bodies sated. Callie could almost fall asleep like this, but there was one thing she needed to clarify first.

"Not to be *that* person, but..." Emmett turned to look at her. "We are... together now, yeah?"

"Do you want to be?" he asked. Callie resisted the urge to roll her eyes.

"I shouldn't," she said. "You were a colossal dick this week."

"True, but my colossal dick makes up for it, right?"

Callie jabbed her palm into his shoulder, shoving him as he laughed.

"I want to be with you" he said sincerely, a hint of vulnerability shining through the mirth on his face.

"Exclusively?"

"Just you. If we're doing this, I'm committed."

He watched her as she considered, anxiety building the longer she stayed silent. Callie decided to put him out of his misery, smiling softly at him as he rolled onto his side to face her properly.

"Good," she whispered, "me too."

Emmett sagged into the bed like a weight had been lifted from his shoulders. He gathered her in his arms, pressing his face into her hair.

"Wait!" Callie giggled, flailing her free arm in the general direction of the ceiling. "The light!"

Emmett grunted, reaching over her to grab his discarded pants. Blindly, he flung them at the wall behind him. By some miracle, the throw was a direct hit, the fabric catching on the light switch and flipping it off in its descent to the floor. Callie's giggle erupted into full-belly laughter, both amused and impressed, as she settled into Emmett's arms, feeling like things were finally looking up.

Chapter Thirty-Eight

EMMETT

The next morning came earlier than Emmett would've liked. He was awoken by the front door of Lichen House rattling in its frame, percussive bangs echoing through the building. Callie was up in an instant, scrambling to cover herself with any piece of real clothing she could find and leaving Emmett to silently curse whoever had interrupted their first morning together.

Pulling on a pair of jeans and a t-shirt, Emmett made his way to the door while Callie scurried off to the bathroom to fix her hair. He shook his head, fighting to keep the smile from his face. With how loud they'd been, there was no way Aaron and Nyla didn't know what happened. Her mad dash to hide her dishevelment was a doomed effort, but he'd keep that knowledge to himself a little longer, let her have a moment of peace before the teasing began in earnest.

Voices sounded from the foyer, and by the time Emmett reached the front door, he already knew who was here and why.

"—you're going to pay for my therapy, and my medical bills from the heart attack you gave me, and every additional hair treatment I'll need now that I'm going completely grey—"

"You've been dying your hair for years, Pratt. I'm not footing that bill."

Emmett cleared the final stair to see Nyla, Aaron, and Tyler in the midst of a heated conversation. Aaron looked much better after a few hours' rest and some attention from Nyla, but he was clearly still struggling. He'd seated himself on the same chair from the night before, and Emmett could see how his chest stuttered with the effort of breathing normally. Nyla was right beside him, hovering but trying her best to be discreet about it. Tyler, on the other hand, was pacing the room, hair wild, face gaunt, and dark circles beneath his eyes.

"Do you have any idea how many years you've shaved off my life?" Tyler demanded, pausing mid-step to jab his finger in Aaron's direction. "Can you sue for that? I swear to God, Klein, I'll throw the book at you. I'll— I'll—"

"I love you too," Aaron said, interrupting his tirade. Tyler's jaw snapped shut. "I'm sorry I scared you."

"You're damn right you're sorry!" Tyler huffed, shoving his hand through his hair for what must've been the dozenth time. He took several breaths, squeezing his eyes shut to calm himself. "Do you know how hard it was not to march over here last night? Nyla was the only reason I didn't. I figured if anyone deserved to strangle you more than I did, it was her."

"That was very considerate of you," Nyla said, amused. "Now, can we please get Suits to the hospital? I'll feel better once he gets the all-clear from a professional."

"I'm fine, Nyla."

She eyed him skeptically.

"Professional." Nyla emphasized the word until it sank in that Aaron wasn't getting out of this. She turned to Tyler. "Can you drive us?"

"I'm not letting him out of my sight for the next year," Tyler agreed quickly, pulling his keys from his pockets. "Sam and Am are on their way here. Do you have anywhere to be, or can you wait for them?"

The question was directed at Emmett, who shook his head.

"We can wait. I was just going for a coffee run, but I'm not in a rush. I don't think Cal has any plans this morning either."

"Where is Callie?" Nyla asked, injecting a deliberately false innocence into her tone. "I heard a bit of a commotion last night. You two finally lose it and try to strangle each other?"

"No strangling," Emmett said, smirking. "Only some light choking."

Tyler sputtered a laugh, just as Callie finally bounded down the stairs. She skidded to a stop so abruptly she almost tipped forward face-first onto the floor.

"Wh— excuse me?" she stammered, her face pale. "What the hell, Emmett?"

"Don't blame him," Nyla said, jumping to his defense before Callie could summon her indignation. "It's not like he's telling us anything we didn't hear for ourselves."

Emmett watched in amusement as the realization dawned on Callie's face. Lichen House was unfinished *and* unfurnished, meaning sound traveled readily throughout the building. The exterior stone walls provided insulation from outside noise, but the interior wood walls did next to nothing. Worse, the absence of furniture meant that the entire building had a prominent echo.

Aaron and Nyla heard every single second of their nightly activities.

"Oh my God," Callie whispered in horror, red creeping up her neck and spreading to the tips of her ears. Emmett couldn't suppress his chuckle, earning him an impressive glare.

"You have no idea how many times I stopped her from screaming at you to tell her what kind of piercing he has," Aaron told Callie, squeezing Nyla's shoulder. She smirked back at Callie unapologetically. "You're welcome."

"Ampallang and pelvic," Emmett answered easily, enjoying Callie's discomfort far more than he should. "And no, I won't show you."

"Ew, I was *not* going to ask," Nyla said, scrunching her nose at him. Mischief flashed in her eyes before she glanced sidelong at Aaron. "I was going to ask if you'd show *him*. For inspiration."

Aaron raised an eyebrow at her.

"Happily," Emmett said teasingly. "Any chance to knock you down a few pegs, FBI Man."

"As much as I'd love to shatter that ill-placed confidence," Aaron droned, "I have no interest in seeing your dick, Coady."

"Your loss," Emmett said, shrugging.

"And I'm not piercing mine, *mi vida*," Aaron told Nyla, rolling his eyes. She pouted, batting her eyelashes at him. Aaron laughed. "Alright, how about this: I've got something on my nightstand at home that's far more... 'effective' than a piercing. If you still want me to get one after *that*, I'll consider it."

Nyla's expression lifted in curiosity.

"Deal," she said cheerily. Emmett caught Aaron's eye, furrowing his brows in a silent question. Aaron didn't answer, flashing a small smirk before changing the topic.

"No kinky sex until you have a clean bill of health," Tyler scolded, slipping his arm underneath Aaron's to help him up. Aaron muttered something under his breath but accepted the help, pushing away from Tyler when he'd found his balance. "Nyla, are you good to help him to the car? I'll drive it up to the door."

"I've got him," Nyla promised, wrapping her arms around Aaron's waist. He didn't grumble this time, a soft smile tugging at the corner of his lips. "Wish us luck!"

Emmett held the door while Nyla walked Aaron to the waiting vehicle. He wasn't perfectly steady on his feet, but Emmett had no doubt he could've walked to the car on his own. Still, Aaron kept Nyla close to him.

"Well, that was mortifying." Callie collapsed onto the floor, lying flat on her back and staring at the ceiling. "I'm just going to lie here and hope the ground swallows me so I don't *ever* have to face those guys again."

"I hate to break it to you, but Sam and Amelia are on their way. You don't have long to wallow."

"Kill me."

Emmett laughed, poking her leg with the toe of his shoe.

"You worry too much." He smiled down at her, catching her eye with a playful wink. "If it makes you feel any better, we'll have the place all to ourselves tonight."

Callie glared at him, but the pink flush of her cheeks betrayed her interest.

Sam and Amelia arrived not long after that, only mildly surprised to find Callie splayed on the foyer floor. After a rushed debriefing on what had happened with Aaron the night before, Emmett and Callie left to grab coffee, breakfast, and enjoy a small respite from the onslaught of teasing that was sure to begin as soon as Nyla let the cat out of the bag to Sam and Am.

"Do you think the food will act as a buffer?" Callie asked hopefully. The look on her face said she already knew the outcome. "You know, 'please go easy on me, here's a bagel.'"

While they were in the drive-thru line, a new message pinged in the group chat, still named 'Bite Me.' It was a text from Amelia, which included only three skull emojis in the message. Emmett didn't need to ask to figure out they'd been talking to Nyla, further confirmed by the shrugging emoji Nyla sent in the same group chat. Their phones had been silent ever since, but Emmett had no doubt they weren't being let off the hook that easily.

"I think that's stretching beyond wishful thinking and into delusional territory," Emmett said, laughing. They were back at Lichen House now, food and drinks in tow. He could see Sam's rental parked near the door, but no sign of Aaron's X5. Even less distractions to keep Sam busy and off of their backs. Callie hung her head with a resigned sigh, stepping onto the gravel walkway leading from the parking lot to the front door. As she did, her heel slipped out from under her. Emmett reacted quickly, grabbing her elbow to keep her upright without dropping the tray of coffees balanced in his other hand.

"Christ," Callie muttered, getting her balance back. "Sorry, I don't know what I slipped on—"

Her voice died the moment she looked down at the ground, blinking in uncomprehending surprise. Emmett followed her gaze to the patch of crystal-clear ice shimmering beneath her shoe. The patch of ice that hadn't been there a moment ago. The patch of ice stretching toward them like jagged fingers from the shadow of the trees.

"Callie." Emmett tightened his grip on her elbow, getting ready to pull her behind him or push her toward the door, whichever was safest. The forest around them had gone deathly quiet, not so much as a whisper of wind disturbing the air. "When I tell you to, you *run*."

"It's daytime," Callie deadpanned, staring at the tree line. The evergreens closest to them shifted, too deliberate to be natural. "It's daytime, and the drone—"

Faster than either of them could react, the trees buckled with a resounding crack, toppling to the ground. Emmett yanked Callie back as twigs and pine needles scattered from the impact, the crash echoing through the Basin. Callie screamed, and Emmett watched in confused horror as the Chehwinoo materialized between the shattered trunks, slinking through the underbrush. It clung to the shadows, avoiding the sunlight, creeping toward Lichen House and the wall of artificial darkness it cast.

"The door!" Emmett braced himself to sprint, but Callie stopped him.

"It'll get there before we do!" She was right, and Emmett cursed his blind instinct. "The car!"

They pivoted, but the Chehwinoo chose that moment to leap. It lunged from the woods, its skin hissing and spitting steam where the sunlight touched it. Callie fell back against Emmett as the creature landed with a symphony of shrieks, blocking their path to the parking lot even as it dissolved before their very eyes.

"What the fuck is it doing?" Emmett asked no one in particular, his legs instinctively taking him toward Lichen House. Callie kept pace with him, the bags of food and tray of coffee long since splattered across the dirt. "It's almost like—"

The Chehwinoo leapt again, landing with an earth-shaking thud directly between them and the front door. It scuttled backward, sheathing itself in the building's shadow, its skin knitting back together the longer it remained in the dark.

"It's herding us." Callie's words stuck him like a thorn in his chest. It was impossible... the Chehwinoo didn't have that level of intelligence. At least, it never did *before*.

"We need to—"

"*DUCK!*"

The command was followed by a series of staccato gunfire, peppering the Chehwinoo from behind. It screamed in rage, recoiling like a spider splashed with insecticide. Emmett and Callie dove to the ground until it was quiet again, only the angered wailing of the Chehwinoo disturbing the silence.

"Son of a bitch," Amelia cursed, shouldering Ephraim's rifle for another shot. "Is this asshole a kamikaze now or something?"

"It'll be dying alone," Sam said cheerfully, slipping out from behind Amelia. He had Aaron's handgun, aiming it at the Chehwinoo as he side-stepped to where Emmett and Callie were huddled in the dirt. "When we said we wanted something to wake us up, I was thinking caffeine."

"I'll take that under advisement," Emmett panted, helping Callie up while Sam provided cover. Amelia had reloaded and was aiming for the Chehwinoo's chest, but just as she released the trigger, the creature dove left. The bullet shattered its shoulder, leaving its heart intact.

"Did that look... deliberate?" Sam asked. Emmett and Callie remained quiet. "Shit, alright. Sure. Why not?"

"Get in here!" Amelia yelled, lining up another shot. Sam took a couple himself, his aim far worse than hers. One bullet veered off the side of Lichen House, the other embedded into the Chehwinoo's leg. "Ideally, *before* Sam shoots a hole in something he shouldn't!"

"I am much more adept at filling holes than making them," Sam said unapologetically, following Emmett and Callie as they made their way to Amelia. She ushered them inside, holding the creature in the rifle sight until they were clear. When everyone was safely indoors, she slammed the door shut and bolted it. Even through the walls, they could hear the creature's angered screeching.

Then, the door shook.

All four of them stopped, staring. Frost began to form first on the handle, then the frame. Amelia's lips parted in shock, Sam blinked in stunned silence, and Callie took a step back. Emmett remained rooted to the spot, waiting, refusing to breathe—

With a crash, the front door of Lichen House crumpled to the floor.

"Fuck!" Amelia was the first to move, shooting at the blackened, skeletal arm that reached through the now-open doorway. Her bullet went through the Chehwinoo's palm, splashing slush and shards of ice in an arcing pattern across the floor. Sam grabbed her hand and pulled her along as they all broke into a run, looking to Emmett for guidance. He knew Lichen House didn't have a back door, but some of the windows were big enough to escape from. The problem was that most were on the top floor, and all were bolted shut. He mentally calculated the farthest point from the front door they could reach, veering everyone into the kitchen.

Behind them, the screams grew quieter. He could hear the Chehwinoo's nails scraping the stone floor, scrambling for purchase, but the noise came no closer. Pausing, Emmett looked back. While the creature had been able to knock the door down, it didn't seem to be able to cross the threshold. At least *that* rule held true.

Still, he wasn't taking chances. With Sam's help, he shifted the new shelving unit in front of the door, blocking the Chehwinoo's path to them.

They waited, trapped in a weighted silence, until an ear-splitting shriek tore through the air and, shortly afterward, the temperature in the room began to rise again. For all its bluster, the Chehwinoo didn't, or *couldn't*, follow them inside. With a shaking breath, Emmett slumped against the wall.

"That was new," Amelia spat, glaring daggers at the ground like it had personally offended her. "I don't like 'new.' New is bad."

"In this case, I'm inclined to agree," Emmett muttered. He caught Callie's eye, and she shuffled closer to him. "It was doing that on purpose, right? Calculating the risk versus benefit of sun exposure, defending itself from being shot in the chest? That was all... intelligence, right?"

"It seems like it," Amelia said, a troubled waver in her voice. "Intelligence that it didn't have before."

"How did it get here without us noticing? Did something happen to the drone?" Callie asked Amelia, her arms wrapped around her middle in self-comfort. Emmett laid his hand on the small of Callie's back, wanting to pull her into a full embrace but unsure if she'd welcome it. Their relationship was so new, even with supernatural death monsters running around, Emmett felt the unbearable weight of measuring his every move carefully. "Did the battery die?"

"No," Amelia answered, staring hard at her phone screen. Her brow was furrowed in frustration, tapping away at something. "I've been checking it every half hour, and I have a monitoring program set up that alerts me to any major movements. According to our heat map, it's still in the same spot."

"So, this is a second one?" Emmett didn't even want to consider the possibility, but once the thought entered his mind, he needed to voice it. Amelia slowly shook her head, still staring at her phone.

"No, that doesn't make sense with anything we've learned so far," she said.

"Neither does it busting down the door," Emmett argued, "but it did that just fine."

"It didn't come inside though," Amelia reminded him. "It's... bending the rules, not fully breaking them."

"If it's not a second creature, then how is it in two places at once? How did it move without triggering the drone?" Callie wondered aloud. Amelia was silent for a few seconds, and then her face paled.

"No fucking way... that's— no. It can't have..."

"What?" Sam prompted. Amelia met his gaze, her eyes wide with shock and a touch of fear.

"I think... I think it did this on purpose. It found a way around the drone."

"How?" Callie demanded, coming over to look at Amelia's phone screen. She held up the device so they could all look.

"There's a cold front moving in from the North," Amelia explained. "I've been watching it for a few days now. It's bringing temperatures that are similar to the Chehwinoo, so I wanted to make sure I had tabs on it. I thought it was just going to skirt the edges of Somerton, but... look."

She pointed to an area of the heat map that was dotted with dark blues and blacks, forming a slight curve. It dragged from the town border to roughly a mile from the Chehwinoo's last known location, and then it veered off on a diagonal. Almost like the creature had waited until the weather system got close enough for it to move through, blending into the naturally cold temperatures of the Basin in winter.

Almost like it was trying to throw them off its trail. And worse, it worked.

"You're telling me it *planned* this?" Emmett gaped at the two women, struggling to comprehend what he was hearing. "It figured out we were tracking it somehow and it *adapted*? Waited until the weather was cold enough to mask its movements and snuck up on us during the day, when we wouldn't be ready for it?"

"It looks that way."

"It's getting stronger," Sam murmured, furrowing his brow in thought. "Something must've changed, right? It didn't do this randomly, did it?"

"I don't think so," Amelia agreed. "It'd be too convenient. Something definitely changed, I'm just not sure what."

They were quiet, thinking, for several minutes. Then Callie gasped.

"The explosion!"

Emmett blinked, realization dawning.

"That must be it," Callie continued, determined. "When the dynamite went off, it triggered some sort of shift. I don't know what, exactly, but it makes sense. We theorized that the Chehwinoo was tied to the mines somehow. Then there's a cave-in, and the next day, the creature has inexplicable intelligence? No way that's a coincidence."

"You're right," Amelia said, tapping on her phone screen. "It can't be a coincidence. I'm updating Nyla; she and Aaron are coming back from the hospital. He's pretty battered, but nothing life-threatening. Ty went back to the station to bring George up to speed. We need to come up with a plan, and we need to do it *now*, before things get worse."

Chapter Thirty-Nine

CALLIE

"Okay, a lot of what I'm about to tell you isn't publicly available, for good reason."

Clary's voice was strong, despite the trepidation on her face. Not long after Amelia texted Nyla about their encounter with the Chehwinoo, Lichen House was overrun with people. The sudden changes in the creature's behaviour worried them all, and it felt like there was a noose tightening around their necks. Before, they had time. They could figure out their next steps, plan, calculate. Now, they were facing a ticking clock.

Callie supposed they were *always* facing a ticking clock, but now the droning metronome was too loud to ignore.

Nyla, Aaron, and Tyler arrived first, followed by Sheriff Mason, and Clary. It took Sam and Emmett a few minutes to remove the barricade they'd placed in the kitchen, the absence of adrenaline proving that the shelving was much heavier than they originally thought. Once the way was clear, Tyler and George joined them in erecting a temporary front door. By that time, there was a buzzing electricity in the room. The fact that Clary was present indicated that this meeting would be different from their previous ones. Anticipation tickled the back of Callie's neck.

Nyla gave Clary the floor, and the group fell silent as she spoke.

"I had a Zoom meeting with the Onakwe band council in Madison yesterday afternoon. It took some persuading, but I was able to get access to highly se-cretive information that can help us. But there are ground rules." Clary shifted uncomfortably, and Nyla reached over to take her hand. Callie couldn't imagine how difficult it must be, divulging sensitive cultural information to people who weren't entitled to it, even when considering the dire circumstances. "If I don't elaborate on something, please don't press. Ideally, I wouldn't be telling you *any* of this, but the band council has given me permission due to the circumstances. They just ask that you not spread the information outside of this group."

"You have our word," Aaron promised, eyeing everyone in turn. Callie nodded emphatically and, once everyone had expressed their willing agreement, Clary visibly relaxed.

"Thank you. Now, let's start at the beginning." Clary pulled out her phone, presumably where she'd taken notes. "As you all suspected, this is not the first time the Chehwinoo has caused trouble in Somerton. The Chehwinoo spirit is as old as the Basin itself, and it made itself known to the very first tribe in the area. When the Onakwe people settled here, long before Wisconsin was colonized, the spirit warred against the local people. It's one of the very rare volatile nature spirits— most are passive, even benevolent. This one is made of anger. It wanted the Onakwe people to leave this land, but that wasn't possible at the time. When the spirit started killing the townspeople, possessing the locals and using their physical bodies as a tether to our realm, the elders decided to act."

Clary took a deep breath, scanning her phone and considering her next words carefully.

"I need to skip over the specifics, but they used some of their cleansing and binding rituals to contain the spirit inside the Basin. The process is complicated, and it requires some kind of natural element that is resilient enough to contain the spirit's power *and* endure the inherent challenges of thriving in the wild. The elders decided to use an element that was abundant in the Basin, one they'd come across many times in their hunting trips."

"Topaz," Nyla murmured, her eyebrows bunching together. Clary nodded in confirmation. "It *is* bound to the mine."

Callie thought back to the pieces of artifacts found in the tunnels. The eerie glow of the Chehwinoo's unnatural eyes.

"The Chehwinoo spirit has been bound to the natural veins of topaz running through the Basin for hundreds of years," Clary corrected. "It's broken out several times, as you already figured out from your research, but it's never been fully *free*. Even now, the Chehwinoo is limited to using only a fraction of its power."

"You mean to tell me this thing has a higher body count than some of the most prolific serial killers in the world and it's *not even at full strength*?" Amelia gaped, blinking rapidly. "Jesus Christ."

"We need to stop it before it frees itself," Aaron agreed, staring at the floor in deep concentration. "If it *can* free itself. Clary?"

"I'm not sure," she said honestly. "The council explained the details of the Chehwinoo's confinement, but not if it was able to break free without outside help. I would assume the topaz itself would need to be compromised somehow. That's how the spirit was able to start possessing people before."

"The damage caused by the factory build released it, just like we thought," Callie said. "And we can assume that past town construction disturbed a portion of the topaz veins, temporarily releasing the Chehwinoo. That's probably why references to the mine were destroyed, too. To discourage people from trying to reopen it."

"It also explains how it started *thinking* in a matter of hours," Aaron said, humming in thought. "The dynamite must've damaged more of the mineral vein, just like Callie said."

"That's exactly right." Clary smiled tightly. "Stamkos' nightmare factory project set things in motion this time around, but any damage to the topaz deposit will strengthen the Chehwinoo."

"So, wait," Sam interjected. "If the Chehwinoo has broken out before, how did it get trapped again? Did someone bind it every time?"

"No," Clary said, tapping her phone screen. "The binding ritual has only been done once. Every other time, one of a few things must've happened. Either the locals determined that something they did unleashed the creature, and they reversed it—"

"Like covering up the topaz they'd unintentionally exposed," Nyla added.

"Or the area was abandoned for a time, and the Chehwinoo had no choice but to go dormant until people returned. The spirit is tied to the topaz, so it can't venture outside of the veins' limits. I suspect that's why it hasn't come directly into town, the topaz probably stops before crossing town lines."

"In theory, then, we could locate the point where S&S disturbed the topaz vein, cover it up, and the Chehwinoo is back to being trapped in the Basin, right?"

Emmett suggested, his arm hooked over Callie's shoulder. She did her best to ignore the searing heat where their skin connected, but it was difficult. Every time Emmett spoke, she felt the soft vibration of his voice through their contact. The man was infuriatingly distracting, and Callie was convinced that he was doing it on purpose.

"Sure, but there's a problem with that," Tyler said, frowning. "The original damage is *already* covered. The Hovel was filled in shortly after it was discovered, likely by Stamkos' crew. Does that mean covering it won't work this time?"

They were quiet for a moment, considering the implications. Suddenly, Nyla jolted upright.

"Diamond," she whispered in shocked awe. "Guys. That's it! That's why there was such a huge gap between Carver and Diamond! They filled in the Hovel and trapped the Chehwinoo again, but—"

"But then Diamond started blasting and opened up a *new* vein, one that obviously wasn't fixed when the second bout of dynamite went off." Aaron finished for her, his expression darkening. "Damnit."

"Covering it up again is only a band-aid fix anyway," Tyler dismissed. "Stamkos isn't going to ditch his precious factory easily; he's made that abundantly clear. Even if we manage to undo the current damage, who's to say they won't unearth *more* topaz in the process? The more they disturb, the stronger it'll get. If it breaks completely free, then we'll have a bloodbath on our hands." He paused, reconsidering his words. "Well, a *bigger* bloodbath."

"We need something more permanent than just burying it and hoping for the best," Nyla agreed. "It's a miracle that it's only been unearthed a handful of times as it is."

"Actually..." Clary began, looking uneasy. "Less 'miracle' and more 'strategic.' While I was talking to the band council, I started to wonder the same thing. How hasn't the creature been let loose more often? As it turns out, that's by design. The full story of the Chehwinoo is known only to the Onakwe people, but there has been one consistent exception made. Every time Somerton elects a new mayor, a representative from the Madison band council meets with them and warns them about the Chehwinoo. Some listen, some don't. That's why the appearances are so sporadic."

"You're telling me that James Carver *knew* about the Chehwinoo when he signed that contract with Stamkos & Stein?" Nyla demanded, anger flaring in her eyes. "And he did it anyway?"

It was hard to imagine, but Callie had no doubt that Clary's information was good. They'd considered the fact that Carver knew about the mine and that was why he'd pushed back against Stamkos, but what if that wasn't all? If Carver knew about the Chehwinoo, then his reluctance made more sense. It also made his failure to stand strong that much more damning.

"To be fair, the contract Carver signed was for a slightly different blueprint that didn't cross into Chehwinoo territory," Amelia gently reminded her. Nyla still looked angry, but her shoulders sank. "Likely, Stamkos wanted more land and didn't see any good reason why he couldn't have it. Maybe he thought Carver was just being stingy, or maybe he was tired of negotiations and decided to ask for forgiveness instead of permission. I wouldn't put either option past him."

Pushback. Territory. Negotiations...

A thought struck Callie, but it wasn't fully formed. Something they'd forgotten? Or something they didn't yet understand? The epiphany writhed just outside the edge of her consciousness until she retraced her steps, familiarity bursting to life when she got to the contentious contract negotiations between Stamkos and Carver. The coincidence of the mine tunnels burrowing under Lichen House. The only reason Aaron was standing next to them now, alive and mostly in tact.

The struggles she'd had securing permits for Tara and Ed.

"Oh my God," Callie breathed, her voice so fragile that Emmett jolted and grabbed her shoulder, like she was about to pass out and he intended to catch her. "Lichen House is part of the mine, isn't it?"

She phrased it as a question, but Callie knew deep in her gut that she was right. Historical buildings were always a nightmare to navigate when it came to renovations, but the delays she faced with Lichen House went above and beyond standard roadblocks. None of them had had time to consider the extent of the implications of Aaron finding his escape through Lichen House's cellar, but it had been lingering in the back of Callie's mind. They were too relieved at Aaron being alive to question how he managed to get from the mine to the cellar, but now...

One look at Clary's grimace told Callie that she'd hit the nail on the head.

"Yeah, that was something else the council mentioned," she said apologetically. "Lichen House was originally built as lodging for the miners. After the decision was made to destroy all records of the mine, they couldn't really maintain that it was living quarters for miners that, officially, had no business being in the area. The band council and the mayor agreed to just let the building rot, but when the Gallagher's started looking into renovating the property, they revisited the original maps. One of the back-up entrances ran right underneath Lichen House."

Callie felt the knowledge swirl and settle in her stomach, warring with the disappointment, anger, and futility she'd been battling since the start of this nightmare contract. She'd already given up on Lichen House and Orville's retirement, but the truth that she was fighting a losing battle from the very beginning stung. Emmett's grip on her shoulder eased into something more comforting, grounding her in the moment.

She could break down about the unfairness of it all later. Right now, she needed to focus. Callie laid her hand over Emmett's in gratitude.

"Did you know?" Nyla asked, turning to George. "Did Bill?"

George swallowed harshly.

"I didn't know," he said slowly, his expression ashen. "As for Bill, he never said anything to me about it. If he knew, he kept it between himself and James."

"From the way he reacted to seeing the Chehwinoo, I doubt he knew, *mi cielo*," Aaron said, his voice low. "Or, if he did, he didn't really believe it."

"At the end of the day, we're still cleaning up some billionaire's mess." Sam rolled his eyes. "Does it matter which one made it?"

"How much money do you think small town politicians make?" Amelia questioned, staring at Sam with disbelief. "I can promise you it's not *billions*."

"Not the point," Nyla said, waving off the exchange. "Sam's right. It doesn't matter who takes the blame for the Chehwinoo's release. The only thing we need to care about is how to stop it. For good."

"I can help with that, too" Clary said, drawing attention back to her. She held up her phone. "The council was gracious enough to translate some old texts for me. They may not be willing to get directly involved, but they don't *want* the Chehwinoo running free."

She scrolled.

"Why won't they get involved?" Callie asked. "We could use any help they can offer."

"I'm not sure, to be frank. I didn't feel like I could ask anything I wanted, so I'm only speculating. I think it's a 'not my circus, not my monkeys' situation. But they can't completely wash their hands of it either, because if the Chehwinoo breaks free than it *will* be their circus and their monkeys. That's why they gave me the details I need to perform the binding rituals."

"Are you serious?" Nyla's face lit up. "You know how to stop it? You can do that?"

"I can't give you the specifics of the rituals themselves," she said apologetically. "But yes, I know how to do them. And I'll have to be the one to perform them."

"Are you sure—?"

"I'm sure," Clary said resolutely. "You guys have been risking your hides for months. It's my turn to get out there and kick some monster butt."

"What do you need from us?" Aaron asked.

"I can gather the ingredients myself," she said. "The less you know about the process, the better. I can at least tell you what each ritual will do, though. The first one is a binding ritual, slightly different than the original one used to trap the Chehwinoo in the topaz. It's designed to bind the spirit to the host body."

"Does that mean if we kill it, both the human *and* the spirit will die, instead of just being ejected?" Sam piped up, sounding hopeful.

"Unfortunately, no. It does the opposite. You can't *kill* a spirit. If I bind the Chehwinoo to its possessed body, the result will be a monster that is essentially invulnerable."

"That sounds like the worst possible idea," Sam said flatly. "Please tell me there's a step two?"

"Of course." Clary snorted. "The second step is another binding ritual, but this one is... bigger. More of a sealing, of sorts. With the Chehwinoo spirit stuck in its host body, it'll be a lot easier to confine it. The elders used topaz because there was an abundance of it, enough to contain the spirit's power. This way, the power will already be contained within the host, so we don't need something as big as a mineral vein to trap it permanently. Think of it like double-bagging the kitchen trash. We can find something sturdy, something that can't be disturbed by accident."

"Hang on a second," Emmett held up his hand, like he was waiting to be called on in class. "You just said that the power will 'already be contained in the host.' Does that mean the first part of this plan actually *releases* its full power?"

Clary grimaced.

"Yeah... that's the risky part. To bind the spirit to the host, I need to bind all of it. The first part of the process is freeing the part of the Chehwinoo that's still bound to the topaz. There will be a tether point, some part of the topaz vein that houses the majority of the Chehwinoo's spirit. You'll need to find it and break it, completely severing its ties to the Basin."

"So, for a moment, we'll be facing a full-strength Chehwinoo that we can't kill?" Sam gaped. "Yep, we're dead."

"We'll need to have everything prepared," Nyla said while Amelia hushed Sam. "If we can minimize the time between the first ritual and the second, we have a better chance at coming out of this alive."

"It'll all be compounded into one big ritual," Clary assured them. "In theory, the Chehwinoo shouldn't be at full strength for more than a few minutes."

"A few minutes is a lot of time for a creature that moves as quickly as the Chehwinoo does," Aaron pointed out, humming in thought. "Will it still have its known weaknesses? Water? Fire?"

"It should," Clary said. "But it'll be stronger, more resistant."

"How long will it take you to get the ritual ready?"

"About two days."

"Great, that gives us enough time to come up with a plan." Aaron grunted, rolling his shoulders with a wince. Callie hoped that two days would be enough for him to recover, at least a little. They were at a stark disadvantage without Aaron at his full strength. "Let's finish this."

Chapter Forty

EMMETT

The days passed in a blur of unbroken tension. With the Chehwinoo challenging the established rules, no one knew what it would try next. The uncertainty solidified into a thick fog of dread, clinging to all of them and making it impossible to rest. They needed to, though, or they wouldn't be able to enact Aaron's plan.

Clary confided in him about what she needed to perform the ritual. Not the exact steps or ingredients, but what she needed from *them*. Aaron took that information and turned it into a trackable plan, something that Emmett knew he couldn't have accomplished with so many unknowns at play. Not for the first time, Emmett was grateful Aaron was on their side.

The first order of business was to find somewhere safe for Clary to perform the ritual. She needed to be outside the Chehwinoo's territory, not just for her physical wellbeing, but mentally. Emmett didn't fully understand it, and he didn't need to. Clary told them that she needed a degree of separation from the spirit's domain so she wouldn't be influenced by its own wants and desires. She didn't elaborate after that, and no one questioned further. As far as Emmett was concerned, her word was more than enough to convince him.

Nyla, Clary, and Emmett scouted the outskirts of the Basin while Aaron rested. The hospital visit confirmed that he suffered some gnarly internal injuries, but nothing that would keep him down for more than a few weeks as long as he didn't push himself. Emmett almost laughed at that. With Nyla in harm's way, Aaron wasn't going to sit back on his laurels and wait. At least he didn't need to worry about accompanying Nyla into town for the foreseeable future.

In a matter of days, it seemed like the local hostility toward Nyla had reached an all-time high. After the initial surge of hate caused by the ridiculous article, things had largely settled back into a tenuous normal. Now, things had gone from bad to much, much worse. The Chehwinoo was operating at an entirely new level of efficiency, and the sudden spike in disappearances over the last 48 hours returned attention to Nyla. Then, word of Aaron's accident spread among the townspeople, and hostility turned to borderline violence. She'd joined Sam and Amelia on a supply run the day before but it was cut short when the cashier refused to serve them while Nyla was present. They were ejected from the store, and Nyla resigned herself to helping in ways that kept her out of the public eye, but Emmett could tell it pained her. It pained him, too. The unfairness of the situation permeated the air like toxic fog, one he feared would linger long after the Chehwinoo was gone.

It didn't take them long to find a spot. A small clearing, tucked away behind a shallow ridge just east of Lichen House. It was sheltered from both inclement weather and prying eyes, far enough from the road that they wouldn't be spotted and close enough to the Chehwinoo's domain that Clary could easily reach out and work her magic. Once they'd settled on their location, preparations moved quickly. Emmett spent most of his free time securing as many fail-safes as he could. Between him and Amelia, they'd gotten their hands on a portable air quality tester. Fire was an effective weapon against the Chehwinoo, but it wouldn't do them any good to accidentally blow themselves up. They needed to test the air in the mineshaft before introducing a spark.

All the while, Emmett had to forcibly stop himself from thinking about Callie. Maybe he should've waited to kiss her until all of this was settled; his mind was constantly split between the task at hand and remembering the feel of her body beneath him.

When this was over, he was taking her on a proper date. Flowers, chocolate, the whole shebang. For now, though, he had to be content with casual touches and stolen glances.

Even with all of their preparation, go-time came before Emmett knew it. He was ready, they all were, but he didn't feel it. A deep sense of dread wormed its way into his stomach, and Emmett did everything in his power to not let it show on his face.

"I'll be in a deep state of meditation for most of this, so I'll need someone with me," Clary said uneasily. Emmett wasn't sure if she was uncomfortable with the thought of being vulnerable or requesting help. Maybe both.

They were in the clearing, checking and double-checking their supplies. The weather was cooperating as much as it could; skies were clear, cloudless, and blue. The temperature was lingering just below freezing, meaning they were all dressed in winter gear. They were ready.

"I'll stay with you," Callie volunteered, and Emmett's pulse slowed to a reasonable beat for the first time in days. "I can monitor the radio and keep everyone in the loop, just like last—"

Callie stopped before she finished her sentence, and her gaze flickered briefly to Aaron, who smiled ruefully.

"Let's hope no one gets buried alive this time," he joked, and Emmett saw Callie's shoulders sag in relief.

"You should stay here too, *mi sol*," Nyla murmured, so quietly that it was almost like she didn't want to be heard at all. Aaron's smile vanished in an instant, his spine snapping to attention.

"Nyla..." he began in a soft warning.

"You're still injured," she argued, gaining confidence as he met her suggestion with resistance.

"I was injured when we killed the first Chehwinoo, too," he countered. Nyla narrowed her eyes at him.

"That was different," she said. "We lured the Chehwinoo to us. This time, we won't be staying in one place. While Clary is performing the ritual, we'll be underground, searching for the tether. You won't be able to camp out and cover for us, not in a damn mineshaft."

"I'm not letting—"

"She's right, Aaron," Emmett cut in, drawing a sharp glare from Aaron. Emmett set his mouth in a firm line, meeting his glare with determination. "You'll do better work here. You can keep an eye on things, defend the girls if this gets messy. I'd feel a lot better knowing Callie wasn't guarding Clary alone."

"And I'd feel a lot better if I wasn't sending Nyla into the belly of the beast *without me*." Aaron huffed a breath in agitation, seeking support from anyone who hadn't spoken up. He didn't find it.

"Sam, Tyler and I will go in through the collapsed tunnel," Amelia said, her tone appeasing. During the rescue efforts to find Aaron's body, they'd cleared a small entrance into the tunnel once again. It wasn't large enough to fit equipment through, but it was enough for them to squeeze in. "From everything we've researched, that should be the closest entry point to the tether. There's three of us, so it makes sense that we take the more dangerous route. Then Emmett and Nyla can go in through Lichen House's cellar."

"I won't let her out of my sight," Emmett promised, clapping a hand on Aaron's shoulder. He let the full weight of his gesture rest on Aaron, making him wince in pain. A twinge of guilt ricocheted up Emmett's spine, but he needed Aaron to understand that he wasn't at his best. From the flash of resignation on his face, Emmett guessed it worked.

"Neither will I."

Sheriff Mason's voice startled all of them, clearing his throat authoritatively.

"George?" Nyla questioned, raising one eyebrow at him. George dipped his chin in acknowledgement.

"If I'm understanding all of this, we have one shot to put this thing down for good. We need all hands on deck, and that includes mine."

"What about the station?" Amelia asked.

"I'll have one of my seniors keep an eye on things," George said. "He'll be under strict orders to waylay Stamkos' movements and report any activity to Agent Kelley. With luck, he won't try to resume operations today, but if he does, my guys can hold him off. Right now, I'm needed here."

Aaron seemed to consider this for a moment, and then he sighed.

"Fuck," he muttered, pushing his hand through his hair in frustration. "I don't like this."

"I know, Suits," Nyla smiled at him, twining her fingers with his, "but it's the right move. You know it is. You also know that I can take care of myself."

"That's not the point," Aaron said, a spike of worry cracking through his frustration. He glanced around at their unorthodox assembly —a bricklayer, a lawyer, a spa owner, an admissions counselor, an athletics trainer, a small-town sheriff, an active FBI agent, and a wilderness guide. "I trust all of you implicitly. But we've had too many close calls lately. I'm not comfortable being on the B team for this."

"Technically, Clary's the A team," Nyla argued with a teasing lilt. "Without her, none of this happens."

"She's also not in any immediate danger."

"Spiritual danger, maybe." Clary shrugged.

"I can't put a bullet through a spirit."

"I would argue that's what you've been doing for months," Sam pointed out. Aaron rolled his eyes.

They were silent for a while, each of them weighing the inevitability of what they were about to do. This was it. While far from the first time Emmett embarked on a suicide mission with the people in front of him, the air pulsed with a different energy. There was a tone of finality to Clary's plan that wasn't present before.

The last hunt. The last kill.

The last Chehwinoo.

"Come back alive," Aaron ordered, meeting each of their gazes in turn. He ended with Nyla, the cold authority in his eyes softening to a warm desperation that he couldn't hide if he tried. "That's not a request, *mi vida*."

"Make sure I have something to come back to," Nyla countered, wrapping her arms around Aaron's waist in a tight hug, despite his sling. Releasing him, she turned to face Emmett and George. "Let's go, we're losing daylight."

Chapter Forty-One

CALLIE

As everyone prepared to leave, Emmett pulled Callie aside. The concern on his face looked a lot like irritation, but Callie knew better now. She laid her hand gently on his chest, contrasting the dark glare she gave him.

"Don't do anything stupid," she warned, hoping she looked intimidating. "Be careful. Listen to Nyla. Don't let—"

"I'll come back to you, Cal," Emmett promised, his lips twitching in amusement. "It might be in more than one piece, but I'll come back."

Callie scowled. She didn't find the same amusement in his words that Emmett clearly did.

"One last thing," she said, grabbing his sleeve as he turned to leave. With impressive strength, she yanked his arm until he bent forward, and Callie surprised him with a ferocious kiss. A groan caught and died in his throat, smothered by her tongue. When they parted, Callie held Emmett's gaze. "End this."

A wolfish, almost manic smile lit his face.

"I plan to."

With that, Emmett joined Nyla and George as they piled into the sheriff's patrol car, taking the road that would lead them to Lichen House. Sam, Amelia, and Tyler left shortly after, opting to walk to the mineshaft entrance. From the clearing, it was closer on foot.

Clary, Aaron, and Callie fell into a tense silence until the sounds of their retreating friends faded into oblivion, leaving behind a sense of dread and purpose.

Wordlessly, Clary began to remove a series of items from her bag. Aaron took a steadying breath, checking his gun before safely holstering it.

"What can we do?" Aaron asked her, and Clary shook her head.

"Nothing right now," she dismissed. "I need to meditate for a while first, until I find the thread connecting the spirit to the tether point. Once I find it, the others can destroy it. Then, I'll need someone to hand me what I need for the second half of the ritual."

Clary moved easily around the clearing, draping a stunning, handwoven blanket over the frost-encrusted ground. She then placed several small bundles of plants tied with string in the corner of the blanket, followed by a stone bowl. The bowl held what looked like soot, but Callie couldn't be sure, and she didn't ask. Like Clary said, if they needed to know, she would tell them.

"I need you to be as quiet as possible," she instructed, carefully unbraiding her hair. She took several deep, rhythmic breaths before stooping forward, unlacing her boots and removing her socks. When that was done, Clary stepped onto the blanket. Moving to the center, she gracefully sank to a seated position, her legs crossed and her palms resting on her knees. Clary looked up at Callie, then Aaron, flashing them a cocky smile. "Tell the others if they find the tether, *do not break it*. Not until I'm ready. Understood?"

"You guys catch that?" Callie held up the walkie-talkie, her thumb on the comms button. A chorus of cracked affirmation sounded through the channel. "Understood."

"Good," Clary squared her shoulders, pulling her phone out of her pocket and tapping on the screen. In a few seconds, an even tempo began to play, like the ticking of a particularly loud clock. "There's a burlap pouch in my bag. When I tell you to, grab it and bring it to me."

Aaron and Callie nodded.

"Alright," Clary said, releasing a long breath. "Time to hunt."

The next thirty minutes passed by uneventfully. Callie should've been happy about that, but she couldn't shake the building anxiety that cranked up yet another notch every moment nothing happened. Aaron looked far more at ease than she felt; she suspected he'd done at least a few stake-outs during his time with the FBI. He was probably used to this, the palpable tension in the air clouding only Callie's mood.

They'd heard from both groups, everyone having safely found their way into the mines. Amelia was still annoyed that the weather was too cold to make use of the drone, so they didn't know where the Chehwinoo was. It was only a small comfort knowing that it couldn't reach Callie, Aaron, and Clary. It could reach the others, and that was more than enough to make Callie stress.

"Got you, motherfucker."

Clary's sudden whisper had Callie jumping out of her skin, despite the softness of her voice. Aaron's head swiveled to face Clary, his hand hovering over his gun.

"Claire?"

"The thread," Clary informed them, her words steady but low, like only half of her attention was in the clearing with them. "I found it. It's... cold. I guess that's not surprising."

"What do you need?" Aaron pressed, keeping his own voice as quiet as he could while still being heard. Clary shook her head, just slightly.

"I'm following it back to the tether," she explained almost dreamily. Her left hand twitched to life, reaching beside her until her fingers brushed one of the plant bundles. She picked it up, holding it in her open palm above the stone bowl. "Have they found it?"

"Guys?"

"*Still searching,*" Nyla's voice answered, crackling through the speaker. "*Amelia?*"

"*Nada,*" she responded. "*Will we know it when we see it?*"

"You'll know," Clary assured them. "One of you is close... I can almost feel you."

"*Creepy.*" Sam was quickly shushed as Amelia cut the line.

"Don't do anything until we give you the go-ahead," Aaron said into the radio. "When you find it, tell us, and hang tight."

"*Yes, sir.*"

Nyla's mischievous lilt made Aaron smile for the first time since the group had split up.

Another twenty minutes passed in silence, and Callie felt herself start to fidget. She was cold, the chilled wind having long since seeped through her coat and into her bones. Trying not to disturb Clary, she wiggled in place, flexing her fingers and breathing into her hands.

Aaron raised his eyebrow at her, silently asking if she was fine. Callie nodded.

She was considering taking a walk when Clary inhaled sharply. Callie spun on her heel at the same time as Aaron, both of their attention fixed on Clary's hand. It shook, crushing the bundle of herbs in her tight grasp. Callie moved to step forward, but Aaron held out a hand to stop her. Clary's face pinched in concentration.

The bundle of herbs disintegrated in Clary's hand, crumbling to fine dust that littered the ground beneath her. Callie watched in awe, certain that she could *feel* the ritual working.

Until, that is, she saw Clary's face.

"What's wrong?" Callie demanded, rushing forward. Before she could reach her, Clary was sent flying backward, like an invisible force had collided with her head. Her neck snapped back, the sudden movement making everyone wince, as her torso slammed into the earth with a loud crunch. Callie sprinted to her side, getting there before Aaron, who'd paused to raise his gun and survey the area. Callie couldn't blame him; it truly looked like Clary had been shot right before their eyes.

"Are you okay?" Callie pressed, grabbing Clary's elbow and helping her stand. Clary shook her head, a look of panicked rage contorting her features. She snatched the walkie from Callie's outstretched hand, her knuckles turning white with the force of her grip.

"What the hell are you doing?" she hissed, jamming her feet into her boots so she could pace in the snow. Clary ran to the other side of the clearing, frantically pawing through her bag. "I didn't give you the signal yet! Why—"

"*What are you talking about?*" Emmett's voice responded, sounding both concerned and confused. "*We haven't done anything.*"

Clary paused, her fingers twitching over another bundle of herbs.

"What do you mean?" she asked. Callie took a tentative step toward her. "You're not at the anchor yet?"

"You told us to stay clear," Emmett argued. There was some shuffling, and then a new voice came over the line.

"All calm on our end, too," Amelia informed them, sounding worried. *"We haven't even found the damn thing yet."*

"Clary, what's happening?" Aaron sounded much calmer than everyone else, but the urgency in his words was palpable even through his controlled demeanor. "Did something go wrong?"

"I— I don't know." Clary blinked, uncertain now. Callie silently took her hand. "I felt one of you getting close, so I was reaching for the tether attaching the creature to the topaz veins, and then it just... snapped. I thought—"

Before Clary could finish her sentence, Aaron had his phone pressed to his ear. Callie felt the knot of dread in her chest tighten until she could no longer take in a full breath.

"Kelley, it's Klein." The clearing was quiet enough that Callie could hear the other person respond, but not so silent that she could understand their words. "Do you still have eyes on Stamkos?"

A pause as he listened. Callie turned back to Clary.

"Does this mean the Chehwinoo is free?" she asked, feeling a knot of dread form in her stomach. Clary shook her head.

"It's damaged, but not completely cut," she explained. "We can still do this, we just need to move quickly."

Aaron's voice interrupted Callie's next question, sounding strained.

"Can you check?"

Callie watched his face carefully, watching as it morphed from tense to confused to ultimately settle on frustration.

"Okay, thanks Kelley. Keep me posted."

"Where is he?"

"His car hasn't left the motel," Aaron said, readying his weapon and moving to the perimeter of the clearing. "The front desk is refusing to give out any information on his movements, and we don't have a warrant to get into his room."

"So," Callie finished for him, "his car is there, but he might not be."

"Am? Did you find anything about more blasting plans in Stamkos' computer?"

"No," Amelia answered Nyla's question, sounding as frustrated as Aaron looked. *"But that doesn't mean there aren't any. I only have access to his laptop. If he planned anything from his phone, I wouldn't know unless he synced all his communications."*

"Which he almost definitely didn't." Callie sighed. "Especially if he thought he was under surveillance for any reason."

"I can guarantee he didn't," Amelia continued. *"Carver was very clear in his messages to Stamkos that blasting was strictly off the table. That's also probably why he buried Mac Diamond's employee file under three levels of restricted access."*

"My guys confirmed that there isn't any work going on in the Basin today, at least not on Stamkos' dime," George's voice added. *"Whatever happened, it wasn't at the factory."*

"Damn," Aaron muttered, pushing his hand through his hair. Callie hadn't known him long, but she already recognized the gesture as a nervous tic. "And you guys are absolutely sure you didn't damage anything down there? Even by accident?"

"We didn't," Nyla assured them. *"What does that mean?"*

"It means," Clary murmured, her mouth forming a hard line, "you're not alone down there."

Chapter Forty-Two

EMMETT

As the ominous words echoed through the tunnel, Emmett's spine tensed. Nyla was sandwiched between him and Sheriff Mason, holding the radio in front of her so they could all hear and speak clearly.

"Claire? How close are we to the tether point?" Nyla asked. There were a few beats of silence before Callie's voice answered.

"She's trying to find you. Hang on a second." The line went quiet for another breathless moment, and then Callie came back. *"The tether is a lot weaker now so it's hard for her to tell, but she thinks you're close. Like, practically on top of it."*

Nyla's expression became troubled. Emmett could guess what she was thinking already.

If there was unauthorized construction that damaged the tether, they would've heard it. Felt it.

"We'll keep moving," she said, making eye contact with both Emmett and George for confirmation. They nodded in turn. "Can you still perform the ritual, Claire?"

"She's nodding. I think we're good to go," Callie said. Nyla closed her eyes, gathering her composure before holding the radio up to her lips.

"The Chehwinoo is a lot stronger now," she reminded them, "We need to find out what happened and fix it before it figures out what we're doing, if it hasn't already. The sooner we finish this, the better."

"I texted German, he's on standby with the others," Tyler said, his voice crackling through the speaker.

"Nyla?"

Aaron's voice now, low and commanding. Nyla pressed her lips together.

"This just got a lot more complicated. Clary says the tether is hanging on by a thread. She's not sure if it'll be able to hold against the Chehwinoo if it tries to free itself, and that's if it tries right now. *The longer it's unstable, the stronger it'll get. At some point, it'll be too powerful for Clary to control."*

Nyla closed her eyes, processing the information.

"How much time do we have before that happens?"

"Hard to say," Aaron answered. There was a delay in his responses, listening to Clary's explanation while condensing it for their sake. *"As long as that shred of tether hangs on, it won't be able to resist the ritual. If it breaks completely, though, we might have an hour. Maybe two."*

"Shit." Emmett read the uncertainty on Nyla's face, answering for her with a confidence he didn't feel. "Alright. We'll get it done. Be ready."

It was hard to believe Clary's claim that they were close to their goal. Emmett held the flashlight aloft, illuminating the next few meters of their journey. The air was damp and chilled, but not unnaturally so. The deeper they travelled, the more signs of past excavation they encountered. The dirt smoothed beneath their feet, making their descent easier, but increasing the echo of their footsteps. While the beginning of their excursion was clumsy and unrefined, they were clearly in the official mineshafts now, and Emmett wanted to believe that was only a good thing. The possibility that they weren't alone down here shredded that hope.

They moved in silence, Emmett leading with the light, Nyla in the middle, navigating, and George pulling up the rear and providing cover. When the floor dipped into a low-slung curve, Emmett stopped dead in his tracks. The air coming from around the bend was ice-cold, the sudden temperature change struck him so sharply that he has to gasp for breath.

"We found it."

Nyla's voice was hushed, whispering into the radio. Emmett's body thrummed with anticipation, knowing the end of their ordeal was practically in sight. All he had to do was round this last turn.

"I'm ready," Clary's voice answered, louder than Nyla's. Emmett flinched as her words echoed, and he realized there had been sound before. Dripping water, creaking rock, shifting dirt, burrowing animals. Now, it was silent.

"Come on," Nyla said, her small hand pressing reassuringly on Emmett's back. The touch shook him from his stupor, and he quickly stepped forward.

As soon as he cleared the bend, the tunnel opened into a gaping cavern. Even with the glow of the flashlight dominating the room, Emmett could tell it wasn't the only source of light. He swung the beam in a wide arc, his heart thudding wildly in his chest when he finally saw it.

"Jesus Christ," George cursed, his voice rusty from disuse. Nyla stayed quiet, but her expression was one of shock.

On the far side of the room, embedded in the rock, were hundreds of softly glowing mineral threads, snaking through the dirt and debris like veins under pale skin. Following the largest of them, Emmett found that they converged on one spot, a larger facet of stone that shone brighter than the rest, casting the air in an eerie yellow light that mirrored the eyes that hunted them.

The tether stared at them, pulsing, like an alien heart pumping spiritual lifeblood into the ground. It was nothing short of otherworldly. The longer he looked, the more he felt like the tether was looking back at him, like it was alive in its own way. Tiny pinpricks of ice crept up Emmett's spine. He'd stared down the Chehwinoo many times in the past; more than once, he'd been the last sight the creature saw before it was forcefully ejected from its latest host. The cold terror he felt when faced with a dominant predator was sobering, almost humbling. This was different. This fear was bone-deep, ancient, like he'd stumbled upon something he was never meant to see.

"Is that... a pickaxe?"

Nyla's question brought Emmett back to the present, following her gaze to the stretch of dirt in front of the heart. A tool lay abandoned at the base of the rock, too modern to be from the original excavation.

"I think we figured out what damaged the tether," Emmett said, furrowing his brow. Somewhere in the back of his mind, he'd held onto the hope that this was an accident. Some animal, perhaps, or an idiotic human. Seeing the pickaxe, so deliberately discarded next to the giant glowing heart-rock, squashed that idea. Someone had taken it upon themselves to come down here on a solo mission, and they'd left in a hurry. The question now was: who?

The answer scratched at the edges of Emmett's consciousness, but he didn't want to acknowledge it. Didn't know what it meant. How to handle it.

"Guys? What's—?"

A gunshot rang out, clear and sudden in the still air. Emmett didn't even have time to duck as the bullet ricocheted off the rock and embedded itself in the ceiling.

"What the fuck?!" Nyla whirled as George leveled his own gun in the direction of the shot, barking at whoever was hidden there to come out with their hands up.

"Nyla? Was that a gun? What the hell is happening?" Aaron's voice now, frantic.

"It wasn't us!" Amelia quickly interjected. *"We're still in the tunnels."*

"Who's there?" George demanded. Emmett was just beginning to consider the repercussions of stomping over there himself when movement caught his attention. As the shadows shifted, a man stepped out of them. A man they all recognized with varying levels of disgust. A man that, dejectedly, Emmett expected to see.

"Of fucking course," he squeezed his eyes shut, hoping that when he opened them, this would all go away. "What are you doing here, Stamkos?"

Chapter Forty-Three

INTERLUDE

Aaron

Aaron didn't think his heart could stop beating while he still lived, but he came close when Emmett's aggravated voice sounded through the radio, speaking the name of the one man who could bring their whole operation to a screeching halt.

His grip tightened on the walkie, struggling to remain silent as he pieced together what was happening from the tidbits of sound still coming through the line. Nyla clearly had kept her finger on the comms button, allowing Callie and him to eavesdrop on the conversation.

Good girl, he thought fondly.

"What the hell are you doing here?" George demanded. There was a long minute of silence before Stamkos' insufferable chuckling pulsed through the connection.

"If nothing else, I can grant James his devotion to discretion," Stamkos said. *"I'm here to clean up your mess, of course. What else would I be doing in such a... quaint environment?"*

"Our mess?!" Emmett's voice now, hard and angry. *"You have no idea what you're dealing with. Turn around and walk away before you get yourself hurt. And yes, that is a threat."*

"Charming. Is that how you plan to deal with the Chehwinoo? Bully it into letting you do whatever you want?"

Silence descended over them. Aaron's limbs felt frozen, locked in place, as he tried to process what he was hearing. Adrian Stamkos, talking about the Chehwinoo.

"How does he know?" Callie whispered, eyeing the radio suspiciously. Aaron held it up so she could see that he didn't have the comms button pressed. They could speak freely. "How *long* has he known?"

"Something isn't right about this," Aaron murmured, feeling the ache in his ribs pulse in a feeble reminder of why he wasn't standing next to Nyla in that mine. "Kelley said that no one has left the motel all day. If Stamkos is down there, he must've left before dawn."

"Why? What on Earth could he be doing down there?"

Aaron wished he knew.

"What a timely reminder that you don't know everything," Stamkos continued. Aaron resisted the urge to snap at him to shut the fuck up. He could picture the scene easily; Nyla, Emmett, and George all staring at Stamkos, utterly dumbstruck by his words. *"There are powers at play here that you don't understand, Ms. Jameson. Now, stand back. I have a business to run."*

"Oh, fuck you," Nyla hissed. There was a scuffle, just enough to make Aaron's heart race, before she spoke again. *"You can take your business and shove it up your ass!"*

"Nyla," Emmett said in a gentle warning. Aaron fought down his surge of pride. If he was right, Nyla had tried to launch herself at Stamkos again.

"Such animosity is unbecoming of a bright young woman," Stamkos prompted, confirming Aaron's guess. *"You know, I almost had you arrested over that little scrap in the woods."*

"Not by any of my guys," George growled. *"You've been nothing but trouble since you showed up here in that damn flashy car. I should've told Bill to kick your ass back to whatever nepo-baby hellhole it crawled out of."*

Stamkos laughed, loud and long.

"What makes you think Bill had any sway over me?" he asked, still chuckling. *"Somerton was in trouble long before I showed up. You country bumpkins dug your own grave and now you're just looking for someone else to bury in it. Hell, I'm the saviour in this story. If I hadn't swept in when I did, there wouldn't be a Somerton to speak of. Your town is cute, but it's not smart. It's certainly not worth the effort you're all putting into sinking it."*

From behind them, Clary made a panicked noise.

"What?" Callie demanded, rushing over to her. She didn't step on the blanket, but she hovered as close as she could. "What's happening?"

"The Chehwinoo knows something's wrong," Clary muttered, staring at nothing. "It's... searching."

"For us?"

"I'm not sure," Clary blinked, bringing herself back to the present. "They can't let Stamkos damage the mineral veins any more than he already has. I only have a tiny window to cut the spirit's ties to the topaz, bind it to its host, and then to another vessel. If he releases it before I'm ready—"

"Can you start now?" Callie asked, her attention flickering between Clary and Aaron. "Be ready to bind it as soon as Stamkos makes his move?"

"It's not that simple," Clary argued. She hesitated, then held out the bundle of herbs in her hand. "I have from the moment I set this aflame to the moment it burns out. These are dried and delicate plants. They'll disintegrate in less than ten seconds."

Aaron remembered how quickly the bundle had turned to ash when Stamkos damaged the topaz initially. Clary wasn't exaggerating; they only had seconds to work with.

"Shit," Aaron said, squeezing his eyes shut. There *had* to be a solution here. There had to be.

"You're the worst thing to ever happen to Somerton," Emmett snarled through the radio. *"You and your pathetic factory. If it weren't for you, none of this would be happening in the first place! Now you expect us to believe that you're the solution?"*

"That's not true."

The statement was so small, so quiet, that it took Aaron an uncomfortably long time to understand that it was Nyla who'd spoken.

"Mi vida?" he whispered, his thumb flinching over the comms button. What was she talking about?

"Nyla?" Amelia said, her tone echoing Aaron's concern.

"Stamkos isn't the worst thing to ever happen to Somerton," she explained. *"I am."*

Time slowed to a crawl, a sick feeling uncoiling in Aaron's stomach. She was buying time. Nyla was smart; she'd likely realized the severity of their situation. Clary had told them how important it was not to break the tether until she was ready. Nyla was stalling, distracting Stamkos until they could get him away from the tether. That was her plan. It had to be.

Even as he told himself that, Aaron couldn't shake the dread hovering at the edges of his mind.

"*Bullshit,*" Emmett said vehemently. "*Nyla, you're the best thing to ever happen to this town. I'd bet my life on it.*"

"*I'm a plague, Em,*" Nyla argued, and from the sound of it, she was close to crying. Aaron felt the sniffle like an electric shock, his entire body jolting with the need to comfort her. *Why* hadn't he gone with them? "*I was so focused on turning Somerton into something it's not that I didn't stop to think. If I had just kept my head down and did what everyone wanted me to, James never would have made that deal with Stamkos in the first place!*"

Silence followed her outburst, only punctuated by a sharp curse. Aaron didn't know who it came from, but he wholeheartedly agreed with them.

"*I told myself that this was all a huge mistake,*" Nyla murmured. The steady flow of voices cut off briefly, and Aaron knew without a doubt that she'd taken her thumb off of the comms button. He scrambled to say something, to connect the line from his end, but Nyla's voice returned a moment later, a little farther away. Someone else had taken the radio from her and was letting them listen in. "*A coincidence. The factory, the Chehwinoo, James, Bill... I wanted to believe none of it was connected. It was just a series of unfortunate events that clashed all at once. And now I know that James was fighting so hard because he knew about the Chehwinoo, and I pushed him into doing something anyway! Now we're here, and you're here, and I can't pretend anymore. James brought Stamkos in because of me. I should've left well enough alone,*" Nyla insisted, her tone hardening. "*I didn't. And now, James is dead. Bill is dead.* Half the town is dead, *and the other half hates my guts. I brought this on us. Now I need to fix it.*"

As Emmett jumped in to deny any fault on Nyla's part, Aaron's sick feeling crept up his throat. While everyone was caught between the whiplash of Adrian Stamkos showing up in the mine and Nyla admitting she'd been carrying more guilt than any of them knew, Aaron was clinging to the underlying desperation in her words. Desperation, fear, and stubborn resolve.

Nyla hadn't wanted Aaron to stay behind for his safety; at least, that wasn't the only reason. She knew there was a chance they might not all make it out of this alive, they all did. But the determination in her tone told him that Nyla decided that if anyone was going to put themselves in harm's way, if they had a choice in the matter, it would be her. She also knew that Aaron would never let her. The realization hit him square in the chest, crushing him until he was sure he'd been caught in another cave-in.

Nyla was prepared to die, and he wasn't there to stop her. Before he could think better of it, Aaron lifted the walkie to his mouth.

"I refuse to let you throw your life away for a town that doesn't give two shits about you," Aaron snarled. If anyone was confused by his words, they kept quiet. "Emmett? Get her out of there. Now."

"No." Nyla's voice was strong and defiant. Aaron closed his eyes and took measured breaths. *"I'm finishing this, Aaron. No matter what."*

"Ah, Agent Klein!" Stamkos' jovial tone made Aaron's skin crawl. *"Believe it or not, I'm happy you're alive."*

"You won't be by the time I'm done," Aaron said. He released the radio button, shoving the device into Callie's hand. "Take this. I'm going after them."

"Aaron, you can't!" Callie insisted, reaching for his arm. "You're still—"

"I don't care," he said, cutting her off before she could spout the same arguments Nyla had given him. Whether they were valid or not didn't matter. Not now. "Things are going belly up and I'm not going to sit here and wait for shit to hit the fan. You know as well as I do that if anything happens, Nyla isn't letting anyone else take the fall. Don't ask me to listen to my girlfriend sacrifice herself through a damn radio, Callie. *I'm going after them."*

Callie's mouth formed a hard line, but she didn't say anything. Instead, she lifted the radio to her lips. When she pressed the button, though, a loud static whine cracked through the air.

"What?" Callie blinked at the radio, pressing the button again and again with no change. "Hello? Guys?"

"Is the battery dead?" Aaron demanded, stepping closer, his retreat momentarily forgotten. "Maybe it's—"

A scream drowned out his next words, and then the clearing erupted into chaos.

Callie and Aaron turned in time to see Clary convulse on the blanket, her spine rigid, her body spasming. They rushed to her side, just as two people burst through the cluster of trees behind them. Aaron spun on his heel, gun raised.

"Klein!"

Kelley and Andrews.

"What are you doing here?" Aaron asked, crouching next to Clary and looking to Callie for any kind of explanation. She offered none.

"I got worried when you called about Stamkos," Kelley explained, holstering her own weapon before dropping to her knees next to Clary. She bracketed her head with her palms, keeping her from thrashing too wildly. "I left one of the deputies to watch the motel. Then I heard a scream on my way here. What's wrong? Is she overdosing?"

"No, it's nothing like that," Aaron assured her.

"It's complicated," Clary wheezed, her body still twitching. Callie breathed a sigh of relief.

"Are you okay?"

"I'm alive," Clary said, bereft of her usual confidence. "The others, are they okay?"

"We lost communication," Aaron told her, and made eye contact with Kelley. Silently, they came to an agreement. "I'm going to the mine now."

"The Chehwinoo is free," Clary said, coughing. "I don't know if Stamkos did something or if it freed itself, but it's power is spiling out of the topaz faster than I can track. In about 10 ten minutes, we'll be dealing with a full-strength spirit."

"Does that mean we can't trap it?" Callie asked, panic in her eyes. Aaron watched Clary's face as she considered her answer.

"Not necessarily," she said, her eyes flicking to her bag. Wordlessly, Callie grabbed it for her. "I have something here... for emergencies. I hoped I wouldn't have to use it."

"Is it dangerous?"

"Yes."

"Will it kill you?"

"Probably not, but it's possible."

Aaron paused, thinking.

"Will it work?"

Clary nodded.

"Do what you have to do."

Aaron stood, summoning his adrenaline. His injuries were worse now than the last time he took on a Chehwinoo at less than his best. Regardless of how the next few minutes played out, Aaron was going to *hurt*. He didn't care, though. Not when all of their lives were at stake. And now, with Kelley and Andrews providing Clary and Callie the protection they needed, Aaron was free to go after Nyla.

He just prayed he wasn't too late.

Chapter Forty-Four

EMMETT

Emmett greatly preferred when things were simple.

Evil monster killing civilians? Take it out. Simple.

A pretty girl he liked, and who liked him in return? Kiss her. Simple.

Whatever was happening in the underground network of mine tunnels beneath the Basin was anything but simple.

After Nyla's confession, revealing to everyone that she was carrying far more weight on her shoulders than they could've guessed, Stamkos had been suspiciously quiet. Emmett was torn between refuting Nyla's guilt and letting this play out— the longer they kept Stamkos' attention away from breaking the tether, the better. Clary needed time, and right now, keeping quiet was giving her that. Part of Emmett still hoped that Nyla was just playing up her emotions for the sake of causing a distraction, but the pain in her voice was real. Whether this was a ruse or not, there was truth to her guilt, and Emmett had to forcibly bite his tongue.

"You do have an overinflated sense of self-importance, don't you?" Stamkos said after nearly a full minute of silence, almost giddy. "I wish you'd said something earlier, Nyla. Good God, you think all this happened because of you? I've been in land acquisition talks with James for *years*, long before you moved to Somerton. Then again, you knew that already, didn't you?"

"What?" Nyla demanded, stammering in confusion. Stamkos shook his head almost fondly.

"You can't possibly think I didn't know about your spyware," Stamkos continued, shrugging his shoulders. He was wearing a hideously-coloured Henley, the sleeves rolled up past his forearms. He was smeared with dirt, confirming that he was the one who'd been picking away at the tether before they arrived. "I admit, it took me longer to notice than I'm proud of. Your friend Amelia is good at what she does. I'm sure she found my conversations with James."

"We know you were friends," Nyla said defensively. Emmett glanced down at his hand to confirm he was still holding the button on the walkie. His brow furrowed as he took in the red light, the error message on the screen flashing NO CONNECTION. "That doesn't mean you've been planning this for years. Your business expansion plan has been in the works for ages, you would've started building long before now. You're lying."

"Sweet girl, why would I lie about this?" Stamkos donned a cold imitation of sympathy on his face. "James and I have been discussing the possibility of opening an S&S facility here for many, many years. We could never come to an agreement that worked for both of us."

"What changed?" Emmett demanded, partly to keep Stamkos talking, partly because he was genuinely curious.

"Property lines," Stamkos said, his lips twitching like he'd made an inside joke.

"That's impossible," Nyla argued. Stamkos gave her a smile that was supposed to be reassuring but came off almost clinical.

"I can show you the initial contracts." Stamkos shrugged. "Those were all done in person and on paper, so there wouldn't have been any electronic copies for your friend to steal. Everything is outlined, including James' reluctance to hand over the property in the first place. He built a warning into the damn fine print. Clever, except he was a fool to think I wouldn't have a team of lawyers going over it with a fine-tooth comb."

"That's why you broke into Carver's house." Emmett gaped, blinking at Stamkos in the eerie light. "You wanted the contracts. To cover your tracks."

As the information sunk in, Emmett felt frozen. Nyla, to her credit, didn't falter.

"Bill told me that *my* antics pushed Carver into doing something radical. Everyone blames me for this, and now everyone is blaming me for trying to *stop* it! You're *lying.*"

"I'm not," Stamkos assured her. "Bill blamed you purposely."

"Why?"

"Because I told him to."

Nyla fell silent, struggling to connect the dots. Emmett couldn't remain quiet anymore, not as the certainty in Nyla's eyes wavered.

"You're leaving something out," he accused Stamkos, stepping up beside Nyla and planting a hand on her shoulder. "Why waste time turning an entire town against one person? You had a reason. What was it?"

A shuffle of rubber on dirt sounded from across the cavern, and then Amelia appeared from one of the connecting tunnels. She was followed closely by Sam and Tyler, evaluating the situation as quickly as they could. Stamkos raised his hand in a friendly greeting.

"Can I expect to see Agent Klein and Ms. Quinn scurrying from another shadowed corridor?" he mused, raising an eyebrow at Nyla. "You collected quite the team; I'll give you that."

"What was the reason?" Emmett repeated, his tone leaving no room for interpretation. Either Stamkos answered their questions, or he wasn't leaving the mine in one piece. With a dramatic sigh, Stamkos leveled his attention on Emmett.

"The original contract included a much larger parcel of land than what I eventually purchased. Unfortunately, the owner of said land was too stubborn to sell it back to the town. He went around James and made a private sale, iron-clad and perfectly legal, to an optimistic young woman looking to build a wilderness retreat."

"You... you wanted to buy the Willow," Nyla whispered, less of a question and more a statement.

"Correction, I was *in the process* of buying the Willow when Oscar screwed everyone over with his traditionalist values. It was an annoying development, but not enough to dissuade the company from plowing on. We just needed to rework some things, not to mention fight with James over it all. Without your land, the factory would be 'too close to its territory,' he said. I thought he was spouting nonsense, but it looks like I owe his headstone an apology."

Emmett was rooted to the spot, shock and disbelief warring with confusion and anger. He wanted Stamkos to shut up. He wanted to tell Nyla to stop blaming herself. He wanted to drive that pickaxe through the heart of the topaz deposit and put an end to this nightmare.

"You knew all along and yet you—"

"Oh, come now, don't be ridiculous." Stamkos snorted. "You can't honestly tell me you all believed this supernatural garbage straight out of the gate. Why would I?"

As much as Emmett wanted to disagree, he had a point. An ancient, angry ice demon trapped in the ground didn't exactly sound like a plausible roadblock.

"Still, this build wouldn't have happened without James' support," Stamkos said, sighing again. "To keep him happy, I told him that I would gladly move the factory if he provided more land. As I understand it, that's why he and Bill were so adamantly trying to run you out of town. When you proved to be more resilient than they expected, I got tired of waiting."

Nyla was deathly still, staring at nothing. Emmett risked moving his hand from her shoulder to her bicep, squeezing in reassurance. She didn't even glance in his direction.

"Oh, and make no mistake, even if I *had* the Willow, I would've expanded deeper into the Basin eventually. There's far too much valuable real estate in this area to simply leave it as-is. So, truly, Ms. Jameson, none of this is your fault. Although I do wish you'd managed to deal with the creature on your own. I hate getting my hands dirty."

Stamkos brushed his hands on his slacks, like he was finishing a particularly gruelling presentation.

"Why were you blasting out here?" Amelia's voice startled Stamkos into turning slightly, regarding her with mild interest. "You hired Diamond after construction began. The blast site isn't anywhere close to the factory. What were you doing out here?"

Emmett breathed a quiet sigh of relief. Amelia's question served its purpose; Stamkos considered her for a moment, content to answer, giving them more time to come up with a plan.

"I already told you," he explained, shrugging. "I'm cleaning up your mess. After the unfortunate incident over the summer, and James' convenient disappearing act, I began to suspect there was more going on in Somerton than I originally believed. Without James, however, I was sorely lacking a reliable contact. I had my legal team investigate Somerton's records and we came across this beautiful topaz mining operation."

Stamkos waved to their current surroundings, pausing as his attention snagged on the glowing heart once again.

"I really do owe James an apology," he continued. "When I discovered the old mining plans, I assumed that he'd made up the Chehwinoo nonsense to cover up future plans. I thought he was going to cheat me, bring in another industrial operation and drop it in my backyard. I wanted to figure out precisely what I was dealing with. That's what Mr. Diamond was hired to do; uncover the mine, find out what James was so intent on hiding. I never could've guessed the poor bastard was telling the truth. Then you all had to go poking your noses around that old blast site and I couldn't abide by that either, so I called in an old friend to finish the job Mr. Diamond started."

"And I suppose it was pure coincidence that you showed up at the same time we did?" Amelia asked, her expression skeptical. Stamkos shrugged.

"You can't think I wasn't keeping an eye on you after I found your spyware," Stamkos said. "I *was* hoping to arrive before you put yourselves in any unnecessary danger, but I underestimated how quickly you were planning to move. If Jerry hadn't been on standby, we may have missed you entirely."

Nyla had fallen deathly silent, staring at Stamkos with wide, unblinking eyes. Emmett could almost see the gears in her mind whirring, revisiting every inter-action she'd had with the town, viewing her struggles through a new lens.

"There now, are we all happy that everything's out in the open?" Stamkos clapped his hands together decisively. "Wonderful. I truly am sorry you all got tangled up in this. I hope you can see that I bear you no ill will, outside of my newly acquired stitches courtesy of Ms. Jameson, of course. Regardless, I'm willing to put that in the past if you will simply leave me to my business. Construction has been on hold for far longer than we planned, and we're quickly getting to the point where it'll be difficult to recoup our losses by next year's third quarter. Here's what I'm going to do for you."

The next few seconds happened slowly. Stamkos reached down to grab the pickaxe, heaving it over his shoulder and preparing to swing. George and Tyler shouted at him to freeze. Sam and Emmett flinched forward to stop him.

"I'm going to break this rock, the Chehwinoo will go free, and you lot can chase it across State lines to your hearts' content. Honestly, I don't care what you do. I just need it off my land. Finding replacement workers has become a substantial headache."

Amelia's head whipped around to peer behind her, her mouth opening in shock. Nyla grabbed Emmett's arm in a vice, a warning sprouting to her lips just as a blast of frigid wind billowed through the cavern. The gust was so strong that it knocked them clean off their feet, sending dust and debris spinning through the air.

Someone screamed. Emmett wasn't sure who.

When he regained his balance, he already knew what he'd see. Standing behind Adrian Stamkos, crouched like a grotesque spider scuttling along the cavern wall, fangs dripping with congealed water, was the Chehwinoo.

Chapter Forty-Five

CALLIE

As Aaron disappeared into the trees, following the same path Sam and Amelia took earlier, Callie refocused her attention on Clary. She was coherent now, at least, but she was drenched in sweat and her skin was mottled and red.

"What can I do?" Agent Kelley asked, and it took Callie far too long to realize she was speaking to her.

"Don't let anything into the clearing," she said, jerking her chin downward at the blanket. "And don't step onto this. We need to be as quiet as possible to let Clary work."

"Done." Kelley nodded to Agent Andrews, and they both stood. "Yell if you need help. We'll do a perimeter check."

As their footsteps faded, Callie reached out to take Clary's hand.

"Are you sure about this?" The answers Clary had given Aaron weren't exactly reassuring. Clary nodded, squeezing her eyes shut as she slowed her breathing.

"It's the only way, now that the spirit's all but free." Clary shifted, reaching for the herb bundle again. "You'll have to help me, though. I can't do it alone."

"Tell me what to do, and it's done."

Clary smiled.

"When I tell you to, I need you to light this bundle on fire. Hold it over the bowl for as long as you can. When your fingers get hot, drop it into the bowl and step back. And, whatever you do, don't touch me. If I try to grab you, move out of the way. Do *not* let my skin come in contact with yours. Understood?"

Callie agreed. Mollified, Clary took a small purple flower from her bag. It was dried and pressed, so delicate that the petals were ripped in several places.

"I only get one shot at this, so it needs to count," she explained. "Here's what's going to happen. I'm going to eat this flower, and it's going to amplify my awareness. With luck, it'll guide me to the nearest forest spirit, which *should* be the Chehwinoo. Once I find it, I can try to suppress it. If I succeed, we'll have a subdued spirit ripe for binding."

"And if you fail?"

"Then we're all dead."

"I guess you'd better not fail then," Callie said with deliberate nonchalance, despite the rampaging fear in her stomach. Clary answered her bluff with a smirk, taking a deep breath and holding the flower to her lips. She murmured some words in a language Callie didn't recognize, and then she popped the bloom into her mouth.

There was a distinctive shift in the air as Clary chewed. She placed her hands palm down on the blanket, grounding herself. Her chest rose and fell in even intervals, her breath leaving her mouth in small puffs of steam. For a tense moment, Callie wondered if she couldn't find the spirit.

And then Clary's body seized.

Her spine locked into place, her arms and legs going rigid. Callie scrambled backward as a low keening sound rattled out of Clary's throat. Her back bowed off the blanket, her mouth opening in a wordless scream. Her eyelids fluttered shut and then burst open again, revealing an otherworldly glow. Clary's eyes were shining a bright, unnatural gold, the same colour that Callie had seen stalking them from the shadows the night Emmett had held her hostage in the back of his vehicle.

Clary's fingertips began to turn blue, and Callie knew she'd done it. She'd found the Chehwinoo.

Now, she just had to beat it.

Chapter Forty-Six

EMMETT

Adrian Stamkos didn't have time to scream.

Emmett lunged forward, either to pull Stamkos out of the way or intercept the Chehwinoo, he wasn't sure yet. Before he made it even a single step, the creature leapt from its position, landing on the uneven ground with a concussive bang that had them all scrambling for balance. With deadly precision, the Chehwinoo's arm shot forward, aimed directly at Stamkos. He had the wherewithal to duck, but the creature was faster.

The Chehwinoo's claw pierced through Stamkos' ribcage, directly below his heart. Stamkos' eyes bugged, a splatter of blood staining his lips. Emmett forced himself to his feet, looking for something— anything he could use to help. With his attention flitting around the cave, he didn't notice Tyler had pulled his gun until the first shot nearly shattered his eardrums. He instinctively dove to the ground, dragging his body over to where Nyla was readying the flamethrower. Tyler shot again, and this time the bullet pierced through the Chehwinoo's chest, dead center.

Its scream stuttered to a halt, saliva clinging to its fangs, so thick with slush that it reminded Emmett of mucus. He waited for the rapid melting that followed a direct hit, but it didn't come. The creature looked down at the gaping wound in its torso, an almost curious expression on its skeletal face. Stamkos gurgled a protest, perhaps a plea, Emmett couldn't tell. The Chehwinoo's attention snapped back to him, hissing vapor over his muddied skin. Stamkos inhaled to scream, but the Chehwinoo drowned out the sound with a symphony of cracks and shatters. Then, the light changed.

Bright yellow tendrils of light burst from the Chehwinoo's injuries, sparking like lightning, arcing from the creature to Stamkos.

Emmett watched in horror as the light invaded Stamkos' mouth, his nose, his *eyes*— any and every orifice it could reach. Then, they began to merge.

The spirit wasn't jumping from body to body, not this time. The Chehwinoo screeched in pain as its ribs cracked open, its brittle, blackened skin falling away to reveal jagged shards of ice decorating its insides. The ice shot forward, piercing Stamkos' arms and legs, hooking into his flesh and pulling him into the sunken cavity that had formed. Stamkos tried to scream, tried to fight, but it was useless. He was pinned, and the Chehwinoo was too strong.

Emmett peeled his eyes away from the unfolding horror long enough to find the others in the dark. Nyla watched in fascinated terror while George turned away, staring hard at the ground. Emmett wished he had the strength to turn away himself, but he couldn't. He was transfixed by the grotesque way the Chehwinoo's broken bones acted like teeth, biting into Stamkos' body as he was absorbed into the cold and rot. Sam, Amelia, and Tyler couldn't see what was happening from their vantage point. Emmett was thankful for that.

"Clary! What do we—?" Nyla's question cut off as she spun to look for the walkie. Emmett held it aloft and pressed the comms button again, but he was met with nothing. No static, no voices, nothing. He tried again, turning the walkie on and off, but it was useless. Amelia tried hers with the same results.

"No way," Emmett muttered, checking his phone. It, too, remained silent. Even their flashlights were dead; he hadn't noticed before due to the light coming from the topaz veins. Whatever power the Chehwinoo unleashed, it had managed to completely isolate them.

"Fuck!" Amelia cursed, hoisting her rifle in the air. She took aim at the Chehwinoo and fired, but the bullet passed through its stomach with nothing more than a faint grunt of pain. Emmett checked the flashlight on his phone, hoping against hope that this one tether to the world above this damn cave still worked. White light illuminated the ground in front of him, and he breathed a sigh of relief. They may not have cell reception, but they had light. It would have to do.

"New plan!" Nyla called out, pointing the flamethrower at the Chehwinoo.
"Duck!"

A burst of flame shot from the nozzle, scorching the Chehwinoo's left leg. It
screeched in fury, whipping toward Nyla even as its torso stitched back together,
sealing Stamkos' lifeless body inside. The flames licked at the creature's dead skin,
leaving bright white gashes along its thigh and hip. The Chehwinoo lunged out
of the way, skittering to the far corner of the cavern. Nyla dropped the nozzle,
letting the flames die out. While the flamethrower was helpful in close quarters,
it wasn't the most effective ranged weapon in their arsenal.

Panic warred with the desperate will to live as they recovered from the shock
of seeing Stamkos swallowed by the very creature he'd freed. Part of Emmett was
hoping that, once Stamkos was dead, the Chehwinoo would somehow cease to
exist. Some kind of poetic justice, or something. No such luck.

"We need to get to more closed ground!" George barked, readying his gun.
"Back it against the wall and head for the Lichen House tunnel. Don't turn your
backs on it!"

Emmett did as he was told. He didn't have a weapon on hand, so he reached
out to pluck the rifle from Nyla's back. She helped him, shrugging out of the
strap. Slowly, keeping his gun fixed on the Chehwinoo, he began to inch back
the way they'd come. Nyla kept pace with him, glancing over at Sam and Amelia,
who were flanking the creature with Tyler. They were scattered but still making
progress.

The ground was crusted with jagged frost; firm enough to provide friction but
brittle enough to crunch under their shoes. Emmett felt each step like a shock, his
legs vibrating with the sheer amount of adrenaline coursing through his blood.
The Chehwinoo watched them, yellow glowing eyes far too intelligent for a feral
beast, and then it moved. Like a viper striking its prey, the Chehwinoo pushed
off using its back legs, soaring across the cavern until it skidded to a sudden stop
behind them, blocking their exit. Its jaw cracked open and a high-pitched wheeze
clamored from its throat, slightly melodic, with enough intention that Emmett
felt cold fear snake around his heart.

Was it... trying to *talk*?

"Oh, fuck no," Nyla muttered under her breath, having come to the same conclusion. She raised the flamethrower and blasted the creature, but the Chehwinoo was ready. It swiped with its skeletal hand, hooking the flamethrower in its claws. The hose snapped like frayed twine, dripping gasoline onto the shimmering dirt floor.

George fired a shot at the Chehwinoo, striking it in the jaw. The creature screamed at him, spittle and steam sputtering from its gaping maw. George yelled for them to get out of the way, but the Chehwinoo was too fast. It lunged at them, and Nyla only just managed to swing the flamethrower's decapitated fuel pack in front of her before the Chehwinoo's teeth clamped onto the metal. It shook its head, ripping the pack from her hands and slamming it into the cave wall.

Emmett grabbed Nyla and yanked her back out of the way as the creature lunged again. George fired off two more shots, but the bullets were barely slowing it down. The Chehwinoo sank into a crouch, preparing to launch itself at them again, but it was suddenly thrown backward, like it was struck in the chin. The creature screeched in outrage, clawing at its own skin, the light in its eyes blinking yellow then... white?

Confusion rippled through them, almost tangible in the chaos.

It recovered quickly, shaking off the momentary debilitation and coming at them again. Tyler circled it, aiming his gun at the Chehwinoo's joints. He shattered a kneecap, dropping the creature to the ground. With the Chehwinoo blocking the Lichen House tunnel, they had no choice but to redirect to the entrance Amelia, Sam, and Tyler had used. If they could crowd into the tunnel, they forced the Chehwinoo to attack from only one direction. They could retreat, keeping their weapons trained behind them, making sure they weren't ambushed.

They just had to get to the tunnel first.

The Chehwinoo was recovering quickly, its leg regenerating faster than before. All of their previous strategies flitted through Emmett's mind at lightning speed, dismissing each as they cropped up. Before, they were dealing with an animal. Vicious, bloodthirsty, and dangerous, yes, but driven by instinct. Now, the Chehwinoo was something different. Something that could think, plan, and react.

On its half-formed leg, the Chehwinoo loped toward Amelia, who'd aimed the rifle at its shoulder. Sam collided with the creature's good leg, making its step falter so Amelia could retreat. Emmett shot a bullet straight through its eye, watching as the light began to blink white again.

"What's happening?" Nyla yelled, hovering near George now that her weapon was a shredded pile of junk on the cave floor. The Chehwinoo screeched again, its voice breaking half-way through, almost like it was annoyed. "What's wrong with it?"

"Don't look a gift horse in the mouth!" Tyler ducked and rolled out of range as the Chehwinoo regained its bearings, digging its claws into the ground for purchase. It may not be the same creature they were used to fighting, but it was still just *one* creature. As long as they kept moving, the Chehwinoo wouldn't be able to target any of them cleanly. It roared, shards of ice flying from its crooked mouth, coating the rocks beneath it in thick, splattered slush. Its screams shook the rock above them, dislodging loose dirt and stones. The damn thing was going to cause a cave-in if it didn't shut up.

The others realized it at the same time as Emmett, and the rush to get to the tunnel became priority number one.

As if his thoughts willed it into being, several large chunks of the ceiling crumbled and fell to the ground in clusters that struck the rock below with echoing thumps. Emmett braced himself against the vibrations assaulting his knees, fighting to remain on his feet. The Chehwinoo scuttled to the far side of the cavern, folding in on itself to protect its glowing core. The path to their escape tunnel was temporarily clear.

In unison, they began to sprint for the exit. Emmett skidded to a halt, swerving as another brief collapse blocked his way. Nyla collided with him, stumbling into his back and pitching them both forward until Emmett caught his balance. He held an arm out, blocking her from running ahead as the rock settled, dislodging dirt and roots above them.

"We need to get everyone out!" Nyla insisted, clutching his arm in a vice. Emmett wasn't sure if she was going to push him aside or hold on, and he didn't give her the chance to decide. He grabbed her shoulders, pulling Nyla into a crouch with him behind the nearest rock. It provided little cover, but it was something. A reprieve. Somewhere to catch their breath before the nightmare continued.

"The tunnel is still open," Emmett confirmed, squinting in the darkness. Between the six of them, there were enough light sources scattered throughout the cavern that he could make out the important details, but everything moved in flashes as they left the circle of one light and entered another, like a failing Halloween decoration. "If we can get there before the Chehwinoo recovers, we have a chance."

"Go." Nyla shoved her palms against his arm. "I'll hang back and distract it, give you all some time."

"Are you crazy?" Emmett said, remaining firmly in place. "I'm not leaving you behind, Nyla. That's suicide!"

"This is *my* mess, Emmett! I need to—"

"Oh, shut the fuck up!"

Nyla blinked, shock silencing her at his outburst. Emmett had never yelled at Nyla before, but he couldn't stop himself now. Adrenaline, fear, frustration; whatever the emotion, it had words spilling from his mouth before he could stop to think about them.

"This isn't your fault, damnit! *None of this* is your fault! This all happened because rich men love money, that's all. Period. Point blank. Full stop. *The. End.*"

Emmett glanced over his shoulder, searching for the others, for the creature. They didn't have long, but he needed to make Nyla understand this if he was going to trust her to keep herself alive. He *needed* her to stay alive.

"I've been a shit friend," he told her, panic and desperation loosening his tongue. "I know that, and I'm sorry. I wish I realized it before now. I had no idea you were struggling so much with the town, Nyla. I should've."

"I didn't tell you—"

"That doesn't matter," Emmett insisted, clasping her arms tightly, resisting the urge to shake her into listening. "If I was around more, if I paid attention, I would've known. I would've been there for you, I would've done something!"

"There's nothing anyone could've done," Nyla argued. The light of her torch flickered, catching the sheen of tears in her eyes. Emmett's throat tightened. "Stamkos made sure of that."

"Exactly," he said, willing her to understand. "Somerton, Carver, Bill, Stamkos, they've all been working against you from the start. You're not the problem, Nyla. You've never been the problem."

Her jaw snapped shut, staring at him with wide, unbelieving eyes.

"You can't die here. If you do, they win." He stopped, reconsidering. "No, forget them. Live for the people who care about you. Don't throw your life away over some stupid misplaced obligation. You *have* to forgive yourself, Nyla! For me. For your friends. For Aaron. *For you.*"

The Chehwinoo screeched, the pained sound bouncing off the walls, distorting its location. Emmett looked around again, making sure they were still safe for the moment, when suddenly Nyla was in his arms.

She wrapped him in a tight, clinging hug, burying her face against his muddied jacket. Emmett returned the hug instinctively, clutching her with every ounce of emotion he could muster. It was brief, barely a handful of seconds, but it was enough to unlock the stress knotting his stomach.

"I think it's about time to get out of here," she said, pulling away from him and getting to her feet in the same motion. She smiled, extending her hand to him. "Shall we?"

With the cavern now dotted with freshly-fallen debris, their route to the exit was convoluted and hazardous. The Chehwinoo was doing much the same thing they were, assessing the new environment and determining its course. Emmett didn't wait, pulling Nyla along behind him as he navigated the broken maze of rock and dirt. The exit tunnel was in sight, but not yet within reach when the creature made its move.

It lunged into the air, its claws digging into the ceiling to anchor it. From there, the Chehwinoo sprung, splitting their group in two with its landing.

Tyler was closest to the tunnel, but he held back until Amelia was alongside him. Sam shook off the frost that had collected on his sweater where the Chehwinoo leapt over him, sprinting for the tunnel entrance. The creature was between him and safety, but he wasn't deterred. Sam ducked and weaved through the Chehwinoo's swipes, diving to the ground in a painful-looking slide as it snapped its jaws at him. He was nearly clear when the Chehwinoo struck again, its claws hooking into the fabric of Sam's jeans and tugging him to a stop.

"NO!" Amelia screamed, firing shot after shot into the Chehwinoo's torso. It paid no attention to the bullets peppering its blackened skin, its sole focus locked on the prey it could reach. Amelia darted forward to intervene, but Tyler caught her wrist. *"SAM!"*

There was a sharp inhale of breath, and then the Chehwinoo's head whipped in a different direction. Sam didn't wait to look, scrambling forward until he was out of immediate danger. Emmett turned, expecting to see George, gun in hand, aiming for a second shot at a vital point. It occurred to him belatedly that he hadn't heard a gunshot.

Then, he saw Nyla.

She wasn't behind him anymore. In a flash, she'd darted to Sam's aid and now she was crouched, one knee on the ground for balance, her left hand wrapped tightly around the Chehwinoo's spindly calf, her right hand twisting something into the thin flesh of the creature's ankle.

Her pocket knife.

Even from his vantage point, Emmett could see the frostbite taking over Nyla's hands where she touched the Chehwinoo. With a pained yelp she tore herself free, rocketing backward now that Sam was safe and the Chehwinoo's attention was on her. Emmett rushed to aim his gun at the Chehwinoo's head, hoping to hit its jaw, its teeth, something to disarm it.

What's happening up there, Cal? We can't keep this up much longer!

With the radios and their phones still out of commission, Emmett had no way to check. He just had to hope.

The Chehwinoo panted heavily, and for one fleeting moment, Emmett thought they'd succeeded in hurting it. Tentative elation built in his chest, promptly obliterated as the Chehwinoo howled. The sound was low, eerie, making shivers erupt over his entire body. Again, its eyes flickered white, and the creature reeled like it was in pain. Blindly, its limbs began to flail in half-hearted attacks on the air, spinning like it was looking for something. When it turned to face the perimeter of the cavern, it froze. Emmett realized what was happening a fraction of a second before the Chehwinoo's arm thrust forward. It struck, its claws a blur in the softly glowing cavern, colliding with the cave wall at the center of the pulsating topaz heart. In an instant, the world went black.

Muttered curses sounded from all around, Emmett's vision slowly returning as he wielded his phone like a weapon. The artificial light barely broached the all-consuming dark, letting the Chehwinoo camouflage itself in the shadows. They wouldn't have known where it was at all if not for the flickering yellow glow of its eyes that surreally floated through the backdrop of blackness, blinking just above the orange cast of Nyla's torch.

In less than half a breath, the Chehwinoo skittered forward and slammed its claws into her leg.

Nyla's scream of pain rent the air in two, breaking as the Chehwinoo jerked her off her feet. The torch smacked against the ice-encrusted rock, still alive, illuminating the scene in horrific flashes. Her shoulder slammed into the ground with a resounding thud that made Emmett cringe. She dug her nails into the dirt, scrambling for purchase as the Chehwinoo dragged her toward it, two of its claws buried in her calf. Nyla kicked with her free foot, her heel connecting with the creature's cheek. It howled at her, ripping its claws from her flesh and reeling back to strike with its teeth.

Emmett's body went numb. No one was close enough to do anything. When Nyla saved Sam, she'd put herself firmly out of their reach, unable to get back to the safety of either group before the Chehwinoo doused the lights.

"NYLA!" Emmett hollered, sprinting toward her. Her three intact limbs fought to propel her to safety, scrambling toward Emmett as she spotted him running to her, the Chehwinoo's fangs snapping at the air mere inches from her face. With another lunge, it would surely—

Thwack!

The Chehwinoo recoiled, screeching in pain and shaking its head. Emmett looked up and, with a surge of hope, spotted the source of the sound.

Aaron dropped to one knee beside Nyla, the barrel of his gun clutched tightly in his right hand. The butt was dusted with snow, and Emmett realized he'd used it to bludgeon the Chehwinoo's skull from behind.

"Aaron—!" Nyla gasped, wincing from her injuries. Aaron didn't stop to answer her, hooking his free arm under hers and hoisting her to her feet. His sling was gone, and Emmett could see the sweat clinging to his hair even from a distance. He must've ran to them as soon as the radios died. Nyla let out a sharp cry as her injured leg took some of her weight, but she remained standing with Aaron's help.

"Clary has a back-up plan," he panted, clutching his side once he was sure Nyla wouldn't topple without his support. "We just need to buy her time."

The Chehwinoo recovered from Aaron's blow, deciding that George was easier prey. It skulked toward him, hissing and clacking its teeth. George's gun had long since run out of bullets and was now discarded at the mouth of one of the tunnels. The Chehwinoo struck out with its arm, and George barely managed to dodge it before it was striking again. Sam tackled the Chehwinoo's back leg once more, knocking it off balance long enough for George to put some distance between him and the creature's mouth.

Outraged, frustrated, and desperate, the Chehwinoo shook Sam free from its body and leapt, landing directly in front of Emmett. Aaron had brought another source of light with him— one of the industrial flashlights they'd used on their previous expeditions— so they could see much more of the space now. Emmett unloaded his rifle into the Chehwinoo's chest, even knowing it wouldn't kill it. The creature kept coming, frozen spittle flying from its mouth, its fangs glistening in the inconsistent light, its eyes trained on Emmett's throat.

The yellow glow once again flickered white, just for a moment, but it was enough.

Emmett threw himself out of the way as the Chehwinoo shook itself. It roared, confusion making it revert to the more feral animal they were used to facing. Tyler's hand clamped down on Emmett's shoulder, helping him out of harm's way, before the light in the Chehwinoo's eyes flickered again.

Then, it went out.

Everything came to a screeching halt. The silence in the cavern was deafening, cloaking them in an unnatural stillness that sent chills through Emmett's body. The Chehwinoo froze, its claws stretching toward Emmett and Tyler. Slowly, its limbs began to twitch, until the soft sheen of frost began to spread from the ground to its body, coating it in a thin layer of pristine ice. Then, the ice began to change. It shrunk, cracking and condensing into something more solid, more present, simply *more*.

Before their eyes, the Chehwinoo turned to a brittle stone, devoid of life, of anger, of everything. They waited, too afraid to breathe, for the other shoe to drop. The next problem. The next danger. The next thing that would ruin their victory. It didn't come, and, slowly, a bone-deep knowing settled among them even as the air began to warm.

It was over.

Uncertain calm fell on the room. For a moment, none of them knew what to do. What to say. The adrenaline they'd felt mere moments before remained thick in their veins, unable to accept that the threat was gone.

But it was.

The threat was gone.

The Chehwinoo was dead.

The truth of that knowledge uncorked the pressure in the air, the world roaring to life with the disbelieving shriek of triumph that erupted from one of them. Emmett didn't see who. Hell, it might've even been him.

"Holy shit," Nyla said, laughing. She fell to the floor, letting exhaustion take over as she rolled onto her back, staring at the ceiling. "Holy shit!"

"Holy fucking shit!" Amelia echoed, mirroring Nyla's actions. Soon they were all lying on the dirt ground, catching their breath, revelling in the unbelievable truth that that'd won.

They'd fucking won.

A thick, satisfied haze fell over them as they lay there, letting reality sink in. With the adrenaline finally seeping from his muscles, Emmett felt the cold more than ever before. It wouldn't be long until he started shivering, but he didn't care. Couldn't bring himself to care even if he wanted to. He welcomed this cold— the normal, natural cold of deep earth, of buried rock.

"Hey, Aaron?" Sam tilted his head back to look at the top of Aaron's head. They were spread out in a loose half-circle, with Sam and Aaron on each end. Emmett had George on one side, Nyla on the other. Amelia was sandwiched between Tyler and Sam. It felt... right. Almost. One person was missing from their group, and Emmett knew his heart wouldn't fully calm until he could hold her again. Aaron shifted, tilting his head back to look at Sam.

"Yeah?"

"Did I see you pistol whip a fucking ice demon to rescue your girlfriend?" Aaron smirked.

"Yeah."

Blinking, Sam turned his attention to Nyla.

"Woman, if you don't suck that man's dick tonight, I will."

"Ha!" Nyla barked a laugh, her whole body shaking with joy and relief.

"Sam!" Amelia said, groaning. Emmett could hear the smile in her voice, though.

"How about you take over when my jaw gets tired?" Nyla offered.

"Deal."

"Do I get a say in this?" Aaron asked in amusement.

"Nope." The reply came from both Sam and Nyla at the same time, and that was the final push. They all descended into a fit of laughter, nearly manic in their relief. Emmett felt tears collecting in the corners of his eyes, felt his cheeks begin to ache, his stomach shaking, aggravating his many bruises. He didn't care.

Happiness choked him, giving him the energy he needed to stand up once their laughter subsided. There was a girl he had to see.

Chapter Forty-Seven

CALLIE

When Callie was thirteen years old, her mother was hit by a car.

It was a hit and run with witnesses, and it didn't take long for the cops to track the man down. He'd been drinking, and when asked why he ran from the scene, he explained that he thought he hit a deer. Callie was angry at him now, but at the time, she didn't have the energy. The collision put her mother in a temporary coma, and they weren't sure if she would wake up again.

Seeing her mother in that hospital bed was hard. The waiting, the not knowing, that was harder.

The same feelings coursed through her now as Callie helped Clary to her feet. She looked exhausted— sweat soaked her skin, her hair hung in tangles around her face, and her eyes were bloodshot. The battle to overpower the Chehwinoo had taken almost everything out of her, but she'd succeeded. While she didn't fully explain the process, Callie pieced together the gist of what happened. Whatever that flower was, it connected Clary's mind to the Chehwinoo. To contain it, she had to overpower its consciousness. She did, but not without a heavy physical toll. Clary assured her that with some rest and medicinal tea, she'd recover. Callie hoped she was right.

The spirit was bound to a small, carved talisman that Clary had procured specifically for this purpose. The Onaqwe band council in Madison made it for her, and the elders were already waiting with a secure, undisclosed location to store it long-term. As soon as she was able, Clary was to bring it to them wrapped in a downy-soft rabbit skin she pulled from her backpack when she woke up.

Agents Kelley and Andrews had returned a while ago, summoned by Clary's unnatural screaming. Callie had to physically stop them from interfering, which was how she figured out that neither of them knew the full extent of what they were dealing with. That was probably for the best.

Losing contact with the others had fallen to the back of Callie's mind while she helped Clary, but now it was front and center. The ritual worked, yes, but had it worked in time? As much as she wanted to make a break for the nearest cave entrance, Callie couldn't leave Clary behind in this state. Besides, she didn't know which tunnel the others would take to leave. She might miss them entirely if she picked the wrong route. Logically, it was better to stay put and wait.

That didn't make it easier.

After a painful half hour, Callie heard rustling in the trees. Clary was resting in the back of Agent Kelley's vehicle, closer to the main road. Agent Andrews lifted his gun, just in case, but Callie knew the cadence of the male voice that carried through the woods. She broke into a run before Emmett fully came into view, and then she was in his arms.

"You're alive!" Callie cried, squeezing as tightly as she dared. Emmett returned her embrace, burying his nose in her hair and inhaling deeply.

"We're alive," he confirmed. "Barely."

"Where's Claire?" Nyla asked, and Callie couldn't suppress the gasp that left her when she saw her friend. Nyla was limping heavily, her leg bound with bloodied fabric that looked like it used to be Aaron's jacket. Aaron had her arm hooked over his shoulder, stooped low to help her move. From his staggered breaths, he wasn't faring much better.

"I offered to carry her," Tyler told Callie when he saw where she was staring, "but you know Aaron. Overprotective hard-ass."

"I offered to carry him, too," Sam interjected, "but he's not ready to admit that he's cripplingly attracted to me yet, so he turned me down."

"I thought you liked his Mama Bear Override?" Nyla teased, spotting Clary in the back of the nearby SUV. Tyler rolled his eyes.

"I think you greatly underestimate how much this man annoys the shit out of me."

"Come on," Aaron said to Nyla, ignoring the jabs at his expense. Callie had to admit he was a good sport about it all. "Let's get you to the hospital."

"I think that goes for everyone," George announced, releasing a bone-weary sigh. "Does anyone know how to file paperwork for this?"

Tyler nudged Kelley with his elbow.

"Tag, you're it."

Kelley raised a skeptical eyebrow in his direction.

"How about this," Nyla proposed. "Group outing to the emergency room followed by drinks at the Willow while we fill everyone in on what the hell just happened. Sound like a plan?"

Callie smiled, locking eyes with Emmett.

"Sounds like a plan," he answered for them. Then, his lips twitched in amusement. "As long as we setup shop around a campfire. I think it's been long enough since any of us sat and watched the stars."

Chapter Forty-Eight

EPILOGUE

Nyla

In the weeks following Adrian Stamkos' death, Nyla's world was flipped on its axis more times than she cared to count.

Everyone was coping differently with the aftermath of their multiple brushes with death. Sam and Amelia were perhaps the least affected, returning to their home in Philadelphia with promises to keep in touch and a visit during the next semester break. They'd wanted it to be sooner, but between this trip and several impromptu weekend getaways, they had no paid vacation left to take. Tyler drove with them as far as Chicago, jumping at the chance to see Chia again. That was the last Nyla had seen of the three of them.

The owners of Lichen House finally reached their limit with setbacks and unexpected complications. As Callie had guessed, they already agreed to sell the business to Stamkos & Stein. While the deal was on hold given the sudden passing of one of the founders, Orville's firm was no longer in the picture. To everyone's shock, he acted like Callie's outburst over the phone hadn't happened. She was able to return to work without issue, but Orville's retirement plans had been put on hold. Emmett was still trying to convince her to start her own firm, and he was making some progress, but she was reluctant. Nyla wasn't sure she needed to, though. Her outburst had humbled Orville, just a little. Whenever Callie spoke of work now, she did it with an air of burgeoning confidence she hadn't had before.

Emmett's boss was a little pissed about losing the Lichen House contract, but they would recover. Ephraim was the bigger problem. He was out of a job, and his physical abilities limited his options for further employment. Emmett was trying to get him a clerical position with his company, despite Eph's continued protests. Nyla hadn't heard if they'd made headway on that.

Aaron had come out the other side of this case in better shape than he'd been in before, proving to be the only truly happy outcome of their ragtag group. Collaborating with Callie to unearth the intricacies of Stamkos & Stein had ignited a passion for the corporate espionage subsector of private investigating. He was in the process of reworking his business model and obtaining the right paperwork, which had him traveling between Somerton and Chicago every few days.

That left Nyla.

From the beginning, Nyla planned for her to take the brunt of the fallout. This nightmare started with her, and she wanted it to end there, too. So far, she'd succeeded.

Rescuing the townspeople from an ice demon did nothing to improve her reputation, considering no one knew about it. Instead, the face of S&S's failure to implement their factory fell to none other than her. It started as a rumor— Nyla wasn't sure who came up with it— pinning the blame for the project's issues on Nyla's protests. Quickly, the story morphed into an exaggerated tale of a hotheaded female businessowner causing mayhem for the town, raising hell about a project that would bring new money and job opportunities to a dying rural population, all fuelled by a renewed interest in the bogus article that Kelley confirmed traced back to Stamkos. The delays, the accidents, even some of the deaths were attributed to her, unofficially of course, and Nyla's position as a pariah was more concrete now than ever. With that came a wave of bullying far worse than she'd experienced when she first moved to Somerton.

The restaurant staff refused to serve her. Advertised sales suddenly ended when she reached the cashier. Any product she asked about was out of stock. Nyla was unwelcome in Somerton, and the townspeople wanted to be sure she didn't doubt that. Even in death, James Carver and Bill Hannaford got what they wanted. At least, when Aaron wasn't around.

It was bitterly amusing. Nyla noticed right away that Somerton's behaviour toward her shifted when Aaron was in town. The locals weren't friendly, exactly, but their hostility was veiled. He'd made no secret about his willingness to defend his girlfriend, and Nyla supposed that people were more scared of Aaron than they were of her. Understandably. Still, she kept the extent of her problems with the townsfolk a secret from Aaron.

He'd probably be angry with her if he ever found out about it, but Nyla couldn't bring herself to dampen his newfound enthusiasm for his job. If she told him that Clary had to get her groceries for her, or that people threw eggs at the Willow when his X5 wasn't parked out front, he'd insist on staying in Somerton with her until things cooled down. She wouldn't let him. His life had been on hold since the start of the investigation, and Nyla refused to make him wait on her any longer. So, she held her tongue, rinsed the egg off the windows, and prayed Aaron wouldn't notice the spike in the water bill. That was largely wishful thinking. Aaron noticed everything. It wasn't long before he switched vehicles with her, stating he wanted to bring her old beater into Chicago to get a few things fixed for her. He said he was worried about her driving an unsafe vehicle, but Nyla knew better. He may not have realized the extent of her poor treatment, but he knew something was going on. Without fail, Aaron was doing everything he could to protect her.

It was time Nyla returned the favor, which is exactly what led her to George's office that Sunday evening.

"You want me to... what?" George furrowed his brow, evaluating her with that hard stare of his. While the events of the last few months alienated Nyla from the rest of the town, she'd finally found a friend in the newly appointed Sheriff. "Nyla, I—"

"Just for an hour or two," she insisted, smiling politely. She kept her expression confident but subdued, not too eager, but not too reluctant either. Nyla *needed* George to believe she was sure about this, even if her gut was still screaming at her to stop before it was too late. "I promise no one will be in any danger. You have my word."

"I'm not worried about that," George grumbled, folding his arms over his chest. He appraised her for a moment, taking in everything about her posture, her expression, and her tone. Nyla waited patiently. Eventually, he sighed, sinking his top teeth into his bottom lip as if to stop his next words from leaving his mouth. "Are you sure about this, Nyla?"

"I'm sure." Nyla fixed him with a determined stare. She *wasn't* sure, but George didn't need to know that. "Two hours, George. That's all I need."

Her solution had come from the most unlikely source. Jerry Leichester, former personal assistant to Adrian Stamkos, appeared at her door one morning with a coffee and a plan. He wasn't friendly, exactly. Nyla almost slammed the door in his face before he could speak a single word, but he'd stopped her just in time to prove he'd come in peace. As Stamkos' right-hand, Jerry would likely be moved to a different role in the company, meaning he was about to get a substantial pay-raise. He also wasn't particularly fond of Somerton, and together, seated at the dining table in the Willow's canteen, Jerry and Nyla had come to a tentative truce.

They figured out an agreement that would work for both of them, but Nyla needed to get George to agree to their plan, first.

He was quiet for so long that Nyla thought he'd deny her request. With a reluctant nod, George grunted an affirmation. She should've felt relief, to some extent. Nyla just felt numb.

"Thank you," she said, standing in one fluid motion. Her legs shook, but they didn't give out. "Should go without saying, but... keep this between us?"

George barked a humorless laugh.

"You've got no worries there," he droned. "I like you, Nyla, but I'm not risking my job for you."

"I'd expect no less," Nyla said with a wink. She could see that George wanted to say more, likely to try to convince her out of her plan, but she left his office before he could form the words. If he argued with her, she'd give in. She couldn't afford to let that happen now. "See you around sometime?"

"Anytime, Jameson," George answered, smiling impishly as he uttered her last name for the first time in several weeks. Nyla scrunched her nose at him in a playful glare, waving at the remaining officers in the lobby as she made her way to the parking lot. None of them, except George, waved back. "Take care of yourself, alright?"

"You too, Sheriff."

The door swung shut behind her, and Nyla didn't look back.

She took her time getting back to the Willow. Before making her way there, she stopped at all of her favourite spots in town. It took a few hours, but she wanted to make sure she didn't miss anything. Sure, the people were cold to her, but she had *some* good memories before the bullying ramped up. *That* was the Somerton Nyla wanted to remember; the one full of possibilities. Of new beginnings.

The slow ascent into the Willow's parking lot normally provided Nyla with a sense of peace. This lodge was her home, her pride and joy. When the townsfolk were particularly callous with her, when she felt the weight of her 'otherness' pulling her down into the depths of sadness, the Willow was her safe haven. Here, she wasn't Nyla Jameson, social pariah. Here, she was just... Nyla. Owner, caretaker, wilderness guide.

Those days were over.

The knowledge lodged itself in her heart long before her fight with Aaron outside Clary's. She'd known for months now. She just wasn't ready to admit it. Now that the Chehwinoo was gone, though, there was nothing left to distract Nyla from the inevitable: her time at the Willow Lodge had run out.

Aaron's SUV was a much smoother ride than her old rig, she couldn't deny that. It was nice, in a way, to pull into the lodge for the last time in a representation of the life waiting for her after today. Nyla parked the SUV in the middle of the lot, surveying the property with a practised eye.

Winter was in full swing now. Snow coated the pavement and grass, blanketing the trees and casting the lodge into a crystalline glow against the blue sky. It was beautiful. Beautiful, and perfect for her plan.

Nyla didn't bother going inside. The sun was dropping behind the trees, so daylight was limited. She crunched through the snow, sticking as close to the buildings as she could, stepping on bare patches of dirt whenever possible. Her footprints would likely melt long before anyone noticed, but she didn't want to take chances.

Rounding the main building, Nyla couldn't suppress her grin. Betty stood sentinel at her post, chugging away, keeping the lights on while she was out.

"Hey, girl," Nyla whispered, propping open the electrical panel on the back of the building. Betty rumbled, quieter than she'd been in years. "You know I trust you, right?"

Nyla knew generators couldn't talk, but she imagined that Betty was reassuring her that she already knew what had to be done. With the electrical panel door safely shut, Nyla sank into a squat. Her leg still ached from the damage it sustained in the fight with the Chehwinoo, but she'd finally stopped limping. A small collection of heavily insulated cables snaked from behind Betty, but Nyla didn't care about those. She reached around to the connection at the back, where a slight nudge would cause it to come loose. Usually, that wouldn't be a problem. The lights might flicker, or go out entirely, but it wasn't dangerous.

The next thing she did was reach for the garbage bin. With a heave, she tipped it on its side, much the same way that Bill had the night he attacked her. Garbage scattered across the snow, and one of the bags tumbled to a stop practically on top of Betty, blocking the heat vent. Nyla didn't normally leave substantial amounts of garbage in the bin for long, knowing that the scent would attract predators. Given recent events, though, she figured it would be understandable that something so mundane slipped her mind.

Stepping back, Nyla observed her work. It was basic, at best, but that was the point. Anything too complicated would immediately be suspicious. She needed to make it look like an accident, one that's been waiting to happen for a long time. Only time would tell if she succeeded.

"Give it your all, Betty," Nyla encouraged, ignoring the sting of tears threatening to spill. "I know you can do this."

With a deep breath, Nyla turned to make her way back to the parking lot. She hadn't decided what she wanted to do while she waited for the Willow to ignite, but she'd figure something out.

The sound of tires on packed snow made her heart leap into her throat. Nyla schooled herself as quickly as she could, trying to look casual. She wasn't doing anything wrong, at least not optically. She owned the Willow, she was allowed to walk around the property freely. There was no reason to think that she was up to no good.

Another set of tires, and Nyla's heart stopped altogether.

She had the momentary thought that George had changed his mind about helping her. If he did that, though, wouldn't he just call the fire department right away? Is that what he did? The two vehicles in the lot didn't sound big enough to be fire engines. Did George show up personally, to talk her out of it?

Nyla didn't have long to wonder. When she emerged from behind the Willow's main building, her fear melted into an unsettling combination of relief and anxiety.

"Nyla."

Aaron's sad smile told her that, somehow, he already knew what she was doing. Nyla opened her mouth to assure him that she'd thought this through, that he shouldn't be here, but then other voices made themselves known.

"You've got some fucking nerve, *Jameson*," Amelia taunted, crossing her arms over her chest and raising her eyebrow at Nyla accusingly. "After everything we've been through, you didn't think to tell us that you're blowing up the Willow?"

"I'm not blowing it up—" Nyla shook her head, refocusing. "Why are you here? You should all be home, far away from Somerton."

"Come on, you didn't think we were going to let you commit insurance fraud all by yourself, did you?" Sam grinned, slinging his arm over Amelia's shoulders. "You can't have all the fun."

"I didn't want to get you involved—" Nyla started, but Amelia held up a hand.

"Bullshit," Amelia snorted. "If we can take down ancient demons together, we can handle a little coordinated arson."

"Is it arson?" Emmett asked, appearing behind Sam with Callie in tow. Callie raised her hand in a small wave, her other hand still twined with Emmett's. "We're not technically lighting anything on fire. Cal?"

"Don't look at me," Callie said. "I work in small claims. Aaron?"

"You could make an argument for arson," Aaron mused, "but I'd personally aim for criminal negligence."

"Either way, they're both federal charges," Callie continued. "So, if anyone blabs, we all go down."

"Should we do a blood pact?" Sam asked, looking far too excited at the prospect.

"It's *fraud*, not witchcraft." Tyler appeared too, carrying a set of folded chairs from the back of what Nyla could only assume was Sam's infamous Tacoma.

"Aw man," Sam pouted, "and here I was excited to get naked and dance under the full moon."

"Guys, seriously," Nyla said, worry clouding her joy at seeing everyone again. "I appreciate the support, but none of you should be here. Pratt, you're a federal agent. Callie, you're literally a lawyer. And Aaron—"

"We all know what's at stake, *mi vida*," Aaron said softly. "We're not leaving you."

"Damn straight!" Clary's voice startled Nyla the most. She hopped down from the bed of the rusted red pick-up, holding an armload of blankets. "In for a penny, in for a pound. We've even got a story ready."

"We're all staying at the Willow for a fun weekend getaway with friends," Amelia explained. "I say we set up a bonfire, get a little tipsy, and cement our alibi."

"I've got a Bluetooth speaker here," Tyler added. "Blast some music loud enough and we're not going to notice anything amiss until it's too late."

"Not to mention the smell of burning wood won't be weird with a bonfire going," Amelia concluded, and Nyla had the sneaking suspicion that most of the details of this alibi were her doing. "Now, who brought the marshmallows?"

"I've got the booze!" Sam whooped, scurrying to the back of his truck as Tyler arranged the folding chairs in a wide circle around the nearest fire pit. Nyla stood, rooted to the spot, as she tried to process what was happening.

"How did you even know I was doing this?" Nyla asked Aaron when her mouth started working again. She met his gaze, and the silent answer there was easy to pick out. "Jerry."

"He didn't want you to be alone. He called me while I was with Pratt and Chia, so of course, he insisted on coming along. I wasn't going to tell the others, but Jerry beat me to it. He called Amelia a few days ago, so they were already on their way to Wisconsin by the time I found out."

He paused, scrutinizing her features as Nyla took all this in. She knew that Jerry wasn't doing all of this out of the kindness of his heart. He was a major player in the future of Stamkos & Stein, and the Somerton factory had become a money-sink that he now needed to deal with. Eliminating the Willow from the equation would serve as the final nail in the coffin for the expansion plan, proving that recovering their losses at this stage would be nearly impossible. The insurance payout for Nyla was a bonus, a happy side effect. But calling Aaron, her friends, so she wouldn't be alone? Well, perhaps Jerry had a bit more heart than she initially thought.

Perhaps the future of Stamkos & Stein was in better hands now.

"Nyla, are you sure you want to do this?"

"I'm sure," Nyla insisted. As painful as her decision was, she didn't doubt her reasoning. "This is the right thing. There's too much pain here. The Chehwinoo might be gone, but who's to say it'll never come back? Something could happen to the talisman, we can't know for certain. We can't stop people from coming to the Basin, but we can stop them from coming to the Willow."

"We can find another way." Aaron suggested gently.

"I can't afford to keep it," Nyla admitted with a wry smile. "And if I sell it at this point, Jerry might just torch it himself. Besides, you were right."

He waited, letting her find the words.

"I wanted to thrive here," she said. "But I can't. Somerton doesn't want me, and there's nothing I can do to change that. It doesn't mean I have to give up *everything*, but I need to let go of the life I wanted here. It's not going to happen, and that's okay."

Nyla said the words with conviction, willing herself to believe it. She wasn't quitting. She was just adapting.

"I'm ending this, Aaron." Nyla met his gaze, feeling a spark of confidence for the first time in weeks. "I can always start again."

"With a little support this time," Aaron told her. "I know you're not keen on moving to Chicago, but do you think you could handle living there long enough to figure out our next move?"

Nyla smirked, affection for him welling in her chest.

"Okay, but only if you're naked as much as reasonably possible."

"I was planning on it."

Aaron enveloped her in a tight hug, and Nyla let herself bask in his warmth for a few precious seconds before reality interrupted them.

"Let's get this party started!" Sam cheered, blasting the P!nk song of the same name from Tyler's speaker. Sam slapped his open palm on the hood of his truck. As ancient and questionably built as the vehicle was, Nyla couldn't deny that it had a certain charm. Jumping into the pan of the truck, Sam whipped his sweater off over his head. "Jesus! It's freezing!"

"It's winter!" Amelia reminded him, laughing in disbelief. "Put your damn shirt on before you get frostbite on your nipples!"

"No way," Sam gestured for Tyler to throw him a beer can, catching it in one hand, "this is not a shirts-on occasion. I don't think anyone besides Am and Ty would appreciate me whipping out my equipment, so 'Dicks Out for the Willow' is off the table. 'Nips Out for the Willow' will have to do."

"You heard the man," Emmett elbowed Callie's shoulder. "Nips out, Cal."

Callie raised an eyebrow, experimentally reaching for the hem of her shirt. Emmett's expression dropped immediately and he wrapped his arms around her middle, stopping her in her tracks. Laughter rang out, doubling as Tyler joined Sam in the truck bed.

"Nips out for the Willow!" Tyler's shirt came off, joining Sam's on the ground. With a comical shiver, Tyler cracked the tab on his beer and began gulping it down. "This was a terrible idea, Fisher."

"Well, if you two are in on this," Emmett let Callie go, shrugging out of his jacket and starting on his shirt buttons. "Toss me a drink, Cal."

"EVERYBODY FREEZE!" Sam shouted, grabbing Tyler's arm and shaking him aggressively. "It's finally happening! We get to see the man, the myth, the *legend* in all his glory!"

Emmett snorted, shrugging out of his shirt to a chorus of whoops and cheers from Sam as he dramatically swooned, forcing Tyler to catch him before he tumbled out of the truck bed. Emmett ignored him, climbing into the truck and taking a drink from Callie. Sam recovered immediately, reaching over to flick Emmett's nipple piercing.

"Dude, fuck off," Emmett said, but he was laughing. "That hurt!"

"That's good quality steel, too." Sam hummed thoughtfully. "Watch it with that thing, Cal. You might chip a tooth."

Emmett elbowed him as Callie smothered her mouth with her palm, hiding a giggle.

"That just leaves you, FBI Man!" Sam taunted at Aaron, who was still wrapped tightly around Nyla. She felt his chuckle rumble along her back, leaving him in a puff of warm air against her ear. "Come on, let's see those chocolate coins!"

"Oh my God," Amelia groaned. "I'm so sorry, Aaron."

"He's too old for fun, Sam," Emmett said, huffing derisively. "He'd break his back just jumping up here."

"Leave grandpa alone," Sam said back. "He can still manage a polka. Maybe even a jig, after a drink or two."

"Careful," Tyler said, laughing, looking conspiratorially at Aaron. "You guys didn't go to college with this maniac. He may be *boring* now, but you're looking at the reigning keg stand champion of 1046A Jericho Boulevard."

Sam and Emmett immediately descended into a chorus of boos, refuting Tyler's claims. Aaron sighed in Nyla's ear, pressing a quick kiss to her cheek.

"Excuse me, *mi cielo*," he said dramatically. "I need to go remind these children who they're dealing with."

In a mixture of shock and excitement, Nyla watched as Aaron— calm, collected, professional Aaron Klein— let his jacket slip to the ground, tugged his cashmere sweater over his head, and hopped the side of the truck bed in one fluid motion. He held out a hand toward Callie, who tossed him a can of beer. With Sam and Emmett already taken off guard, Aaron punctured the bottom of the can with Nyla's pocketknife, popped the tab, and chugged the entire contents in a matter of seconds. A chorus of cheers erupted from the men, all jostling Aaron in good-natured amusement.

"See, that's just not fair." Amelia shook her head with a smile. "He's smart, fit, attractive, *and* he can toss back a cold one like it's nobody's business? What factory spit him out and where can I get one?"

"He's one of a kind, I'm afraid." Nyla smirked. "Looks like you're stuck with your current model."

"Yeah," Amelia sighed, feigning disappointment. Nyla saw the affection in her eyes, though, shining brightly as she stared at Sam. A smile tugged at the corners of her mouth. "I guess I am."

"How long do you give it before they admit defeat?" Callie asked, still chuckling. Clary checked her imaginary watch.

"Right... about... now."

"Fuck, shit, damnit," Tyler whined, trying not to touch the side of the tuck with his bare skin as he leapt to the ground, searching for his shirt. "Why do I go along with your dumb ideas?"

"Because you have unwavering faith in my ability to have fun," Sam answered him, reaching for his own sweater. When all the men had regrouped, fully dressed, Nyla set to work building a bonfire. The busywork kept her from glancing over at the Willow, scanning the darkened sky for traces of smoke.

"So, what's your plan when you get to Chicago?" Amelia asked, handing her another wood split. Nyla hummed in thought.

"I haven't thought about it much," she admitted, "but hopefully the insurance payout from the Willow will give me enough to put a down payment on a new property somewhere. In the meantime, I'll probably try to find work in my old field."

Amelia blinked at her in shock.

"Your old field?" Her eyebrows lifted high, exchanging bewildered glances with Callie and Clary. "I kinda thought you always worked in nature."

"Not at all," Nyla said, laughing. "Want to guess what I used to do?"

"You won't," Aaron told them, shaking his head. "I didn't believe her until I ran a full background check."

"Stripper," Sam guessed immediately. Amelia rolled her eyes.

"See, I might actually believe that."

"Come on, what was it?" Emmett prodded. Nyla grinned.

"I was a financial data analyst for the Bank of America."

Stunned silence descended on the group, all except Clary and Aaron, who'd known for some time. Eventually, laughter erupted.

"You've got to be kidding me," Tyler scoffed. "You're right, Klein. I *never* would've guessed that."

Nyla just shrugged.

They fell into easy chatter after that, distributing drinks and roasting sticks until a pleasant haze wrapped around them, making the night seem less important. Less monumental. Nyla laughed. She smiled. She joked. She teased. Her friends' support lifted her from the edge of a bottomless pit that was threatening to swallow her. She was reminded again that she wasn't in this alone, not this time.

When the fire caught, Nyla knew it immediately. Emmett noticed first, seated across from her where he could see the Willow in the space between Nyla and Clary. His face shifted, and Nyla knew from the subtle tension what she'd see when she turned around.

If nothing else, Nyla was grateful that fires moved quickly, especially with old, wooden buildings like these. As long as George was true to his word, firefighters wouldn't be dispatched to the Willow until roughly an hour after the first signs of smoke were reported. By then, most of the lodge would be ash.

Nyla knew every inch of Willow Lodge by heart, so thoroughly that she could tell which room was being swallowed just from a glance. The fire spread from the generator to the lobby, consuming the overpriced guest chairs that she and Clary had lugged over the Willow's hilly parkway one by one. The lobby was where she and Clary had met, back when Nyla still believed Somerton would grow to accept her in time. Where a fierce knock on her door at five in the morning led to her first altercation with Bill Hannaford, and a toppled garbage can led to her last. Where she'd cried on the phone with her dad after the town denied her permit application for the 6th time, preventing her from doing any serious renovations. Where she'd learned of the first disappearance and dismissed it as a part of life in the Basin.

The canteen was next, engulfed in billowing smoke before it was tainted by flames. Nyla always liked the canteen, despite its many flaws. It was where Clary taught her to cook. Where she and Aaron had bonded over questionable sandwich toppings. Where they realized they couldn't be apart any longer. Where Nyla decided she loved him.

Nyla watched as the flames swelled over the pile of firewood stacked against the back wall. They licked at the nearest cabin, her cabin, nestled just behind the Willow's main building. Nyla had chosen it because it was close, but also because it called to her. The cabin was her home for four years, and now it was disintegrating before her eyes.

More and more memories flooded her, overlapping and fragmenting in disorganized chaos until Nyla couldn't separate them anymore. Her life in Somerton, everything she'd worked for, crumbled through the cracks in her mind like water slipping through her fingers.

For once in her adult life, she didn't try to stop the tears. They flowed freely, silently, collecting in her wool scarf and making the skin of her neck itch. Without Aaron's arm around her, steadying her, keeping her in the moment, Nyla wasn't sure she'd still be sitting upright.

Soon, the Willow would be gone. It was already difficult to pick out the individual buildings in the massive cloud of smoke, and what was left wouldn't stand up to well-fed flames for long. Nyla was just starting to squint at the obscured outline of the lobby roof when the first wails of a siren crept up the mountain road.

"Looks like that's our cue to lay on the dramatics," Amelia said, ruffling her hair and pinching her cheeks to redden them. "Do we need to run through the story again?"

"I'd like to once again motion for the addition of aliens and/or space robots," Sam announced solemnly. He was met with a chorus of boos from Emmett and Tyler, who were already getting to their feet.

"I'll grab whatever water I can find," Callie said to no one in particular. Nyla smiled at her, sinking further into Aaron's embrace.

As they all scattered to prepare for their roles, Nyla bid a silent farewell to Willow Lodge. For all the heartache, frustration, pain, and tears, the Willow would always be special to her, even when it was long gone.

"You did the right thing, *mi cielo*," Aaron whispered into her hair. Nyla nodded mutely. She knew that, deep in her heart, she knew. Her tears would dry, her hurt would heal, and Nyla Jameson would carry on as she always did. This time, with a few more friends at her side.

Aaron held her tighter as the firetruck at last pulled into view, lending her his warmth against the chilled wind threading through the sentinel of evergreens.

ACKNOWLEDGEMENTS

How many times can I say thank you before it gets annoying? We're going to find out!

Seriously, thank you. Readers, friends, family, supporters, pets, Diet Coke, coffee, peanut butter M&M's, you've all kept me going through this long and arduous process. Some of you may remember that *Camouflage* was supposed to come out last year. I won't get into details as to why that didn't happen (life stuff, it is what it is), but by last fall I had a choice to make. Rush to get the book done by Christmas and release a story I wasn't confident in, or wait. As much as I hate missing a deadline, I hate misrepresenting a story more. So, I took the time.

Camouflage was a labor of love, emphasis on the labor. I had so many goals for this book; namely, I wanted Nyla's story to come to a clean, satisfying close with no loose ends. I have timelines, maps, character sheets, notes, and frantic nonsensical scribblings all over my desk just trying to make sure I didn't miss anything. It was frustrating at times, and extremely satisfying at others. And now, it's done! It's done, and I'm not crying. You're crying. Shut up.

I hope you love the ending of the Somerton story. Nyla, Aaron, Sam, Amelia, Callie, Emmett, Tyler, Clary... they've all cemented their place in my heart, and hopefully yours too. This won't be the last you see of them, though. I always like to write little short stories that take place in previous worlds, so be on the lookout for those. The best way to stay up to date is to subscribe to my newsletter or stalk my website/socials.

Thank you all, and happy reading

ABOUT THE AUTHOR

Victoria Jayne Saunders is an author of new adult horror, romance, thriller, and fantasy. She lives in Newfoundland, Canada, with her husband, three cats, two dogs, and one very cranky lizard. She graduated from the Memorial University of Newfoundland in 2016 with a BA in English Language and Literature. She loves DIY, reading, writing, and forgetting to eat when she's playing too many farming/life sims.

ALSO BY

Deus
A society of were-sharks accidentally dissolves a human trafficking ring to rescue a hapless college student. Also, Greece.
Ebook and paperback available here (Amazon, if you're reading this as a physical copy)

Kill Bite: Book One of the Topaz Trilogy
Find out how we got here if you haven't already (in which case... why did you read this?) Follow Nyla and Aaron as they discover the truth behind the disappearances that started it all.
Ebook, paperback, and hardcover available here (Amazon, if you're reading this as a physical copy)

Prey Drive: Book Two of the Topaz Trilogy
Again, little confused if you read this one first... but just in case, here it is!
Ebook, paperback, and hardcover available here (Amazon, if you're reading this as a physical copy)